T0354747

THE
SANGUAVIS

WILLIAM A. J. DUFF

ARCHWAY
PUBLISHING

Archway Publishing books may be ordered through booksellers or by contacting:

Archway Publishing
1663 Liberty Drive
Bloomington, IN 47403
www.archwaypublishing.com
844-669-3957

Interior Image Credit: William Duff

ISBN: 978-1-6657-5885-7 (sc)
ISBN: 978-1-6657-5887-1 (hc)
ISBN: 978-1-6657-5886-4 (e)

Library of Congress Control Number: 2024907139

Print information available on the last page.

Archway Publishing rev. date: 04/05/2024

Far Lands of Evellior
Untris
Requilit
Great Sea
Civit
Maciv
Fairy Woods
Meridine
Mertris
Neciv
Pleniris
Sout

CHAPTER 1

"The past holds terrors beyond nightmares because the past was real. Nightmares and dreams are all in our minds, but our pasts are reminders that there are things in life that we wish to be awakened from but cannot be. That is the truest horror of life."

There was once a land called Pleniris. This land was divided into four kingdoms, each occupying one of the corners. To the southeastern corner was Istimus. To the southwestern corner of Pleniris was Meridine. To the northeastern corner was Venirit. And to the northwestern corner was Requilit. These four kingdoms were ruled each by four kings and their queens. Throughout the lands of Pleniris was one belief that a singular god created their world and all who lived in it. The peoples of these lands believed that upon dying, if their faith was appreciated by their god, their spirit would ascend into the skies to be with him. If they were not worthy of his love or to be with him, they would descend into the ground and rot with a being only known as the Hellruler.

The Hellruler was a being of pure evil and he was the sworn enemy of their god. He was once the son of their god, the most beloved in fact, but was banished from his home when he was young for wishing to be like his father. He has legions of demons at his disposal, and they try to meddle in the affairs of the humans. These were the lessons that were taught to those of royal blood. The royals of Pleniris believed that only those who shared their blood were worthy of possessing the knowledge of the history of their religions. The only knowledge that the non-royals would have received about the religion they believed in was stuff that would be said in a church such as old tales involving their god or people close to him. The knowledge kept only to the royals was information relating to Hellruler, the true nature of demons, or the very secret truths about their lord.

In the kingdom of Requilit, the royal family had a little more sympathy for the non-royals of their kingdom. They did not let them know *all* their secrets, but they did tell them that they should try to work harder for what they were praying for because it would not just simply happen because they asked and prayed. The king and queen of Requilit were named Kentrin and Eleana. Kentrin's father was the king before him. His father was not a nice man. He fully believed that the "shit-smelling peasants," as he called them, were not worthy of the royal family's attention or mercy. He treated the people of Requilit like animals and punished them as such, if not worse than animals. He did not share a single bit of information with the people about the secrets of the religion. Any time the people came to them for prayers he would spit at them and turn his head away. He would even put some to death if they asked a second time after he sent them away.

Kentrin's mother, however, was beloved and kind. She sympathized for the people of Requilit and taught Kentrin that every life was sacred and deserved equal treatment as if they were royals themselves. She told him that when he was king, he could bring light to the darkness his father left behind. He agreed to do so, and that is what he did. When his father died from choking on a bone from the leg of a chicken, he sat by his deathbed swearing an oath that he would treat the people as they should be treated. He of course would keep the very vital secrets of the church only to the royal family, but he would tell them everything besides that.

When he became king, he was only thirteen years old. His mother watched over his upbringing until she died on his seventeenth birthday. His first change he made as king was turning the old slave houses into church houses where he would entrust priests and preacher to spread the ways of their beliefs, along with the few secrets he was able to share. Requilit was the only kingdom out of the four that openly taught some of the secrets of their belief. Many people snuck over the borders of the kingdoms to hear more of their god they could not hear from their kingdom. The result of this was greater belief in religion and the increased power of the kingdom of Requilit. It eventually became the most powerful of the four.

The power of the kingdom was based on the strength of their believing numbers. The more people that believed in the kingdom meant there were more willing to fight to keep that kingdom safe. Therefore, due to the secrets the Requilit kingdom held, they were the most powerful of the four. In the center of the four kingdoms was a large mountain known as the Shrieking Peak. It gained its name for the sound it makes when the wind picks up and blows past its peak above the clouds. The sound is like people screaming in fear and agony, terrifying those who hiked the paths around the mountain. There was a rumor that a great evil lurked in the massive cave system twisting through the mountain. The entrance was located at the top and stretched through the bottom under the earth. Those who tried to venture inside to see what was inside were never seen or heard from again.

When Kentrin reached age eighteen he met Eleana at a party he was holding for his one year annuversary of being king. By this time, the kingdom of Requilit was prospering and its reputation for its beliefs was very great. At the time she was sixteen when they had met and after a few years, when she reached the age of eighteen, they got married and she became their queen. She viewed the people as equals with the royals but understood that some of their secrets should remain secret upon hearing them. Their marriage was beloved by all, and no one opposed it. The other kingdoms heard of the wedding and sent letters congratulating them. After four years of them being queen and king, Eleana gave birth to a son whose name would be Kerstas.

⊰⊱

The year was 854 nearing the end of the cold seasons. Kerstas was seven years old at the time and was getting dressed for the weekly service where the peoples in a certain area of the kingdom would attend to hear about their god and lessons on how to honor and serve him. He was putting on a pair of pants and a white shirt that had a string tying holding the collar and the top half together. The room he was in was made of stone and had a large window overlooking the many houses and streets of the capital. There was a bed with a thick fur blanket on it that kept young Kerstas very warm during the cold nights of the chilling season. The blanket was made from a bear that his father had killed on a hunting trip a year prior.

His father had taken him on the trip deep into the woods near the border of Meridine. These woods were inhabited by many species of bears, boars, and other forms of wildlife. He had killed three bears on the trip. One he made a blanket with, he made a coat with another, and the last he made a carpet for his bedroom. He mounted two of the heads on both sides of his throne in the main hall of his castle in Requilit's capital. The meat from the bear, along with other animals he and his men brought back, provided a large banquet for the royals of Requilit. Kerstas was a very well-mannered boy. He loved the people of the kingdom and had a conversation with those who would, whether it would be about their beliefs or just how the weather was that day. The people loved him and respected him. There was talk throughout the streets and small villages that he would be a terrific king when he came of age. The proper age to become king was either upon the death of the father or when the father passed on the title, which he would be able to when his son would turn sixteen. When the king's son turned eleven, he would begin his training to rule the kingdom by learning its history, studying its towns and the ways of living, and the responsibilities of taking care of the people.

There came a knock at the door. It was one of the servants of the royal family. His name was Rengeon, and he was Kerstas' favorite. Ever since he was able to walk, Kerstas played with Rengeon, and he would always ask him when he could speak his name. They were as close as friends as anyone could be. Rengeon was rather lanky, and his hair was always knotted up like he had gotten in a fight with an animal just before entering the room. He was a young boy not older than the age of fifteen. Kerstas was nearly half of his age, but that did not stop their friendship from forming. When he was young his parents were killed by a group of bandits that were robbing his house. Kerstas' father found him hiding inside of a tree stump during one of his hunting trips just moments after the attack. Kerstas' father had the guards with him search the woods and hunt down the ones who murdered Rengeon's family. They did, and Kerstas' father took him in. He was around Kerstas' age when that happened. Kerstas had been born the week after.

"Hello, young prince," said Rengeon. "You slept in a lot. The service is nearly over. Your father won't be very happy with you if you missed a service." It was midday, an hour after the start of the service, which occurred twice a week. The first was at the start and the second was at the middle of the week.

"Good morning, Rengeon." Kerstas' voice was light and ending the stage where it was cracking. Rengeon walked into the room and stood Kerstas in front of the mirror hanging on the wall. The metal around it was a fine gold in the shape of two dragons wrapping around each other and meeting at the top. From their mouths came silver flames curling around the inner frame of the mirror to their lower legs.

Kerstas could see himself in the mirror. His golden hair was sticking out in different directions from waking up. His eyes were a deep blue like staring into an ocean. Rengeon adjusted his collar and nodded.

"You are ready, Kerstas. Go on before your father kills the both of us." He walked Kerstas out of the room, closing it behind him, and leading him down a white stone hallway with paintings of old men and women on either side.

They walked down a set of stairs curving downwards to the left. The railing was golden, and the frame was dark wood. He came into a large room with many round tables that had white cloths draped over them. There were wooden chairs seated around the tables, and the walls had many paintings depicting winged people battling horned monsters. His father told him one day that the paintings were of angels fighting demons during the last holy war. He walked through the room and into another, which was the main entrance. It was down a small set of stairs with golden rails and wooden frames. There was a large circular image painted on the ground that depicted two eyes intersecting in the pupils. His father never explained what the symbol meant. He only said that it was an evil symbol, and it was never to be drawn or shown to anyone outside of the castle. It was the darkest secret that the royal family held, kept for generations before history was first recorded. His father said that when he was crowned king, or when he would come to his death bed, he would tell Kerstas the secret of the symbol.

Rengeon opened the doors to the front of the castle and the light blinded Kerstas. When his eyes adjusted, he saw the city in front of him. There were many buildings to see. Some were tall and some were short. To the left he could see the marketplace, which was a large circle of shops around a fountain where the people would drink water from. To the right was the service hall his father was in. The two walked down to the hall and when they got there, the people were crowded outside of the door trying to listen in to what was being said. They turned and saw Kerstas. They bowed and all made a path to the front for him. He could see his father staring at him. He was sitting behind a man standing behind a podium. There was an empty chair on the other side of the man, who had greying hair and was wearing a long white robe.

Kerstas lowered his gaze to the floor. He felt embarrassed for being late to the service. He walked past the people in the hall who were all staring at him. A few were whispering about how he was late and other words that would not be heard except between those in the conversation. He sat in the chair that was empty. His father looked over at him. His eyes alone spoke words saying that he was ashamed of him and that *it* was to happen again as punishment. Kerstas' mind went into a spiral. It had been months since *that* had happened. He had almost pushed it from his mind. He wished that he could.

Kerstas loved the people, but he did not like their beliefs so much. Because when *that* would happen, he would pray for it to end and never happen again, but it continued. For two years *it* had happened as a punishment for being late or being disrespectful in service. Of course, his father had no idea what *it* was. He only knew that the preacher and the others at the other service halls would keep him in a dark room to teach him what he did was wrong, and that he will learn his lesson. His father agreed only if he would be returned by sundown. They agreed.

The preacher asked everyone to bow their heads and close their eyes. "Oh, great lord, thank you for another wonderful service and another day of living. We pray that you gift us more so that we may thank you again at our next service. Thank you, Lord." They all opened their eyes and stood up. They all started pouring out of the building returning to their homes and the market. His father nodded at the preacher and the preacher smiled. He waved his father goodbye and grabbed Kerstas' shoulder. He stood him up and threw him inside of the back room. He turned the lights off and slammed the door, locking Kerstas inside.

As every time before, Kerstas tried feeling his way around the room to try and escape, but there was no luck. He huddled himself on the floor and his eyes started to water, wondering why and how he could allow *it* to happen. After nearly an hour passed and he heard the front doors open, close, and then lock. There were whispers from multiple men approaching the door. It clicked and opened. There were five men, all in white robes, standing in the doorway illuminated by the sun. it was the only light that entered the room, like a small ray of light at the end of the tunnel, but this tunnel should have been destroyed and never dug out again.

The man in front lit a candle with a match and the others

grabbed Kerstas. They dragged him out and into another room on the other side of the podium. Inside the room was a small bed with purple sheets on it. Two of them tore the shirt off his back and tossed him on the bed. They tied his arms to the posts against the wall, laughing as he screamed. His pants were thrown to the ground around his ankles, and he felt excruciating pain in his ass. He tried to pull his hands free, but it was no use. They were too restrained. His struggle simply made them tighter. Hours passed, each taking turns and repeating them over and over. The sun had set and by the time it had, Kerstas' legs were covered in blood, spit, and semen. He had nearly passed out from the pain. He was heaving and sobbing. They were all laughing and they all but one left.

He grabbed Kerstas by the hair and untied his wrists. "You tell your father about this, and we will make a fool out of you in front of the whole kingdom!" He threw him to the ground and left.

Kerstas got up from the bed and pulled his pants back up and retying his shirt. The residues on his legs made his pants cling to him. He limped his way back to the castle and laid down in his room. He curled up in a ball and stared at the stars outside. He asked himself why men of God would do such a thing to him. To anyone. For two years this had happened. he would someday find a way to end it. He swore that when he would become king, he would put all of them to death for what they had done to him. He closed his eyes and fell asleep. His back was throbbing from the pain. Some day he would end it.

Nine years had passed since that day. The year was now 863. Kerstas still had not been able to find a way to tell his father what the preachers were doing to him without feeling that they would hurt him or make him out to be a liar. They continued to do the same thing without mercy and threatened him more and more until he had gone nearly insane from the stress and paranoia.

His father still believed that what the preachers were doing was simply keeping him inside a dark room for a few hours until he learned his lesson. If his father knew what was truly happening, he would put them to death. At least he would like to. If he did, he would have been afraid of his reputation being the same as his father's by killing holy men of God for something he could not say. The people would ask questions and spread rumors of the king hating their lord and trying to remove it from the kingdom, which would result in Requilit's armies being less powerful and at a disadvantage to the other three. Kerstas kept quiet about it, but he was still determined to put them to death when he became king. There was only one month left until he turned sixteen, which was when he would become eligible for the crown.

<hr />

When Kerstas turned four his mother became pregnant and gave birth to a girl who they named Inerium. She was born with black hair, a freckled face, pale skin, and beautiful blue eyes. Her eyes matched Kerstas'. He did not like her at first because she was attracting all the attention in the family, but he grew onto her and played with her every chance he got.

Her birthday was close to Kerstas'. They were nearly two days apart, so when he would have a celebration of birth, she would share it with him. He did not mind. He was her best friend as well as her brother. It was an inseparable friendship, both in blood and life. When he turned sixteen, she would turn twelve. She was very well-mannered and was even called the "perfect example" of what parents would want in a child. She had much sympathy and love for all life and even paid respects to insects when they died or when she would accidentally step on them.

She never misbehaved in service and was never late. This was mainly because Kerstas told her that there were bad things that would happen if she did not follow the rules and obey every order their father told them. She never had to endure the pain that Kerstas went through, and was still going through, for nearly ten years. If they even laid a hand on her he would sentence their deaths even without being king. He would do it with his own hands if he had to. The more times that it happened he lost more and more faith in their lord they called so great. If he was so loving and caring, he would end their lives for causing that much trauma to a child. And who knows how many others.

He was lying in his room staring at the ceiling. A knock came at the door and his father walked in. He was smiling. "Hello, son."

"Hello, father," he said. "Is there something you need?"

His father walked over to the window and looked over to the mountain towering in the sky. "How are you feeling about next month? You become a year older and become of-age."

"I am indifferent about it. There is a long time to wait until I become king. You have a lot of time left before you would give it to me."

He looked over at his son. "I would not be so sure about that, son. I had a vision last night that I would die soon. I am preparing you for the worst. When I die, I would entrust you to our whole kingdom. You are ready to rule Requilit. I know it."

"Father, I am only fifteen. I am not fit to rule an entire kingdom!" In most cases a son would be worried about his father talking about his death, but Kerstas' was too nervous about having to rule a kingdom to process it.

"I said you are ready, son. Your mother will be there with you. She has been by my side this whole time. She knows how to rule a kingdom just as well as I do, if not better." He looked back outside. "You will have a coronation on your birthday and on that day, you will become king. I will send out the letters to the other kingdoms to receive their appraises." He left the room after taking one last glance at the mountain. He shut the door behind him.

Kerstas sat up in his bed. He was trying to process everything he was just told. It was too overwhelming for him. He got up and looked outside of the window and peered over to where his father was staring. His eyes fixed themselves on the mountain in the distance. The clouds had parted just enough to see the top. There was a hole near the top that appeared to be a cave and he suddenly got the feeling of being watched and his heart skipped a beat. He quickly shut his curtains and hid himself from the mountain's gaze. The feeling went away, and he calmed himself.

Another knock came at the door. "Who is it?" He asked.

The door opened and Inerium was standing there wiping her eyes on the sleeves of her white dress. She came running into the room and hugged him tightly. "I had a nightmare."

"It's okay, Ineri, it was only a dream. They aren't real." He had given her the nickname Ineri when she was six when she was trying to say her name at a party, she could only say that part of her name without getting shy. She called him mean for calling her that, but she kept the nickname as if it were her own.

"But it felt so real. I saw daddy dying and you had been taken away from me." She sobbed harder and wiped her eyes again.

Kerstas dried her face with his blanket and told her to stop using her sleeves because she'd ruin her beautiful dress. She eventually stopped crying. She never cried in front of anyone besides Kerstas. Before she had come into the room, she had checked the hall to make sure no one was watching her, and then she had started to cry. She wanted to make sure she did not seem weak or upset to the other royals or people. They would worry for her, and she did not want that stress on them. She had been like that ever since she was five. When she cried in front of her mother or father, they would just tell her that princesses shouldn't cry, and they would ignore her crying. Kerstas was the only one in the family that would listen to her and try to comfort her.

"Don't worry about it," Kerstas said. He remembered what his father had just told him. Did she have the same dream he did? Did they both see the future, or was it just a coincidence? He was not sure, but it was enough to worry him. He stood her up. "Come on. Let's go look at the garden outside. That always cheers you up."

He led her out into the hall and to the right. They walked to the end and made a left. There was another hall that looked just like the previous one. There were more pictures of old people and some young, all related to Kerstas. At the end of the hall was a set of stairs that spiraled down to the floor below. They followed them to a long hall. At the end of it was a set of double doors decorated with golden flowers and silver vines. He turned the rose petal doorknobs and the doors opened, revealing a large courtyard filled with many beautiful plants, flowers, and trees.

This was Kerstas' great great grandmother's garden. She planted the seeds when she was a young girl. From that day, she had tended to them and when they would die, she would replant the seeds that fell from the previous plants and start the cycle over again. The women of the royal family have kept up this tradition for four generation, and soon to be five when Inerium became ten. They would replant the seeds until their next born would come of age so that the beauty of the garden would remain forever until the end of time. The plants here had come from all over the land of Pleniris. Merchants and other royals had given his great great grandmother every different type of beautiful plant they could acquire for her. She was a very kind and beautiful woman. Everyone from all four kingdoms loved her and her generosity. She did not care about the laws and would grant hospitality to anyone who needed it.

That was until she was in her late age, when her daughter had come in her twenties, that one of the mercenaries from one of the other three kingdoms was sent to assassinate her. No one knew who had sent him. The only hint to her murder they got was that it was a royal who had paid him. After this incident had occurred, the four kingdoms were thrown into a war that lasted until Kerstas' grandma came of age to marry his grandfather. He stopped the war by striking fear into the hearts of the peoples of Pleniris that he would personally hunt down and murder every royal who dared lay a hand on his family. Scared by his threat, the other three kingdoms backed down and Requilit was the victor by default. This struck further fear into the hearts of the other kingdoms because they did not know who had killed Kerstas' great great grandmother, and they were terrified that his grandfather would find out one day and lay waste to their kingdoms and claim them for his own.

It was eventually found out that it was a commoner from

the kingdom of Meridine who had loved her but had never met her. He decided that if he could not have her then no one could. He paid an assassin fifty silver pieces that he had stolen to kill her. He did and the assassin was put to death in front of the kingdom of Requilit the same day. The second day after was the service to honor death. The entire kingdom of Requilit attended it, along with the royal families of the other three kingdoms. The royals of Meridine felt embarrassed because someone from their kingdom ordered the kill so they gave the family of Requilit five hundred gold pieces in compensation. The Requilit royals were thankful for the money and Kerstas' grandfather stored it away for himself. When Kentrin had come of age and was crowned king, he used the money to rebuild and refurbish the homes of the people in Requilit. He had also used the money to buy more supplies from the smaller farming and mining islands around Pleniris for the people and royals of his kingdom.

They walked around the garden smelling the lovely scent of the flowers. The pollen made Inerium sneeze. It sounded almost like a pixie fairy sneezing with how soft it was.

"What's that one called?" She asked. She pointed to a group of yellow and purple flowers that slightly resembled an eye if one were to glance over them.

"That's a Aifuryowa flower. Our grandmother got it from a merchant that was selling the seeds at the border between the southern kingdoms."

She looked at them again and smiled. "They're really pretty." They walked down the path further passing other flowers with many different colors, some of which thought to have not existed before. The shapes and sizes were of every form imaginable. There were large ones that were red and had blue stems, some with green petals and orange stems, and small ones the size of a thumb with multi-colored petals that almost looked like a sunset when looked at right. They turned a corner into the section of vines and other such plants. There were many different vines that were as thin as a finger and as thick as a tree trunk. They twisted and turned in all sorts of ways. It hurt Inerium's head trying to follow one of them through its labyrinth of tangles. On the outer edges of the garden were large trees arranged in a short and tall pattern. In order they were tall, short, tall, short, short, and short. This pattern repeated around the room and lined out perfectly from start to finish. Unless one marked their starting tree, they would not be able to keep track of when they started because of how perfectly they lined up. The colors of the leaves were unique and very different than any other tree on the island of Pleniris. During the hot seasons they would turn a beautiful orange and red color as if they were on fire. During the cold seasons instead of the leaves falling off, they would turn into an icy blue and silver color and would shrink a bit, making them all look like a sheet of ice circling around the room.

She asked Kerstas to walk around the garden a few more times until she was satisfied. She continued to ask what the plants' names were even if she asked previously. Whether she forgot them or not, she still liked hearing her brother explain them to her. She loved her brother. it was not in a weird incestuous way, no, but in an older brother who is your best friend in the whole world kind of way. Once they had done their third circle around the garden, Inerium told Kerstas she was feeling hungry.

He walked her back through the halls and into the kitchen where two women were kneading bread dough. They looked up. They were twins, roughly around their mid-twenties. They both had brown hair and green eyes. Their skin was slightly scarred from burns from both the kitchen and their previous times before working for the Requilit royal family.

Before working for the Requilit royals, the twins worked for a slave trader and were exploited as sexual providers to those who bid the highest and won the auctions. When an auction was held, the winner would take one, or both, of the twins to a back room in the slave house and have their way with them. Kentrin found them one day when he was at an auction. (He disliked the act of slave trading, and he would buy them and either offer them a job for actual pay or he would let them be free to live their lives as they wished.) He disguised himself and bought out their entire slave house. When he was offered to have his way with the twins, as far as he wanted, he killed the slave captain and offered them a job under him, where they would be safe from harm. They agreed and became his personal cooks. They were the best he had. There were many cooks under the royal family, but the twins were to cook only for him and his wife. Eventually Kerstas and Inerium would be added to that list. They were proud of what they did. They were happy to be honored to cook for the royal family, especially knowing the fact that the family enjoyed their cooking. They were hired at fifteen, and they were trained by the previous cook of the royal family. They outdid the previous cook with their first ever dish and he tried to kill the twins. Kentrin did not approve of the cook's behavior, so he sent him away to work elsewhere. Since that day the twins were his head cooks for him, and they learned new recipes with as many different ingredients as they could so they could continue to impress Kentrin and his family until they were either relieved from service or when they met their deaths.

They were standing next to each other. There was not much difference between them. The only defining characteristic between the two was that Tsuin, the one on the left, had a burn scar on her left cheek, and Tsuon, the one on the right, had one over her right eyebrow. They loved to put their hair down over their faces to cover the scars and make Inerium guess which twin was which. She almost always guessed right every time. There was perhaps one, maybe two, times that she had gotten it wrong. They had played that game with her multiple times a week ever since she could say their names.

"Hello, Tsuin and Tsuon," Inerium said cheerfully.

The twins smiled and in unison said, "Hello, young princess, how are you today?"

"She had a nightmare earlier, so I took her on a walk through the garden," Kerstas said.

"Aww, I'm sorry," Tsuon said. "Don't worry, though. It is just a nightmare. I once had a nightmare that my sister Tsuin here had turned into a giant bear and tried to eat me." Tsuin made a roaring noise at her and Inerium started to laugh along with the twins. "Do you want something to eat?" She asked.

Inerium thought for a moment. Her eyes lit up. "Do you remember that delicious dessert you made me a year ago? The one with the berries on top?"

Tsuon smiled. "Of course. You loved that one and begged me every day for a week to make you one for every meal." She chuckled lightly. "Give me about half an hour and I will have it ready for you."

The twins began making the dessert for Inerium. Kerstas was not hungry. His appetite was robbed of him when he was told about inheriting the throne in just two weeks. He took Inerium into the dining hall in the next room over. They sat down at one of the round tables and waited for her dessert.

"Hey, Brother, can you tell me that story?"

"Which one?"

"The one about the dragon and the golden city."

"That one has a bad ending, though." Kerstas said. He told Inerium many stories. He would make them up to get her to fall asleep at night and had kept it up as a nightly hobby for the past eight years. Her favorite story was about a dragon that turned a golden city into ash with his powers. Kerstas had a dream one night when he was eleven about it and retold it to her when nothing else would come to him. She loved it and made him retell it at least once a week.

"Okay. Once upon a time in a faraway land there was a great dragon. He had many wings and had a beautiful set of ten eyes. The dragon had his parents taken away from him when he was very young, and the dragon swore that he would get his revenge on the ones who took them away. So, the dragon followed the ones to their home in a great golden city in the sky. The people had a large army ready to fight against the dragon and they fought for many years. Finally, the dragon used his powers to their fullest ability and melted the city and turned the gold into ash. When there was no one left in the city, the dragon had nowhere else to go besides back to his home to live alone. But, before he could leave, a man of golden light chained the dragon to the ground of the ashen city around him and left him there to spend the rest of his life. All alone without anyone to talk to besides himself."

"But one day I will go and see him!" Inerium shouted. She always said this at the end of the story. She always told herself and Kerstas that she would see the dragon from his dream and be his friend. She had given him a name when she was five. She nicknamed him Dorgy the dragon.

Every now and then she would sit in her room and play pretend with straw stick figures. There were many different scenarios she would play out from a trapped princess to a house party. She loved getting her stick figures and sending them into a cave (under her bed) and trying to save Dorgy from the evil wizard that trapped him. She built the figures from straw she got from the stables and twigs she found on the ground under the trees in the family garden.

Tsuin brought out a small plate with the dessert on it. It was a small tart with a red crème filling. There were three small purple berries around one edge of it and a red berry sliced in half occupying the rest of the dessert's surface. The crème filling was coming out over the edge of one part of the dessert. The crust around the top edge appeared like an ocean's wave around the top, and the crème was like the water coming from it. "Here you go, little Inerium." She smiled and returned to the kitchen.

Inerium picked up the dessert and took one of the halves of the frusia berry off. She ate it, followed by two black berries. She bit into the tart and the crème leaked out of it onto her face. She made a mmm sound followed by a "yum" and continued eating it. When she reached the last bite, she picked up the last fruits on the tart and ate them together. She licked the red crème off her face and finished the tart. "Thank you!" She shouted out towards the kitchen.

There was a pause for only a second and a loud "you're welcome" answered her thanks. She brought the plate back to the kitchen and Tsuon took the plate from her to clean. "We're glad you liked it, Inerium." They washed the plate and put it next to the others laying on a damp white cloth.

Kerstas walked Inerium back through the halls to her room. He opened her door and led her inside. Her room was small but had enough room for her to play around comfortably. Her bed was in the corner of the room, and she had a dresser at the foot of it where her clothes were kept. There were a few paintings around the room that she had painted. They mostly were simple paintings of what were at first to be her family but had turned into paint splotches on a canvas because she had gotten frustrated due to mom's arms being longer than her legs. She got scared of it, thinking she had drawn a monster, and threw her small cup of paint at it. In the corner of the room, the one next to the door, was her small pile of straw figures. A few feet away from it was her collection of straw and twigs that she would use to make more figures. There was a large cloth over an odd object near the twigs and straw. When Kerstas went to uncover it, she dove in front of it and told him he couldn't see it yet.

"What is it?" He asked. He was curious about what it was.

"You'll see when it's finished." She checked the cloth to make sure it was fully covering the object under it. It was.

"Fine then, but you better finish it soon." He turned to leave the room. He shut the door behind him and returned to his room. It was getting dark outside. The sun was setting over the hills. The shadows were stretching to meet his room. He lay in his bed and closed his eyes, falling asleep until the next day.

CHAPTER 2

There were many mysterious things in the lands of Pleniris. The most mysterious was of course the Shrieking Peak in the center of the kingdoms, but the second most mysterious was the concept of magic. The beliefs in Pleniris were that their lord, the Hellruler, the angels, and demons were the only beings that could possess any abilities that would fall under the definition of abnormal. The angels had flight and holy powers, Hellruler and his demons had evil powers of manipulation and other such things, and their lord had the ability to create and destroy anything he pleased. However, there was a separate form of power in the world of Pleniris. This power was commonly called magic and was called evil by the priests and preachers throughout the lands. Those that either possessed, or thought to have possessed, this power was burned in front of towns and kingdoms for blasphemy against their lord. The holy men of the lord in Pleniris thought that if humans possessed magic, they were evil and puppets of Hellruler, or that they were trying to imitate their lord's power to be like him. Regardless of the reason, it was seen as evil to possess any power that could be related to magic.

There were instances where street magicians, who could not use actual magic, were burned at a stake because a holy man saw him performing and believed his magic was real. When he learned that the street performer was fake, and he was responsible for the death of an innocent, he was brought to the ruler of Istimus at the time, King Seretix, and was put to death. King Seretix's reputation dropped a little and he was called a priest killer because many people did not appreciate when a "man of the lord" was killed, especially by a royal family member.

There was, however, an actual form of magic in the lands of Pleniris. In an older age, it was taught only to the royals of the kingdoms. The most common magic mostly dealt with the natural elements of the world which were air, water, earth, and fire. The limitations of what could be done with this magic were unknown because new spells and practices were being developed all the time. There were other magics that dealt with the forces of dark and light. These were the powers that the angels and demons naturally possessed, which deemed them forbidden to anyone including the highest of the royals that could use magic.

When an old king in Meridine who lived nearly five hundred years ago used dark magic he was possessed by a demon. They used their powers together and they conquered the lands of Pleniris for years. It was not until the year 402 that a hero from Istimus with no name was blessed with holy magic and fought the demon-possessed king. There was no victor in the battle. No one knew what happened to the king or the hero. There were some rumors that the hero became king of Meridine in the previous one's place There were other rumors that the demon-possessed king had run away to another island and lived out the rest of his life. Eventually the rumors boiled down into myths and legends until all that could be said for certain was that the king was possessed, and he fought the holy hero.

The information here was found in a book that was kept in the library of the castle in Requilit. Kerstas had read it when he turned thirteen. He told Inerium stories he would find inside of it. One day when he was reading it his father told him he should never let anyone outside of the family know about the book because the information kept inside of it, and the other books on the same shelf, were forbidden for anyone to know. The authors of the books were all unknown. There was no credited author or any titles for that matter. The book covers were all blank but had thousands of pages of old texts talking about their lord, magic, and other such things only royal members were allowed to know.

There was one book at the end of the shelf that was a little under thirty pages long, but the pages were thick. Kentrin's father had told him that the pages were supposedly made from actual skin, and the ink made from blood. He was not completely sure what it was made from, but this book fascinated Kerstas the most.

The book spoke of a world in a separate reality created by a greater being with no name. The only mention of the being was in the first sentence. It read, "The son of the Grand Creator fell into a deep sleep, and from his dreams came the Nightmare."

The first few pages of the book explained that the Nightmare was a realm of different worlds layered on top of one another. If one were to stack plates on top of each other, each of those plates would represent a world in the Nightmare. Each one was different but had only one similarity: they were all created by the Grand Creator's son's dreams. The rest of the book talked about one layer called D'vilsik. There was a second half to this layer called Nelivesk, and it connected through a large hole in the ground that cut through the layers.

The history of these two worlds was one. Nelivesk was a world like Pleniris until a cult tried to resurrect an evil deity known as Muhest. The history was explained for nearly a thousand years until an event happened called the Rupturing. This was an event that the cult tore a rift into the layers to D'vilsik and released the monsters in that layer. They destroyed Nelivesk and the last five survivors escaped into D'vilsik to live. The rest of the pages seemed to be torn out. There were at least a hundred more pages left of the book and they were nowhere to be found. Kerstas repeatedly read the book trying to come up with theories on what happened to the last five survivors. None of them were correct to the actual answer, but the closest he got was that the last five had found a way to escape the Nightmare and go into another reality. The true fate of the five would seemingly never be truly known.

<hr />

There were only two days left until the coronation. Kerstas' father had continuously checked up on him and asked him about how he was feeling about becoming king. Kentrin would give him a refresher course on how to keep his loyal guards in check and a bunch of other things that he did to keep his kingdom orderly. The *punishment* happened two more times and each time only drew out Kerstas' hate for the church even more.

He respected the belief, but the main issue was that he continuously prayed to save him and end the punishment, but nothing helped. The more he prayed, the more he felt ignored and unloved by the lord who supposedly gave unconditional love and saved those who prayed. This, however, was clearly a lie in Kerstas' mind because if it were all true, he would not endure the pain he felt by the very people who spoke so highly of their lord.

Out of all the secrets the royal family kept, the darkest of them all was that the lord they prayed to and loved truly did not care for them. Kentrin kept this from Kerstas because he feared that he would push his son away from him by saying the deity that created everything cared about his people about as much as a human cared about a pile of animal shit. Kerstas, however, learned this sinister truth about his lord the last time *the punishment* happened. It occurred to him because if it weren't true, then why? Why would holy men of that god be so cruel? The answer became quite clear. It was the same answer as to why Kentrin's father did not give any attention to the people of Requilit. He did not care.

The only thought in Kerstas' head was him putting those holy men in front of the entire capital and putting them to death for what they had done to him. This was his goal for years. To put those damned people to death for *their* sins.

Inerium walked into the room. Kerstas was standing in his window looking at the mountain as he had done multiple times a day for the past few days. "Hey, what are you doing?" She asked.

He turned around. "Hey, Ineri. Nothing, just looking outside again." He took another glance at the mountain and shut his curtains.

The truth was that he continuously looked at that mountain for two reasons. The first was because his father and his father before him loved to stare at the large mountain in the distance. The mystery of it fascinated them and they wanted to discover its secrets for themselves. However, they were terrified of the mountain because they had frequent dreams of it at night. In the dreams they would see a creature of shadow bearing yellow eyes glowing in the darkness. The creature would beckon them to come inside his cave. When they would he would grab them and fall into the pit inside the cave. Before they would hit the bottom the creature would whisper "come to me" and they would wake up. The dreams started occurring when Kentrin's father was nearing his age to become king. The same happened with Kentrin. When he was nearing his sixteenth birthday, he started having the dreams. Now, it was happening to Kerstas. It would continue to happen until Kerstas turned sixteen. It was unknown why this happened and why it only happened to the kings of the family, but it was a cycle that had lasted for three generations. The mountain seemed to almost all to Kerstas at night as the creature did to him in his dreams.

"You liar. You've been staring at that mountain every time I've come in here for the past week."

"It's hard to explain, Ineri, but the mountain seems to be calling to me somehow. I have the urge to go to it every time I look at it."

"I know what you mean. I want to go to it, too." Inerium had not been having dreams like Kerstas had, but her mind was gifted with something special. She always got an odd feeling in the back of her mind when she either looked at the mountain or when she heard about it from someone else. This special part of her mind was a mystery to most, but not to her mother. She knew exactly what was special about Inerium's mind, and only they were to know. The males in the Requilit royal family weren't the only ones who had secrets connected to the abnormal.

The males had their connection to the mountain and the dreams they had about the creature. There were more, but the secrets were lost to Kentrin's father. He failed to tell Kentrin because he thought no one besides him was worthy of knowing the truth. The females of the royal family in Requilit had a different connection. The females had a mental connection to the realms between the planes of the living and the dead. They could hear whispers and other things from beyond the plane of the living.

The special abilities of the females in the royal family began when Eleana, Kentrin's wife, turned seven. She started seeing things in her dreams before they would happen, sometimes either moments or even years. No matter the time, she still would see the events before their occurrence. A year later when she turned seven the images and thoughts would appear in front of her and around her. For example, she would have been walking down the street and she would see in her mind a man falling and twisting his leg. Then, almost directly after or a moment after, it would happen. This began to grow more and more frequent until she decided to go to a person who she thought might help. This person was a supposed witch named Majosei.

Majosei was not a witch capable of spells and elemental magic, but she could craft magical remedies and project her mind into the realms beyond to gain knowledge. She was branded as evil by the church and cast away. They could not burn her because she had received a royal pardon from Eleana's mother. Eleana was escorted outside of the capital with two guards who were to always watch over her. They were greeted by Majosei in the woods a mile out from the walls. She brought Eleana into her shack near the heart of the woods. The three entered the woods on horseback but when they had almost gotten to the heart of the forest, they knocked off the guards and Eleana. The horses ran back out of the woods leaving the three with Majosei. They walked nearly a quarter mile into the center of the forests' heart, and they reached her old wooden cabin.

The cabin was overgrown with weeds and leaves and there were tree branches growing into her windows on the sides of the cabin. "Come in," she said. "But you two must stay outside." The guards were hesitant at first, but Eleana reassured them.

Inside the cabin was a small table with a blanket draped over it. There were many candles lit around the room ominously illuminating the room. There were two chairs sitting across from each other at the table. A cushioned chair was set in front of the fireplace at the right of the room. The fire was out, however and the room was chilly. She sat down in one of the chairs and told Eleana to sit across from her. She took the blanket off the table and a red glass orb was sitting in the middle of it. It was resting on a golden stand that appeared like a clawed hand was holding it in place.

"What is it you seek from me?" Her voice was old and cracked at every other word. When she would finish a sentence, she would often follow it with a hoarse cough that sounded like she had smoked out of a pipe for her whole life.

"My head has been filling with visions of things recently. I could see people getting hurt and soon after it would happen in front of me."

Majosei scratched her wrinkled head. Flakes of dead skin fell off onto the floor and got stuck in her nails, which had not been cut or trimmed in a long time. She hovered her hands over the red glass ball and started to chant a few words in a language Eleana could not understand. The language was old, and the mere sound of the uttering made her feel a little tired. "Greyant -Mayee-Sayeetay-tayough-sayee-tahee-trayooth"

The words sounded like gibberish to Eleana, but when Majosei finished speaking, the room filled with wind, dimming the candles, and smoke filled the glass ball. There were quiet whispers coming from the glass and faces could be faintly seen swirling in the smoke.

"What is that?" Eleana asked.

Majosei cracked her knuckles on the table and stretched her legs out. They made a loud cracking sound like she had broken them. She grunted and straightened herself. She peered into the glass. "This is a Spectrin Orb. These were common in an older age among magic users. They would use it to peer into the future or into the minds of others to gain knowledge." She peered closely into it. "I see. I see. Your family has many special affinities to its blood. On one side, the kings and men of your family have a tie to the great mountain and that within it. On the other side, the queens and women of your blood have ties to the witch known as Sybralem, who was the first of her kind. From her blood, the women of your family gain some of her power and can use its abilities to some extents. What is happening to you right now, Eleana, is that you can use your mind to understand the world. For example, you could ask if something happened or not, and your body would subconsciously react to it in a positive or negative way."

They talked about some of the other benefits and a few secrets about her blood and the sun started to go down. She returned home and fell asleep.

CHAPTER 3

There were many secrets linked with Eleana's family's blood. All of which could be traced back to Sybralem, the first witch. In the older days, before the time of Kentrin's grandfather's rule, there were many magic users across Pleniris. At the time they were more feared than hated. Magic was not common knowledge in those ages, so when someone would see a magic user lift a table or catch a ton on fire, they would be terrified because they did not know what had happened. The only ones at the time who knew about magic, and some of the knowledge that comes with it, were from a village in the kingdom of Istimus near the great sea.

The village was a peaceful one and had no conflicts with any other village. They fished in the sea and provided food for the neighboring villages. That was true, until one of the women was fishing at the wrong place and the wrong time. It was late at night because the fish were hungry and eager for a meal under the great reddening moon. The red moon aroused many superstitions throughout Pleniris. They believed that when the moon changes color the demons of Hell ascended into the living world and impregnated a chosen woman. When the moon reddens, all men refuse to lay with their wives because they feared the idea of being possessed by a demon and put a devilish seed into their wives.

The woman sat in her favorite spot holding a line out into the water. The spot was a cliff that hung out over the water. The outer edge of the moon started to turn red. The woman felt a hard tug on the line, and she jerked the pole she held. She grabbed the string with a cloth by her side that she would use to prevent slicing her fingers open and started to pull her catch from the sea. When the catch was pulled all the way up, she dropped it on the ground beside her out of fear.

The catch was like no fish she had caught or seen before. It was black and was nearly the size of her forearm. There were horns growing out of its head, eight to be exact, and its eyes were attached to its head by elongated tubes like a snail's. There were four fins on its side and one tail. Its back was lined with spines from its neck to its tail.

The strange fish jumped around on the ground and opened its mouth and closed it again. It looked at the woman and stopped jumping. It seemed to freeze in place and fixate itself on her. The woman did not know what to do. The moon turned fully red, and the reflection of the sea made the water appear like blood.

"What is your name?" The fish asked. His voice was deep and loud yet sounded like a whisper. Its mouth was filled with rows of jagged teeth.

This of course startled the woman. It was of course uncommon for a fish, or any animal, to speak. "My, um, name is Sybralem. I am from a village nearby. How are you talking to me?"

The fish paused for a moment, shifting his eyes around, which made Sybralem a little nauseous looking at it. "My name is Grigori. Your kind does not particularly like mine. I am what you would call a demon in your tongue. I took this form because I thought it would appear a little less frightening. I was of course wrong."

"You are a demon?" She asked. "Why are you here, then?" She gasped. The thought suddenly occurred to her. Was he here for that? Was he choosing her as a carrier?

"I think you may have the right idea." He laughed. "I can't do that, though, in this form." The fish's body engulfed in smoke and in its place sat a man with orange eyes and wore a dark cloak.

The woman straightened up. "If you are going to, then go ahead." Secretly Sybralem wanted this. She had not planned it, but ever since the year prior, she had wished she would be chosen so she could destroy the village she lived in.

On the day prior, she was fishing with the other women of the village of Sylahm. A few of the men came from the woods behind her and asked her what she had caught. She told them she had caught about six fish since she started an hour before, and they smirked. They said they had another fish for her to catch. They proceeded to pin her to the ground and violate her. When they finished, they threw her in front of the rest of the village and told them that she offered to pleasure all four of them at the same time. The villagers laughed at her and called her the whore of Sylahm.

She told herself that she would find a way to get back at them. She had heard that the moon would bleed on the next night, so she snuck out and started to fish, hoping that she would be chosen to bear a child from a demon.

It was a tradition in Hell that when a demon chose a woman to inseminate on the night of a bleeding moon, they would protect the woman until the child was born. The demon would protect only that woman and no other until the day of the birth. There were some situations in the past where a woman chosen on the bleeding moon night would ask for favors from the demon and often it would grant them.

Sybralem was chosen. Grigori did the act and when he finished, he said, "The deed is done."

She nodded. She enjoyed it. Demon or not, she did not care. If it was good, the sex was appreciated. "Grigori, can I ask something of you?" She asked.

"Sure, go ahead," he said.

"Can you give me some way to get back at the villagers for humiliating and violating me?"

He thought for a long moment. "I do have an idea. It was a very old practice in the old ages. It was mutually considered forbidden even by God and Hellruler due to the unholy act."

"What is that?" She asked. The moon darkened and was surrounding Grigori's silhouette in the darkness. All that was visible in the bleeding light were his eyes in his shadowy form.

"People used to gain power through the consumption of higher beings. In the older ages there were a few people who had eaten demons and angels and received great power from the act. When one would combine the souls of a human and a higher being, a new soul was made that was filled with power from the higher being, but the human would remain mortal."

The act was considered forbidden by all kinds because the results of the act could not be entirely determined. It was greatly feared because one of the humans who had eaten an angel that had fallen from the sky grew hungry for more power. He used old rituals to summon demons and other angels to consume. By the time the human had turned thirty, he had consumed over fifty angels and demons. The power he gained was too much for even the archangels to handle, so their Lord banished him to a prison built in the center of Hell.

"And you expect me to just simply eat you?" She asked. The idea was both out there and was forbidden by everything that could think.

"That is right." He smiled. "I will revert to my aquatic form, and you will cook me. Devour me and I will be a part of you, protecting you from all harm. And when your child, our child, is born, I will materialize once more and continue with my what you would call life." He laughed. "I think it is a good deal. You get my power during the time I am with you, and you can do as you wish to those villagers you so despise."

The thought of course was insane, but to participate in an act that was forbidden by *God* was too intriguing of an offer to pass up. She had nothing to lose, and an eternity of punishment in Hell was in her mind worth it. "I'll do it," she said.

He laughed once more. It was dark and evil. His body turned into smoke, and he was the multi-horned fish again. She put Grigori inside of a sack that she brought with her to put her catches inside of. "Ack," he said, followed with a gagging sound. "These fish reek!"

On most nights when she fished, she would return with the sack no less than halfway full. She was dedicated to keeping the fish count high because the villagers that stood higher on the totem pole liked to gorge themselves and leave the poorest with next to none, if not none.

The moon was still red. It was not as dark as before, but it still was in its bleeding moments, like a healing scab that got scraped on something. She carried the sack she had back to the village. When she returned the villagers were all asleep. There were some whispers and laughs coming from inside the houses farther up the street who were most likely drunken men. Even more likely they were the ones who violated her before. She laid the sack by a small tent for a person to pick up in the morning to give out. She took out Grigori and walked on to her house.

She arrived at her home, which was a shack that had a partially caved in roof from the heavy rain that came a few days before. Nothing was destroyed from the cave besides the roof of course. She carried Grigori's fish body to a stick that was hovering over a pot in front of the fireplace. There was a small straw bed in the corner that was close enough to the fire to keep warm, but far enough away to still get chills from the wind that blew through the window at night.

She picked up the stick from the stand it was laying on and shoved it through the mouth of Grigori. With a struggle he managed to say that the rod tasted nasty, and the rust cut his mouth. The phrases that followed were a mess of gargling and muffled groaning. She lit the fire and waited for the wood to be fully aflame. When the flame was high, and the air was hot around it, she moved the rod over the fire.

The stand the rod was on was designed so that she would not get burned. The legs on both sides of the stand were connected at the bottom to hold it in place. The right side held the rod in place, with a place for it to lock into on the left side. There was a cloth wrapped around the lever on the right side of the bar so she would not burn herself. The flames started to lick Grigori's fish body, slowly cooking it through. A few of the scales fell off into the wood below. Grigori did not scream. Of course, the heat probably reminded him of home and relaxed him. He seemed to have fallen asleep. Or maybe the body was dying, and his spirit could not talk through it anymore and he was just hovering around waiting for Sybralem to eat him.

After about ten minutes or so she slowly started rotating the rod so the fish would get evenly cooked. Another five minutes passed, and it was ready. She grabbed a pair of tongs that hung on the left leg of the stand and grabbed a plate. Sybralem pulled the bar back and locked it in place on the left side of the stand. She pinched the body of the fish near the middle and gently pulled it off onto a cutting board. She cut off the head and carefully sliced the meat away from the center carcass. She divided the fish into four pieces, each about three to four inches long and two inches wide.

She sat down at her small table in the middle of the room and poured a glass of milk taken from the cows a few houses down. She went into her pantry in the corner and pulled out a few vegetables she picked from the garden behind her house.

She picked up a fork and knife and closed her eyes, about to pray for the meal, which was very ironic considering she was about to eat a demonic fish corpse.

"Go ahead. When you finish the meal, I will be in your mind and be able to provide any wishes you so desire," the voice of Grigori said. "At least within my limitations."

She started with the small potatoes and veggies, taking a few drinks of milk, and moved on to the fish. She picked the meat apart with the fork and knife and started to eat it piece by piece. The meat tasted surprisingly delicious. She had forgotten to season it, but the taste of the skin and meat was fine by itself. She finished the food and tried to pray once more. She stopped herself because she figured at that point her lord turned his sight from her when she ate Grigori.

She sat up from the table and suddenly felt dizzy. "Hello, Sybralem," Grigori's voice said. "So, what do you want to ask of me?" His voice was echoing in her mind.

"Anything, hm?" She asked. "Give me some power. Let me kill them in the village. I want payback for what they did to me."

There was a dark laugh that shook her soul, and she felt

a sharp chill run through her body. Her eyes started to burn, and the tips of her fingers turned numb. "Do as you wish. My power is yours. You can simply speak a command and it will happen. There are limits, but you will figure that out along the way."

She exited her house and pointed towards the church. "Burn." The words were whispered, and when she said it, a tingle surged through her arm towards her fingers. The church erupted in flames instantly and two people ran out of the doors, which had fallen behind them. The church collapsed and the smoke was shot in all directions around the charred wood on the ground. The sparks and flames flew to the other rooftops and started to light them ablaze.

The villagers started to run out of their homes screaming and crying in fear. Some were on their knees in the streets praying to their god and others were cursing him. Sybralem laughed manically and burning more houses and buildings.

Some of the villagers started to notice that the fire continued to grow in the places she was pointing. They started to gather more and more people, picking up tools and torches made from the damage. They started to make their way to her. Some of them started to throw their weapons and torches at her. It did no good. She simply waved her hand, and they flew away. Some of them flew back and hit the ones throwing them.

She saw the ones who had violated her. She curled her fingers into a fist and pulled her hand towards her. The men levitated and flew over to her. They were grunting from the pain and struggling to free themselves. "Why are you doing this, Sybralem?" They shouted.

Her eyes had turned a dark purple, and the sclera of her eyes had turned black. "You know why." These words were the last that the men heard. She twisted her hand and pointed her index and middle fingers at them. Their bodies started to turn red as if they were metal being held over a fire. They started to scream, and she waved her hand again. Their mouths were sewn shut and liquid fire poured from their eyes. The rest of their bodies started to leak the liquid from holes that started to form, and they melted into a pile of flesh, bone, and nearly melted organs.

The rest of the night that followed was quick. She spoke the word "kill," and all the other villagers had their necks snapped. They collapsed to the ground and the rest of the village burned to the ground. She sat in the center of the village watching the corpses burn in front of her. She had arranged them in a pile so they would burn all together. It pleased her to watch their bodies turn to ash. The village she grew up in was burned by her own hands. Was she upset? Of course not. In her mind she saw them as corrupt and that they deserved it. She mercy killed the elders of the village. The children, however, were killed in the fire because the parents left them unattended. That she was upset about, but she pushed the thoughts away. Her goal was complete, and she had other things to worry about. She had a child to birth and raise.

She left the village after she slept in front of the burning pile of corpses. She decided to venture towards the neighboring villages and make money from her newfound powers. From her came the imitating wizards and witches who performed fake magic on the side of the streets for money. Many of the other villages spoke about Sybralem's village burning down, but they did not know how it was.

The following months of Sybralem's life were of her traveling the lands and making money for her child. Grigori continued to aid her and keep her safe from harm. When she had her child part of her power was transferred to her. Her child was the grandmother of Eleana's mother. She would be the great grandmother of Eleana, and the reason of the royal family of Requilit having gifted females. The term 'witch" started to grow among those who feared the magic users and the witches adopted the name as their own term, as a joke to say they accept not being liked, and that even the greatest fears of man could not take their power from them. Only death could separate them from their power. And there were some witches, however, who even death could not separate from power.

CHAPTER 4

The day had come. The day of Kerstas' coronation. He was getting dressed in his room, with the help of Rengeon. He still stared at the mountain at night and had more vivid dreams about the inside of the caves. He occasionally would see a vague image of the rumored creature inside the caves that lead throughout the peaks. When he would see the creature inside, he would always be coaxed to peer into a hole that stretched seemingly infinite into the earth. When he would look closer to try to see the bottom, if there was one, the creature would groan, shake his head, and kick him into the hole. He would start to fall, but before he could see the bottom of the hole, he would wake up. The curtains would be opened with the cave staring at him like an eye in the mountain.

Kentrin entered the room. He was wearing a proud smile on his face seeing his son getting dressed for his coronation. The customs for the coronation have been the same for over four generations, around the times of the demon-possessed mad king of Meridine. The customs were that the current king would stand in front of the throne and perform a speech about respect, ruling, and religion. After the speech, the king would ask his successor to stand in his place in front of the throne, and the king would place a new crown on the heir's head, declaring him the new king. It was, of course, still a law that until the king dies that he will be the ruler of the kingdom, but a new king can be named even while the old king lives. With this scenario, Kentrin would declare Kerstas the new king of Requilit, and he would be the new ruler. Kentrin, however, would still have influence in the kingdom as a secondary king, who could give orders and keep the people in line, but Kerstas would take all the burdens of ruling Requilit on himself. Kentrin would of course be there to help until he died, but until then he would help Kerstas.

The queen during the ceremony would smile and sit quietly, as did everyone else, until her son was crowned. When the crown would be put on his head, the people in the audience would stand up from their seats, drop to their knees, and bow to their new ruler. The queen would then walk in front of her son, kiss him on the forehead, and curtsy, declaring how proud of a mother she is to see her son become king.

The next custom for the coronation is that the to-be king was not allowed to eat after waking up. This was because after the coronation there was to be a great feast, and everyone in the kingdom was to eat at it. It was the greatest feast, greater than the yearly cold-season feast thrown to celebrate the survival of another year. The people are always overjoyed to see how much the new king can eat. In the people's eyes, the more the king can consume at a feast or banquet represents him having a fire in his belly that will drive their kingdom to greatness. During Kentrin's coronation feast he had eaten through six platters of food before asking for the dessert to be brought in, and then ate three portions of it. The people believed that this was meant to mean he would be a great leader and had what it took to lead the country. And it was true. He undone the fear his father had put on the kingdom and its people and looked after his subjects. He was a great king, and the people were holding high expectations for his son, who was to be crowned in a mere hour.

Kerstas was led out of his room into the large room down the stairs, and further through the winding halls into the main throne room. Inside the room were rows upon rows of chairs stretching from the throne at the back to the entrance in the front. Beside the golden throne with red cushions on it were two chairs, both on either side of it. All the chairs were crafted of the finest wood in the kingdom, cut from trees in the grass lands near the Great Mountain. These trees are very special. They are called the King's Trees, earning their name because they are somehow naturally attuned to the heirs of the royal families of the four kingdoms. When the king is nearing the end of his life, the trees start to grow leaves. Up until this point the trees grow, appearing dead. When the king is nearing his end, and the next in line is to be crowned, the trees will bloom beautiful golden leaves and produce golden sap. The branches as well start to almost turn golden from the vines wrapping around them turning to the holy color. The trunk of the tree turns a beautiful dark brown, with an almost black void appearance at night. When the night approached, the leaves would reflect the moon's light and cast beautiful golden rays of light around them.

When the time comes near for the next king to be crowned, the branches, vines, and leaves will fall off to be collected and taken to the castle, where the servants and other workers will decorate the throne room with them. The scenery would resemble the vines curling around the walls and wrapping around the left and right side of the throne in the center. The golden leaves would be sprouting from the vines and the sap would hold them together until the ceremony was over. Using the very best leaves and vines the weaver of the royal family would weave a crown for the king, fitted perfectly to his head. The vines and leaves would hold their beautiful golden hue until it was nearing the time for a new king, and it would then wither away to dust.

Once the ceremony was over, the servants would then take the vines and leaves down and burn them in the center of town. The smoke would turn into a beautiful gold, while also choking out those who stood too close to it, and the ashes were collected to be used as a form of incense for the throne room.

Kentrin's crown was almost completely withered. He kept his in his chambers above his bed, where every king would store their crown because it would be bad luck for the crown to lose leaves out in battle or wandering about. It was rumored that if a king were to wear his crown when it was not required to, the leaves that fell would cause his life to shorten. This was never proven, but it was still best to avoid proving. There was only a singular leaf that held its golden color on his crown. The rest had either fallen off or shriveled into nothing. The vines were unraveling from their braided shape and had started to split apart.

This, however, was not told to Kerstas until a moment ago. It was tradition to keep this secret from the heir until their coronation day. And this secret was only kept to the king and his heir. No one else in the kingdom, not even Eleana or Inerium, could know about the crown and its association with the king's lifespan. If Eleana or Inerium were to find out about it, they would worry and become paranoid when they would see a leaf fall off, or even see that Kentrin's crown was nearly done for. This would indeed cause her great distress and would not bode well for the coronation of her son, whose crown would show how much of his life is left.

The hour was approaching. There were twenty minutes left until the ceremony would begin. The guards were standing at the doors keeping the people out. Some were trying to force the doors open just to see the new king-to-be. There were many thoughts going through Kerstas' mind, but the one that was going through his head the most was that when that crown was to be put on his head, he could finally expose those men of God for what they did since he was a kid. They deserved to be punished and whatever sentence should be carried out for them, in Kerstas' eyes, was not enough. He wished that they would suffer eternally in Hell to be treated as he was for so long, but for them it would last for eternity.

Kerstas sat down in his chair next to his father's throne. The room was beautifully decorated with the golden leaves and vines from the King Trees. The sun was rising above the hills and pouring light into the room, making the gold shimmer even more brilliant than before. Kentrin was sitting in his seat. He was proud of his son. Eleana was on the other side of the throne in her chair, and Inerium was given a small chair next to Kerstas.

A few moments passed by of silence and occasional glances from one another. Kerstas kept forming a smile, which his father thought was from him becoming king. While this was correct, it was not for the exact same reason. It was for the fact that *when* he became king, he would finally get his revenge on those holy men. He was not going to keep the churches from having priests. He was planning on having the people elect their own new priests from each church after the old ones were gone.

The time had come. The time for the ceremony. The sun had fully come into the room and the golden leaves were reflecting the light so brightly that if one were to stare at one for a few seconds they would think they had gone bright when they looked away. The guards opened the doors and the people started to pour in. All the people were gasping and pointing to Kerstas when they saw him. There were whispers going between them. Some of them could be heard, and they were talking about how they believed he would be a great king and would make his father proud. Some of the other comments were about how pretty the scenery was and that it was very bright. The kings of the other three kingdoms had shown up. They were to be seated in the front row in specially made seats. In the absence of the kings of the other three kingdoms, their sons and wives were to be trusted to rule. Each of the kings had two guards to protect them if it was needed. They were to stand guard on the far wall within a distance to apprehend one trying to assassinate them.

Each pair of guards bore the insignia of the crest of the four kingdoms. The crest of the Requilit guards was red and shaped like a diamond. The crest of the Venirit guards was yellow in the shape of a circular orb. The crest of Meridine was in the shape of a green eight-sided shield. The crest of Istimus was the shape of a blue rectangle. The king of Meridine was a large man, but not in fat. He was muscular and had a long black beard paired with his black hair pulled back in a bun to keep it out of his eyes. He was very scary looking, and he continuously eyed over Kerstas with a dark look in his eyes, which he assumed was just the king's way of things in his kingdom. The king of Istimus was rather lanky with light brown hair and looked like he did not want to associate with anyone around him. This was obvious because his hands shook when someone came up to him to say hello, followed by him sneaking away when they were not looking. The king of Venirit could not make it

Once all the people were seated, which all of them were not because there were so many, Kentrin stood up from his throne. "Hello, everyone. Thank you for joining us on this very special day. And thank you, lords, for going out of your ways to attend this ceremony." The room silent. "This day is special because my son Kerstas is going to be crowned as the new king of Requilit. He has turned the eligible age, and I believe he is ready to be my successor to the throne." He suddenly stopped. He looked at the mountain through the doors. "And now, a few words from the head priest of our grand cathedral here in the city." He sat back on his throne and started to rub his eyes. His crown lost another leaf. It started to unravel slowly as the priest walked onto the stage.

"Greetings, everyone! I am so happy to see you all gathered today for this special day." He turned towards Kerstas and smiled. There was a quiet laugh that came from his throat that only Kerstas could hear. He turned back to the people in the room. He continued about a speech talking about scriptures and God and other such holy things that made Kerstas' skin burn from the memories of those years of torment from them. Soon it would be. Soon it would be time that he could show all the people what they did to him and let them pay for their actions.

When the priest finished his speech, he finished with an "amen" and walked back to his seat. Kerstas had been so filled with rage that his legs were shaking up and down. He had to place his hands on his knees to stop them. A whisper started echoing in Kerstas' head and he looked out towards the mountain just as Kentrin did. He seemed to stare off for hours.

Kentrin started to call for him and put his hand on his shoulder. Kerstas snapped out of it and looked at his father.

"Son, it is time. Stand in front of the throne."

Kerstas stood up and walked over to the throne. Kerstas stepped out of the way and a few servants walked down the aisle with a crown on a red pillow. The crown was woven by multiple vines and many leaves were growing out of it. The sap that was used to hold it together was perfectly traced along the gaps in between the vines. The time was so close. The time he had waited years for. The servants knelt before Kerstas, and Kentrin picked up the crown. "As the king of Requilit, I, Kentrin, name Kerstas, my first-born son, the new king of Requilit." He started to lower the crown on Kerstas' head.

Suddenly, a scream came from outside, and everyone turned around to see what had happened. A few people came running through the doors trying to get through the crowd. Through all the panicking, the only words heard were "soldiers" and "dead."

A bunch of soldiers suddenly rushed through the doors and strung a few of the people up on spears. They cut the heads off some of the others around them and charged towards the front where the kings were. The crest on their armor was not present, so it could not be told which kingdom they were from. They all wore masks to cover their faces aside from their eyes. The guards around the room ran at them to protect the royals, but they were killed as well. They were pinned against the walls and chairs by spears. Two of them grabbed Kerstas and dragged him down the aisle. Eleana and Kentrin grabbed the soldiers and tried to pull them off Kerstas, but it was too late. Two other soldiers rushed in and drove their swords into the backs of the king and queen. They both gasped and fell to the ground. The guards for the other kingdoms had managed to safely get out during all the chaos, but it was not to be said about those of Requilit.

Kerstas cried out and lashed at the guards. They laughed at him because he could not reach them to do any harm. He lurched towards a part of one of the soldiers' legs that was not covered in armor and bit hard. His teeth sank into the skin and drew blood. His teeth went deeper, and the soldier kicked him off. He grunted in pain and punched Kerstas in the head.

The blow was heavy and Kerstas started to fall unconscious. He took one last look at his parents, who were gasping for air on the ground next to each other. The two soldiers that had stabbed them held their swords to the throats of the king and queen and opened them up. The last thing Kerstas saw was his parents coughing up blood with tears in their eyes.

CHAPTER 5

The ceremony was so chaotic that, in all the mess, no one noticed that Inerium had made it out safely through one of the hidden passages in the castle. As a younger girl Inerium wandered around the castle. Due to the bloodline connection to Sybralem, Inerium got fluttering feelings around the entrances to secret passageways, and she could every now and then hear voices telling her, or hinting at her, how to go into it.

When the first blood was drawn Inerium snuck towards the far wall close to where she was sitting. There was a painting of an old king of Requilit that was hung up. She pulled on it and it opened like a door. She climbed up into a hole in the wall and shut the painting behind her. No one had noticed through all the cries and fighting that she was gone. She crawled through the tunnel and entered a small room used for storage. There were old clothes and some small cleaning supplies used by the servants who lived in the castle due to their homes being destroyed prior to their duties under the king. She listened through the door for anyone on the other side. When she realized there was no one there she opened the door and entered a hallway near her room. She went into her room next and hid under the bed.

Inerium laid under the bed for a few moments making sure

no one was planning to come in. She grabbed a doll she had made in the likeness of her brother and opened a hatch under her bed (which she had discovered a year prior when she was pretending her dolls were in a cave) and jumped down into the hole below. The hatch shot above her, and she continued down the tunnel that was hidden below her bed her whole life. At the end of the tunnel was a large room that was shut off from the rest of the castle. There were no doors to lead into a hallway or bedroom. The room had a small table and a few dolls that Inerium brought in to play with. The room was used as a support for the other rooms above and around it. There was no knowledge that the room existed, and it was not known how tunnels were dug into it leading through the castle into more rooms just like it, which then led to accessible rooms through secret passages like the hatch in Inerium's room.

She picked up another two dolls she had made for her parents, but they burst into flames and the ashes fell on the ground. She looked at Kerstas' doll in her hand, and it was still okay. The history behind the dolls was that she had made them use the hair of the person the doll was in the likeness of. In some way they were voodoo dolls, but they were not used for dark purposes. They were simply used so that Inerium could attune her mind to the linked person and feel if they were okay, mentally, or physically. Other than the fact that she saw her parents die in front of her, the dolls turning to ash would have been a clear indication that they were dead, had she not known about their deaths. Knowing that Kerstas' doll was not harmed made her feel a little bit better.

There were two tunnels on the wall opposite the one she came in from. One led to the kitchens and the other led to an old cave that existed on the eastern wall of the city. She chose this tunnel and crawled through it for around a minute. The stone was wet and grew colder the farther she went in. There was a decline as she crawled further towards the cave. When she reached it, she dropped down a few feet into the cave, which was freezing and dark. There was a faint light coming from further into the cave. She followed it, watching her steps so as not to fall and hurt herself. When she reached the brighter area, she could see the end of the cave. The ground had a puddle of water sitting in the middle. It looked like it could be a pool, but there was no bottom to see because of how deep it went. She walked around the pool and headed on towards the light. Her eyes started to adjust to the light as she stepped into the field outside of the walls.

She was not sure what to do. She could not go home. There was no home to go to. Her only remaining part of home was Kerstas, and he was currently being taken away on a carriage towards the south along the main road surrounded by an army of calvary and foot soldiers. She decided to head out to a village close by that she visited as a younger girl. The people who lived there were nice and they loved Inerium.

The village was about a half-hour walk away. The sun had started to creep towards the western horizon. The stables were near where she had come out at. It came to her that getting a horse would make her journey better. She made her way along the wall, which was darkening from the shadows, growing larger as the sun set further. After a few minutes had passed she made it to the stable unseen. There were a few soldiers standing guard. They did not bear the insignia of her kingdom. They were the crestless soldiers who attacked the castle. Two of them were drinking flagons of alcohol laughing their asses off and three others were sitting in a circle around a fire roasting a pair of chickens they had killed from a farmer living nearby. Behind them were four horses. Two were brown, one was black, and the last one was a beautiful white stallion with a crimson red mane and tail. This horse was Inerium's, at least to her. She had never officially been gifted him, but the stable boys considered him her horse. And the horse claimed her, too, as his rider. She would sneak out of the castle walls (even before she knew about the secret passages) and feed him apples and hay for a few minutes and take him riding around the wall to let him exercise. She named him Snowfire, after the way it looked when he would run, as if his mane and tail were blazes of flame on a snowy field.

The other three horses of course were fed and loved by Inerium, but Snowfire was *her* horse. She was determined to get him. From the position she was standing in, Snowfire was the closest to her and the soldiers were on the other side of the stables looking in the opposite direction. She ushered out a whistle that was loud enough for Snowfire to hear but quiet enough that the soldiers could not. The horse started walking over to Inerium. His hooves were crunching on the ground, but the soldiers were too drunk to pay attention to the sounds. She jumped on him and grabbed the red leather reigns on him.

One of the soldiers stood up and stretched his back, almost stumbling over. He turned and saw Inerium on Snowfire. She froze in fear.

"Hey, you!" He called out. The other soldiers quickly turned and drew their swords and spears. One of them had a crossbow with a quiver of brown feathered arrows in it. She whipped the reins on Snowfire, and he dashed off away from the stables.

The men charged at her and started swinging their weapons at her. They did not know it was her. They only knew that some girl was running off with a horse, and they were ordered to kill everyone inside the city who tried to escape. They missed all their swings, and she whipped the reigns again. Snowfire ran faster and left them behind.

The man with the crossbow called out a signal and the others stopped and moved out of his way. He aimed and shot the crossbow at Inerium. The string was released, and the arrow flew towards her. It barely missed her head but still grazed her left ear. There were a few more arrows shot, but they all missed her.

After ten minutes of riding, she arrived at the village. It appeared safe and untouched by the soldiers. She rode to the stables and tied Snowfire up to them, feeding him some hay and water. She ran to one of the larger houses and knocked on the door rapidly. An older man opened the door and smiled.

"Hello, Inerium." The old man's voice was shaky and hoarse. "What brings you here so late in the evening? Isn't your brother's coronation today?"

Her eyes started to tear up. "The castle got attacked. These men came in and-"

Her voice was cut off. She started sobbing too hard to talk. The man hugged her and brought her into his house. It was old, but it was cozy. A fire was burning in front of a pair of chairs. A table was sitting next to a window with a chair sitting on both sides of it. She could see a larger straw bed in the next room. One of the sides was more worn than the other and the blankets were more fixed on the other. It was like half of the bed was just made and the other had been used by him. She did not ask about it out of respect. One thing her mother taught her a lot of was respect and manners. She assumed that there used to be someone in his life who would share those extra places with him at one point in life, but not anymore. A part of her mind as well was telling her that this was true, and she knew it was for the better if she did not bring it up.

He was cooking a stew in a metal pot over the fire. It smelled wonderful. There was an aroma of potatoes, meat, and other vegetables that blended and blessed her senses. "Would you care for some stew I made? It has rabbit in it." He made himself a bowl and reached for another.

Inerium nodded. She sat down in the other chair by the window across from him and started eating with a wooden spoon. The food was delicious. She paired the soup with a slice of bread he had on a shelf where he stored his meats and vegetables. She drank some water to wash it all down and thanked him for the meal. A thought suddenly struck her. What happened to Tsuin and Tsuon? The twin cooks back at the castle. As it was unknown to Inerium and Kerstas, they had gone out the day before to get some special spices for the big dinner that was to be held for Kerstas, but they heard about the attack and stayed around the Istimus kingdom where they were getting the spices. They were safe from harm in the inn they stayed at, worrying about their masters back home. When they learned about the deaths of Kentrin and Eleana, they were devastated and prayed to their god that Kerstas and Inerium had survived. Whether it was a miracle of God or not, they survived, nonetheless.

"Thank you for joining me, Inerium. I haven't shared a meal since my wife passed away. It has been almost five years since it happened." His voice was shakier. He took another bite of his food. "I don't mean to trouble you with my problems. I know you are going through a lot right now, and I am sorry. What do you plan to do?"

She wiped some tears away. "I don't know. I want to find my brother and get him somewhere safe."

"Where is he at now?" The old man finished his bowl. He took it and her bowl to clean it in a bucket of water.

"When I escaped the walls, he was being taken down the Eastern Road away from the city. I want to find him."

"Hmm. They might be taking him back to their kingdom. If you were to follow their path, you might be able to figure out who is responsible for this madness."

She got up from her chair and stepped outside. The people were stepping out of their homes. They saw Inerium and smiled and waved at her. They asked what she was doing at the village, and she explained what had happened. They were sad to hear about it and a few were scared that they might come for the village next and kill them all, too. This started to worry the villagers and one started to panic and pray on his knees. She told them not to panic and that it would be okay. This somewhat calmed them down, but they were still on the edge of terrified.

"How did you escape?" A woman in a torn green dress asked.

"I snuck out through an old tunnel under the castle. I rode Snowfire here. He kept me safe from the soldiers as we were heading this way."

The man that was still freaking out froze. "You mean that they *know* you went this way?" His voice increased in levels of fear. It was true. They saw her come this way to the village. That means that if they really wanted her dead then that means only one thing.

There was suddenly a sound of thundering hooves closing in from the distance. Inerium looked over and saw over a dozen calvary soldiers charging towards the village with weapons drawn out. Their yells and shouts could be heard even from the distance they were at. The older man's eyes grew wide, and he grabbed Inerium's shoulders.

"Inerium, grab your horse. Ride East to the border. Tell them that you have urgent news about the attack in Requilit and you must speak to the king. They should escort you to the main city in Venirit where the king will be. Ride East until you see the forest. Find the main path through it and it will take you directly to the border of Requilit and Venirit. Go now!" He rushed her towards Snowfire, and he lifted her onto him. He untied the reigns and handed them to her. He smacked the ass of Snowfire, and he galloped off East.

Inerium turned to look back at the village as she was rushing away, and the old man was smiling and waving at her. She waved back and an arrow flew through the back of his head through his eye. His hand twitched and tried to reach to pull the arrow out, but he fell to the ground.

She cried out but she knew she could not stop. The moment she tried to think about turning around to help, her head filled with images of her being killed by the soldiers, so she kept on riding. She felt guilty for turning her back on them and leaving them for death, but it had to be done. She knew the king of Venirit knew of the attack, but she had to let him know that the ones responsible were heading down the Eastern Road that leads South. She whipped the reigns, shouted, "Yah," and Snowfire galloped faster East, with the forest coming into view.

CHAPTER 6

Inerium had made it to the forest. After minutes passed of scanning the edge of the forest for a path, she found it. There was a large gap in between the trees where a dirt pathway slithered through. The trees were tall, and the leaves were coming to life and reflecting the sunlight with a beautiful green color as the sun was rising. She had camped out when the sun set and ate some small vegetables she found growing out of the ground along the way. She had a leather drinking pouch in the saddle of Snowfire's saddle and used it to collect some water \from a nearby stream. The weather was peaking from changing over to the hottest part of the seasons, and the sun was shining very brightly. The heat could be felt radiating off the forest, and the denseness of the woods would most likely increase it further.

There were a lot of rumors that circled around the forest that connected the kingdoms of Requilit and Istimus. There were some rumors that said that the woods were haunted by the ghosts of those who died inside, and there were others that said it housed woodland elves who used an old form of magic to keep themselves hidden from the outside world. Whether they were real or not, Inerium had heard far more stories told by her grandmother when she was alive. She had told many various stories about the "old woods of the north," as she called them.

The stories Eleanor, Eleana's mother and Inerium's grandmother, had told to Inerium were what she would tell her to go to sleep. Some tales were of the elves rumored to live there and others were about a dark part of the forest where a dark race of elves lived and practiced the dark magic that was forbidden from use. She had to travel through the woods many times to gather the plants she used for her grandmother's old garden that she loved to visit, and for the many rare spices and herbs for her meals and medicines.

She ignored all the fears going through her head and pushed on into the forest. The heat was strong as she progressed further down the path, increasing more the longer she and Snowfire traveled. Minutes passed and she started to sweat. When she looked behind her, she could no longer see the opening where she had started from. The path had twisted and turned through the trees until the sun could barely seep through the leaves above. The leaves were a dark green, lit only a little by the sun, and the wood was a darker brown than common trees. They were a lighter color than the King's Trees near the mountain, but they were close to it. The area was dark due to the little sunlight coming through, and the air was both cold and hot at the same time. In one area Inerium would feel the burning from the sun, and other areas she would get chills where the sun refused to look.

Snowfire was beginning to grow thirsty. He kept swaying more and more as they trudged on. "It's okay," she said, "we will find water soon."

After a few more minutes of continuing the path Inerium suddenly stopped. She listened closely and could faintly hear water splashing. She pulled the reigns towards the noise and

Snowfire followed in its direction. They wandered off the path and cut through the trees, Inerium nearly getting hit in the face by low hanging branches. A few twigs and leaves got caught in her messy hair. They made it into a small clearing and saw a small pool of water, and beside it was a beautiful red stag whose horns were great in size. A prize in the eyes of a hunter. He was a massive creature, with his head at least six feet from the ground. His horns were a great white color with some of his fur growing onto them. they sprouted out like a tree's roots in the ground. His eyes were a fearsome black that could pierce the soul of one who looked at them.

The stag looked at Inerium on Snowfire and stared at her. The silent, cold stare pierced her like a sword and the eye contact did not break. "It is okay," she said, "we are not going to hurt you." The stag almost seemed to understand her because after she said it, he lowered his head and continued to drink the water.

Snowfire walked to the pool and Inerium got off him. She refilled her drinking pouch as Snowfire drank from the pool. The stag continued to drink unbothered from their presence. His breathing was the only sound that could be heard, aside from Snowfire's breath and the occasional chirp of birds flying overhead.

After the pouch was filled up, she drank the pouch dry and refilled it. The trip had parched her, and she needed hydration. She put the pouch on Snowfire's saddle and decided to take a bath. The water itself was quite warm for how cool the air around the pool was. It was nothing like the hot baths she took back at the castle. She took off her dress and set it on a rock on the bank. She took off her leather shoes that were made for her during the last warm season past. She unclothed the rest of herself and got into the pool. She tore her brassiere up and used it as a scrubber to get the dirt off her. Even if it meant that her breasts would not have any support, she would rather be clean than not. She dunked her head in the water and soaked it for a few seconds and slung it back when she raised her head from the pool. When she finished cleaning herself, she found a section of the pool where the wall was solid rock with no dirt at all. She rested her back on it and used her arms to hold herself above the water. She closed her eyes and took in the area, relaxing in the warm pool.

Inerium opened her eyes and looked around. The stag had disappeared and so had Snowfire. She quickly got up and reached for her clothes. She threw on her shoes and slipped her blue dress over her. The skirt had ripped when she picked it up due to the end getting snagged on a sharp end of the rock. The damage was not too bad, but the tear ripped one of the sides up to her waist. The cloth clung to her skin as she walked due to her being wet from the pool. Every step she took was colder than the last as the chilling wind blew towards her through the trees.

Inerium saw prints on the ground that matched Snowfire's. She followed them through the woods and found a pile of shit he had left behind. It was not too old, but it was not fresh either. It had been there long enough for flies to swarm it and eat at it. She continued to follow the prints farther into the woods until they stopped suddenly. She looked around on the ground to find any other signs that Snowfire could be nearby, but there were none.

There was suddenly the sound of a twig snapping behind her. She quickly spun around to see what the noise was. There was nothing there. The leaves above rustled, and she looked up to where the noise was. In the branches was a large person crouched down staring at her. She gasped and stepped back. The person jumped down and stood upright.

It appeared to be an elf, but not as they were described to her in old tales. In the old tales the elves were said to have green skin, pale eyes, and very short. This was not the case at all. The elf standing before Inerium stood around seven foot tall, had light brown eyes, and had blonde (almost white) hair braided down to his lower back. His hair was over his ears, so she could not tell if the old tales were true about their pointed ears, and his skin was in fact not green. It was a tone like one would see in the center of a tree when it is cut. He wore a long white robe that wrapped around his body tightly and his arms loosely. He was carrying a large wooden bow on his back with a vine-woven quiver for his arrows made of sticks and feathers. He looked at her and seemed to study her as he looked up and down her body, like he had never seen one of her kind before. It was likely that this was true, because it had been ages since a human and an elf made contact of any sort with one another. The elves had boiled down to being mythical creatures that existed in fairy tales and old stories who had traveled off to a faraway land to live in peace away from the rest of the world.

She raised her hand and tried to wave at him. He flinched in fear and reached his hand for his bow.

"No, it is okay." Inerium put her hands down. "I do not mean to hurt you or anything. I was saying hello."

The elf stood still, his hand still near his bow. His stance lowered slightly as if he were ready to lunge backwards and fire an arrow at any moment. Inerium thought for a moment to figure out how she could deescalate the situation. She smiled at him and slowly walked towards him, like one would to a horse. She would inch closer to him, pausing when he would twitch and close his hand in to his bow. She continued to tell him she meant him no harm and that she was friendly.

She was close to the elf, very close. She was close enough that she could reach out and touch him if she stretched out enough. the elves breathing was calm, yet his eyes were opened enough to know he was ready for anything to happen. A feeling suddenly came into her, and her mind flooded with an idea to try. It was difficult to explain what went through her head, and how it did, but it made sense to her, and her gut feeling backed it up.

She walked to the tree next to her and put her hand on it. Her grandma told her in an old tale that the elves were very in tune with nature and could almost sense how the plants and trees were feeling. Inerium used this story to help her. She placed her hand on the tree and the elf looked at her. He moved his hand away from his bow and slowly walked over to the tree her hand was on.

He placed his hand on the tree next to Inerium's hand. Her heart was racing. He closed his eyes and took a deep breath. He held still for a moment, holding his breath as if he was listening to the tree talk to him, and let it all out. He opened his eyes and looked at her. He smiled and reached his hand out to hers. He spoke a word in a foreign language and led her through the woods. They passed by many trees. Inerium tried to count them as they passed, but she lost count after she reached the fifties.

They reached a clearing in the woods where one massive tree stood. the tree stood higher than all the others and was so round that it would have taken ten men to wrap around the tree, with their arms fully extended holding each other's hands. He led her to the tree and said a few more words in his language. He pointed at his hand and then at the tree.

She put her hand on the tree's trunk and looked at the elf. He walked up to her and said a word, gesturing that he wanted her to say it. "Mo-thee-array-trayee," he said as he made the gesture. She repeated the words, and the tree grew warmer. Part of the bark opened suddenly like a door and a large tunnel was dug through its inside into the ground.

He led her down into the tunnel. The door shut behind them. It was pitch black in the tunnel, and the air still somehow remained warm despite being underground. The elven man said another word and a small flame appeared in his hand, illuminating the tunnel. The roots trailed down further, almost as if they were manipulated by magic to create the passage, they were traveling in. The flame did not seem to burn the elf, despite radiating a strong source of light from it. After a minute or so of walking down through the tunnel, the area opened, and the roots curled around the edge of the tunnel's exit.

The next area they entered was magnificent, almost as if she had entered a dream. There were large sources of light on the ceiling from seemingly nothing besides magic. That is exactly what it was. Magic. The elves had separate divisions of magic that they used in the old tales, deriving from the six natural elements of the world, which were air, water, earth, fire, light, and darkness. The one Inerium was traveling with was an elf who could use pyro-based magic, which was the fire element. Not every elf had the gift to use this magic, but there were so few who could not that it was written that they all possessed the ability.

There were large houses made from stone and tree roots connected by stairs and ladders in the large, cavernous room. At the bottom of the area was a large pool of water reflecting the sky above, which was able to be seen from a hole in the top of the cave. There were many elves that looked like the one Inerium was with, all walking together along the paths to the many buildings and hanging stone platforms with wooden archways connected to each other forming a ceiling. On some of the platforms were fountains of marble producing crystal-like water, and the water would refill from the water below with water magic used by water magic gifted elves. One elf was tasked to keep up the flow of the water, but she had done it for so long that it was like breathing for her and she did not have to think about it to keep the flow going.

The platforms and other structures had been formed from the elves who could use earth magic, and the other water craftsmen helped by using the water in the vines to lead them down into the shapes they were now. The fire and air gifted elves used their magic to create warm steam that kept the air at a constant comfortable temperature year around, even in the coldest and hottest of seasons.

The elf led Inerium down a set of wooden stairs that curled in a spiral down onto a platform with a golden wood railing circling it. They walked down and passed by a pair of elves walking side by side and talking. They were also wearing white robes matching the one accompanying her. They had gold words in a foreign language, most likely theirs, lined on the edges of the robes. There was a golden line underneath the lettering that ran along the robes under the letterings. From Inerium's understanding, the gold lining on the robes meant they were either royals or they were a higher class than the one with Inerium was.

As they passed the two elves, he bowed to them and they did the same, but only half as low as he did. They continued and passed over a few more bridges and platforms. It seemed that they were heading towards the large platform in the center that was suspended by thick vines on eight different parts of the platform. At young ages the Elven kids would run on these vines from end to end despite their parents telling them not to because it was not safe. There were a few doing it as they entered the large platform. One was all the way at the end, and the other three were on the others about halfway across them. Inside the large platform were three large thrones. The one in the middle was taller than the other two, and they were all a beautiful gold-painted wood with the same writing around the edges of them. The handles on the throne were carved to resemble water flowing, and the back of the chair had a carving of two stags facing each other standing proudly on a cliff. The horns of the stags extended past the throne, and their eyes were large silver jewels that glimmered in the sun's reflection.

In the thrones were three elves. The center one wore a large crown of silver, with sterling leaves dangling from the top. He was wearing a large necklace like a stag's antlers and wore a glittery silver robe with golden lettering around the neck and edges of the robes. His eyes were a golden brown.

The elf on the left throne was wearing a silver and gold alloy circlet with a bright green jewel in the center of it, where the metal looked like branches twisting together. His eyes were green, and his lips were painted green on the lower lip. His eyes were also green, but they were brighter than the greenest leaf in the warmest season. It was as if the color was created from his eyes.

The elf on the right throne was beautiful beyond measure. Looking into her eyes was like looking into a sky full of stars shining as brilliantly as ever. Her smile was kind and warm, and her dress was blue and silver, with depictions of fish jumping over ocean waves. She was wearing a silver necklace that had a blue crystal being held by silver waves. It could be assumed that she was an elf who possessed water magic, which was correct. She was the one who kept the water flowing into all the fountains and who formed the tunnel into this beautiful elven city. She was the wife to the man on the center throne. The elf on the left throne was the son of the other two. These three were the highest class of elves.

The elven man with Inerium bowed in front of the three, and she did the same. The center elf asked a question in their foreign tongue, and the elf with Inerium responded. They held conversation for around a minute, gesturing to Inerium and back around to other places. She was confused, but she remained bowed until she was told otherwise, even if she embarrassed herself in the process.

"Rise up," the center elf said. His voice was soft spoken yet firm in tone. It was a voice that could put one to sleep, but make you do anything it asked all the same. "What is your name?" Inerium was confused that the elven man knew how to speak her language. She thought that they only knew the elven language they had been speaking in.

"My name is Inerium. I am the daughter of King Kentrin of the Royal House of Requilit." Her voice was trembling from how nervous she was. Until now she thought that elves were only a myth.

"Inerium. Forgive me. You are probably confused as to why you were brought here. I am Evindal, king of the woodland elves. This is my wife Aylisen and my son Ellisar. We welcome you to Olmenor, one of the last elven cities in these lands. One of our scouts saw you and your horse at the pool near the borders of our lands."

Inerium was shaking beyond control at this point. She was happy that she did not have to bow anymore. Her back was hurting from being bent over for so long. "Where is my horse?" She asked. "Where is Snowfire?"

"Snowfire?" Evindal asked. "What an interesting name but fitting in a way." He looked over at his wife and asked her something in his tongue. He turned his head back to Inerium. "Yes, he was brought to the place where we keep our mounts." He pointed over to a place where stairs made of tree roots curled around the wall and led outside where the sun and moon would shine into the elven city. Outside of the cavern was a small clearing where they built feeding grounds that their stags would stay at. They could come and go as they pleased, but when they heard the whistle or call of their rider, they would come running to them, ready to go where they were led.

She started to walk towards the bridge that led up to the stairs, but Evindal stopped her. She turned towards him. He stood up from his throne and walked over to Inerium. He was at least around seven foot tall. His near-white hair was braided into three braids. Two of them were on the fronts of his shoulders and the middle one was on his back with the rest of his hair. His face was like marble, and it seemed as if he did not even have pores with how his face was, like it was cut from marble.

"Come with me," he said. He started walking across the bridge towards the stairs. As they walked across the bridge, the lower levels of the city could suddenly be seen. There were houses on platforms held in the air by vines with bridges leading from one another, and stairs and ladders led to the higher level that Inerium and Evindal were on. There were other elves in plain white robes walking among the bridges and paths. Some had younger elf children with them playing with each other and running in circles around their parents. The difference in classes in the elven community could be easily seen from the difference in robes. There were plain white robes on elves (and some with silver lettering) on the lower levels, and there were robes with golden lettering on elves (along with the royals) on the upper level of the city of Olmenor. Even with the most seemingly perfect race known to these lands, they still separate their people by class. However, the difference in classes were not divided to be negative on those of the lower classes. They were divided because the ones with the higher-class robes had more of a responsibility in the councils and duties of Olmenor compared to those of the plain and less ravishing ones. They made it to the staircase leading out to the surface and they began heading up.

"Inerium, correct? There is something I must ask of you. I know it is a lot, but I have no other choice." They made it to the top and the sun was setting. The sky was a dark purple that faded into an orange towards the West. To the left was a large pile of straw and berries for feeding. Snowfire was helping himself to the pile along with two white stags and a black stag.

"I need to head to the kingdom of Venirit and talk to the king. I must tell him that my brother is still alive and being taken South. I was told they could help me get him back." She had not forgotten for one second what was at stake. Kerstas needed her, and time was running short. She was fearing that the other kings in the other kingdoms were in danger from the ones who killed her parents.

"I know that you need to save your brother, but how can you when the way out of the other side is blocked by evil magic?"

Inerium stopped. She was about to run and hug Snowfire, but the new news puzzled her. "What do you mean? What evil magic?" She asked. The concept of magic existing was already a big slap in the face for her, especially with the existence of elves on top of that. The idea of evil magic also existing was of course needed to have good magic. There must be a balance between good and evil, but the thought of *what* evil magic could do was scary to Inerium.

"We are not the only elves in these woods, child." His voice suddenly held a weight of fear on them. The warmth of his voice suddenly had a chilling undertone to it. "A long time ago, in an age when man was still young, we elves ruled these lands as our own. Then, when man came to gain powers beyond their comprehension, they started a war with us. They used unnatural magic on us to drive us away, and those of us that remained had to go into hiding as to protect our own."

"Why did you all not go away with the rest of the elves?" Inerium asked. The question was innocent, but she thought it came off a bit rude, like she did not want them living in Pleniris, which was not the case at all.

"We woodland elves have a connection to these woods, whether it is physically, ancestrally, or spiritually. Those of us that already lived in the woods remained while the rest of our brethren went on to the lands beyond the great salty waters." He looked out in the direction directly in front of the exit of Olmenor. The woods almost seemed fouler in a way. Inerium got an uneasy feeling in her stomach when she followed his gaze into the woods. Evindal took a deep breath. "You feel evil, too? Yes, that part of the woods is corrupt. A few centuries ago, about a dozen elves ventured out to gather some food and supplies. On their way, they encountered an ancient relic in the old city of Nellenor. The item corrupted them and turned their skin a charcoal grey and gave them dark powers. They put a spell on the surrounding woods and trapped us inside, and if a passerby were to stray away from the main path and come into our lands, they would be trapped forever by the evil magic. What I am asking of you is a lot, I know, but if you want to escape these woods and save your brother, then this is the only way to ensure you can."

Inerium thought on it. She knew she needed to save Kerstas no matter the cost. To do that she would need to get out of the woods first. She nodded her head. "I will do it." She meant the words she said. in her eyes there was no other choice but to do this. How else would she save him? She was the only one who knew where he was, or the fact that he was still alive.

"Good." Evindal smiled and put his hand on your shoulder. "There is more to you, young princess. There is magic in your veins as is in mine, but I sense something stronger than even that." There was a tone in his voice that almost seemed that he wanted to say more about the thought, but he decided not to. He held his tongue about it and cleared his throat like he was disposing of unspoken words. "What you need to do is ride your horse to Nellenor and find the old relic that corrupted our brethren. I do not know how many are left but beware of their magic. I do not even know its limits."

"Where is the city?" Inerium asked. She could tell from the sun setting that North was almost directly ahead of her. The sun was almost fully submerged below the skyline.

He pointed forward, around Northeast. "That way. It is about a mile or so in that direction and when you start to see the decay increasing, you will be close." He lowered his arm and sighed. "It is late, though. Perhaps it can wait for one night. What do you say?"

Inerium wanted to just hop on Snowfire's saddle and run off to Nellenor, but she was exhausted. She had traveled all day through the forest and her mind and body needed rest. She smiled and nodded her head.

Evindal smiled and put his hand on her shoulder. They walked back down the stairs into Olmenor. Where the sun had left the view of the city, the lights on the ceiling grew brighter and reflected in the water below, creating a crystal-like, almost unnatural, surface. "There are places to sleep over there." He pointed to an area away from the platforms in the center. There were small buildings like cabins made of wood and polished stone built into the walls of Olmenor. There were at least three dozen of them on the wall. They all had a small balcony to overlook the city and a few windows to look out at the sky and at the other cabins to greet neighbors if one wished. On the left-hand side of the cabins (on the right if you were on the balcony looking out) was a small opening that led off.

The cabins on the upper levels had ladders in these openings that led down to the bottom level cabins. At the bottom of the ladders was a wooden platform that was built as a large, interconnected balcony for the lowest level cabins. From this wooden platform were rope bridges that crossed the gaps between the cabins and the platforms that made up the city of Olmenor. If one were living on the highest cabin and wanted to go to the city, they would have to go onto their balcony, scale down their ladder, and walk out across the bridge into the city.

Evindal told Inerium that she could have one of the cabins on the higher levels, because the others had been occupied by the other elves of Olmenor. She was told that when the sun rose the next day that she was to join him and the other high council elves for a meeting. He bowed his head and turned away to return to his throne.

Inerium walked across one of the four bridges that crossed the water below. She looked down and could clearly see herself in the reflection of the water. She smiled at herself and headed towards the ladder on the wall. There were nails in the wood on every fifth step on the ladder holding it onto the stone. She clutched the wood and began climbing up. She made it about halfway and turned her head. She was already so high up and could see everything in the city. It was much larger from the height she was at compared to being at the floor level of it. She made it to the top of the ladder and stepped onto the balcony of the cabin she was to stay in.

She shut the gate where the ladder was and leaned over the balcony railing. The city was beautiful in the bright moonlight. The pool below was shimmering from the moon and the ceiling lights. The wooden tops to the platforms reflected the light and gleamed beautifully. The water had started to form spirals as it trickled down from the fountains around the city. There were a few elves still roaming the paths and looking at the stars above. Inerium yawned and stretched out her arms.

She opened the wooden door to the cabin and stepped inside. The inside was beautiful and cozy. There was a fire burning in the wall, in what seemed to be a fireplace with no chimney. The fire was burning without any wood or coal. The fire was just burning on its own, and it was not hot. It made the room a perfect medium temperature to balance the fire and the cold stone. There was a cotton-sewn bed with a soft yellow blanket and fluffy pillows to match. She took her shoes off and quickly ran and jumped onto the bed to keep her feet off the cold ground. She covered herself up with the blanket and stared out of the window to the left of the bed. She could clearly see some of the city and all its magnificence. She turned onto her left side and closed her eyes.

CHAPTER 7

Kerstas opened his eyes. He was lying on the floor of a cart being pulled by a black horse. At the front of the carriage was a man with short brown hair wearing a set of armor holding a whip. He was the driver of the carriage. Across from him were two soldiers with their hands on their swords. Their armor had no symbol or crest to show which kingdom they belonged to.

He sat up and rubbed the back of his head. It ached badly from being stuck. His back was sore from the awkward position he ended up lying in after being thrown onto the carriage. His rms were tired and his whole body hurt. His eyes adjusted to the light and the sun was just starting to peek out around the sides of the mountain.

The large mountain was staring at them as they were traveling down the road. The party he was with had about six carriages, ten mounted soldiers, and about a dozen or so foot soldiers that were not in the carriages sitting down. Inside the carriages were probably about another dozen, maybe even two dozen, soldiers. He moved his gaze around to see if he could find the leader of the group. His eyes fixed themselves on one at the front of the party riding a large brown horse with white, almost grey, spots on his hide. The man had a very expensive-looking armor set on and had a gold-hilted sword, whose scabbard was the same. The hilt and scabbard combined to form a full picture engraved in them. The image on the two created a two headed dragon whose body curled around the scabbard and ended near the tip of it. There was a great mistake, though. At the end of the scabbard was a symbol. But before Kerstas could get a good look at it, the wind blew the man's red cape over it and covered it.

The two sitting across from Kerstas saw that he was awake and sitting up. "Hey, look who finally woke up," the one on the left said.

The other one chuckled and scratched his chest under his armor. "We were thinking you had gone and died on us. I was starting to worry." He laughed again and burped, almost puking.

The road they were on was close to the mountain. Just barely in the distance he could see the large King Trees towering over the smaller trees surrounding the mountain. The shadow of the mountain covered most of the lands around them. There were some small villages that they had passed. Kerstas could see them getting smaller as they grew farther away from them.

"Who are you all?" he asked. "Why have you done this?"

"Be quiet," the one on the left said. We would have done away with you already if it weren't for that damned prophecy." He quickly paused and his eyes widened. He had slipped up.

The other soldier looked at him. His black beard was tangled up in the chin strap of the helmet he was wearing. "We were told not to mention that. That is supposed to be a secret. If word got out that he knew about it, chaos would erupt out of every corner of these lands!"

"I'm sorry. It slipped out. It won't happen again."

The soldier with the beard nodded. "Good," he said. He looked back at Kerstas. "We are ordered to keep silent about a lot of things. What you can know, though, is that because of the prophecy numbskull, here, spoke of, we were ordered to do what we did. That is all I can say."

"I do not care about prophecies and orders. You all murdered my family and took me from my kingdom. You murdered and slaughtered them. No excuse justifies that." Kerstas looked back at the mountain. He grew chills down his neck and shivered a little.

The sun was starting to come up and the air was warming. With the hot seasons peaking, the heavy armor the soldiers were wearing caused them to sweat much more. The leader of the party held his hand up and let out a loud whistle. The party came to a halt.

"Time for the morning meal," the soldier on the left said. He was heavier set so of course he was excited to hear that. He quickly jumped off the carriage and ran to the clearing where some of the other soldiers were setting up a large fire and clearing some weeds for a sitting area.

The last remaining soldier on the carriage stood up. He pulled out a leather rope. "I am sorry, king Kerstas." His voice was near a whispering level so no one could hear him talking to him. "I need to restrain your hands. Forgive me." He tied up Kerstas' hands and stood him up, leading him off the carriage.

"Why are you being nice? You all killed my family and everyone I knew. What reason should I have to forgive you."

"I know," he whispered. He walked away from the group out of earshot. He turned towards the rest of the soldiers. "He has to take a shit!" he shouted out. A few of the soldiers waved as a sign of hearing him and returned to watching the fire, which a large portion of meat was being grilled over on a metal slab. "Drop your pants and crouch on the ground. Pretend you're shitting."

Kerstas was confused, but he did so anyway. He dropped his trousers and squatted down to the ground. There was a bush in between him and the soldier for privacy, at least by appearance. "What is this about?" he asked.

"I had to separate us from the group so that we could talk privately." He looked around to make sure no one was eavesdropping on them. "I owe you my life, King Kerstas. Your father saved my life. He was traveling the other kingdoms and came across my village when it was being raided by bandits. I was just a young boy back then. He saved everyone he could, and his men killed all the bandits. He made sure I was okay and took me and my family to the king of our country. I was recruited into the ranks of his army and raised as a soldier. I owed my life to your father, Kerstas. I did not know what was happening the other day until it was too late. Our orders were simply to accompany our king to your coronation. Then, when the ceremony began, we were given orders by our captain to kill everyone in Untris, Requilit's capital. I did not know what we were getting ourselves into. I was told that I was supposed to meet you once the ceremony was over and you were to start your travels across the kingdoms. I heard the screaming, which at the time I thought was cheering with all the noise, and when I came int, I saw what had happened."

Kerstas was silent. It took a few moments for him to process it. How many of them truly knew what was going to happen? He felt more sympathetic towards the soldier. *He* did not kill his parents, of course. He should not be blamed for the actions of his comrades, those who were under orders. When recruited in the ranks, refusing order meant treason, therefore death by hanging or beheading. He suddenly remembered what his goal was. His revenge. He now had two revenges to carry out. He had to kill the ones who ordered the men to murder his family and people, and he had to have his revenge on the priests who violated him for so long.

"What is your name?" Kerstas asked.

"My name is Barnabin, sir." The politeness was odd for Kerstas. It was very formal, as if he was the soldier's king and not whoever his real king was.

"I am not your king. I am no one's king now. My kingdom is dead because of these men. Why do you still treat me like one?"

One of the soldiers hollered out for them. "Hey," he called out. It was the fat one from the carriage they rode on. "You all coming? Little man of his size can't hold that much in him, can he?" A few of the soldiers around him laughed at his comment.

"Coming!" Barnabin shouted. He stood Kerstas up and helped him put his clothes back on. It was hard to do with his hands being restrained. "We will talk later. But I still call you king because you earned the title. Kingdom or not, you are still a king, Kerstas. Even if you are not my king, I still hold respect for those who wear a crown, and where you are Kentrin's son it makes that all the better in my book." He walked Kerstas back to the other soldiers and sat him down.

Barnabin was handed a bowl, and it was filled with small chunks of cooked greasy meat and a piece of bread. He started eating. The man who filled his bowl looked at Kerstas and smirked. "You want some of this, boy?" He laughed and walked away, filling the bowls of the other soldiers who were waiting for their food.

Kerstas was starving. He of course had not eaten since the day *before* the coronation, as it was tradition for the king to be hungry for his first Feast of the King.

Barnabin leaned closer to Kerstas. Not too close to arouse suspicion, but close enough to make it look like his side was hurting and he was relieving pressure off it. "Wait until we are about to leave, and I will give you some to eat. I cannot give you a lot because they might suspect thievery, but I can give enough to nearly satisfy you.

"Thank you, Barnabin. I would knight you as my own if I could. You are a good man." He faintly smiled and quickly wiped it off his face before the other soldiers could see.

"Really? Why would you do that, sire? I cannot even follow the orders of my own king."

Kerstas glanced at him. Barnabus had a sad look in his eyes. He believed that he was a disgrace to his kingdom and to his king, but that was not the case. "Barnabin, there is no dishonor in going against orders you morally believe are wrong. *You* can make the choice to do an unholy order or not. If I were your king, I would be proud of you for disobeying the order to help murder an entire city for my own paranoia."

Barnabin smiled. "Thank you, Kerstas. If you, no, *when* you get your kingdom back, can I become a soldier and fight for you?"

Kerstas nodded. He coughed from some dust that flew in his mouth from a soldier who was walking by. He glared at the soldier and returned to stare at the horizon, where the sun was now rising fully above. The soldiers were talking amongst themselves about a lot of nonsenses. Some were bragging about how they had their way with some of the women in Untris, (the capitol of Requilit) and some were talking about how they could not wait to get back home. He overheard a conversation with a group of soldiers that were sitting about ten feet away from him.

"Do you really think it is about him?" one of the soldiers asked.

"No, but the king seems to think so. Who are we to question him?" The soldier was large and had already downed three bowls of the greasy meal. The juice was all over his body and soaked into his beard. There was a third soldier in the group who had not said a word the whole time and they both looked at him. "What do you think?" he asked.

The soldier looked up from his bowl. He had barely eaten any of it. He was a very scrawny man whose eyes were almost buried in his skull. "I do not know. I feel bad for the boy. He has been through so much in just a few days. I understand what the prophecy says. The time is nearing, and he was the next crowned king in Pleniris, but can we truly assume that *he* is the one that will start it?"

The other two looked at the ground. The look in their eyes showed their doubts about the situation. They of course were loyal to their king, but that did not mean they felt truly enthusiastic about what he ordered them to do. They did not say another word about the topic. They continued with their meals and Kerstas turned his gaze to the Shrieking Peak.

They were a way away from the mountain, but still close enough that they could hear the awful sound from it. The wind picked up and traveled through the crevices and edges on the mountain, creating a shrieking noise that echoed all around the land. It sent chills up the spines of the soldiers and some of their hands started to shake, splashing some of the grease on the ground and themselves.

Barnabin had his bowl refilled. His hands were not as shaky as the others, but they were still shaky, nonetheless. "You are a prince, Kerstas. Your family possessed nearly all the knowledge in the kingdom about the lands and beliefs. Far more than my own king. What do you know about the peaks that scream with the wind?"

Kerstas felt the feeling of being watched from behind him. He looked at the mountain and saw a small part of the cave above. It was not very clear, but the flat surface in front of the entrance was easy to pick out from the jagged points. "My dad told me some about it. He said that the men in my family all inherit a sort of curse, as he put it, and that we all are always drawn to the mountain. It starts as soon as we are about to become king. We begin to have vivid dreams of going inside and meeting with the creature within, and it torments us until our hair comes of age. I do not know what truly lies within those caves in that mountain, Barnabin, but I do not wish to meet it."

Barnabin shivered. "I see. What do you think it is that lies within? A monster? A devil? *The* Devil?"

Kerstas shook his head. "I do not know. All I know is that at least four generations of my family have been haunted by it. My father told me, the day before the attack, that he always felt like he was being watched from the cave residing on the peak of the mountain. I, too, felt that feeling. It was like the creature was staring at me while I slept and while I was awake."

Whether it was a devil or any monster, Kerstas did not care. No matter what the creature was it still was a burden for his family to carry. A burden they knew nothing about, yet they knew so much about it. Suddenly a soldier stood up and cried out, "Archers, get down!"

A storm of arrows suddenly started to fall from the sky. Three soldiers were impaled by at least half a dozen arrows. They fell to the ground and all the other soldiers jumped up, drawing their swords. "Where are they?" One asked.

They all frantically looked around trying to find them. The sound of bowstrings releasing was heard from the East. A soldier pointed over to the direction he heard it from. "There!" The soldier and a few more behind him charged towards the direction of the noise, which came from the woods in the distance. The rest of the soldiers that stayed behind held up their shields, ready for another storm of arrows to come from the sky.

Barnabin quickly held up his shield above Kerstas and walked him over to a large rock in the ground. They ducked behind it to hide from any aerial attacks. Another soldier joined them. "What are you doing, Barnabin?" He asked.

Barnabin quickly grabbed another shield from a fallen soldier a few feet away from them. "You know the prophecy, Geremi. What would happen if he died here? Do you want that yet?"

The soldier shook his head. He held up his shield above his and Kerstas' head. Another wave of arrows flooded the sky and impaled five of the men who were still running around the camp like beheaded chickens.

"What are you guys talking about?" Kerstas asked. He kept hearing more and more about the prophecy about him, but he never got a single hint or fragment of what it said about him. Barnabin told him not to worry about it, that if he were to know then it would happen. He said it was important for Kerstas to stay in the dark about the prophecy or else it would not happen.

Whatever the prophecy was, it was clearly important enough for him to be kept alive, at least for the time being. "Thank God this rock was here to keep us protected."

"Do not thank that man. He is not with us. He never was. I learned that long ago. If he was with us, then we would all be happy together. My family would still be alive, and those damned priests would have been executed already."

Barnabin and Geremi looked at Kerstas. "Why would you say that? He is our lord, and he has protected us through all this, has he not?"

Kerstas scoffed and spat on the ground. "You two have saved us, and I thank you for that. All *he* did was sit up there on his little throne of clouds and laugh at our suffering. That is what he did to me all my life!"

Barnabin and Geremi did not know what Kerstas was talking about, but they knew it was for the better if they did not ask about it. They knew it was personal and he had his reasons. Knowing what the prophecy said in its entirety, they knew it was for the best they did not dissuade him from his path.

The cries and sounds of swords clanging filled the air. Many limbs were severed. Arrows were loosened. Heads were mounted on spikes. It was a bloody battle. Finally, however, the soldiers that had taken Kerstas were victorious in their fight. They beheaded the leader of the group and mounted his head on a spike with the next two well-dressed soldiers who had ridden on horses with him into the fight. Barnabin, Geremi, and Kerstas all stood up from behind the rock and looked at the remains of the battle. Many of the soldiers were dead but there was still enough to have a small army to fight if there was another attack. The soldier with the cape cleaned blood off his sword and sheathed it. He stabbed the spike in the ground that held the leader's head and placed it in the ground. The other soldiers moved the bodies into a pile around the spike and started to pour oil on them. When all the bodies were gathered, and their bodies looted of all coins and weapons that were not damaged, they lit the pile on fire. The stench of smoke, burning wood, and charring flesh filled the air. It choked out a few of the soldiers standing nearby and they covered their faces with the collar of their shirts under their armor.

A few of the soldiers started to pray and thank their lord for their victory and for not being killed off in battle. Kerstas cleaned some dirt off his pants, and he walked to the group of soldiers that had gathered near the fire. The leader of the group was doing a head count of those who had not fallen from battle. After the counting, there were around three calvary soldiers, fifteen non-mounted soldiers, the leader, and Kerstas. Of the nearly fifty soldiers that the party started with, only twenty remained alive. Four of them were injured from their wounds and had nearly bled out. Their wounds were bandaged by the only remaining field medic of the group, and they were drinking water to keep from passing out.

Barnabin patted Kerstas on the back. "At least we won. We may have suffered a lot of casualties, but we still won. That is all that matters."

Geremi looked over at the two. "Are you siding with him, Barnabin?" He asked."

Barnabin shot him a look that told Geremi not to talk about it. "Do you want to be on his bad side when shit hits the fan? When does it come into place? His father saved me when I was young. The least I owe him is protection, and that is our duty anyway is it not?"

Geremi paused. He nodded. "I guess so, yes. I will help, too, but make sure this stays between us. If the rest of the group found out we were personally making sure he stayed protected, they would flip."

Kerstas thanked them both. No one else had heard their small conversation. Three of the six wagons had been destroyed during the fight, and their wood was used as kindling for the fire, which was now blazing high in the sky. The stench of the bodies left a foul smell in the air which nearly made one of the men vomit.

The caped man looked at Kerstas. "I see you survived. Good. We live to see our world still intact for now. My name is Malgrin. I am the group leader of this party, but of course you knew that. We are taking you to our kingdom because our king believes you to be the subject of a prophecy that he founded years ago. I do apologize for what we did, but it is in the past. We must move on. I understand if you hate me and everything to do with this group, even the kingdom I am from. All I ask is that you cooperate with us. We are supposed to protect you until we reach our king. Until then, you are ours to protect." He looked around the party of soldiers. To them he said, "If any of you lays a hand on Kerstas I will personally execute you for treason. He is a king, after all."

"Which king do you belong to, Malgin?" Kerstas asked. "You are simply following orders. I do not entirely hate you for that. Your king ordered you and your men to kill my family and all who lived in Untris. Who were the men who killed my parents specifically?" He looked around the group to see if he saw the soldiers who killed his parents. He did not.

Malgrin looked at him. "I do not see them, either. I believe they died during the fight. I cannot say which king I belong to. We were sworn to keep secret just in case there were spies hiding amongst us who would wish to start a war between the kingdoms over this matter."

"Your king ordered the death of a king and queen of a kingdom, while also killing all of those who were present at a coronation. What about that does *not* call for an act of war, sir?" Kerstas looked up at the mountain. The peak could just barely be seen behind the clouds and smoke.

Malgrin nodded. "You do have a point. I do not know what will happen. Maybe another kingdom will come up in your defense, but I am not sure. I cannot predict the future, though I wish I could. I do apologize, Kerstas." Malgrin mounted his horse, and the other soldiers readied the carriages to go. They all packed up the supplies and salvages from the battle and put them on one of the carriages.

Kerstas, Barnabin, and Geremi sat on the carriage loaded with supplies because there was not enough room on the other two carriages for them. The party set off down the road. The sun was shining greatly down on their heads as it started to lower into the West behind them.

CHAPTER 8

Inerium woke up the next morning as the sun seeped through the top of Olmenor. The bed she slept in was so comfortable and she felt like her slumber during the night had lasted for a year. She got up from the bed, her hair a mess, and looked out of her window into the city. The other elves were walking down to start their jobs and business for the day. There were a few who had clearly just woken up, and there were also some who had been up for hours waiting for the sun to shine through to greet them on a new day.

One elf was walking on the bridge below her towards the inner city of Olmenor. She turned around and saw Inerium. "Hey, human!" she called out. "Come down. You must see this before you miss it!"

Inerium went to dress herself. Her old clothes were gone. In their place was a new set of clothes perfectly folded on the table by the door. She held up the shirt in the light to see it. It was green with golden leaves along the collar and broke down into two parallel vines leading to the bottom of the shirt, where the vines and leaves continued to circle around the bottom of the shirt. The pants were black and had golden vines on them as well. There was one on the sides of each leg leading down from the waist to the ankle part, both circling around the waist

and ankles. The shoes she was given were made from the hides
of the stags who passed either in battles or from natural means.
The shoes were warm and fit perfectly on her feet. The whole
outfit was surprisingly a perfect fit. It was as if they were made
with her exact measurements. She put it all on and rolled the
long sleeves up to her elbows.

Inerium stepped out of the cabin and climbed down the
ladder. She jogged over to the elf who called out to her. "What
is it?" she asked.

"Follow me." The elven girl was no more than a year
older than her, if even that. Inerium did not know how the
ages worked in Elven terms. The girl was beautiful. She had
bright blonde, almost-white, hair that trailed down in a long
braid to her lower back. She was wearing a red dress that was
cut off around her thighs. The dress almost looked like she was
wearing fire. Her shoes were red leather and she had fur orange
socks on. Her skin was pale, almost perfect in a way. Her voice
was soft and soothing, one that could put a person to sleep if
she were to sing them to sleep.

She led Inerium down the bridge towards Olmenor. "Climb
off here." There was an opening in the side of the bridge where
the branches did not connect. A path led down away from the
bridge down to the lower levels of the city.

Inerium followed the Elven girl down the path. The sound
of the fountains splashing on the pool below filled the air,
drowning out any sounds besides it. They reached the bottom
level of the city and walked down another path towards the
cavern wall. The lower level was filled with family-sized cabins
and small shops for simple trading and bartering. There were
gardens growing around some of the cabins in the fronts where
makeshift gardens were placed. The water droplets that came
off the fountains watered these gardens, which supplied the rest

of the city when they were fully grown. They followed the path down towards the wall.

At the end of the path was a small gap between it and a part of the stone wall that stuck out like a narrow walkway. The elven girl jumped over the gap gracefully and turned around to look at Inerium. "Coming?" She asked. She smiled and giggled.

Inerium looked at the gap. It was not up high, but the drop was still enough to scare one who had a fear of heights, which she did. She took a few steps back and started off with a running go. She reached the edge and leaped over the gap. Her feet contacted the edge of the other side. She started to lose her balance and began to fall backwards toward the water below. The Elven girl quickly grabbed her arm and pulled her back. Inerium stumbled forward and was caught by the waist. Their eyes met. Inerium got a closer look at them and noticed that they were blue but had a flare of red in them that circled around the pupil to the outer edge of her iris.

"I got you, clumsy." She let go of Inerium and adjusted her shirt that almost came undone. "We are almost there. You don't need to miss it." She grabbed Inerium by the hand again and led her down the walkway. They passed behind a few waterfalls and circled around most of the city. She stopped her at a small circular area in the stone that looked out onto the city.

The scenery was perfectly aligned in the center. Two waterfalls crashed down on both sides of the circle, creating ripples in the water. The sun was starting to rise higher in the sky, and it began shining though the top of Olmenor. The light glistened on the city and reflected off every droplet of water that fell from the walls of the city. The reflections in the pool created a beautiful scene of the sky circling above with the city's buildings sewn into it, creating an image like Olmenor was floating in the sky among the clouds.

"Beautiful, isn't it? She asked. She stood next to Inerium.

"Yes, it is," Inerium said, just remembering that she had stopped breathing from the sight of the city.

"Just wait. There is one more part of it." She turned Inerium's head back towards the water. She pointed towards the throne room above where the royal elves sat. "Look there. Here she comes."

Queen Aylisen walked out to the railing on the platform and overlooked the city. She smiled and stretched out her arms. The water suddenly started to swirl around in the center of the pool and create a whirlpool spiraling down into the depths below. The spiral inverted and shot out towards the opening in the top. The water spouted out towards the walls and the water trailed down the stone, creating one singular circular waterfall around Olmenor. The circle they were standing on had a part of the cave above it that split the water around them.

From the outside of the circle this visual would of course have been magical, indeed, but inside the circle was magnificent, something one could only dream of seeing. The view from inside the circle appeared that the two were standing inside of an aquatic portal leading into an old city of magic. It was like something from a fairy tale. Inerium and Kerstas' grandmother may have not even come up with such a design of imagery. If she were still alive, Inerium would have loved to tell her about it; about the elves, the magic, all of it.

The elven girl turned to look at Inerium. "My name is Choleira. I am what they would call a rarity when it comes to the magic I have. I was born with the affinity of two forms of magic. I have water and fire magic at my disposal."

"My name is Inerium. Thank you for showing me this, Choleira." Inerium smiled. "It was beautiful." She did not have much knowledge about magic, so it was unknown to her that having two forms of magic was indeed a great rarity. Rare enough that less than a handful of people was gifted with it.

Choleira smiled and giggled. She moved her braid over her shoulder. She started to shuffle her feet. There was a long moment of awkward silence between the two. Finally, she spoke. "When do you plan to leave for Nellenor?"

For a moment Inerium had forgotten about Kerstas and her mission to save him. The thing Choleira showed her distracted her from it. "Shit, I almost forgot." She quickly turned around and started to go along the path back towards the top of Olmenor.

Choleira quickly followed her. "Hey, wait up!" She caught up to Inerium and slowed to her pace. She was light on her feet and was much quicker than the average human. "Take me with you."

"What, why?" Inerium asked. "You just met me. Plus, I am a human, and you are an elf."

They had reached the gap and Choleira jumped across just as gracefully as before. She turned around and waited for Inerium to jump. She did with a running go, and just as before she almost slipped off the edge into the pool below. Choleira caught her and pulled her up. "Because what would you do without me? You cannot even make a jump across this gap here without stumbling off. Now what kind of friend would I be if I let you go alone, Miss Clumsy?" She giggled and led Inerium back up the trail.

"Hey, I am not *that* clumsy," Inerium said sassily. She stumbled over a small rock on the ground after saying these words and Choleira caught her."

"Uh huh. What was that, then, hm?" She smirked.

"Nothing. That rock was not there before I tripped on it."

Her face turned a little red. She was of course embarrassed at tripping over a simple rock, but the teasing from Choleira did not make it any easier for her. They had reached the middle level of the city and were making their way up to the highest one.

A male elf approached them. He had a neatly braided beard and pulled-back hair. His clothes bore silver vines on them, and he had blue eyes that went well with the blue clothes. "Choleira, what are you doing?"

"Brother, I was just simply showing her around. There was no harm."

"No harm? You do not know what these humans are capable of!" He scoffed and sneered. Their kind are the reason we must hide here in the first place!" His voice was whiny, almost like a child's.

"Just because she is a human does not mean she is capable of the same evil that her predecessors done to our kind centuries ago. All those who did that to us are long dead now."

"I do not care. Her kind are monsters. They drove us into hiding like animals. We have not seen the world outside these woods for generations because of them!"

"Hey," Inerium said, cutting in. "No one in my whole kingdom even knew you even existed. I am the only one most likely out of the whole land that knows you all are real. How are we to blame if we do not even know about you?"

Choleira's brother was silent. He had no words to say. He almost spoke but no words came out. He simply sighed and said, "I guess you have a point. But it was still the humans that drove us here."

Inerium shook her head. "Humans who were in possession of dark magic, the most powerful of the six forms of it. Anything that had that power would overpower you. Even one of your stags in possession of that power could potentially lay all of you to waste."

He nodded. "I am sorry. We elves were taught that humans were evil, and their nature was the reason that we had to live like we do. Let me start fresh. My name is Korlyn. You have obviously met my sister Choleira."

Choleira patted Inerium on the back. "It is okay, Inerium. I never thought of you as evil." She winked at her and giggled.

"Thanks, Choleira," Inerium said. She smiled. "I do still have to find out what is cursing these woods, though, and save my brother."

"Well, then I am coming with you," Choleira said.

"No, you are not." Korlyn said. "It is too dangerous."

"He is right," Inerium said. "This is my journey. I am sorry. It was great meeting you, Choleira." Inerium started to walk up towards the higher levels of the city, back up the path they took down.

Choleira went to follow her, but Korlyn stopped her. He took her into the house and shut the door behind them. Inerium looked back at their house. Her eyes alone said she had wished Choleira would have tagged along, but she knew it was not safe, and she would feel so bad if something happened to her. She cast the thoughts away and continued up towards the top of Olmenor. When she reached the top, she was greeted by the king. He smiled and said hello.

"Hello, King Evindal."

"Did you enjoy Lady Aylisen's show? It happens every morning, but they all seem different somehow, always more beautiful than the last." He was looking out at the water over the branch railings. "I saw you and the girl from below watching it. You two got along fast, despite you being human."

"Choleira? Yes, she was very nice to me. Your wife did a

lovely job with her water magic. What does me being a human have to do with her liking me?"

He sighed. "That is not for me to say, but she has a gift of knowing how someone is just by looking at him. It is like she can almost look into their souls and read their whole character like a book with a glance. I cannot even explain it, but she saw something in you she liked. That is all that matters, Inerium."

"So, when do I begin my travel to Nellenor? She asked."

"Come," he said. He led her across the bridges and up the stairs to the stable section above. Snowfire trotted over to Inerium, and she began to pet him.

He pointed over towards the darker area of the forest. "This path will lead you to Nellenor. Do not stray from the path, or you will find yourself lost forever. When you reach Nellenor, make your way through the city and find the large castle in the back. I suspect that whatever is corrupting the forest is most likely being kept in there. If you happen to come across dark elves there, please stay safe. Use this to protect yourself." Evindal pulled out a short sword. The blade was a light, almost white, silver metal that had a half sun carved into the base of the blade. From the sun came branches with small leaves on them growing out of it towards the tip of the blade. The hilt was a light brown wood with black leather wrapped around the handle. "This is Solef, a sword imbued with light magic. Take it as a gift, and as a weapon to use against the dark elves. Dark beings can only be harmed by dark or light magic, as well as light beings can only be harmed by light or dark magic."

"Thank you, King Evindal." She tied the scabbard around her waist and sheathed Solef. Evindal hoisted her up on Snowfire's saddle and she started to make her way down the path in the woods.

Inerium did not know what she was going to do when

she got to Nellenor, but she knew that she had to find an evil
artifact, lift the curse on the forest, and continue her journey
to save Kerstas from his kidnappers. The farther she traveled
into the woods towards Nellenor, the grimmer the woods
became. The wood on the trees started to darken and the air
became almost bitter tasting. A fog started to accumulate and
grow thicker to the point that the trees in front of her were
nearly invisible.

A foul smell started to linger in the air. The smell was
that of rotten corpses, and something near sulfuric and decay.
She had a creeping feeling that she was getting very close to
Nellenor. Through the trees she could see a fence taking shape
through the fog. When she got to it, a sign was on the ground.
It had fallen off the gate. It had been worn down and stepped
on by mainly animal tracks and the occasional rain. She picked
it up and tried to read it. it was written in some form of elvish
that she could not read.

"It reads Welcome to Nellenor," a young girl's voice said
behind her.

Inerium quickly turned around, startled, to see Choleira
petting on Snowfire. "What are you doing here?" Inerium
asked.

"I could not let you go alone, silly. My brother was not in
the best mood about it, but he said that he trusted you enough
to take care of me." She giggled. "But of course, I can take care
of myself, and if I was not here, who would take care of you
and your clumsy self?"

"You still should not have come. You do not know what
is in there."

She shook her head, smirking. "And you do? I am an elf. I
at least have an idea of what magic they possess. I also can see
through a good amount of illusion magic if any was present.

Inerium opened the gate. It creaked open, and some rusted flakes fell off the hinges. The bottom of the gate, which was dragging on the ground from wearing over time, left a large indent in the dirt where it opened. She got on Snowfire and Choleira jumped on behind her. They made their way through the gate and walked through a courtyard of overgrown weeds and rotten tree stumps. The sky and atmosphere itself almost appeared green as they made their way further in. The mist was thinning out after they had traveled about a minute's way past the fence gate.

As they made their way through the courtyard, the silhouettes of buildings started emerging from the shadows and taking shape among the misty veils. The buildings lined the courtyard on both sides leading parallel down the courtyard. They had all been destroyed from what the two could tell. They appeared that they had either burned down, rotted away, or that they had simply been demolished by Lord knows what. There were splintered boards and shattered tiles all over the ground around the buildings. Ash surrounded the burnt ones like a ring of salt one would circle around their beds to keep witches or evil spirits away.

"Look at that," Choleira said. She got off Snowfire and walked over to one of the houses on the right. The roof had been caved in and three of the four walls were still intact, but only barely. The door at the front was blocked by the debris from the caved roof.

"Stay here, Snowfire," Inerium said, and followed behind Choleira. They walked inside through the gap where the wall had fallen. Inside was a table beside the window which had become a hollow hole in a wall above a small pile of shattered glass and shredded wood lying on rotting boards that once made up a beautiful floor that most likely held up a family for possibly their whole lives, if not even generations before.

What Choleira saw, however, was not just this broken window. What she saw was far more upsetting. As much as it was upsetting that the window (whose frame once was a near perfect arch that hosed stained glass depicting a dream-like forest with birds flying overhead and deer eating grass) was broken, the most upsetting sight was what she saw in a room at the back of the house. They walked through the maze of jagged boards and displaced stones towards the back. How Choleira saw this was a wonder, but when Inerium saw it, she felt the urge to fall into tears. What was beheld in the back room of the house was a scene most heartbreaking.

On the floor there was the charred corpse of a woman reaching outwards to the opposite side of the room. Behind her was a man curled on the floor a few feet away from her curled into a fetal position. When the two followed the woman's arm to where she was reaching to, the remnants of a baby's cradle were in shambles, burnt, on the floor, under a charred, ash-covered blanket was the ashen corpse of a baby, whose head had caved in over time. One of the baby's arms were held upward towards the ceiling, while the other had fallen off and crumbled to dust next to its side. Inerium suddenly heard in the back of her head the faint cries of a baby and the screaming of terrified parents. The flames licking the walls and the roof caving in around them. What could have caused such a thing to happen? *Who* could have caused this to happen?

"Let me feel my daughter," a voice said. The voice was a woman's, soft and sorrowful. "Bring her to me, please." Inerium heard the voice in the back of her mind, just like the baby's cries. She reached down and gently picked up the baby's ashen body like one would pick up a newborn kitten. A few small grains of ash fell, but none of the body was disturbed or dismantled. She gently placed the baby's body down next to the mother.

"What are you doing?" Choleira asked.

Inerium nodded towards the mother. "Thank you," the voice said. Suddenly the room grew cold, not freezing but like a chill one would get from being watched or when they would eat dinner and their fork would graze the surface of the plate and make that God awful noise.

Just as the chill went up both Inerium and Choleira, a pale mass of smoke emerged from the body of the mother. The smoke took shape as the woman, wearing a dress. The woman had the pointed ears of an elf and long hair trailing down to her elbows. She was cradling a baby swaddled in the same blanket that was lying charred in the corner of the room. The baby started to cry and jolt around.

"Shh, it's okay," the mother said in a soothing voice that could put almost anyone to sleep if she told a story to them. "My little Ivara." She looked at the two girls standing before her. "Thank you both for setting my soul at peace. I have spent ages trying to be reunited with my Ivara. Now that I am, we both can ascend to the Heavens. Thank you." They faded away into smoke, and as they did, the smoke shifted into golden dust that flew into the sky until it was no longer visible.

"Well, that was something." Choleira said, not knowing any other phrase to use.

"She is in a better place. I cannot imagine how long she had waited to be with her child again. But now she can be with her forever." Inerium watched the ashes crumble away and be carried off by the wind. They turned around and walked out of the house, Inerium wiping a few tears away. "We should continue along. The main building should be here somewhere."

They followed the center path of the city, continuing their way from before. In the distance a tall tower-like building was forming through the mist. As they grew closer, the buildings on the sides became more and more rotten. The debris became ash, and the plants became small twigs and shriveled up things simply sprouting from the ground. The wind blowing caused the ash and small debris to kick up in the wind. Inerium and Choleira had to cover their faces to avoid getting anything in their eyes or mouth. When they got closer to the tall building, the path on the ground started to become littered with thorns and splintered bones. The dirt was stained with blood and the atmosphere around it almost seemed green, like poison.

The tower was tall. It was less of a tower, and more of a tall, thin building that stood tall like a tower. It had very few windows and where they did, small balconies curled around them to look out from. At the bottom of the building was a large walkway of stone that turned into steps, leading up to a rotted pair of doors with green stained glass depicting the scene of a dragon with leaf wings flying in the sky. The dragon was seen from the top, where its wings spread out and took up most of the room on the stained glass. They approached the doors and behind them they could hear the screams and cries of dozens of voices coming from all directions aside from in front of them.

They quickly ran inside and slammed the door behind them, not turning around due to being so afraid to see what the screams came from. When they caught their breath and calmed their minds, they looked around the room. There were small tables strewn about with chairs by them. Some were upright while others were on their sides on the floor, which had a large green rug on the black wood floor. The left part of the room had a staircase leading up to the second floor, which had a balcony wrapping around the top of the first floor that overlooked the room they were in. The railing was old and rusted and looked like metal branches woven into the wood it stood on.

There were a few rooms on the bottom floor, but when they tried to look in them, they were all locked. The inside of the house had a horrid smell of old blood and dust. They headed upstairs towards the second floor. Inerium had a dark feeling growing in the pit of her stomach. She felt something was wrong. Choleira was starting to feel it too. Was it the fact that there were no dark elves around? Was it the uneasy thought that they were surrounded by ghosts like the woman from the house? Or was it simply the dark power of the artifact taking its toll on them? Neither knew the answer. The feeling was one that swelled out from the soul. There was no true explanation to the uneasy feeling they felt. The only sure thing was that the feeling was there, and they were correct to feel it. Something was terribly off in the main hall of Nellenor, and it was a truly terrible thing indeed.

There were voices heard seemingly inside the walls. They were whispering foreign tongues that resembled the Elven speech from Olmenor, yet they had dark undertones to them. Choleira could hear them. She said she could translate a few words they had said but not enough to make out a full sentence or phrase. There were three doors on the balcony of the second floor. One was in the center, one was on the left wall, and the last was on the right wall. Inerium walked to the left wall, which was the closest to where they were standing. The door was unlocked. She turned its golden knob and opened it. The doorway led to a long hallway filled with old pictures that had faded away or had been burned to ashes. The few intact pictures that remained were mainly humanoid portraits, but the faces were faded or scratched out.

As they walked down the hallway, the pictures seemed to talk to them just as the walls from the previous part of the building did. The walls were covered in old peeling paint that once depicted a tree whose branches stretched from the center of the hall to both ends at the beginning and end of it. There were golden leaves on the branches that occasionally blew away from the branches in the wind. The end of the hall had another staircase leading up to a higher floor. They followed it up, avoiding putting their hands on the railing because of the mold and decay on it, and entered another hallway like the one they had just exited on the second floor. This hallway had paintings on the wall as well. These, however, were not faded. The paintings were all landscapes and faraway lands. Some were hand painted by the ones in the house, noticeably by the sloppy styling and the small paint fingerprints on the frame around them.

The paintings that were not hand painted by the people who once lived in the house were beautiful and almost as if they were formed from angels' dreams. There were great lands in the skies on some and others had beautiful, secluded forests with animals eating grass and berries on them. The end of the hall had a door like the one below. The know this time was silver. Choleira turned it, saying it was not fair that Inerium had opened both the front door and the other doors. Inerium motioned her to open it, and she did so.

As they entered through the door, they entered another room like the entrance of the town hall. There was a chair in the corner of the room, which was next to a door, the same as the one they had just come through. Inerium assumed that the other door entered a hallway that led down a spiral staircase back down into the entrance hall downstairs, which was correct. The main town hall of Nellenor had rooms on the left and right sides parallel to one another. Where one hallway and staircase on the left was, the same would be on the right. Of course, there would be different paintings and paint on the walls, but the layout and rooms would be identical in shape, size, and orientation.

When the town hall was built, the maker intended the main hall to be a perfect mirror image of itself from left to right. They even ensured that magic-gifted builders would make every measurement down to the last centimeter perfect from the center to either edge of the town hall. Why the maker had such a hard-on for the perfect layout of the town hall, no one knows, but it is known that they were *unhealthily* hard for it, enough to have killed one of the builders of the house who had made one room of the town hall a few feet too wide compared to the rest of the other rooms. Which room was this? It was the room in the center back of the hall. The room was both taller and wider than all the other rooms in the hall. It was, in fact, as tall as all three floors of the town hall. This was the room the townspeople used to gather in to discuss politics or who had stolen the fresh killed deer from a woman's house during the night while she was off gallivanting with another man as her husband slept soundly.

There was no door leading back to the center of the room Inerium and Choleira were in. There was simply just a large painting of a lake with two giant elegant swans touching their foreheads together swimming in the center of it. There was a ripple effect swirling out from their bodies creating an almost too-perfect image of the sun in the sky reflecting through the ripples. The painting was like one had taken a photograph of the scene and simply placed it on the wall where it sat now.

Inerium was almost tempted to take it down and bring it home with her. She then remembered that there was no home for her to go to. There was no Eleana or Kentrin to come home to and tell of how the day went.

Inerium's eyes began to water and the saltiness of soon to be falling tears started to make her eyes water more. She went to wipe them, but Choleira beat her to it. She used her sleeve to wipe off her tears. Her hand lit up in a bright blue color and the droplets she wiped off hovered in the air over her palm. They swirled around in a circle a few times and became a singular droplet. Choleira pulled out a necklace she kept hidden behind her top. It was a small vial that had silver branches with leaves on them spiraling from the lid of the vial to the base of it. A small light-colored cork was stopped in the lid. She pulled it out and tears flew in. They shimmered the same bright blue as her hand and then faded back to their clear watery form.

"What did you do?" Asked Inerium.

"Your tears," she said. "We like to think of them as a sort of bond. It is hard to explain. The way I can explain it is that when elves were friends or lovers perhaps, when they felt comfortable enough to cry in one another's presence, the other would collect those tears in a vial like this. When we would collect them, it creates a stronger bond between the two through the magic they hold."

"Tears hold magic?" Inerium asked. This magic was already new to her, so hearing that simply crying in the presence of an elf was magical on its own was a surprising piece of information.

She nodded. She put the necklace back under her top. The silver chain glimmered in the lights of the candles lit on the walls, which they had not paid attention to, thinking it was somehow normal for an abandoned city whose houses had

all been destroyed to have a town hall with still lit candles
to light up the halls and rooms. In a world where magic and
Elves existed, the thought of candles still being lit in such a
circumstance was not far from abnormal.

"Tears only form from high emotions; be they sorrow or
joy. The effects they hold are powerful. If a bond is formed
between two beings who hold one another's tears, their souls
are bound until the tears are either drank or thrown away. It is
like blood magic, where blood bonds could be formed, but tear
magic is the purest form of bonding magic any being can do."

Inerium watched her put the necklace in her top. She
adjusted her hair to get it untangled from the chain. "So, say
if we were to make a bond, how would *I* get one form you?"

Choleira thought about it. "I would have to either be
incredibly happy or upset for me to shed a tear. It takes a lot
of willpower for us to hold them back, but when the moments
come, and we are with those we trust ourselves around, it can
happen. Just wait until we return to Olmenor. Then, I will ask
Lord Evindal to make you one if the time ever came and you
wanted one of mine."

Inerium nodded. "You would wish to do that?" Of course,
they had only just met that day, but regardless, Inerium felt that
she had met a friend for life and would hope that Choleira felt
the same towards her.

Choleira smiled and scrunched up her nose. She spun a
graceful spin and skipped along towards the painting. She lifted
it off the wall and placed it on the floor.

"What are you doing"?

"You will see." Choleira's hand lit ablaze with a crimson
flame, and she burned away the frame around the top of the
painting. As the flames charred away the frame, she pulled the
canvas off it. She rolled up the painting and uttered a word

in her Elven tongue. The word sounded like Shray-inkay. It shrunk down to a smaller size, almost the size of the little finger on the hand, and she used a strand of cloth from her dress to tie it. When the knot finished, she made the remaining strings into a multi-looped bow that almost looked like a flower. She handed it to Inerium. "For you."

Inerium smiled and took it. Her eyes started to tear up. "But why? What am I going to do with this?"

"When you want to look at it or put it up, untie the knot I made, or just slip it off the paper, and it will regrow to the size it once was. When you are finished, repeat the word I said, and it will become this size again. Put the bow back on it and it will remain that way until you decide to open it again." She grabbed her by the hand and led her down the stairs to the opposite end of the room. "And because I had a feeling that you wanted it; you just did not want to say it."

Inerium knew she was right. Of course, she wanted the painting. Anyone who would not want it would be insane. It was true art. True beauty. A masterpiece. Whoever the artist was, and it would remain unknown due to the lack of signature on the piece, truly had a gift and Inerium wished she could collect more of their works.

Choleira led Inerium down the hallway through the door and down another spiral staircase just like the one from before. When they reached the second floor, they tried to open the door in the middle to see what was behind it. When they opened it, they each grabbed one of the two doors and pulled them open. Behind the doors was a hallway whose ceiling had caved in and collapsed into. No matter how much they could try, no amount of their strength could move the rubble to see anything beyond the doorway.

Realizing that the second-floor center room was of no use,

they returned to the bottom floor to go into its center room. Inerium and Choleira each grabbed one of the two handles on the double doors.

"On the count of three," Inerium said. "One...Two... Three!"

They both yanked open the doors of the middle room of the town hall. They creaked open eerily and a cloud of dust erupted from the floor and walls. A hoard of lifeless moans erupted from the dark hallway before them. The candles on the candelabras were not lit. If they were, the air that had blown into the hallway that had been shut off for who knows how long. The smell that came from the hall was the foulest stench of all. It could only be described as an entire pack of animals that had died, and their bodies were left to rot inside of the walls for weeks. The stench was so bad that Inerium nearly vomited from the impact it had on her nostrils. She burped and covered her nose with her shirt. Choleira covered hers too as well and she held up her index finger, as if to say, "one moment."

Choleira said, "I got this," and her palm held a small flame over it. It illuminated the area around them. The walls had completely molded over, and small patches of grass and fungus were growing from the ground, which had split apart by the plants. There were small parts of the walls that black liquid, which had a consistency of tree sap, oozing out of in clumps like blood clots. There were areas where the mysterious liquid was forming into small piles like ant hills on the floor. There were some plants that were covered in the black tar-like liquid, and they seemed to almost be melting from it.

Choleira and Inerium did their best to avoid touching the liquid just in case it could be acid, poisonous, or even somehow its own entity that could possess those who touched it. The hallway was long, almost unnaturally. It seemed to go on forever, at least until they had finally reached the end where they were greeted by a set of double doors. These doors were molded over by grey fur and small mushrooms that had turned black and dark green. The handles were covered in small vines and baby mushrooms. Choleira held her hand up to the handles and burned away the mold so that they would not have to touch it.

The mold burned away, and She waited for the handles to cool down a bit before grabbing it. When she did, she and Inerium opened the doors, which swung away from them. They slowly pushed outwards due to the mold almost being glue holding the doors in place. When the hold of the mold broke, however, they flew open and slammed against the wall of the great meeting room of the town hall of Nellenor.

The room inside the great meeting hall was not what one would expect. When someone imagined a meeting hall, they would expect to see a podium at the end, many rows of chairs, and perhaps a few benches for the people in the back when there were no more chairs to sit in. This was not the case, however. The meeting hall of Nellenor was more like a banquet hall in a castle, like the one in Requilit's capital.

There was a great long table in the center of the room, housing probably dozens of chairs on both sides, with a large chair residing at the front and back ends of it. The wood of both the table and chairs was a dark oak-like wood. They were hand carved, and masterfully at that. The smaller chairs had images of birds flying around the back of the chair, and the large throne-like chairs at the ends had stags butting heads on the backs of them. The legs spiraled down from the round seat of the chairs to the floor on every chair. There were large chandeliers made of deer and stag antlers which held large candles on them, which dropped wax down into small vials, which would then be used to recycle the candles infinitely instead of having to either make new ones or buy new ones.

The room was dim, yet the fire above was glowing bright. It was like the energy in the room was so dark that it was physically pushing the light away from it. And this was true. The dark magic and energy that was in this very room was in fact dark enough to destroy light itself if it were used to its fullest potential.

When Inerium and Choleira's eyes adjusted to the dim room, they could make out the most ungodly sight. Sitting in some of the chairs at the tables were the corpses of elves. Their bodies almost appeared preserved, like they had only died moments before they had entered the town hall. Their skin was shriveled up. Not like a ball sack in the cold seasons, but like when a balloon would be blown up for days and then the air finally released from it shriveled. They were dead for sure, but it was unknown for how long.

The skin on the Elves, however, did not match Choleira's. Her skin was perfect and pale, while the Elves here had grey skin that seemed to crack apart like old paint.

"These are not Dark Elves," Choleira said. "These were like me and the rest back in Olmenor. The artifact must have corrupted them somehow and turned their skin ashy. The are Grey Elves, those who were corrupt by the dark magic of the Void."

"I thought that Dark Elves had control of dark magic," Inerium said.

Choleira nodded. "Some can, but not all of them. The Dark Elves use elemental magic like us, but they use a less elegant way, as some would say. The Grey Elves were a sort of scary bedtime story we would be told as children. They were said to have been Elves corrupt by evil magic. *Pure* evil magic that one cannot simply obtain naturally."

You think that these Elves in the chairs are those? At least some of them?"

Choleira shook her head. She did not know for certain, but it was the best guess. Guessing or not, this assumption was correct. These Elves lying dead at the long table of Nellenor were in fact the nightmarish Grey Elves of the scary stories among the Elven races.

At the end of the long table sat an older Elven man. He was wearing old robes that had been covered in the black liquid from the hallway before. His hair was white and slicked back. There were a few straggling hairs that were falling into his face. He continuously swiped them away, but they kept returning to their stations. Around his neck was a black string holding a pale bone object.

The object resembled an eye of sorts. When one would draw an eye on paper, they would start with the outline of the socket. This was part of the shape of the unusual object. There was one vertical socket and one horizontal socket, both meeting in the center of it. The two sockets were enclosed in a bony circle holding all four corners of the sockets in place. In the middle was a perfect place to put a pupil, or one's eye if they would want to. The older Elven man kept clawing at it, not like an itch, but like he had to continuously confirm its existence with him.

He looked up and saw the two had entered the room. He had only noticed when the door slammed shut behind them. "Hello, newcomers," the man said. His voice was frail and scratchy, like he had inhaled smoke from a bonfire and had not coughed it away yet. "We have not had visitors in a while." He gestured at the table of the corpses of the other Grey Elves.

"Come, have a seat. Dinner is about to begin. The cooks will be out shortly with our feast." He looked over towards a door to the left, where he believed the kitchen was.

Inerium and Choleira glanced at each other in worry. Did the man not know that the Grey Elves at the table were dead? Did he know and did not care? Was he simply playing a game with the two girls and delivering the same fate to them as he may have to his fellow kinsmen? They did not know, but to avoid the last choice happening sooner than it would, they sat down at the table, keeping distance from the dead bodies.

"Thank you two for joining us." My friends here are very thankful for it, as am I. We have not had guests here in a while, and I was starting to miss people outside of these here." His eyes, which were a dull green, got wide. He gestured at one of the corpses on the opposite end of the table they were on. He flew his hands up and said, "no no, I am sorry. I do not mean anything by it, Aldrig, I was just making small talk with our guests." He looked again to the door on the left, impatiently waiting for it to open with a long line of chefs with plates of delicious food over their shoulders to feast on.

"What is your name?" Inerium asked, trying to stay on his good side, and trying to keep the image out of her head that he was talking to a dead body.

"My name is Greilyn. These are my other companions. We set out here from Olmenor about a few days ago to find some food to take back. We stopped here for a few nights for some shelter. The cooks here said they would provide us with a good meal for staying. They should be out any minute."

Choleira leaned close to Inerium. "I think that thing around his neck is the artifact that Evindal mentioned. It must be creating some sort of illusion on him."

"Is there a way to break it?" Inerium asked. "He has to know that whatever he is seeing is not real."

"I assume that if we can separate that eye thing from him it will break the illusion, and maybe the curse around this forest as well."

Inerium understood. She stood up. "Hey, Greilyn, can I get a closer look at your chair? I have a strong admiration for furniture."

"What are you doing? Are you insane? And what kind of excuse is that?"

"Trust me."

Greilyn looked at Inerium, puzzled. He looked over at the corpse beside him. "What do you think?" He paused for a moment, as if a response was coming from it. "Okay." He returned his gaze to Inerium. "He trusts you, so I will, too. I cannot stand up from my chair, but you can admire the woodwork if I lean forward. Come, young one."

Greilyn leaned forward in his chair the relic clunked on the table. His eyes flickered to it to check if it was still there, and he returned his eyes to Inerium. She walked over to him, trying not to cover her nose from the nasty smell of the decaying corpses. When she reached the chair, he was sitting in she looked at the back of it. It was the same as the one on the opposite end of the table, but she pretended not to notice for the sake of hoping that this plan would work.

This is a very nice chair, mister Greilyn. Would you perhaps be taking it with you to Olmenor when you return?"

He nodded. "Why, of course." He sat back in the chair. "This fine craftmanship cannot simply stay here. It must be sat in by the finest of Elves."

Inerium waited for him to look again to the door on the

left. When she realized that it may not be coming any time soon, she pointed. "Is that door opening?"

Greilyn quickly turned around. "It is about damned time."

As he turned towards the door, Inerium quickly leaned in and grabbed the relic around his neck. She jerked it away from him and the string snapped off. The relic started to burn in her hand, and she dropped it on the ground. The burning was not like fire, no, it was just the feeling that her hand would have melted away if she held onto it any longer.

He quickly stood up. "What are you..." He paused and looked around the room. His eyes fell in sorrow, and he let out a wheezy gasp. "How long...? How could this...have..." His body started to shrivel like the others around him. He let out a final breath as he sat down in his chair once more and looked around the table. "What happened to me?" His skin started chipping like old paint and he crumbled into a pile of ash on the chair. A cloud of dust erupted from the ground where he had not been up in such a long time. All that remained was his clothes.

Inerium picked up a spot of cloth from Greilyn's robes that had not been covered in the black liquid and wrapped up the relic. She put the relic in the pocket of her clothes and walked back over to Choleira. "I did not know that would happen."

"No one could have known, Inerium. At least now his soul could be at peace with his fellow brethren."

The room grew a chilling cold, and a freezing wind blew in from the hallway doors, which had swung open from the force of it. Whisps of smoke emerged from the mouths of the Grey Elves and formed into a phantom form of their corporeal bodies. They turned to look at their bodies and sighed. Their gazes led to the large chair where Greilyn sat at. His ashes swirled in a circle and a phantom took shape of his corporeal form as well.

"My friends, how long has it been since we have properly conversed?" He asked.

The one he called Aldrig spoke. "I cannot say, master Greilyn. We know as much, if not less, as you do."

"Then, my friends, we shall return to Olmenor and ask our loved ones how long we have been gone. I believed it only to have been a couple of days."

One of the Elven men on the left spoke. "I cannot wait to see my lovely wife again." He smiled and clapped his hands. "She must miss me so much, and I bet she is worried sick."

"I can second that," another said beside him. "I bet she already has a meal prepared for me and my son on the table." He licked his lips. "It already makes me hunger for it."

Choleira looked at Inerium. She shook her head, to silently tell her that she did not need to tell them the truth.

Greilyn's phantom nodded at the two girls. "Thank you two for freeing me. Now, we shall return to Olmenor. Goodbye." They all faded away into the golden dust that the mother and daughter had become in the house from before, and they flew off into the direction of Olmenor.

Choleira and Inerium left the meeting house of Nellenor and returned to Snowfire, who was patiently waiting for them by the house she told him to wait by. They hopped on him and rode on back to Olmenor.

The forest had lost its dull and morbid look, and the green was returning to it. The mist was fading away back into the sky and life was already starting to return to its proper form. They had started to reach the edge of the forest around Olmenor when Choleira noticed something to her right.

"Oh no. They know." She hopped off Snowfire and

slowly walked into the direction she looked at. Inerium got off Snowfire as well and followed behind her.

When they stopped behind a tree, they saw the phantoms of the Grey Elves kneeling beside tree stumps growing out of the ground. They were most likely no more than four or five feet tall. "What are they doing?" Inerium asked Choleira.

"A tradition of the Elves we have here is that when one dies, we bury their bodies with a seed from one of the trees in the woods. We plant them and the trees that grow are like gravestones for us. We place a rock on the ground next to them with the name of the deceased written on it."

"Oh, I see." Inerium said. Her eyes started to water again. "It is so sad. They thought they were gone only for a few days when it was years. Maybe decades. Maybe even centuries."

Choleira readied her sleeve to wipe Inerium's tears. They did not fall. She calmed her mind and shook her head, to erase the thoughts of sadness from her mind. They walked to the stables of Olmenor, leading Snowfire behind them. Snowfire started to feed some hay and drink some water. They continued down into the city of Olmenor and walked over into the throne room where Evindal and his wife and son sat. The fresh air and the scenery in the city were so much more refreshing compared to that of Nellenor's.

Evindal looked up and saw the two approaching the room. He stood up and walked over to the archway connecting the throne room to the bridge that Choleira and Inerium were currently walking across.

"Choleira. Inerium, you are back. And I can feel that the curse in the woods is lifted. You are free to continue your journey, Inerium."

"Thank you, Lord Evindal." She pulled the relic from her pocket. It was still wrapped up in the robe from Greilyn.

"There was only one of them left. The rest had died off long ago." She started to unfold the cloth. "This was what was causing the curse. Greilyn had this around his neck. When we took it from him, he died, too."

As the cloth fully unveiled the bone eye, Evindal quickly covered it back up. He wiped his hands on his robes. "Do you not know what that is?" His voice was shaky. His hands were trembling in fear. "Take that thing as far away from here as you can. Whatever you do, do not listen to its temptations. That relic is pure evil."

"What is it, my love?" The Elven queen asked. She looked at the cloth, which was now covering the eye, and reached to uncover it.

Evindal quickly grabbed her hand. "No. It is the eye. *That* eye."

She looked at Inerium and took a step back. "You need to continue your journey to Venirit. Save your brother, Inerium. As my husband said, do not listen to anything that thing may say to you. It will never lead to good."

"Can I not just break it apart?" She asked. "Can't I just throw it away somewhere?"

Evindal shook his head. "No, I am afraid not. This relic has more secrets than probably even the Lord you all worship up above. I know that no amount of force or magic even an angel could possess would be able to break the bones apart. And do you think that Greilyn in Nellenor did not try to throw it away? It played tricks on his mind. He gave into it. That relic has a mind of its own, and it will not allow itself to be cast away so lightly. Keep it on you as you have been. Do not lose it or give it away, though. When you arrived here, I assumed that you had a gift of sorts. I now know that at least *one* of those gifts is the ability to naturally resist the dark, at least a little bit. It is a rare gift, little Inerium. My mother was the only other one I knew that had it. No matter how dark or tempting something was, she could look at it like it was nothing. She could have been offered the most powerful form of dark magic imaginable for the exchange of nothing, and she would laugh in the offeror's face at the idea."

"I see," said Inerium. "I will set off for Venirit when I can. I just need to say my goodbyes to you all." She turned around to Choleira and sighed. She did not want to say goodbye to her new friend. They had only known each other for roughly a day, but she felt that they had been friends for years. Her eyes teared up. "I. I do not know how to say it."

Choleira hugged Inerium. Her eyes started to water as well. "I do not want you to go. Please do not say goodbye, Inerium. We had such a fun time together. After all these years I finally feel that I have a friend."

"She will not have to say it," said a voice that had just entered the room. It was Korlyn, Choleira's brother. "She can go with you, if she wants to."

"Korlyn?" She asked. "What are you doing here?"

He smiled. "I brought a few things of yours that I knew you would want to take. I do not wish you to go, but I have not seen you this happy in years. I would hate to have that taken from you." The bag was a light brown and had leaves drawn all over it in small colored images. Some of them were good and others were poorly drawn like a child drew them. This was the case. She got the bag from her father as a last gift before he died. She had drawn leaves on it on the anniversary of his death every year since his passing.

She turned around to Inerium. "See, you will not have to go." She hugged Inerium again, this time a lot tighter, almost crushing the breath from her body. "I am coming with you, Inerium. No matter what you say I will not change my mind."

I do not plan on it."

The two girls said their goodbyes to Korlyn and the three royals of Olmenor. As they were leaving, the three royals gave Inerium and Choleira each a gift. From the three Royals, Inerium received a glass vial matching Choleira's from Evindal, a ring made of water from Lady Aylisen that gave her the ability to control water to an extent if she wore the ring, and from Ellisar she was given a small knife that matched Solef.

"This knife is the younger twin of your sword you have there," Ellisar said. His voice was deep despite how young he looked. "It also has the possession of light and can snuff out any darkness from those that are corrupted by it. The name of this small blade has not been given. You can call it as you wish, or you can just call it Solef's smaller twin. This is my gift to you."

Choleira received a long bow with branches carved into the wood from Evindal. The string was strong and would never fray no matter how many arrows were loosened from it. Lady Aylisen gave Choleira a quiver of arrows. The quiver had waves spiraling around its leather body and small fish dancing above them. The arrows were made of water and ice, and if water was in the quiver, arrows would be infinite. From Ellisar came a cloak that he had woven, which would keep the wearer warm in the cold and cool in the heat. It would keep whoever wore it at a comfortable temperature so that they were always at their best, while being protected from harm.

"Try out your bow, Choleira," Lady Aylisen said.

Choleira pulled out her bow and pulled out an arrow from the quiver. The shaft of the arrow was ice, and the tip was almost like a rock. At the end where feathers would usually be tied were watery strands that would manipulate the air around it to navigate to its intended target no matter how far it was or where it would move to.

She drew her string back and loosed an arrow at the far wall of Olmenor. It sailed through the air and landed in the center of the large circle they had stood on that morning when Lady Aylisen did her morning water show.

She thanked the three Lords. And so did Choleira. They turned and left back up towards the top of the city. They reached the stables of Olmenor and readied Snowfire, who had a mouthful of hay in his mouth.

They got on him and he whinnied. "Where is East, Choleira?" Inerium asked. Choleira pointed to the right, where an old pathway was cut through the woods. "Then off we go." She directed Snowfire towards the path. "To Venirit."

CHAPTER 9

The night had come. The road that the caravan had rode on was rough and bumpy. The stars overhead was shining brightly next to the moon that illuminated the whole land around them. The mountain stood in the distance like a colossal beast watching them as they traveled. The great trees shimmered around the mountain in holy magic light, almost brighter than the moonlight. When the silver shimmer of the moon and the golden gleam of the trees, it created a wondrous collage of colors that only the richest of people could imagine. The caravan had stopped a couple times to let a few of the soldiers piss and shit in the bushes nearby. When the other soldiers were not looking, Kerstas, Barnabin, and Geremi all helped themselves to the food and drink in their carriage. They did not eat a lot, but enough that would go unnoticed by the inventory checkers of the caravan.

On top of the roughness of the road, the caravan was constantly going up and down slopes and hills, which had started to give Kerstas motion sickness. For the past hour or so Kerstas and the other two had been asleep on top of the sacks of vegetables. Barnabin was kicking the wall of the carriage behind him from the nightmare he was having. Kerstas, however, was sleeping soundly. At least he was until the dream turned sour.

In the dream he was walking along the halls of the castle in Requilit with his father Kentrin. They were talking about the honor in ruling a kingdom and about how the people will love him. They walked out onto a balcony looking over the whole kingdom. The sun was beaming down on them.

"Son, when my time comes, there is something you need to do."

"What is it, Father?" He asked.

Suddenly the sky darkened out. The sun got blacked out and a fiery ring formed around the void in the sky where the sun stood. The wind started to pick up rapidly and buildings started to get ripped up by massive air spirals coming from the clouds. Lightning struck the ground in the distance and started lighting everything on fire. The whole horizon was ablaze under the eclipsed crimson sky, and Kentrin got sucked into the air. Kerstas grabbed Kentrin by the arm and tried to pull him back.

Kentrin cried out in pain from a large piece of wood that had pierced his side. "Son, the next eclipse is not far away. When it arrives..." The wind dragged him away and pulled him into the cyclone of air. The whole horizon shifted, and the eclipse now stood over the mountain peak, covering the whole land in a dark crimson shadow. Kerstas' eyes started to burn but he could not look away from the void of the eclipse.

There was a rumble in the air so low that it shook the whole ground like an earthquake and destroyed the smaller buildings in the kingdom below. The ground crumbled away and all that remained was the castle and the great mountain. Kerstas' vision started to blur, and a voice started echoing from the mountain. "Come to me, Kerstas. Come to me." Kerstas blacked out and fell on the floor of the balcony.

Kerstas woke up from his dream, sweating profusely. He

dried his sweatier areas and sat up. His head was pounding, and his eyes were still burning a bit, like when soap would get into someone's eyes. They traveled a long way since Kerstas was last awake. Perhaps ten miles maybe. If not more. Kerstas realized that they were heading towards the East, and not the South anymore. He realized that meant, according to what he remembered from the old maps, he would look back at the castle, that they were on the Southern Road towards Istimus. They were still in the territory of Meridine, however. He could tell this because the great mountain was still to his left. When the mountain would start to trail behind them and get farther away, they would be in the Istimus kingdom territory.

Barnabin woke up and sat upright. "Are you okay, Kerstas?"

He turned his head towards Barnabin. Not towards him, but towards him. "Just a bad dream, Barnabin. You do not need to worry yourself of it." He looked off at the mountain. His body started to slightly shiver, despite it still being warm even at night from the hot seasons.

"It's the mountain, isn't it?" He asked. "It is bothering you again."

Kerstas fully turned to look at Barnabin. Geremi was starting to wake up, but he simply turned over with a grunt. "It is always bothering me. It is in my blood for it to bother me. It is a curse that me, my father, my grandfather, and all his fathers before him carry. It is a curse bound to us until death, Sir Barnabin. And I do not know how to fix that curse."

There were crickets chirping in the grass around them, harmonizing with the occasional toad croak that would drown out all other noises besides it. The throbbing from Kerstas' head lessened a bit. It still hurt but it was now bearable to only an annoyance level.

"Perhaps, maybe, do you think going to the mountain

would fix it?" He asked. "I mean you said that every guy in your family has always been drawn to it. Maybe going to it will somehow end it."

Kerstas sat on the thought. He sat on it for a while, almost long enough that if his hand was the thought, it would have been asleep already. "It might work." He looked up at the mountain. "But it terrifies me. What if going to the mountain is the whole reason for this curse existing? That the whole reason this curse plagues my family is so whatever is in that mountain can have us. I do not know why it would want us specifically, but I do know that it does. And knowing that, I refuse to give that creature what it wants."

Barnabin nodded. The carriage in front of them hit a bump in the road and it knocked one of the soldiers off on his ass on the dirt.

"Halt!" The driver of the carriage in front of them called out. The caravan stopped and Malgrin turned around on his horse, trotting over to the soldier who cried out.

"What is it?" asked Malgrin. "What is this for?"

"One of the men fell off, sir. We were stopping to get him back."

Malgrin looked over to the soldier who was standing up. He dusted off his pants and straightened up his uniform. "Do not let this happen again, soldier, or next time you will not get back up."

The soldier nodded. "Yes sir." His voice was childish, as if he were just hitting puberty. He jumped onto the side of the carriage and tried to kick his leg over the railing to get back inside.

Malgrin shook his head in disapproval and returned to the front of the party. "Let's move!"

The carriages started moving again. There were small

mountains in the distance to their right. Their peaks pierced the clouds. Not passing them like the great mountin to their left, but scratching them, almost tickling the clouds. They were the mountains that bordered the land of Pleniris and the neighboring land that Kerstas was never told of.

In reference to geography, Pleniris lay between two lands. To the North was the ancient lands where his grandmother told him the Elves were born and claimed their magic from. And to the South was a land like the one they were currently on. Part of the Southern half of it was frozen over, and Kerstas was told only that of the lands. He knew not what kind of beings or races could even possibly live there. The land was truly mysterious and the large peaks, who stood on the horizon like teeth on a saw, separated the lands of Pleniris from its mysteries.

As a young boy Kerstas often thought about what could be in the lands to the South, but not even his grandmother knew, and she had traveled all over the lands. She would occasionally tell stories of Elves and magic. Kerstas barely believed them, but Inerium ate them up like candy. She loved hearing about the adventures of the Elf king slaying dragons, or an Elf princess being saved by an adventuring human. No matter how outlandish or fantastical the stories were, she always loved hearing them. Kerstas of coursed loved hearing them because it fed his imagination, but due to his traumatic experiences with the priests in Requilit, his mind was often preoccupied with getting revenge and the thoughts of what he would do when he could finally enact it.

Kerstas did once ask what was beyond the mountains in the Southern part of Pleniris, but when his grandma heard the question, she would usually avoid it with another story or simply pretending to hear Eleana or Kentrin calling her name and she would leave the room.

"Here take this. It has been a few hours since we last ate." Barnabin tossed a small red fruit at Kerstas. He caught it and looked around to make sure none of the soldiers were looking. They were not. He took a bite of the red fruit, and it made a crips tearing sound as he tore a piece off with his teeth. The juice of the fruit leaked out of the areas his teeth sank into and even from a distance, one could see the fresh juice from the fruit soaking into the empty space where the piece had been removed from the body.

He took a sip from a small pouch of water that Geremi had stolen from the corpse of one of the soldiers. It was small, but it held enough water for two glasses to be poured into. The water was very cold and refreshing. It tasted off mixing with the taste of the red fruit, but it did not bother Kerstas. Food was food. Water was water. Whatever satiated his hunger and thirst was enough for him. Barnabin tore into another red fruit like Kerstas.' It was not as juicy as Kerstas', which he knew because he intended the better one to be for the future king of Requilit.

"So, what was home like, Kerstas?" He asked. "You know, before…"

"It was nice. Everyone was so friendly and kind." He remembered the priests that tormented him for hears on end. "Almost everyone. There were a few who needed their asses handed to them, then cut off and fed to them."

"I see. So even the promised king that is to bring true peace to the land has a few grudges against people."

Kerstas furrowed his eyebrows. "What did you say?" He took another bite from his fruit.

"I did not mean to say that. It slipped out. Forget it. It was not meant to be said. it is secret." His voice was panicked, fearful.

"I cannot forget it, Barnabin. What did you mean?"

He sighed. Whether he was supposed to keep it a secret or not, he let it slip. There was no taking it back now. Kerstas was already having thoughts in his head about what it could mean, and he had no plans to stop them from growing and multiplying. "Okay, so there was a prophecy the king from our kingdom heard. It drove him insane for years, fearing it. I did not hear much of it, but what I did hear was that when the next heir to a throne was chosen and crowned, that king would be the one to bring down all the kingdoms of Pleniris and turn them into their own singular kingdom under his rule. And naturally that you were the next king to be crowned, *you* were the one who the prophecy spoke of."

Of course, the thought of it was insane. Kerstas was still young. Very young. In some people's eyes he was still a boy, not yet even a man. Yes, he was eligible to become the new king of Requilit, and technically he *is* the king of Requilit, but that did not change the fact that he was still a boy at the age of sixteen who had not seen the outside walls of his kingdom any more than the outside of his mother's body when he was in the womb.

His mind, however (unlike his body) had been put through both thoughts and experience like an adult. From a young age up until the final days he had with his parents, he had been mistreated by those who claimed to be servants and prophets of the Lord. He had gone from a faithful, Lord-loving, boy to a young man who could not even stand to hear the idea or mentioning of it. What was not mentioned about Kerstas was that any time he had heard mention of the Lord or anything to do with him, a small pit burned in his stomach. Were it rage or disgust, he could not tell. Perhaps it was both. Perhaps it was his body trying to recreate the feeling that the priests had forcefully given him for years, and it associated the feeling with any mention of the Lord. Perhaps even all of these things were true about Kerstas' situation, but whether they were truth or lie, that pit in his stomach grew more and more, burned hotter and hotter, as the years passed by.

There were times when Kerstas would wonder if his hatred towards the priests and the Lord would have affected his reputation as Requilit's king, but was it such a bad thing? He often thought about it. Whether it was in the back of his mind or at the front lines of his thoughts, the thought lingered. He was sure, though, that if he had told all the people during his coronation of what the priests did to him, they would understand his standing. If they were in the same position that he was in, he believed that they would do the same. Hell, he believed that he was doing them a favor for wanting to publicly execute them, and not doing what others would do and mutilate them in the streets or suffocate them in their beds while they were sleeping.

"Hey," Barnabin said. "Over there, do you see it?"

Kerstas looked over to the left where Barnabin pointed. There was a small rocky patch on the side of a small hill they were passing. In the patch was a hole that was dug deep into the ground. The two could not see inside of it due to how dark it was both outside and inside the cave. The caravan halted and Malgrin was riding past the carriages, stopping at each one.

As he passed a carriage, he would top, say a few words, and continue to the next one. When he reached the final one, where Kerstas, Barnabin, and Geremi were he knocked on the wooden railing on the side. Geremi woke up and looked around. He probably thought they were being ambushed again, which of course was not the case.

"We are camping here for the night," Malgrin said. He pointed to the cave. "You three and a small handful of other soldiers will go inside to make sure there are not any bears or any manner of creature that could harm us in our sleep."

Barnabin and Geremi nodded. "Yes sir."

Malgrin began to ride away, but Kerstas called to him. "Hey, Malgrin, sir, what would I use to defend myself?"

Malgrin nodded. "Wait here." He rode towards the front of the party, stopping at one of the carriages behind the first one. He jumped into the back of it and grabbed something from it. He got back onto this horse and returned to the Kerstas' carriage. "Here, take this. The soldiers that passed will not need it anymore."

He handed Kerstas a metal-hilted sword with a long iron blade. It was not razor sharp, but it would do the trick if he needed to use it, and he assumed he most definitely would. He held it in his hand, feeling its weight and trying to find the most comfortable grip to use on it. The sword was not a perfect size or fit for him, but it was at least not too small for him. The sword was heavy, but not unbearably so. He would not be able to easily swing it like a sword fit for him, but if he put a touch more force into his swings, he could do it properly.

The sword came with a scabbard, which Malgrin handed to him after he was done looking at his new sword. The scabbard was nothing special. It was black with the same steel casing around the opening and tip. Kerstas tied it to his pants and sheathed the sword in it. The three hopped off the carriage and watched as the other soldiers started setting up tents and campfires. A small group of about five soldiers left to go hunt some deer or small game animals to cook along with what food they decided would go good with it.

Malgrin waved his hand in a "follow me" motion, and Kerstas followed him. Barnabin and Geremi were right behind Kerstas. They all stood next to the cave, along with two soldiers with black bears, one with a scraggly blonde beard that looked like he had been struck by lightning, and another one who was well sized whose pants were about to come undone from the pressure of the monstrous gut they were holding back. The sizable man was clean shaven, almost as if he could not even grow facial hair at all. His hair was knotted and tangled from his roots all the way down to the ends, where they appeared like a bird's nest on his shoulders. All the soldiers' eyes were a heavy brown color, and the two with black beards were glaring at Kerstas with an intense amount of hate. Kerstas took a few small steps away from them, inching his hand towards his new sword just in case they tried anything.

"You six are going to go inside this cave and make sure that we do not get mutilated as we sleep. There are torches I will provide for you to see in the dark, and if any casualties occur, run straight out at tell me. I will gather all the men and we will take out whatever monster or beast lurks within."

The soldiers nodded and said, "yes sir," in unison.

Malgrin handed each soldier a torch. One by one they went to the closest bonfire to them and lit them ablaze.

Kerstas did not receive a torch. "Do I not get one?" He asked.

Malgrin shook his head. "If something bad happens in there, I would rather a few of those men perish than you. If I were to let a king die in my care, then what kind of soldier would I be?"

"Thank you, Malgrin. I could have sworn, though, you were against me."

He shook his head. "You are a king, and you have done me no wrong. You just must understand that in some situations, orders must be followed." There was a flicker of pain behind his eyes. A fear. A worry. Almost a cry for help. It was only there for a moment and then it was gone.

Kerstas nodded in agreement. This man was the leader of the ones who killed his parents, destroyed his kingdom, and took it from him. He wanted to hate him, but that flicker in Malgrin's eyes somehow made him want to change his mind. Something in Kerstas' subconscious was telling him not to be quick to hate Malgrin, and to wait until he hears everything from him.

Kerstas rejoined the group, whose faces were all greatly illuminated by the harsh colors of the flames from their torches. By greatly, I do not mean to complement their features. There was nothing good really to compliment on these men. It looked like they used to shovel shit from the streets or clean up after the animals before they had become soldiers.

"You ready, boy?" One of the bearded men asked.

Kerstas nodded. The group headed into the cave, which reeked of animal shit, mold, and rot. The cave winded about deeper into the ground until they entered a large room, where most of the foul-smelling animal most likely slept and ate its food. Perhaps there was more than one animal. The piles of bones on the floor, both human and animal, laying in the corner indicated that there was no doubt more than one. Some of the bones were freshly picked at. One of the soldiers pointed this out when he noticed that there was still meat bleeding on some of the bones.

There was a small hole near the bones that led deeper into the cave.

"Hey, Fatass, you go in there," one of the black-bearded soldiers said with a crude tone in his voice.

The large soldier grunted and glared at him. "If I were to do that, *you* would be the one pulling me out of there."

Geremi walked over to the hole and stepped through. He was gone for a few minutes without a word or sound.

"You okay in there?" Barnabin asked.

Another moment of silence passed and Geremi finally appeared in the shadows of the opening. "Sorry. There is a lot more back here. I have not seen any animals, though. But there is something you all should see."

The two black-bearded men walked through the opening, followed by Kerstas and Barnabin. The large man stayed back, due to being too large to fit through. When they were through and on their feet, they looked around the new section of the cave.

The new area inside the cave smelled just like, if not worse than, the previous section. There were bones crushed and broken all over the floor.

"These are just bones, Geremi. What did you see?" Barnabin asked.

Geremi pointed over to one of the walls. There was a large crack in it that had a purple light seeping out of it, like sun rays through storm clouds. The soldiers fought to try to peek through the crack. There were a lot of "Get out of my way" and "fuck you, I was here first" comments repeated by the soldiers, shoving each other out of the way to look inside.

"What is it?" Kerstas asked.

"I can't fuckin' tell, kid. And you aren't seeing it until I find out," the brown-haired soldier said.

"Hey, now, you all have tried your share of seeing. Let him look and try to find out what's in there," Barnabin, said as he stepped away from the crack in the cave wall.

"Oh yeah? Who are you to give orders, Barnabin?" One of the black-bearded soldiers turned around and tensed up his shoulders to appear bigger.

Barnabin shook his head. "We are all the same ranks. No one here has any higher rank than the other."

The bearded man turned to Kerstas and smirked an evil smirk. "Except for this one. He is under all of us." He chuckled deeply. "So, we can push him around all we want."

"No. Absolutely not." Geremi and Barnabin stepped in front of Kerstas. "Captain Malgrin said that we were not allowed to harm him."

"Well, fuck the captain." He grabbed Barnabin and Geremi and shoved them away like one would when they dramatically opened doors to a bar. He grabbed Kerstas and held him up by the collar of his shirt.

Kerstas' mind flashed back to the days when the priests would take advantage of him. He kicked around trying to free himself.

"You little shit are the reason we even came to your damned kingdom in the first place. Our king believed a little fairy tale that happened to relate to you, so he goes and sends us to the other corner of the kingdom. To risk our lives for a fucking kid."

"Put me down," Kerstas said. "Malgrin will hear about this." He said it between grunts trying to catch his breath.

"Oh, will he?" He threw Kerstas at the wall, and he crashed against it with a hard thud. Barnabin and Geremi got back up and stood in front of Kerstas again.

"Leave him alone," they said in unison.

The man shook his head. "The things I had to do when I was there. I killed the damn twin cooks because my king ordered it. Of course, I did *more* than just killing them, but still I had to do it." He laughed a menacing laugh.

Kerstas' heart suddenly stopped. A pool of rage started to boil from his soul, and he clenched his fists in rage. He reached forward and grabbed the under part of the man's arm. He grabbed the muscle and squeezed it as hard as he could. The man dropped Kerstas and shook his arm.

Kerstas grabbed his sword and unsheathed it. He pierced the foot of the man. The man reached down and grabbed his foot, which was pouring blood from the top and bottom of the wound. Kerstas dashed around him and sliced the back of his ankles open. The bearded man tumbled to the ground in agony and stared up at Kerstas, his eyes filled with rage.

"Damn you, boy. You should have been slaughtered with the rest of your damned family."

Kerstas shook his head. "Then I would not have the joy of living this moment." Kerstas smiled and drove the blade into the face of the man. It pierced his right cheek and flew through into his left one. When the blade went all the way through, it made a *clang* as it hit the cave floor. Kerstas left the blade in the face of the man. There was a pool of blood forming around his face, staining his skin.

Kerstas let out a long sigh and turned to the others. "Is anyone going to make his mistake as well?"

The soldiers all shook their heads. Their eyes were wide. The kill happened in only a few seconds, which it had happened by the time they had all turned around to realize what was happening.

The brown-bearded soldier stepped up. "I do not speak for his actions, and I do not wish to. What do we tell the captain?"

Kerstas shrugged his shoulders. "Malgrin said that if anything bad happened to return. We have assessed that there are no animals in here and that it is safe." He glanced at the crack still glowing in the wall. "There is that, of course."

Kerstas walked over to the crack in the wall and tried to peek through it. Suddenly, the sound of rocks cracking and breaking echoed through the cave. The soldiers all frantically looked around to see where the sound came from. They all looked at the opening they had come through as another sound pierced the air. It was the large man trying to fit through.

"I heard you panicking and decided to try and come help. I got myself stuck doing it, though." He tried to push himself back and the cracking of stone sounded again.

"Stop moving, you fat bastard!" The still living black-bearded man shouted. "You will bring this whole cave down."

The large man grunted and shook his head. "Why did they even tag me in this. They knew I could not fit into these places."

"Maybe they hoped that if there was a bear in here it would have eaten you. You would have kept him fed for months." The brown-bearded soldier laughed.

"Stop being mean to each other," Kerstas said. "Fat or not, he is still a soldier, and you all are sworn to protect each other." The soldier looked down at the black-bearded man whose face was still bleeding on the floor with Kerstas' sword sheathed in it. "He does not count. He disobeyed direct orders and tried to attack me. I was simply defending myself."

The brown-bearded soldier stepped up. "I will not say a word against it. He was quite the dick when it came to anything. If I were in your place, I most likely would have done the same." He looked down again at the dead soldier and shook his head. He returned his look to the large soldier who was stuck in the opening. "Alright, big guy, let me see how I can get you free."

The soldier walked up to the large soldier and looked at the stone around him. The stone was cracking around him, and more so in his stomach region. There seemed to be no way to free the man without taking the whole cave with him. There were a few choices he could think of. He could try to free him and risk the cave collapsing. He could kill him and see if it would help, which it would not. The last idea he had was to try to break away from some of the rocks and free him.

The last choice seemed the most reasonable, and he tried it. He used a knife he had to chip away at some of the rocks around the areas that were more stuck than others. The large man could move his legs and arms after a few minutes of chipping rocks, and he moved on to his stomach area.

Kerstas went to peek into the crack in the wall, having not been able to look at it before due to the large man trying to fit through a hole that even *he* said he could not fit through it, yet he tried it anyway. He looked through the crack and he could finally see through it. Inside was a large room filled with crystals. Not like scattered here and there but *made* of crystals. It was like the stone of the cave room they were in was replaced with purple and white crystals. It was beautiful and it seemed to stretch on infinitely. There was a small pathway leading on the floor through the maze of jagged crystals pointing out in every direction.

"What do you see?" Barnabin asked. When the soldiers had tried to look earlier, they could only see bright light and nothing else.

"It is a room full of crystals. It almost does not even seem real." He motioned Barnabin closer. "Come look. Let your eyes adjust."

Barnabin peered into the crack. It took him a quarter of a minute to see the other side of the wall, but he finally did. His only word was "wow."

The brown-bearded soldier tugged on the larger man, and he tumbled inside. The whole cave shook as he crashed onto the floor. He saw the dead soldier on the ground and started to freak out. He hobbled up and tried to run away. He tried to fit through the hole again and the cracks started sounding often. The opening started growing as more and more rocks started to fall on the ground.

"You damned idiot!" Geremi shouted as he ran towards the opening of the cave.

As the large man squeezed through the hole, his leg got pierced by a sharp rock that fell from above. He cried out in pain and the walls started falling apart. Kerstas looked over at the crack in the wall, which was growing more and more into the floor and roof of the cave. The walls started reflecting the purple and white reflections coming from the crack and the wall suddenly broke open. The crystals swiftly grew out of the room and covered some of the walls of the cave. The opening where the large man squeezed through started to collapse. The stone buried him and the rest of the room they were in began to collapse as well. Kerstas ran towards the crystal room, followed by Barnabin and Geremi. The brown-bearded man tried to follow them, but he was crushed by a large rock. The black-bearded soldier made it into the crystal room, and the cave caved in behind them, trapping them inside.

CHAPTER 10

Inerium and Choleira had been riding for hours when they finally reached the edge of the forest. They had found a small hill with a flat top on it to camp at. They had made tents out of the kits that they were given by the elves tending to the stables in Olmenor. A fire was burning outside of their tents that Inerium had started from the branches and leaves around the hill, along with a few they picked up from the forest as they passed through.

Choleira had laid in the same tent as Inerium because she did not want to sleep alone. Inerium did not mind. She had slept alone all her life when she had gotten old enough to, and she had wished for a friend to lie with. Like a sleepover, but the sleepover's games of pretend were not actually pretend.

Inerium had tossed and turned all night. She had dreams of other worlds that she could travel in. There were monsters of unnatural shapes, proportions, and sizes wandering around the planes of the world. She was simply looking into the world, though. They were not dreams where she was being chased by the monsters or exploring an abandoned tomb in them. It was more like she was looking at them through a crystal ball. This was not the first time she had experienced these dreams. She had seen similar ones before. Before her parents and home were taken from her. The dreams were the ones that had given her such a wide imagination when she would play with her dolls.

In one of the dreams, she had a dream that a large dragon was imprisoned in a large field of ashes. He had his arms, legs, neck, and wings chained to the ground. She named him Dorgy and would have times where she would have her dolls go and pretend that they were freeing him.

When Inerium would start to toss and turn, Choleira would roll over and hug her until she would calm down. Inerium never woke from her dreams. They would only lessen their realism and be a little more down-to-Earth.

Choleira had recurring thoughts about the ghosts and watching the grey elf crumble to dust in front of her. She did not want to bring it up to Inerium because she assumed that she was having the same thoughts, and if she was not, Choleira did not want to bring it up. She was right to think so. Inerium had the thoughts as well. She repeatedly saw the ghosts floating around the trees and hiding in the shadows waiting to get her. She was terrified of the thoughts that if she were to meet Kerstas, he, too, would crumble to dust in front of her. That was the most troublesome thought of all. She wondered if he was still alive. Still safe. He was, but if she only knew, it would ease her mind a little more.

Inerium woke up when one of her dream monsters looked at her and started to run towards her. Choleira put her arm around her and hugged her.

"It's okay, Ineri," she said.

Inerium looked up. She had not heard her name be called that in days. It felt like years since she had been with her brother. His nickname she was given by him... It both made her happy and sad to hear it spoken to her again. She looked over at Choleira and smiled. "Thank you, Choli." Inerium gave her the nickname when she had a brain fart and forgot how to pronounce Choleira's name. She only uttered Choli, and Choleira found it cute enough to keep it, and that is when she first called Inerium Ineri. When Inerium first heard Choleira call her that she had broken into tears, and she explained why. Choleira thought she had hurt her, but Inerium explained that she just missed her brother and did not mind the nickname.

"So, Choli, the day is starting. Are you ready to head off?"

She nodded. "Snowfire, come!" From a little hill close by came Snowfire, his beautiful mane and tail flowing in the wind. He was eating on some grass he found and was stripping the area of it all. He had done a large number on the surrounding grass that all that was left around the hill they camped on was mostly dirt and weeds. He whinnied and shook his mane around as he stopped next to them.

Choleira and Inerium packed up their stuff and collapsed the tent, putting it in its little bag where it would remain for many days to come. The sun was already halfway towards its zenith point. The heat was smoldering the land like an oven, and the two girls were already starting to sweat. They drank some water from their pouches, and Choleira used some of her water magic to draw water from the grass around them and refill them. The border to Venirit was close. The Elven Forest was disappearing behind the hills as they traveled further away from it.

They had ridden for about an hour or so when Choleira said she needed to stop to relieve herself. She walked behind a bunch of shrubs that were lying beside the road and squatted behind them. She sat there for a minute or two, wiped herself with a few leaves, and returned to Inerium and Snowfire. The journey continued, and Inerium could not stop thinking about her brother. The memories of playing together in the streets, almost knocking over people, (occasionally doing so without meaning to) and running from the soldiers when they would try to return them to the castle. She and her brother shared so many fun memories together.

What if we can't share anymore memories together? What if he is dead? There will be no one to share these memories with me. These were the thoughts swimming in her mind like a group doing a backstroke in unison. They came with waves and splashes with every thought, and the ripples of her mind only made it worse and made her more sorrowful and more hopeful for her brother's safety. These thoughts were what kept her going. She *had* to ensure her brother was alive and well. *He must be alive. He must be okay so that we can share more memories together.*

Choleira could feel Inerium's hurting. It was her gift after all; to feel and read people. She was exceptional at it. She was terrific. Words were not capable of explaining it. She could meet a stranger she had never met before and see their whole life's story with a simple meeting of eyes. That is why she chose Inerium to be her friend. She read Inerium, almost seemingly into her future, and chose her to be her friend. Some back in Olmenor would even say she could *literally* read minds...

Inerium pulled a coin purse-sized sack out of Snowfire's saddle pouch. It was filled with some large red berries from bushes near the edge of the forest that she and Choleira had collected. They were roughly the size of a large mouse. Choleira called them Errych Berries. They were sweet and grew only in the hot seasons. She said they were delicious in pies and desserts that were made back in Olmenor. The two girls ate a few of them to feed their hunger a bit so their stomachs would not tighten up and cramp from emptiness. There was something more to the berries that Choleira had forgotten about, but she could not quite remember what it was. She knew it was an important thing, but it would not come to her.

The red juices of the berries trickled down Choleira's chin, and Inerium wiped it off with her sleeve. After about five or six berries each, she returned the sack to the saddle pouch. Choleira told herself that when she returned home, she would collect more of the berries, and when she would run out, she would go and get more with Choleira. In Inerium's eyes, she was a best friend for life, and Choleira returned the feeling.

"Hey, did you feel that shaking last night?" Choleira asked.

Inerium nodded. "Yeah, was it an earthquake?"

Choleira shrugged her shoulders. "It woke me up, that is all I know."

The earth shaking from the night before was a violent one. It was like the most powerful earth magic user got angry and decided to shake the earth like a kid in a store shaking a snow globe. They did not know what had caused it, but the whole land of Pleniris had felt it. Everyone from the survivors of Requilit to the fishermen in the most Southeastern corner of Istimus.

They looked over towards the giant mountain in the distance on their right. It was like looking at a beautiful rose with a singular thorn protruding from the bud sleeping in the center of the blanket of petals holding it in place. The golden trees stood around the bottom of the mountain like pollen falling off a flower, pollinating the ground around it as if to let it grow taller. The mountain had looked mammoth from where they were riding but imagining how big it would appear from the bottom of it made Inerium queasy. There was no doubt that this was the same feeling that everyone shared when looking at the mountain. Between the rumors of the creature dwelling within to the screams that could be heard as the wind blew through its ridges, everyone feared the mountain with terror and curiosity overlapping one another.

Inerium had studied the different kingdoms as a little girl. Her mother, Eleana, ensured that she had to learn about all four kingdoms so that she may (both her parents had hoped) find a prince to marry and unite their kingdoms. Inerium of course did not study the other kingdoms for those purposes. She did it to further her knowledge of them and to be able to come up with more scenarios and lands for her to use in her games of pretend. The more she learned about the other kingdoms, the more she would dream about the foreign and alien lands. As much as the dreams scared her, she loved them. They would take her to places she had never been before, and may never go to, but it did not matter to her. She had gone there in dreams and walked their roads and conversed with their people, and that was enough to satisfy her desires to travel there physically.

She had told Choleira about the things she knew about the other kingdoms. About the scary king of Meridine and about the scrawny, not-so-scary king of Istimus. She talked fondly about her home and her family. She would bring Kerstas up a lot, almost to a tedious amount. To some, it would have been a tedious amount, but Choleira loved hearing every word Inerium had to say. She listened with her fullest attention and all her interests were focused on her and her words.

The kingdom of Venirit was getting closer as they continued to ride Eastward along the main road. They could not see the high walls of the kingdom yet, but according to a few small road signs, the kingdom's capital was only a little under an hour away. A few small merchant carriages passed them by. The merchants did not take notice that Choleira had Elven ears or that Inerium was the lost princess of Requilit that the whole kingdom was trying to find. They were singing their little songs, humming, and whistling them without another care in the world. The trinkets and goods in the back of their cloth-covered carriage rattled and bounced around as the wheels ran over the rocks and ruts in the road.

After roughly half an hour passed, Inerium had a thought come to her mind about Choleira. "Hey, Choli, I might need to let you know that you will need to cover your ears when we get to Venirit. Humans might not exactly react normally if they see or hear that an Elf is wandering their city."

Choleira nodded. She took the cloak off her body and put it back on, now covering the bow, arrows, and her ears. Now she just looked like a young girl who liked to wear oversized clothing. Wearing it in the dismal heat would bring up a few questions, but that could be waved off as a personal religious belief or just a simple style of choice. Regardless of which, it would draw out a lot less attention compared to seeing elven ears on a girl with a magic bow with elemental arrows.

The two girls ate a few more Errych Berries and stopped to let Snowfire drink some water. Inerium practiced with her ring by drawing out the water from a nearby pond and refilling her and Choleira's water pouches. Snowfire drank the water as it sailed through the air by his head. He ran over to the pond, which was nearly emptied out, and drank from it. He ate some of the smaller plants banking around the edge of the pond, which was now a dry hole in the ground. When the three were done eating and hydrating, the two girls got on Snowfire and started again heading towards Venirit.

<hr>

The walls surrounding the kingdom of Venirit were drawing nearer. Inerium and Choleira could see, just above the walls, towers where soldiers would watch over to look for invaders or threats to their kingdom. Towards the far end of the wall was a large castle-like building, which was most assumedly the place where the king of Venirit lived.

There were a few issues with Venirit. The first issue was that most of the outer parts of the city, where the poorer people lived, were ruled by the various gangs who tried to claim certain parts of the city. The guards started avoiding conflict with them due to the casualties caused by the interactions. The second issue with the city was that out of the four, it held the highest rates of crime in all contexts, being murder or simple thievery.

Inerium only chose to go to Venirit because the king was friends with her father. He was nice and was the only king, other than her father, who she considered a "friendly sort." The king of Meridine was too scary and intimidating for her, and the king of Istimus was too awkward and reminded her of someone who had proudly answered a question wrong in school and would not let the embarrassment go.

The final issue with the city is that it was very odorous. The sewers were vast in the city, and due to the gangs keeping the guards away, the workers have not been able to fix the backed-out tunnels. Many rumored that there were mutated beasts under the streets of Venirit, but of course they were only rumors. No one had been down to clean the shit and piss-filled tunnels that twisted and winded beneath the whole capital. There was a total of thirteen tunnels that poured out into the lands beyond the capital. The one in the very back, which was protruding out of the wall below the castle like a tailpipe of a car.

These sewer tunnels could be seen pouring out vile liquid filled with chunks of shit and other diabolical substances from its maws. The smell was horrendous even from the distance they were at. The lands around the kingdom were like a swamp. The grass was muddy (a large amount of it not being mud) and filled with yellow and brown liquid. There almost seemed to be steam coming out of the watery areas, with its own aura of heat radiating from it. It felt like a sauna as they traveled along the main road, which had moldy mushrooms growing out of it every so often.

The deeper areas of the swamp had carcasses of animals floating about in its waters. They were mainly molded over and eaten away by maggots and flies. They did not accompany well with the overwhelming aroma that forced itself into the noses of Snowfire, Inerium, and Choleira. The peoples of Venirit's capital had adapted to the smell and have all but forgotten about it. They did not know of the smell of fresh grass or a delicious meal. When food would be served to them, they would receive a small-yet-pleasant whiff of their food and have it overpowered by the odors of their defecations that spilled into their streets.

The path they were traveling on was the only one that had not been flooded by the foulness from the swamps surrounding the capital of Venirit. They approached the giant gates leading into the city. There were two soldiers who were standing guard in front of them holding large halberds. Their faces were covered with thick cloth masks that covered everything below their eyes. They most likely kept these on to avoid destroying their olfactory senses any more than they already were.

The capital of Venirit was not always like this, however. It used to be beautiful and the grasslands around it used to grow the most beautiful flowers. Inerium's grandmother got three or four seeds of these flowers for her garden. Inerium had almost forgotten the garden of her grandmother. The memories came back to her of Kertas showing her the different plants and naming them, saying which ones were poisoned, which ones could be eaten, and which ones went well in a meal table's décor.

"State your business, Peasants," the guard on the left said. His voice was hoarse, like any approaching day could take it away from him.

"I need to speak to your king, Sir." She was looking down on him, which she got a sudden feeling in the back of her head that he did not like, and she got off Snowfire. "I need to tell him about the attack in Requilit."

"You know what happened in Requilit?" He asked.

The other soldier turned his head towards her. "What did you see? Do you know who did it?"

Inerium shook her head. "I do know where they were heading, though. That is why I need to speak to your king. Could you take me to him?"

They looked at each other. They nodded. The right one pulled out a small horn that was dangling from his waist. He sounded three notes: a high one, a low one, and a higher one than the first. He put the horn back on his hip. "Just one moment. You can get back on your horse."

He walked over to her and helped her get on Snowfire. She thanked him for the help, and they all waited for whatever the horn had called or instigated.

After about ten minutes or so, the gates opened only a crack and a line of half a dozen soldiers, hands on their swords, stepped through. They formed a horizontal line next to Inerium and Choleira and clicked their heels together.

The soldier holding the horn smiled and gestured at the line of other soldiers. "These men right here will escort you through the streets to the king. They will keep you safe from the thieves and other nasties that dwell in the ill side of town."

"Thank you, sir. If I could tell my father of your kindness I would." Her eyes grew a sad look in them for a moment at the memory of her father. Her mother. Her home. But she was going to get it back. Right after she saved her brother. That was why she was here. Her adventure through the forest, meeting Choleira, all of it were steppingstones on the path to save her brother.

The soldiers turned around in sync and formed a line. The gates opened wider. The formation they did held the two girls on Snowfire in the center, two guards stood in front of them, two stood behind them, and one stood on the left and right sides of them. The other gate opened to fit the formation through, and they started walking up the street.

As they made their way through the streets, Inerium and Choleira saw many houses and buildings that were run down or boarded up. There were dirty and ragged people either staring at them with disgust through their windows or laying in the street or on their porches gazing at them with their dirt and mud-covered faces. It was heartbreaking for Inerium to look at. It looked like even their Lord had abandoned them and cursed them to live a life of filth, despite being so close to a king who lives lavishly and dines on well-cooked meals.

From the gates, it looked like the entire capital was decrepit and tainted, but after a few blocks, the buildings started to appear more presentable. This was the middle district, where the not-as-poor people lived. These were usually the Smithers or bakers and some specific medical personnel who made only enough to be in the middle class. The sewage odor lifted a little, but only enough that a slightly pleasant bread scent could carry through for some relief. The people of the middle class did not distastefully stare at the party traveling up the main street of the capital, but they did look in a curious manner. A "who are they and what do they want" or "why is that mysterious girl wearing a hood" kind of look.

They passed through the middle district of the capital and entered the high-class district. The buildings here were nice, cleaned to perfection, and the people were dressed neatly as if they were all nobles in some form or fashion. These people sneered and glared at the party, too, but not because they were strangers. They did not care about getting to know people. Most of their personalities were based around their finances and material properties. They barely even knew one another. They would do a slight nod in the direction of another if eye contact was made, but they did not hold conversations unless it was about wealth or gossip going around that they were hungering to hear about. The look they gave at the party, specifically Inerium and Choleira, was the look of "you two are poor. How dare you step into our district and dirty it up with your light pockets."

Light pockets were a term that was made up by the nobles who did not want to be dishonorable by calling the less financial any vulgar names. It simply meant that their wealth was lesser or insignificant compared to the one using the term. Of course, it was not the case considering Inerium was a princess of Requilit, the most prospering (once was) kingdom in Pleniris.

Inerium just kept her eyes forward and tried not to run over the soldiers ahead of her. Her father taught her to ignore those who would look down on her or look at her in any negative way. She had a kind heart, though, so their snares did pierce her heart and made it ache, but she would always clean the wound and hope in some future or timeline they would change their ways.

They had made their way through the streets of the inner district and were standing at the base of the stairs leading up to the castle. Its windows were framed with gold and the stone was a cream color with some places holding moss and vines from its ledges. Three towers stood above the roof of the castle. One was in the middle, the highest one, and two stood beside it, the left one being shorter than the right. They were all blue tiled on the slopes of the towers and each one had three windows lining vertically for each floor they peered out of. The windows were stained glass that depicted images Inerium could not yet make out. The soldiers lined up in a horizontal line again behind Inerium, Snowfire, and Choleira. They were standing guard at the base of the steps. One of the soldiers grabbed the reigns of Snowfire and told the two girls to get off and head up to the doors of the castle.

They got off and started heading up to the large doors, whose long handles were golden, and the wood was a deep blue with parts of it splintering away. Two guards stood on each side of the door. They turned and used their halberds to knock twice on each door. A moment passed and the doors swung inward, pulled by another two soldiers who were inside.

They walked inside the main hall of the castle. The warmth of fires warmed the two girls up. The sweet smell of cakes and fresh meat filled the air. They made their way up another set of stairs and were now in the throne room. The king was sitting on his throne with his advisor to his right. A large table sat in the center of the room with candles burning on it. Empty plates were sitting in front of the wooden chairs lining the table. There were about twenty in total, and the silver plates beautifully reflected the flames of the fires burning on the sides of the room. There was a total of five fires in the main hall. Three were on the left and two were on the right, and a doorway was opened in place of where the third fireplace would have gone.

A guard led the two girls up to the throne and had them kneel down in front of the throne, whose wood was lined with golden accents like a vine would wrap around a tree branch.

"Who are you two?" the king asked. He leaned closer. "Wait a minute. I know you." He stood up and walked over to the two girls. "Are you not going to give me a hug?" He asked Inerium.

She smiled and stood up, Choleira following her actions. She hugged the king of Venirit. He gave her one back, almost crushing the life out of her.

"How have you been, Inerium?" He smiled. "I have not seen you in such a long time. How is your father? I am so sorry I missed your brother's coronation."

"You have not heard?" She asked. Her sadness was as visible on her face as a large zit on a young man's cheek.

"What happened?"

She wiped a tear out of her eye. Choleira patted her on the back. "We were attacked. Another kingdom betrayed us and killed my mother and father. My brother was kidnapped by them, and they were heading South from our kingdom when I escaped the walls."

"It sounds as if they were heading towards Meridine. I always thought that king of theirs had more to him than it seemed. I am so sorry, little Inerium. I wish I had been there. I believe I could have saved them."

She shook her head. "We did not see it coming. They were posted as guards inside the room. By the time the carnage started *inside* the throne room, nearly everyone in the city was killed and piled at the doors. I believe that my brother and I are the only ones left of Requilit. It is in the hands of whichever kingdom betrayed us."

He thought for a moment. He scratched his scraggly beard

and furrowed his greying brows. "Meridine would be the most likely to. It is just South of Requilit, and it does not have to travel through the accursed woods or around the Great Mountain to get there. If it took over Requilit, they could have a military advantage of half of Pleniris."

"If it was them, what do you suppose we do?" Choleira asked. She had not spoken until now, and it surprised both Inerium and the king.

"We cannot declare war, but we can ask the kingdom of Istimus to help us organize a small party to travel to Requilit, negotiate the return of King Kerstas. Once that happens, we will decide what happens next." He turned his head towards the man standing next to him. "Send a courier to Istimus. Tell the king we have found Inerium of Requilit and we need to negotiate terms on having Meridine return her brother to us."

He nodded and ran out of the hall to fetch a courier to send the message. He had quickly written it down on a small piece of paper, which the king then sealed with his wax seal, and stuffed it into his pocket. Istimus was roughly a day or two's journey from Venirit. The hardest part of the journey was not traversing the large swamp caused by the filth of Venirit, but the Cracking Grounds of Vestyr.

Vestyr was the small land in between Venirit and Istimus. In old history the land was beautiful and grew many beautiful flowers that Inerium's grandmother only got to see once. Then, the great fire dragon Vestyr came and burned it all down. He had hoped to burn all Pleniris to the ground, but then a group of knights known as the Knights of the Dragon's Wing stepped in and slaughtered them all and sent them away to wherever they came from. The Knights of the Dragon's Wing consisted of half a dozen knights from a land outside of Pleniris. Some believed it to be the lands to the South beyond the mountains, but their origins were unknown. They bore a cape that resembled the wing of a dragon on their backs. Their swords, which were made from the teeth of dragons, were rumored to be imbued with holy magic, but of course their history of them was only known through history books and old tales. After they had slain Vestyr they disappeared to go find more dragons to slay. Since that day they had never been seen by anyone. Some attention-seeking person might try to say their grandfather was one of them or that they themselves were, but they were all obvious lies.

The land was still burning underground in some places due to the greatness of Vestyr's power. When rain would not come for weeks, the ground would sometimes catch ablaze and cover the whole sky in a void of smoke that would not clear for at least a month.

"I would ask you two to stay here as my guests. In respect to your father and to you."

"Thank you, Sir. How long do you believe it would take for the courier to arrive back?"

He thought about it for a moment. He had taken the journey on horseback before he was king and it took him three days, but he rested for one with many women at a tavern in a smaller village near the capitol of Istimus. "It should take two days for him to arrive, and another two for him to come back."

"Okay, and until then what do we do?"

"The city is corrupt, I know, and I wish there was a lot for you two ladies to enjoy. In the higher-class district is a nice restaurant. Or if you would like to look through the lower districts I would send a pair of soldiers, some of my best, to go with you."

The two girls nodded their heads to show him they

understood. They were feeling quite hungry. "We would like to see the restaurant. We are very hungry."

The king smiled. "As you wish," he said. "I will write a letter for you two to have my pardon so you shall eat for free if you stay here. Everything will be free if you reside here in Venirit. Now, you two will most likely want fresh clothes." He started to wave his hand at his steward, but Choleira stopped him.

"If you allow me, sir, I can clean the clothes with some of my magic." She waved her hand and said an Elvish word that sounded like "Clay Onay." Her and Inerium's clothes glowed a bright blue, and all the filth and grime on them evaporated into steam that dissipated in the air.

"How did you do that?" the king asked.

"It is a talent I have, sir. Sorry if it startled you. It is a secret that me and my family share. We were gifted with magic and would heal others around our home. I would ask if you could keep it a secret as I have, Your Grace."

He nodded. "As curious as I am, I will not ask of it. You ask me to keep it a secret and I shall. It is safe between you, I, and Inerium."

The king called in two soldiers from the next room. "You two escort these girls to The Blooming Gorgot. Ensure the staff that they have my pardon and treat them as if they were my own children. If only they were." His eyes drifted away for a moment, and then regained their commanding stare.

The soldiers bowed and escorted Inerium and Choleira to The Blooming Gorgot.

CHAPTER 11

The group regained consciousness, and they were trapped inside a large cave made almost entirely of crystals ranging from pink to purple shades. They were pointing in every which way and had sharp points on those that had them. A path of a flat crystal surface wound its way through the cave further in. The ceiling was very tall, almost impossibly tall. At least it appeared so to the group. The reflections dancing between the surfaces of the crystals made the ceiling appear nearly infinite. The cave was illuminated by a light without any noticeable source. Everything was clear as day, almost clearer. The colors were so beautiful that it almost did not seem real. Barnabin and Geremi stood up, rubbing their aching arms and necks. The black-bearded man stood up after and tried to touch one of the crystals, cutting himself in the process because he did not realize how close it was.

The man let out a loud "ouch" and woke up Kerstas. He stood up and rubbed the crust from his eyes. The four did not know how long they had been out. The collapse had rendered them unconscious. "What happened?" The bearded man asked. "What is this?"

"I do not know." Kerstas said." I saw this room in that crack in the wall and it opened wider until it just collapsed. I think I saw it kill the man with the brown beard, along with the fat man."

Geremi nodded. "I think it was his fat ass that caused this." He huffed. "He tried to squeeze through the hole he clearly could not fit through, and destroyed the cave, trapping us in here."

Kerstas started walking down the path through the cave to see if there was another way out.

"Hold up, My Lord," Barnabin said. "Let me go ahead. We do not need anything happening to you."

The black-bearded man raised an eyebrow. "*My lord?*" He charged up to Barnabin. "What do you mean by that?"

Barnabin was calm, despite the man being in his face yelling. "His father helped me a lot, Heuron. I owe him my life. Our mission was to keep the boy alive. It remains the same now despite our motivations."

"He is the enemy, Barnabin. Have you not forgotten?"

Barnabin smirked. "The enemy? If you do not remember, we were the ones who barged into his home during his coronation and destroyed his entire kingdom, murdering everyone he loved. All because our king was paranoid about a prophecy that may not even be true."

Heuron sighed. "I hope you know what you are doing, Barnabin. He already has the blood of one of our own on his hands. Literally." He glanced over at the dried blood on Kerstas' palms from the other black-bearded man.

The only one without a weapon was Kerstas. His was still buried in the man he killed, who was now buried under an entire cave. The four men walked down the path of the cave for minutes of seeming the same scenery. It was like walking on a treadmill and wondering why the room would not move with it. Barnabin suddenly froze and reached for his sword. He moved himself into a battle-ready pose.

"What is it, Barnabin?" Heuron and Geremi followed his action. The three gathered around Kerstas.

Barnabin turned his head just enough so that the others could hear him. "Listen closely. We are not alone here. There is something up ahead."

The four held their breaths and did not move. Nothing could be heard for a few seconds, but then the sound of gurgling and rocks grinding together could be heard further down the path. It resembled the sound of someone gurgling water in their mouth while somehow simultaneously chewing on ice. They started moving closer to it, raising their swords higher so they could swing them down when something happened.

The noise grew louder as the path exited out to a large area with a solid flat surface from one wall to the other. Another path was carved into the wall on the opposite end of the room. In the center of the room was the creature making the noises.

The creature resembled a large bull that was made of the same crystals the wall was made of. It had two great horns made of crystals carved in the same smooth and pointed shapes as actual bull horns. Its eyes were glowing a bright red and it was searching for something to eat. There were bites taken out of the crystals along the walls, which the group assumed was what the crystalline bull ate. It looked over and saw the four men standing in the opening. It charged at them and pointed its horns at them. They ducked and the bull's horns locked into the walls around them.

Kerstas noticed that the horns had small runes and markings on them. He could not understand or make out one, but somehow reading them gave him chills all over his body. The bull huffed and puffed and tried to pull its horns out. It was stuck. The four saw the opportunity to escape and they made a break for the other side of the room. When they reached the midpoint of the room the bull freed itself. Chunks of crystals flew out and skated along the smooth floor. The bull roared a gurgling guttural roar and charged faster than before. He swung his head left and right to try to hit the group. He knocked over Heuron and nearly hit Barnabin. Geremi and Kerstas were missed as the bull passed them. Heuron was not bleeding but one of his ribs was at least fractured. He was flung across the room and was almost impaled by the crystal wall.

Barnabin quickly picked his sword up from the ground. As the bull charged them once more, he drove it into one of its eyes. The tip of the sword broke off as the crystal eye shattered on the floor. A silvery metallic liquid spewed from the wound and dripped onto the floor. The bull roared again, and a high ringing tone hovered over the guttural tone of the roar.

Heuron ran over and jumped on the back of the bull. The bull snorted and arched its back. The crystals extended out like a porcupine and impaled Heuron on it. His blood poured out onto the crystals and the bull flung him off, turning around and eating him as his life faded away.

"NO!" cried out Barnabin and Geremi. They charged at the bull with their swords raised. Barnabin's was blunt from the eye, but it could still break the crystals. Geremi stabbed the bull's throat in a place he could see that was open. He pierced it and the silvery blood poured out of the wound. Barnabin stabbed its other eye out and his sword shattered. All he had was a hilt, which he used to break apart some of the crystals on its face. Geremi used some of the broken crystals on the ground to break off part of the bull's right horn. The bull knocked Barnabin out of the way, reared around and kicked Geremi at the wall. He was impaled by the wall. A crystal was sticking out through his mouth. He tried to pull himself off it, but he had died seconds after impact.

The only two remaining were Barnabin and Kerstas. Kerstas picked up the broken horn and clutched it. The bull could not see so it started flailing around in hopes of hitting the two. The ground started to crack beneath it as it stomped and jumped around. The cracks grew bigger as the bull trampled around. Kerstas and Barnabin ran towards the other path and made it inside. The bull roared another guttural roar and leapt over towards them. The impact on the ground the bull made created a huge crack span from where it was standing to the other end of the room. The floor collapsed and the bull fell in. The space under the floor was like a void. The bull disappeared in the darkness and the sound of it hitting the surface below never came. The roars of the bull echoed from the void and continued to do so without end.

Barnabin and Kerstas walked down the path into a new room a little smaller than the previous one. "How long do you think that thing will be falling?" Barnabin asked.

Kerstas shrugged his shoulders. "It killed Geremi and Heuron. I hope it suffers wherever it goes."

The next room they entered had smooth walls all around it, making the room seem like a dome. A large spiral curled from the edge of the room into the center. In the center was a white crystal object buried in a pedestal. A white stone was shimmering from it, catching the attention of both Barnabin and Kerstas.

"What do you suppose that is?" he asked.

"I do not know, Barnabin. But I feel like it could be a trap."

"What makes you say that?" he asked.

Kerstas pointed up near the ceiling. There were holes burrowed around the top of the room circling around it. It looked like a nest of sorts. They only did not notice it before because the light was reflecting the edges making it look like a solid surface. Kerstas grabbed a broken crystal on the ground and threw it into the room. The crystal clattered on the floor and echoed throughout the room. A low humming, buzzing sound erupted from the holes and a few crystal creatures emerged from them. They had translucent crystal wings on their backs that looked like a wasp's. The creatures fluttered down to the floor and looked at the crystal. They looked like human-sized grasshoppers that were made of crystals. The crystals on these creatures were not jagged and spiked like the bull. They were smooth and resembled scales like a lizard. Their faces had six red eyes glowing beneath what looked like a crystal helmet (which was part of their face.) The five creatures that were now on the floor made some grunting clicking noises to each other, which Barnabin said he assumed was their form of communication.

They were holding long crystal spears that reflected the light of the room. If one did not look directly at the creatures, they could easily overlook them with how well they blended in with the room. If it were not for their glowing crimson eyes, the two could lose them easily and never find them until it may be too late. The creatures lifted their heads up in the air and swayed their heads in a circular motion.

"What are they doing?" asked Kerstas.

Barnabin shook his head and scratched an itch on his inner right thigh. "I am not sure. Maybe they are trying to listen for something. Maybe us."

One of the creatures stopped swaying its head and its eyes darted directly over to Kerstas and Barnabin. They froze and their hearts skipped a couple beats before continuing their natural rhythms, at least under such stressful circumstances.

It fluttered its wings, which made a low buzzing sound, and hovered over to the two. It landed on the ground and moved its head around in the odd circular motion from before. The red glowing circles grew bigger and shrunk to their normal as if they were pulsating or flaring like the nostrils of a horse.

Barnabin suddenly realized what the glowing circles were. They were not eyes at all. They were noses, at least as far as he could tell. There were two gaping holes in the sides of its head where assumedly the ears were. The crystal creature had no eyes at all. It had to rely on its other senses to find prey or anything it was looking for.

They held their breath to avoid making any noise that could alert the creature. Barnabin leaned over to his left and picked up a broken piece of crystal that was laying by his foot. He grabbed it and positioned himself to look at the area behind the creature. He reared his arm back that held the crystal in it and hurled it towards the center of the room.

It hit the ground with a loud, high-pitched thud and the creatures all hissed and flew at it, stabbing the surrounding area with their weapons. The creature standing in front of the two turned and joined the others.

Barnabin and Kerstas quickly used their short time to run across the room towards the opening. Their footsteps were heard, and the creatures turned to look at them. They halted in place and held their breath once more. They hummed and buzzed and circled around the two. They closed in further and further until they were almost touching them. When the moment almost came for their dooms, a loud cry came out from the other opening in the room.

A group of ten men charged out of the opening holding up strange looking weapons. There were some that looked like an axe with a string tied around the metal of the blades. Another one was holding a sword that was dripping an odd multi-colored liquid. Some of the others carried the same weapons, but the last one to come out carried a large weapon that looked like a boulder tied onto a log-sized handle. The man was large in both height and muscle. He was like a giant according to legends, eight-foot-tall beings who appeared human. He may have been one of them. The two of course did not know for sure, and they were far too afraid to ask him if they got the chance.

The men bashed into the crystal creatures and swung their weapons at them. Chunks of crystals flew all over the floor and the silver metallic blood splattered and spewed in every direction. The sound of metal clashing with stone rang in the air and the deep chirping and gurgling of the creatures harmonized with it, along with the shouts and grunts of the men. Kerstas and Barnabin were led away by two of the men towards the opening. They shoved any creatures that approached them away and let the other men take care of them. They reached the opening in the wall and were sat on the ground by the two men.

"Are you okay?" asked the man on their left holding one of the axes that had a string around it. The other man was holding one of the swords which was almost dry of the strange colored liquid.

Barnabin and Kerstas nodded their heads. "What were those things?" Kerstas asked.

"Not now. Let's wait until the rest of the group joins us. Then we can talk."

The other men finished their work with the last crystal creatures and made their way to the opening in the wall where Kerstas was. They were covered in silver liquid and had small fragments and dust of the creatures on their clothes and in their hair.

They walked through the long passageway for a minute or so. The men were bragging about the hits they landed and imitating the sounds of the creatures as the hits landed. The cave walls started to have fewer and less crystals on them until it was completely emptied of them. It was just pale stone that had the faintest color of the crystal that had once been there. Small scraps could be seen on the walls where tools and other things were used to pry off the crystals.

They entered a large room barren of any crystals. Only the faint colors and the scrape marks remained. There were tables and chairs set up in the room where some men had already sat at. There were plates of food on the tables that were steaming, as if they had just been prepared and served (which they had.)

All the men sat down at the tables. Kerstas and Barnabin joined them at the one in the middle of the room. When everyone was situated, and a plate and cup were in front of them, a man stood up in the front of the room.

"Today was a good day, men. And we have these two to thank for it. Thanks to them, we were able to take down more of those vile creatures." He held up his cup. "A toast to them, and to their lives which were not taken."

The rest of the men, whose cups were filled with a dark liquid that resembled the alcohol back in Requilit, raised their cups and gave a "here here" to Kerstas and Barnabin.

Kerstas and Barnabin's cups were filled with the same liquid. They held it up to their noses and smelled it. It had a strong scent of a fruit and spice that neither men could name or identify. They both took a sip of the drink, and it went down smoothly with a small burn after swallowing. It tasted good, whatever its flavor was. Barnabin downed it with a few gulps and Kerstas was slowly sipping on it. His palate was not used to alcohol, so it was a stranger to his tastebuds. Despite this, he still drank the full cup and wanted more of it. They both got refills in their cups and drank them again. The other men were already on their third, some of them their fourth, refill. A few of them were already stumbling around and singing unintelligible words in a rhythm of no pattern or form.

The man with the axe that had helped Kerstas and Barnabin sat beside them. "What questions do you have? I assume you have a lot."

"What were those creatures back there?" asked Kerstas.

"They are called the Krysalians. They are made of the same crystals the walls are made of because that is where they are born from. Whatever shape or form they take; they are all born from the crystals that make up the entirety of Krysyn."

"Krysyn?" asked Barnabin. "What kingdom is that?"

The man laughed. "Krysyn is not a kingdom. It is a realm, or at least a layer of one."

"I do not get it," said Kerstas. "A layer of a realm?"

The man took a drink and nodded. "You see, this place you are in right now is a layer of a place called the Nightmare's Workbench. It is a layer of the mind of a boy far older than any of us. Perhaps even your god your people worship. This place is named the Krysyn Depths, and it is one of a near infinite number of layers created by the subconscious of this boy. We are a group known as the Verraks. We travel these layers in search of an old relic that we believe will end the boy's nightmares and free him from his eternal sleep." He downed his cup, had it refilled, and downed it again. "It is a whole lot to comprehend, and trust me I know it is, but it is true."

"How did we get here?" asked Barnabin.

He looked at both Barnabin and Kerstas. "Which one of you was, or has, felt betrayed by their God?"

Barnabin was puzzled at the question, as if it offended him, but Kerstas exhaled through his nose harshly. "Me. I renounce him and anything to do with him. His followers, everyone." He looked at Barnabin. "Not you, you are fine."

"I see. So, you must be Kerstas, then."

Kerstas stopped sipping his drink. He put his full attention to the man. "You know me?"

The man nodded. If one was to understand body language to a perfect level, they would notice that the man's hand was shaking. "Has the eclipse happened yet?"

Kerstas was even more confused. "What eclipse? What is supposed to happen?"

"You are not supposed to know. If you know it could destroy us all."

"Is that about the prophecy of the four kingdoms?" asked Barnabin.

"In a way, yes. But that prophecy is just a mistranslation of the actual events to come."

Kerstas took a drink from the cup. "How do you know about me? And about whatever is supposed to happen during this eclipse?"

The man downed a third drink. "We cannot talk about it. The boss will not let us. The things he can do." His hands trembled more. "I have only heard the rumors. He tells us the information we need to know and that is all. We do not discuss the information. We only use it."

"Where is your boss?" asked Barnabin. "I would like to meet him."

The man dropped his drink. "He is, um, he is." One of the other men came to comfort him. They gave him another drink, and he chugged it dry, licking up the last drops. He caught his breath and calmed himself. "He is everywhere. Here. Now. There. Anywhere. Nowhere. In and out of time. He is wherever he so pleases all at the same place."

"Are you going mad? Is that drink affecting your brain?" Barnabin asked.

The man started screaming in terror and scratching at his eyes and face. The skin started peeling away and blood started seeping out of the wounds. He grabbed his axe and drove it onto the table. He jumped onto the table, took a giant drink from it, doused his head with it, and jumped into the air. He turned his body forward and plummeted his head onto the blade. The axe split his head in two and his brain halves squished onto the table.

"It looks like he talked about the boss." Said the man that gave him the drink.

"This has happened before?" asked Barnabin.

The man nodded. "We do not mention the boss. Or else *that* happens." He glanced over at the man's brain that was leaking juices all over the table along with the blood mixing with it.

"I will take that as we cannot meet him." Kerstas said. He averted his eyes from the corpse oozing next to him.

The room grew cold suddenly, and everyone started scurrying to the back of the room like a family of rats. Kerstas and Barnabin looked to see what it was, and a man was sitting on a chair that was formed from the stone in the ground.

The man was round and short. He had large brown sideburns and a pair of silvery eyes. His hair was messy and some of the hair curled around his ears. He was wearing unusual clothing that the modern-day person would know as a black suit with a red shirt, but Kerstas, Barnabin, and everyone in the room had no idea what it was.

"You rang?" he asked. His voice was deep but had a humorous tone to it. He stood up from the chair and walked over to Kerstas. "I know this drink." He took a long sip from it and drained it. It refilled itself and he emptied it again. "It was created by the fruit from Eden's Garden and the fire spice from the crimson forest tree roots in Locustriad. I made this drink ages ago."

"It tastes very good. What is your name?" Kerstas asked. The men suddenly started backing further into the corner of the room to get as far from the boss as possible. They acted as if their ears were going to fall off if they heard his name. They all covered their ears in fear.

"My name is Spizzer. I guess you could call me Spizz for short. I am what they refer to as the boss. I assume you already knew that, though."

Kerstas nodded. "Why are they so afraid of you?" he asked.

He shrugged his shoulders. "Rumors about me, I guess." He waved his hand around in the air and the blood started flowing back into the head of the guy whose face was split by the axe. His brain was put together, and as his body raised up, everything was mended back together as it was before he went on his manic rant.

The man frantically looked around and bowed his head, bringing his whole body to the ground. "I am so sorry, boss. Please forgive me."

Spizzer smiled. He patted the guy on the shoulder. "Welcome back. Did you learn your lesson?"

The man nodded his head rapidly. His eyes were tearing. "Yes, yes, sir." He ran over to join the other men who were welcoming him back to life.

Spizzer sat down next to Kerstas. "Kerstas, my boy, I am glad to finally meet you. At least this version of you."

"What do you mean?" asked Kerstas.

He smirked and drank another refill of his drink. "I know he mentioned a few things about the eclipse and myself. I am beyond any comprehension your mind can wrap around, my boy. I have seen your future in every possible outcome and every impossible outcome. I am here because of what *your* outcome is. I have a task for you to do."

"What is it?" Kerstas asked.

"I will tell you when the time is right. For now, leave the cave and your path will be laid ahead of you. Take this pouch with you. For the road."

He handed Kerstas a small leather pouch with an odd symbol on it. It looked like an eye with an arrow shot through it. Like a cupid's arrow through a heart. It had words circling it that he could not read. He took a drink of it. It was very sweet and tasted like fiery honey.

"Thank you, Spizzer." He took a few more drinks from the pouch and it refilled. He put the black cork into it and tied it to the waist of his pants.

Spizzer nodded. "You get on now. I will see you very soon."

"How do we get out of here?" asked Barnabin.

Spizzer waved his hand at the wall at the front of the room, and it opened a passageway lit up by many candles hanging from the top. There were no crystals lining the walls. It was plain stone like the room they were in. "Just walk through here and you will be back to your world."

Kerstas thanked Spizzer once again and he walked towards the opening, followed by Barnabin. As they reached the entrance to the passageway, they turned and waved goodbye to Spizzer and the Verraks. They all waved back, still hiding in the corner of the room. Spizzer disappeared in a small poof of smoke and the men slowly returned to their tables and resumed their eating and drinking.

The two headed down the passageway. The smell of sweet-smelling alcohol and delicious food faded away and the odor of animal shit and mold filled the air. The dry walls of the cave started turning moist and the odor grew stronger. The candles were gone and there was a faint light further ahead of the passage dimly lighting the cave floor and walls. The light grew brighter and brighter, and then they were greeted by a fresh smell of grass and clear air. They were out of the cave. They turned to look behind them and the opening to the cave was gone. There was nothing there besides a flat stone surface with a small line arching around where the passageway used to be.

"We are finally out," Kerstas said. "Finally."

Barnabin tapped Kerstas' shoulder. He turned to see what Barnabin was looking at. Kerstas' eyes widened as he gazed upon the Shrieking Peaks. They had somehow come out of the cave to be standing almost at the top of the mountain. The air was freezing, and the wind was blowing harshly, making a shrill, shrieking sound that resembled a choir ensemble of terrorized people. The cave that stared at Kerstas every morning from his window at his home was now just a hundred feet above him.

CHAPTER 12

Inerium and Choleira were standing outside of the Blooming Gorgot. The smell of smoking meat and fresh bread was storming out of the door like a stampede, trampling their noses with the delicious scents. The guards that escorted the two girls walked inside to make sure the workers knew that they were to eat free, and any complaints would go to the king directly. After a minute of talking, the guards returned outside and said, "they are ready for you."

Inerium and Choleira walked into the restaurant. The smell grew stronger, but now mixed with sweet wines and some overpowering colognes that a few men sprayed on themselves to impress the women of the high classes. It of course did not work because when the men would turn away, the women would hold their noses or even try to wave the invisible clouds of cologne away from them. They were set at a table in the middle of the room underneath a large crystal chandelier with orange candles dripping wax into a mold below them.

The large bowl was shaped like a giant pumpkin and the stem collected all the wax, which then trailed down the stem into the pumpkin mold that was now halfway filled with the orange wax. It was a custom at the Blooming Gorgot that when the mold would fill up, the stem would be lit ablaze and the pumpkin would be used as a giant candle until it went out, and then the process would start again. There was a bar to their right at the wall where a bartender was serving drinks.

The bartender was a round man who had red sideburns and curly hair that almost reached his ears. His eyes were a dark brown that looked like glasses of whiskey. He was wearing a white dress shirt with an orange vest over it that matched the color of the wax dripping into the giant gorgot (which was the name of the vegetable that in our world is referred as a pumpkin.) He was talking to a few men drinking their drinks and laughing with them.

The shelves behind him were stocked full of bottles that were from Pleniris and from outside of it. Some of the bottles were in a foreign language that none of them could understand. When a man would ask for one, they would try to pronounce it, and then the barkeep would respond, "ah, yes, the Crimson Moon's tears, one of the more uncommon ones of my collection." The men would always be confused and try to make out which letters matched up to what the barkeep called the drink, but they could never come close to forming one of the three words.

The bottle of the Crimson Moon's Tears was red with a large eclipse on it. There were silver and red streams of blood pouring out of the bottom of the eclipse forming a small river below it. The light shimmered in the reflection of its crimson light, and it caught many eyes when they would sit at the bar looking for something to distract them from their worries or just simply wanting something new to have.

One of the men asked for a glass of the drink, and the barkeep poured him a glass. The liquid was a dark red, almost black, and the man started to drink it. He stopped, looked at the glass, up at the barkeep, and swallowed it. He let out a loud "ahh" sound and continued drinking it.

The barkeep smiled and nodded. He continued pouring more drinks out to the others at the bar and when they were all served, he walked over to Inerium and Choleira's table.

"Hello, welcome to the Blooming Gorgot, what can I get for you?" a pair of menus were handed to them. The words were all written in a golden font and the image of a gorgot was on the front under the name of the restaurant.

They opened their menus and there was a large assortment of food to choose from. There were many appetizers from simple vegetables to fried fish skewers with an in-store-made sauce to dip them in.

There were no items under the main course section of the menu. There was just a line in bold letters that read, "ASK AND WE'LL SERVE!"

The dessert section of the menu also had a bold text, but this one read, "WE ALREADY KNOW!" with a winking smiley face drawing beside it.

The two girls looked through the appetizer section for a few moments and figured out what they wanted. Choleira ordered the grilled vegetables and Inerium ordered the fried fish skewers.

"Drinks?" he asked the two. He wrote down their orders on a small yellow notepad that had many pages torn out of it from previous orders.

The two were unsure of the drinks. They tried looking through the menu for a drink section, but there was not one. The barkeep, now a waiter, smiled again, scratched his right sideburn. "I think I know what you two would want," he said. He walked away behind the bar and grabbed two bottles, pouring one into a wine glass and another into a medium-sized glass. He returned to the table and set the two glasses down. The wine glass in front of Choleira had a light-colored liquid in it that smelled like rich grapes and honey. The medium-sized glass in front of Inerium had a reddish liquid in it that almost appeared pink. It smelled like berries and had a slight lavender fragrance over it.

They both sipped from their glasses and greatly enjoyed their drinks. "Thank you, it tastes wonderful, sir," Choleira said.

"I appreciate it, young Elven girl," he said. "My name is Spenzser. I am pleased to serve both you and the princess of Requilit. Your appetizers will be here shortly." He walked away to the bar to continue serving drinks.

"How did he know who we were?" asked Choleira. "My hood is still on. No one can see my ears." Some of the people in the restaurant were glancing over at the two and questioning why Choleira had a hood on, but they just brushed it off as some religious or cultural thing and thought nothing more of it.

"I do not know," said Inerium. "He also knew who I was without even asking for my name." she took another sip from her drink, licking her lips after.

"I know. Do you think he is magic? Like he can read people like I can?" asked Choleira. She finished her drink and swirled the empty glass around hoping some more of it would appear.

Spenzser returned to the table with two plates that were steaming. He placed Inerium's down in front of her. It had five long wooden skewers with three small fish battered and fried to a golden-brown color impaled on them. Each fish was about the size of Inerium's index finger. Choleira's plate had a small assortment of carrots, potatoes, and other vegetables cut up into bite sized pieces grilled to perfection.

The girls started eating their food. Inerium's eyes widened as she bit into the first fish. It was delicious. The fish meat was soft but flavorful, and the breading on it was seasoned with a little spice for a small kick, but it paired with the sweetness of the fish. She ate through one of the skewers as if she had never eaten before.

Choleira started on her food, using a silver fork next to her to pick up and eat the vegetables. She tried the carrots first and then the potatoes, and then the rest of them. They were all delicious as expected, as if each individual piece could heal any sick person or kill any illness just from how amazing they tasted.

Spenzser returned with the two bottles from the bar and refilled Choleira and Inerium's glasses. "And for your main courses, what will you be having?" The two were silent for a while but could not decide. "I can recommend some things for you. We have the Dragon Wings Platter, the Centaurian Steak, and the Krakenian Stir Fry. Anything you can think of, we have."

"The Dragon Wings Platter sounds interesting," Inerium said.

"I will have the Krakenian Stir Fry," Choleira said, drinking more of her drink.

"Fine choices, girls." He wrote down the orders and walked away to the bar again after putting the ticket on a hook hanging above a window that opened into the kitchen area.

"I wonder what the main courses will taste like," said Inerium.

"I am not sure, but I assume it will be even better than the appetizers." Their appetizer plates were finished off. Inerium had eaten her last fish piece and Choleira had finished off her grilled veggies.

Spenzser returned to their table and picked up the plates. "Your dishes will be out in a moment," he said.

As Spenzser started to turn to walk away, Choleira stopped him. "Hey, Spenzser, how did you know who we were?"

He sat down at the table with them and tapped his finger on the wooden surface twice. Everything around them froze in place. Besides the few workers there. They continued to walk around and serve the food, which then froze in place as they were placed down. Inerium and Choleira's food arrived at them.

"Please eat. You will need full stomachs."

The two girls looked at their plates. In front of Inerium was a plate of a dozen sizzling pieces of meat that resembled chicken wings, but they were slightly larger than usual. There was a bowl of a BBQ-looking sauce.

In front of Choleira was a large plate of mixed peppers and onions, topped off with small pieces of seafood that resembled calamari. The smells rising from the plate were magnificent. They both started diving into their plates, moaning and trying to keep from chewing too loudly. The taste was even better than the smell, and that said a whole lot considering the chef behind the meals.

"Okay, now that you two have at least eaten a little, I must ask something first." A large wooden mug appeared in his hand with an eye symbol carved into it. "Does this look familiar to you two?" he asked.

The girls looked at the symbol and realized that it was an exact match for the relic she had picked up from Nellenor. She pulled it out of her bag. The area around them started to feel dark, almost pure evil.

"Stop that," said Spenzser. Suddenly the aura in the room became normal again without even a feeling of evil.

"What is this thing?" asked Inerium. She held it in her hand and stared at it. "It just seems like a few bones strung together, yet everyone seems to be so afraid of it."

He reached over and grabbed it, taking another sip from his drink. "This relic is something called the Eye of Inanis. It was the first cursed object to be created. It was not created to be cursed, though. It was created near the beginning of time to seal away an evil being named Inanis. The six parts strung together that form this relic represent the six individuals who put him in it." He handed the Eye of Inanis back to Inerium.

"Why does it turn other people so dark and evil when they hold it, but when I do it has almost no effect?" asked Inerium.

"Well, you see, young princess, you have special blood in you. I assume you know that you are a descendant of miss Sybralem, first witch of Pleniris?"

"I am what?" she asked. The wicked witch Sybralem from the old history books?"

"Yes. She was not wicked, though. Are you aware of what happens during an eclipse? When the sun becomes engulfed in darkness and the sky turns to blood?"

"I believe so. They say that demons come out during that time to chase after women. At least that is what my father said."

"In a way he was right. You see, when the eclipse starts, demons do come up to your world, but not to chase after *women*. They seek out *one* woman. They seek one chosen woman, or girl, to be the mother to a special child that they hope would lead the demons into a new age of darkness and rule over the lands of the living."

"How many have there been? How many women have been chosen to do this?" asked Choleira.

He turned his head to her. He took a long drink from his mug, and it refilled itself. "Three so far. Sybralem was the last one. And her child was very special indeed. You all learned about him as a child. Everyone knew him as the Demon-Possessed King."

"*He* was the child of Sybralem. You and your brother are direct descendants of Sybralem and the Demon-Possessed King."

Inerium placed the Eye on the table. "My brother?" You know Kerstas?"

Spenzser nodded. "I do. I know everyone, Inerium. Everyone who will be and has been. I assure you that your brother is safe. You do not need to worry."

Inerium released a relieving sigh. "Thank God. I am glad he is safe. I have been so worried about him. Where is he?"

"I am not allowed to say. There is certain information I am not allowed to speak of, or it will change the timeline, and I absolutely need this timeline to stay straight." He finished his drink and refilled it again.

Choleira and Inerium had finished their plates. Inerium pattered her stomach and let out a little burp. "Excuse me," she said.

Spizser laughed. He took a few more sips from his mug. The symbol faded away and turned into another eye symbol. This one was a normal-shaped eye, but it had an arrow shot through it diagonally. Inerium and Choleira could not make it out, so they did not ask about it. "I am glad you two enjoyed the food here." He looked over at Choleira. "When the time comes, say it." He winked at her.

Choleira's face turned a little red. "O-okay. Um, thank you, Spenzser." She hid her face behind her glass as she finished it off. Spizser waved his hand and it refilled.

He smirked. "These meals would have been free to you two anyway. I frankly do not care for what that king says. No one controls me or tells me what to do. If he were to try to kill me and destroy my business, well I would either kill him myself or simply erase his memory of it."

"You can do that?" asked Choleira. "What elemental magic do you possess?"

"All of them. Or I should say I possess a form that precedes the creation of the elements themselves." Spizser set his cup down. "And there is none that can rival it. That is my power."

"Are you a god?" Inerium asked. "Or God himself?"

Choleira started to shiver a bit. The thought of being in the direct presence of God was no easy thing to process. No one could take it lightly at all.

"No, Inerium. And don't you worry either, Choleira. I promise I am not him."

The two girls sighed. "Phew. That would have been terrifying."

Spenzser refilled his drink and gulped it down dry in a few seconds, refilling it again. He started to laugh a little. It felt heavy, as if it could crush the two girls and take the whole building down with them. "The one you refer to as God, or Lord, is related to me in a way."

"Is he your grandfather or father?" asked Choleira.

He shook his head. "No, he is my great, great, great, great nephew."

Both Choleira and Inerium's hearts stopped. Their stomachs tightened and they felt very nauseous. Spizser waved his hand. Suddenly the nauseous feelings went away.

"I know it is a lot," he said. "But I am telling you two because you are very important to this timeline. That is why I am telling you now—" He looked over at the door. "They came early. They know you are here." He snapped his fingers and time resumed. "I only froze the bar in time. The rest of the world has been moving normally. You two need to head to the castle, and fast."

"Why, what happened?" asked Inerium.

"There is not much time to explain. Just go and run. I promise dessert will be made up later." He cleared the table of all the plates and other dishes and utensils, and two-tapped his finger on the wooden table. The girls had vanished from the Blooming Gorgot and were now standing in front of the main doors of the castle.

"How did we get here?" asked Choleira.

"I think he teleported us here. Anyway, we must get inside. Whoever it is he was talking about, they are here."

The girls ran inside the castle after the soldiers opened the doors and went to find the king of Venirit. He was in his back chambers, as was said by one of the soldiers who escorted them to him. When they reached his room, he was getting ready in a freshly cleaned suit and robe.

"Hello, girls. Did you enjoy your meals?"

"Yes, it was delicious, but sir we were told to rush back because we heard people were arriving."

"Yes. Istimus' king is heading up to the gates as we speak. And we were told that he has brought many reinforcements for us. I guess he already assumed that we needed aid in getting your brother back from Meridine." He walked out of his chambers and the girls followed him.

They entered the throne room, and the king sat down on his throne. The girls stood to his left while his steward stood to his right. Inerium and Choleira's hearts were racing. Meridine was the one who kidnapped Kerstas and murdered everyone she knew, so why was it that every thought in the back of her mind was telling her to run away and hide? Was it what Spenzser said or was it the untapped power of Sybralem's magic that was causing her heart and mind to race? She did not know, but whatever the cause was, she did not like the feeling. Not one bit.

The doors opened and the king of Istimus walked through. He was followed by a dozen yellow-caped soldiers wearing armor and carrying swords. The king looked very snobby. He was wearing a suit that looked like it was woven with gold threads (which were just a very nice yellow color of standard thread) and his sword had a golden hilt on it that had the small depictions of dragons on it (which the hilt was also just standard metal painted with a golden color.) his face was powdered white and had a small beauty mark on his left cheek, which was actually horse shit he had dabbed on his face to appear like a natural mark. His soldiers did well to avoid him, or at least distance themselves from him as best as they could. His hair was tied back in a poorly made ponytail of a gold and brown mess. Little did the soldiers know, he had used horse shit to also color his hair brown in some places to appear like his hair naturally changed that way. It may have fooled the people of it, but the smell was unmistakable. Shit from a horse.

"Greetings, your grace," said Istimus' king. His voice alone told everyone that he was stuck up and egotistical. He rolled his r's and added an accent that he thought made him seem foreign. He would smirk during some of his sentences and maybe form a half smile but never committed to a full one. "I received your letter about Meridine. And I am whole-heartedly ready for whatever the future may hold." He bowed down and he started to slowly fidget around his right pocket.

The soldiers behind him were also doing the same thing; their hands were fidgeting with themselves around the hilts of their swords. Inerium got an even more uneasy feeling that trailed down to a nauseous feeling in her throat. Choleira knew what was going through Inerium's mind, and she got the feeling too.

"Go to the bathrooms in the next room. Go down the pipes into the city's sewers," a voice said in Inerium's head. It resembled Spizser's but it was more serious compared to the humorous tone he had before.

Inerium went to tell Choleira, but she already knew. She heard the command as well.

"Your grace, we need to go relieve ourselves for a moment," Choleira said in a calm voice, trying to hide the fear she was feeling.

"Of course, ladies. It is right through that door and on the left." He pointed to the room they were told to go into by the voice.

The girls walked towards the door and headed through the small hallway to the bathrooms. The guards were carefully watching them leave. Istimus' king side-eyed them, too, as they made their way through the side room. They entered the bathroom, which did not smell as bad as they believed despite how terrible the sewage problem was outside of the walls. Inerium shut the door behind them and locked it. She grabbed a small wooden chair that was in the corner of the room and pushed it against the door, making sure it could not be opened without a lot of force.

"Did you hear the voice, too?" asked Inerium.

"Yes. It sounded like the man from the bar. Why do you think he told us to come in here?" Choleira looked around the room. There was no other way out or in besides the door that was blocked by the chair. "What do we do now?

Inerium shook her head. "I do not know."

The girls walked over to the door and put their ears to the wood, which was quite cold despite the blistering heat outside.

They could faintly hear the voices of the men outside talking, the voices of the two kings most of all. They were discussing the terms of what was to happen.

"And we ride out today to Meridine?" asked Venirit's king.

"Yes," said Istimus' king. "And we will reclaim Kerstas, king of Requilit." He snarled Kerstas' name like it was poison in his mouth.

"I had heard that Kerstas was taken by a large party of soldiers and was heading down the main road towards Meridine. That was a few days ago. He is most likely being held there now."

"Then we should not waste any time. While the sun is still up, we send a letter to Meridine stating that they can either hand us Kerstas willingly or he can be taken by force." It could not be seen through the door, but just by the way he said that last bit anyone could tell he was smiling with his words.

"Does he want to start a war between them and Meridine?" asked Inerium. "He seems very pushing at the thought of going to war with them."

Choleira shook her head. "I do not know, but I can almost read his thoughts. He is almost hoping that it comes to that."

"But why? Why does he want a war? We already lost one kingdom. A war will only lose us another. We cannot risk that."

"Unless that is what he wants. Unless he wants a war because that would mean."

"It would mean what?" asked Choleira.

"It would mean that *he* was the one who caused all this. That Meridine has nothing to do with it. Istimus would be to blame, and with the war, Istimus and Venirit would be joined, so Meridine would stand no chance. And with Meridine gone, Istimus could easily take over the Western half of Pleniris."

"You really think that Istimus is responsible for your parents' death and the massacre of your kingdom."

Inerium got teary-eyed. "My brother's kingdom. He was king. *Is* king. Not only did they take his kingdom, but they took him as well. I cannot forgive them for that."

Choleira put her arm around Inerium's back, pulling her in for a hug. "Hey, it will be okay. You heard Spenzser. He said Kerstas was fine. Maybe Meridine actually has him, and Istimus' king is just a stuck-up asshat."

Inerium let out a little chuckle. "Let's hope that is the case. I do not want this to resort to war, but I also want my brother back. And I will see him again regardless of if there is a war or not."

"Send this letter to Meridine at once," said the voice of Istimus' king. The sound of a ruffled paper was handed to another person who could not be identified due to the door standing between them. The unidentified person ran out of the room and headed towards Meridine to deliver the letter written specifically by the king of Istimus. The only thing that Venirit's king did was sign at the bottom without reading it.

A pair of footsteps started making their way towards the bathroom door. A knock came at the door three times. "Are you two alright in there?" asked Venirit's king. "It has been quite some time."

"Yes," said Choleira. "Some lady things came up."

"I see. Well, when you can come out, the king of Istimus would like to speak to you two." He returned to his throne.

"What do we do?" asked Inerium, turning quickly around to Choleira.

"It is okay. Go on out and speak to him," said the voice of Spenzser. "You two will be okay."

Inerium moved the chair away from the door and unlocked

it. She pulled the door open, and the two girls walked out of the bathroom.

"Hello, ladies," said the king of Istimus. "What are your names?"

"I am Choleira," said she.

"I am Inerium," she said with a tone that was not all that friendly, which not many would have when talking to the one believed to be responsible for the deaths of their parents and kidnapping of their brother.

He smirked a little. "Would you two like to come with me down to this nice restaurant I heard about a few blocks away from the castle?"

They turned their heads to Venirit's king, and he turned his head in a way that said, "he is a king, you cannot refuse his request."

The girls turned their heads back to him and nodded. "Yes, that sounds delightful," said Choleira, trying her best to contain her anger towards the man. It was understandably hard for her not to lash out and scratch the man's face all to pieces. The only things holding her back were that he may be holding Kerstas captive and the fat that she was not willing to get horse shit on her hands.

"Thank you." He turned and started to walk out of the castle. Three of his men stood behind the girls and walked them outside to the Blooming Gorgot, which they had just came from. Not even an hour ago.

⟫⟫◆◆◈⟪⟪

There they were. Standing at the front door of the Blooming Gorgot again. This time, however, they were accompanying the king of Istimus and three of his highest-ranked men. Two of them were average height but had a fierce look in their dark eyes. They were both three wearing long capes that were yellow.

The third one had dark green eyes and had a red cape on. He had a beautiful set of armor that paired with his sword, which had the image of a two-headed dragon curling around the scabbard. At the end of the scabbard was a gold symbol in the shape of a diamond on a playing card. He had a large black beard and stood very tall. He was wearing a red cape, unlike the other two who were wearing yellow ones.

They walked inside the restaurant and were greeted by Spenzser. "Good evening, everyone. How many will be dining tonight?"

"It will be six of us tonight, sir." The king's obnoxious voice was very, well, obnoxious to say the least. He thickened his fake accent to seem even more "fancy" as he believed it to be. "And do please hurry. We are very hungry."

Spenzser smiled. He was clearly annoyed at the king, but he saw the girls and nodded. "Right this way." He led them to a large circular table near the table that the girls had previously sat at. They all sat down at the table and were handed the menus.

"What can I get you all to drink?" asked Spenzser, who pulled out his order-taking notepad, which still had Inerium and Choleira's previous orders on it.

Inerium and Choleira turned around to face Spenzser, who was standing behind them. "We will have what we had earlier." They smiled at him, and he let out a little chuckle.

"And for you four?" he asked, raising his head to look at the others sitting at the table.

The two men with the yellow capes ordered each a pint of blackberry ale. The snobby king of Istimus ordered a glass of the most expensive wine he could get because he thought it would taste the best. Spizser's response to his request was very humorous and he found it amusing.

"You do not want that one. That bottle of wine is very expensive, sir. Even for one as high of a status as you."

The king laughed. "Oh, you peasant, how would you know what wealth looks like? You run a bar. I run a kingdom. Keep your opinions to yourself and I will not have a problem with you."

"As you wish." His eyes suddenly had a dark look behind them. He turned to the red-caped man. "And for you, sir?"

"I will have a flagon of the dragon's breath mead. That sounds good."

"It is, I assure you. After all, I am the owner here." He flashed a hateful stare up at the king and walked off to get the drinks.

"That man does not have any respect at all," said the snobby king. "Who does he think he is telling me what I can and cannot afford. One of you two should teach him some manners," he said looking at the yellow-caped soldiers.

They both looked at each other. "Sir," the left one said. "I do not think it would look good on us if we were to do anything towards the owner of the most popular restaurant in this kingdom, not even mentioning the fact that this is not our kingdom."

The snobby king nodded. "Fine. I guess I will let him get away with it this time. But if he does it again, I will not be so forgiving."

Inerium and Choleira gave each other a look. Spizser returned with the drinks. He sat down the drinks from before in front of the girls and moved on to the others. He sat down the two blackberry ales and the dragon breath mead in front of the three soldiers.

Spizser picked up a glass that had a gold rim on it. The rim was covered in multiple jewels and held a dark red liquid in it. "And here is that wine." He sat the glass down in front of the snobby king.

He raised the glass up and took a large drink out of it. His face scrunched up from the strength of the alcohol content in the liquid. The taste was almost metallic yet tasted like the finest berries on the planet. "Holy shit, what is in this thing?" the snobby king asked. He took another drink, his face contorting again.

"That is our most expensive wine, sir. It is called the Deusanguine Wine. It is made with *very* expensive and rare ingredients."

"It is good, it is just very strong." He took another sip, adjusting slightly to the strength of the contents. "What are those ingredients?" he asked. "Am I able to purchase them from you or somewhere near here?"

Spenzser shook his head. "No. They are secret ingredients and when I say they are rare, I mean it."

"Name your price. I will buy it. I must have this back home."

Spenzser smiled. "Kill the one you call God and bring me the berries from Eden's Garden. That is how to make the purest version of this drink."

The men at the table started to laugh. "You have a dark sense of humor, barkeep," said the red-caped man.

Spenzser refilled the girls' drinks, which had been emptied. "I do, indeed.

"You mentioned a pure version of this drink. Is this not the best one?" asked the snobby king.

Spenzser shook his head. He almost seemed amused that he was still drinking it. "The pure version does not yet exist. I am working on it right now, but I just need the final ingredient for it. And then it will be complete." He had a small twinkle in his eyes, as if he had been waiting ages for the drink to be finished, which was more than literally the truth.

"Well, when it is complete, let me know. I would like to try some of it."

Spizser let out a puff of air through his nose like a silent laugh. "I will try." He looked around, seeing everyone reading off the menu besides the two girls, who already knew what they wanted. The same as before.

Spizser wrote down the girls' orders and moved on to the others. The three soldiers with capes ordered a large bowl of chips with a homemade dipping sauce to share. The snobby king ordered a plate of oysters covered with a wine-mixed sauce. A few minutes passed as the dishes were prepared. The soldiers started talking about a cave that they had stayed by and about how it had collapsed with a few of their men inside.

"Did they make it out okay?" asked Inerium.

The red-caped man turned to his left to look at Inerium, who was in the seat next to him. "I do not know, Inerium." He grabbed one of the napkins in front of him and laid it on his lap. He used his drink to trace words into it using the liquid, being extra careful not to ruin it. When he made sure no one was looking, he handed Inerium the napkin.

The handwriting was sloppy, and it was hard to read. Inerium could not make it out.

"Might I suggest a writing utensil?" Spizser whispered, discreetly handing the red-caped man a small quill with ink dripping off the tip. He grabbed another napkin and began writing on it, hiding it on his lap.

"Thank you," the man whispered. He finished writing on

the napkin and passed it over to Inerium again while no one was looking.

I met your brother. Talk with me after this.

Inerium's heart started racing. She looked up to the man, but he shook his head, as if to say that it is not safe to talk. Inerium was happy. News about her brother, and she can hear if he is safe or not. She may be able to find out who took him and killed her family.

The appetizers arrived and everyone started feasting on them. Choleira and Inerium ate slowly because they had just eaten, as of now, a little over an hour ago. They were also wanting to save what little appetites they had for the main course and possibly the dessert that they were promised.

"Not hungry, girls?" asked the snobby king, his face smothered in oyster meat and the wine sauce. He had almost demolished his plate, despite making a mess of the whole area around him.

Choleira shook her head, holding her hood in place to keep both her ears and weapon hidden.

"Why do you wear that thing?" he asked Choleira.

"I like to hide my ears. They are a little larger than the average person. And it is comfortable to wear in my opinion."

"Okay, I understand that. I, myself, would not wear such a thing, but I will not ask you to take it off."

"Thank you, sir." She lightly bowed her head.

Spenzser returned. "Is everyone ready for their main courses now?" he asked. He pulled out his little notepad.

The two yellow-caped soldiers ordered thick-cut steaks; one medium and one well done. The red-caped man ordered a rack of ribs that were smothered in a rich BBQ sauce, and the snobby king ordered seafood platter called the "Vizs Sea Platter," which consisted of crab legs, a grilled piece of fish, large shrimp, and some other sea creatures no one at the table had heard of.

Inerium could not decide what she wanted. She kept thinking of things to order; decide different combinations to make that would sound good. But none of them caught her attention at all.

After a few minutes of waiting, a menu item appeared in Choleira's menu written in golden writing, like it was just scrawled in instead of printed in. She turned around and saw Spenzser holding his menu up to his chest with a pen in his handwriting in it. It appeared that he had just written something on the menu specifically for her to order.

"I will have that." She pointed at the area on the menu that had just been written on.

Spenzser smiled and wrote it down. "Excellent choice." He walked away and put the tickets up in the window by the bar.

"What did you order?" asked Inerium.

"It was called the Dame Et Clochard. It was a meal for two. We can share it if you don't mind that is." She turned her head away because her face had started to turn pink, almost red.

"I don't mind at all, Choleira," said Inerium. "What do you think the name means?"

She shook her head. "I do not know." She was nearly hiding her face with her hands to try not to be seen reddening more and more.

"Why are you hiding your face?" asked Inerium. "Are you okay?"

She smiled. "Yes, I am okay, Ineri." She looked her in the eyes and held an unbroken stare for at least ten seconds, getting lost in thought and daydreams. "It's nothing."

"Are you sure?" she asked. "Your face has gone almost as red as the Cherryl Berries we have."

Her face grew redder. "Yes. Yes, I am sure." She downed her drink. It helped a little with her nerves, but it did not tone down the redness at all. She was, after all, embarrassed. No others knew the true reason. (At least no one besides herself and Spenzser.)

It would have been obvious to Inerium why Choleira was embarrassed, but her mind was racing here and there about what the red-caped man had said. Her brother was alive, and the man had seen him not too long ago. She was counting down every second that passed, hoping that the one would come that brought her to her brother.

Choleira of course knew what was going on inside of Inerium's mind. She knew where her concerns were lying at. But there was a very small part of her mind that Choleira looked at more often than any other part. In modern terms it would literally be founded in the hypothalamus. But to Choleira, terms did not matter. She knew what she was trying to find, and she found it. Far back in Inerium's head, behind the overpowering desire to get her brother back, was a slowly growing feeling of emotion that she had not felt before. After all, Inerium was young. She was new to those feelings, but Choleira felt, and knew, that they were real enough to be true. And knowing this made her overwhelmingly happy and imaginative for the future.

Choleira had noticed that Spenzser was looking over at their table as he was waiting at other tables and pouring drinks. He would have a grin on his face when he saw the two girls, but his expression darkened when he saw Istimus' king and the two yellow-caped soldiers by him. He carried a large silver platter holding the plates of their food over to their table. He sat it down on the surface that held the large Gorgot and began passing out the plates to them.

Inerium and Choleira received their plate first. In today's world it was a simple large plate of spaghetti and meatballs with only a singular meatball on it. The aroma arising from the plate was unreal. It was a simple dish, but it smelled almost divine. The noodles were arranged into five swirls, like smaller portions on the large-portioned plate. Four sat in the corners and all connected to the center swirl, which held the singular meatball standing in the middle with a small stream of steam radiating off it.

"Here is your food, girls. Enjoy." He smiled as he set the plate between the two.

He sat the other courses on the table in front of the respected persons and they all looked divine, despite of how much he wanted to poison the three that were not the red-caped man, Inerium, and Choleira. They all started to dig in like pigs, Istimus' king trying his hardest to seem elegant, but failing and rummaging through his dish like an animal.

Inerium and Choleira, however, were the most civilized people at the table when it came to eating (or manners in general.) They each picked up their forks and began to twirl the angel hairs around the ends, wrapping them around until the ends of the noodles were finished with their dances. They started to eat their food, and it was even more delicious than it looked (as was expected from Spenzser.)

The girls started on their second swirl of pasta, finishing it just as quickly as the first ones. When they made their way to the middle one, they both dug into it, slurping up the noodles until a connected one started to arise from the pile. Their heads started leaning closer and closer until they were almost touching their noses. They made eye contact, had a small silent pause, and Choleira bit off her end, letting the rest of the noodle fall and dangle below Inerium's mouth. She slurped up the noodles and covered her face once more. Choleira was shaking slightly, only enough for one to see if they could read someone very closely. To the average eye, she just appeared still and unfazed. But Inerium was her best friend now. And she could tell that Choleira was nervous. Or embarrassed. One of the two for sure.

All that was left on their plate was the singular meatball and a few straggling angel hairs, with sauce scattered along the plate's face.

"You have it," said Inerium.

"No, you."

They exchanged the same gesture towards each other for about a minute, both getting a more noticeable grin with every exchange.

Inerium grabbed her fork and cut the meatball in half, picking up one of the two halves. She hovered the fork in the air and sailed it towards Choleira. She opened her mouth and ate half of it. She smiled and hid her mouth as she let out a tiny laugh. She picked her fork up and did the same, almost missing, and stabbing Inerium in the bottom lip.

Inerium ate half of the meatball and tried to hide her face again. Choleira grabbed her hands and shook her head. "Can't hide it from me, Ineri." She smirked. "I've been seeing it this whole time."

Inerium put her hands on the table and was smiling so much that her face started to hurt, but she could not stop. She could not explain what it was that was happening, but she knew that whatever it was, she was happy. That was for certain. The others had finished their plates and pushed them away, showing that they were done with their food. Spizser came up and stacked the plates on top of each other.

"Yeah, you clean that up, boy," said one of the yellow-caped soldiers.

"And follow up with the desert afterwards," followed the other yellow-caped soldier.

Spenzser froze. His eyes turned dark, almost having an evil behind them. He slowly turned his head towards them. "You want to run that by me again, *boy*?"

The one who first spoke stood up. "I said. Hurry the fuck up and bring us our desserts before I knock you on your ass."

Spizser started to laugh. "I would really love to see that happen."

The soldier grabbed his sword and drew it. "Your funeral, asshole!" He went to swing his sword.

Spizser shook his head and grabbed the blade mid-swing. "I do not like violence in my bar." He squeezed his hand and the blade shattered and clattered to the ground. The air grew chilly around Spizser, and he spoke. "Clean it up and shut your mouth." His voice sounded like a whisper but there was a second voice behind it, almost like a gravelly voice shouting at the same volume of the whisper. While the whisper was in standard speech, the other voice sounded like it was another language entirely.

The yellow-caped soldier nodded and grabbed a broom and dustpan from behind the bar. He swept up the mess on the floor and disposed of it in the trash can next to the spot he got the broom and dustpan from. He returned to his seat and would not speak for the rest of the night. All that came out were muffled screams and unintelligible words coming from the closed lips that may never open again.

"What did you do to him?" asked the other soldier, who was about to draw his sword.

"I would not do that if I were you." Spizser raised his hand, curling his ring and pinky fingers to his palm. The air started to grow cold again, and the whispery voice started to creep up again, almost like an evil groan resonating with a light breeze.

"You act like you can do anything. We are the highest ranked soldiers in the army of the great king Vanitar and will not tolerate any insubordination from a simple barkeeper from the shittiest kingdom in all Pleniris!"

A few of the people sitting at the other tables overheard it and decided to step in. One who had a black beard and a small scar over his eye walked up to the soldier. "Do we have a problem here soldier? What did you have to say about our kingdom?" The man's voice was deep and sounded like thunder. He was well over six foot five. Perhaps even closer to seven foot tall. A giant for sure. "I happen to live here, and if I recall, you all are outsiders trying to cause trouble because you can." He reached for a large axe on his back. "Now do we have a problem?"

The soldier grunted and sat back down. The bearded man returned to the bar where he was sitting at before and finished his large drink.

"These people, I swear," said Snobby King Vanitar. "No class whatsoever." He picked up a napkin and wiped off the chunks of meat that were falling off his chin. It was covered in juices and alcohol, which soaked through the napkin and made it a dark blob of paper that now sat on his empty plate oozing out the contents it soaked up.

Spenzser started to rid the table of all the dirty dishes. Vanitar tipped his glass over and spilled it all over the floor. "Clean that up, too, while you are at it. It *is* your job after all." He laughed, followed by snorts and a few extra chuckles that gave off a message that said: *I'm a stuck-up rich asshole that only cares about my own well-being.*

Spizser slowly turned his head from the spilled mess on the floor to the cocky eyes of Vanitar. "Is it? Is it my job to clean this up?" He smiled. The groaning noise returned as he started to talk again. "When I was younger, I was told to clean up my messes and not make others have to deal with my dirty work's aftermath. Now clean it up, mess maker." The under-toned voice was more aggressive this time, almost like the words themselves were blades.

Vanitar nodded his head, as if a recruit was ordered by a drill sergeant, and got down on his hands and knees, licking up his mess. The other people in the restaurant were pointing and laughing behind their cupped hands, to not be seen by him just in case he would try something drastic against them.

"There. It was not that hard, was it?" asked Spizser as he carried the dirty dishes to the back to be cleaned, quietly laughing to himself as he did.

When Vanitar finished cleaning up the mess his tongue was bleeding from the splinters in his tongue, which started to swell up a little. "That bastard! How is he able to do that to us? It's like his voice alone has the power to bend things to his will." He started picking out the splinters and leaving them on the table.

The yellow-caped soldier that had been commanded by Spizser, too, started commenting on it. "Yeah, it was like the moment he spoke all control of my body left and I-. I..." He started crying into his hands. "It was like I was a puppet, and I could have very well taken my own life if the puppeteer felt like it."

"No person can possess that much power. Perhaps a god could, but I will be damned if *that man* is our lord above. If that is the case, he is a cruel motherfucker."

Inerium looked up. "Actually, Sir Vanitar, your lord you

all worship is actually that cruel." Inerium had finally snapped. Her bottled-up rage had topped off and she had to let it out before she passed out from the pressure.

"What did you say, you little brat?" He started to stand up, inching his fingers towards his knife. Spizser quickly turned his head around and tapped on the wood of the bar where he stood at. Vanitar's body snapped back and stuck to the chair like he was glued to it. Vanitar tried to turn his head towards Spizser, but he could not move.

"My family, the ones that you all murdered, knew secrets about your lord that no one else knew. The precious secrets and lies about him and his false histories. And your possible hopes of gaining that knowledge are all gone now because of your stupid delusions. And I want to know where my brother is."

Vanitar sat in silence, still stuck to the chair. "What secrets could your family have possibly possessed, little girl? I am far older and, most assuredly, wiser than you." His voice was even more prissy and snarky now.

"Like I would tell you. You are lucky that you are still alive after what you have done."

"Inerium, please," said Choleira, who was carefully monitoring the minds and behaviors of the others at the table.

Spizser was looking over at their table with a piercing stare. The kind of stare that one would make when they were waiting for the food to come out of the oven or the delivery boy to come trotting through the doorway with a long-awaited package. He of course was waiting for something. And that something was just about to be spoken from a certain snobby asshole's mouth.

"Lucky I am alive?" He laughed. "You pose no threat to me, girl." He pointed at Inerium while looking at the yellow-caped soldier that still could not speak. "Get her. And show her just how lucky she is to be alive. Send out word to our soldiers. The boy dies."

Inerium's heart dropped. Kerstas? Is he the boy he was talking about? "No. You can't!" She stood up and Choleira did the same, standing in front of her with her arms spread out. Her cloak fell off and the whole room turned to look at her ears, which were sticking out from her hair. Her bow was glowing brighter than the candles in the room, contrasting them with a brilliant blue light.

Whispers started getting passed between groups of people.

"An Elven girl?" asked Vanitar. "My oh my you will fetch a pretty amount. Your ears will be worth hundreds of gold pieces easy!"

The soldier started to run over to the girls to grab them. The red-caped soldier stood up and tripped the yellow-caped one.

"Oops," he said. "Too much to drink. He turned around to the girls. "Run." He whispered.

The girls turned away and ran towards the door. More of Vanitar's men were standing at the door, ready for them.

"Girls, over here!" called out Spenzser. They ran towards him, who was standing in the doorway of the back room. They ran through the opening, and he quickly shut the door behind them. "You all are okay for a moment. But they will be after you. And I can assure you that they will be hunting your brother. Do not go to the castle. Head through the sewers out of the city. There is a door in the back that has a large pipe you two can easily go through. I have made sure it was cleaned. Remember that all pipes lead out of the city. Just follow your gut, Inerium. It will know where to lead you."

The girls nodded and they ran through the room of dangling pots and pans, around the working cooks and waiters, weaving through them like a wicker basket. They opened the door in the back of the kitchen and a large gaping hole stood gaping at them from the wall, angling down like a slide. The sounds of rats squeaking echoed up the pipe. The smell was atrocious, but the pipe was thankfully cleaned and scrubbed.

Choleira stepped in first, holding herself at the top. She turned around to Inerium. "Come on, we cannot waste any more time." She held her hand out to Inerium and grabbed it. Inerium stepped in with Choleira and sat next to her, hugging her tight. Choleira pushed them down the pipe. As they went further down, the sounds of rats squeaking started to pair with human wailing and cries for help.

Choleira's grip grew tighter on Inerium's hand as they slid further into the dark sewers below.

CHAPTER 13

Kerstas and Barnabin had started to make their way up the rocky pathway up the mountainside. The air grew colder and colder with every step they took. The wind was freezing, the stone was cold to the touch, and they were hungry. Starving with no food to help them. The wind blowing through the crevices of the mountain made scream-like shrieks that were almost deafening from the top.

"Just a little further, Barnabin," said Kerstas. His voice was hoarse from the climbing. His hands, along with Barnabin's, were bleeding from getting cut by the jagged rocks.

"It's fucking freezing, my lord," said Barnabin, gasping for air, which was very thin being up so high.

"I know. My toes are starting to go numb." Kerstas' fingers were already to the point where touching any surface had no temperature, just pressure. Small icicles started to form beneath both of their noses from the drainage. "But I can see the entrance."

The cave entrance, which had haunted Kerstas' family for generations, was now a few steps above. They climbed on the flat surface in front of the dark maw of the cave. The shrieks of the wind curled around their feet and soared down the sides of the mountain, like a jar of souls being cracked open.

"Now what?" asked Barnabin.

"We go in," said Kerstas. "We did not climb this far to give up."

A chilling wind blew out of the cave, followed by whispers saying things in different languages foreign to both Kerstas and Barnabin. "Come join us, Kerstas," said one of the voices in an ensemble of others.

Kerstas started walking into the cave opening. Barnabin put his hand on Kerstas' shoulder and stepped ahead of him, bracing himself for anything that could come at him. As they inched further into the cave, the more the light behind them faded.

Kerstas and Barnabin had traveled so far into the cave that they had to start feeling around them to make sure they were not about to walk head-first into a wall.

Barnabin stopped walking and felt around at something on the wall. "I think I found something." He rummaged through his small side bag he had and started clicking some stones together. Sparks lit up the damp cave, which had dozens of sharp rocks jarring down towards them from the ceiling. After a few clicks, Barnabin lit a torch that was hung on the wall. The cave illuminated and revealed the winding path that slowly curled down into the mountain.

Their echo of their footsteps grew louder as they traveled deeper into the cave. "What are we looking for in here?" asked Barnabin.

"Remember when I told you at the camp that my bloodline has been drawn to this place? That we believed we were being drawn to the creature lurking within. Well, I want to find out who or what this creature is and why it has been such a burden to my family."

"I see.," said Barnabin. "And what happens when we do find this creature, if at all?"

"I do not know. I guess we will see."

The path stopped curling down and they entered another large space within the cave. In the center of it was a rock jarring from the floor. There were scratches and indeterminable words scrawled out all over it, along with the walls.

The two started to walk towards the jarring rock and stopped when they heard the sudden sound of breath cutting through the silence.

"Did you hear that?" asked Barnabin.

"Yeah," whispered Kerstas.

Footsteps started approaching them from the darkness in front of them. The pattern of the steps had no rhythm to them. Some steps were far apart and slow, followed by a quick follow-up step, followed by another staggered slower step. A figure started to appear in the light of Barnabin's torch. He was tall and was wearing torn clothes that appeared like they were once of high value. The cloak around him was of an animal's skin, which was covered in dust and small fragments of rocks. A pair of red eyes peered at Barnabin and Kerstas from a cracking pale face.

He came fully into the light. He appeared as an older man, with grey hair trailing down his back, but his face was almost wrinkle free. Cracks took the place of where wrinkles would have been, making him look almost like a broken doll. "Hello, Kerstas and Barnabin. I have been waiting for you. Especially you, Kerstas." His voice was soft, but held a weight to it, like he could say die and they would both drop dead.

"Hello. What is your name?"

"I go by many names. The creature of the mountain. The one who lurks in the shadows. Or to some Master. But you all would, by history I would hope, know me as King Daerex, the Demon Possessed King."

"You?" asked Barnabin. "They said you were dead!"

Daerex laughed. "Technically I did. But it was no demon that took possession of me as the stories say. I was born with an old magic that the demons used. Because of that fact I was born a demon-human hybrid. My mother Sybralem the Witch taught me how to control it and use it properly. When the people of Pleniris found this out, they sent a hero who possessed the magic of the Heavens to stop me. It obviously did not work considering I am still here." He chuckled. He sat on the ground. Kerstas and Barnabin joined him.

"What happened, then? We were told you were stopped, and that the hero ascended to be one of the angel warriors for the Lord.

He smirked. "As if. Do you think that man up there holds any praise for those down here? Of course not. You of all people should know that Kerstas."

Kerstas' blood started to flow faster. A rage was bottling up from the memories of the priests from all those years back. "Yes. I do." He clenched his fists.

"And you desire to have your revenge on them, yes?"

Kerstas nodded. "It was going to be my first order as king. To rid my kingdom of those evil men. Perhaps even the entirety of their faith if I can."

"Are you serious?" asked Barnabin. "But the faith of our land has been here longer than we have. Who are we, or you, to question it? The Lord does not treat those well that defy him or speak ill of him."

"Barnabin. I have cursed that man's name for almost my entire life. Those who called him their lord have hurt me and destroyed my life. I was treated as a ragdoll by those who preach his name. And the soldiers who fight in his name and pray to him every night were also the ones who took my family and home away from me." He took a long, deep inhale and blew it all out. "If he allows his people to treat others so harshly without punishment then he is just as bad as them, if not worse."

Daerex laughed. "So, you see the flaws too, Kerstas. That such a praised being could be so cruel, despite learning about his so-called unconditional love."

"You are a demon, though. You are basically bred to hate him," Barnabin said.

"A half-demon, Barnabin. My mother was simply a witch. My father was a pure demon. It is like a demigod, but for demons. Some say we are possibly even more dangerous than the pure-bred demons."

"Why would you say that?" asked Kerstas. Would the pure-bred demons not be stronger?"

Daerex shook his head. "You would think so, right? But that is not the case. Because the half-bred demons have a half-damned soul, that other half is capable of still possessing one of the essences of fire, earth, water, and air. So, a half breed can utilize the powers of two essence elements, one of darkness and one of the four. Combining the two creates a powerful form of the element called dark elements."

"How do you know all this?" asked Barnabin. "What are these element things anyway?"

"My mother taught me everything I know about it. There is too much to comprehend, so what I have said so far is already more than any other human in this land knows. My soul is split in two. One half contains the essence of darkness. And the other half, the human half, contains the essence of the earth element."

"I see. So, combining the two, you possess a dark earth essence?" Kerstas asked.

Daerex smiled. "Exactly, Kerstas." He sniffed the air and let out a whistling sigh. "But the time is coming near. We must be hasty. Kerstas, you must make the choice. Take revenge on those who done you wrong or let them continue living on with what they did to you." What kind of question was that? After all the years of torment... Why would he take back all his promises now?

"Of course. What kind of damned question is that?"

"No matter the cost?" asked Daerex.

"No matter the cost."

A low rumbling laugh erupted from the pits of Daerex's being. "Then let sanity and all be damned."

In a swift turn Daerex swiped his clawed right hand along the neck of Barnabin. Blood started to pour down his throat and onto the stone floor. He clutched his throat and buckled to his knees. He started to cough as his esophagus started to flood with the crimson liquid.

"Barnabin, are you okay?" asked Kerstas. He turned towards Daerex. "Why did you do this?"

Daerex kneeled next to Barnabin. He cupped his hand under his throat. The blood poured into the cupped palm. He raised his hand up to his mouth and sucked up the thick substance, like one does when they are drinking from a soda can and a little bit of their drink overflows onto the top. "A little bitter, but it will do." He bit his hand, his teeth sinking into his skin. Black blood started to pour out of the wound.

Barnabin let out a small croak, holding his hand up to Kerstas. "My...king," he managed to say before letting out a final breath and falling limp, passing away.

Kerstas was shaking. "You killed him. Why did you kill him?"

"You said you were willing to sacrifice anything for your

revenge, young lord. I had to drink his blood, had to take his life, to strengthen myself. Now, you must drink from my hand. My blood will grant you power. You will be able to get your revenge on those who have done you wrong."

"By power do you mean the demon's power?"

He nodded. "Indeed. Your soul will be damned for eternity. Are you willing to accept that?"

Kerstas did not have to think long about it. When one becomes too Hell-bent on revenge, they are willing to do anything to achieve it. Sometimes enough that they become numb to almost all feelings besides their hatred. "I have come this far. Barnabin is dead. I do not really have another reasonable option now."

Daerex raised his hand, inching it closer to Kerstas. He drank from his hand, locking onto it just as Daerex did to cause the wound. Daerex winced as Kerstas' teeth sank into his palm.

As Kerstas drank, he felt large chills, both hot and cold, run through his body. Then, a burning sensation ran through his veins like his bloodstream took a shot of pure alcohol. A sharp pain struck him behind his eyes and his vision turned red from it. He grunted from the pain and fell to the ground. "What is happening?" he asked.

"The pain will subside soon. Right now, your body is adjusting to the swift change in power. As I speak, your soul is being twisted and molded to conjoin your natural essence element with the darkness element. When it is finished, you will be a new being, possessing power beyond any human in this world. Wait for it to awaken, and when that moment comes, you will be complete, Kerstas of Requilit." Kerstas passed out from the pain and fell on the cold stone floor.

Kerstas awoke to Daerex collapsed on the floor wheezing, like one having an asthmatic attack. He sat up. "Daerex, what happened?" He crawled over to him, struggling to move because his body was sore and tingling.

Daerex coughed. "It is almost complete. Your transformation. When it is done, I will die, and you will be just as, if not more, powerful as I once was."

Kerstas' body was slowly starting to recover its strength. His senses seemed almost improved, like they were dialed up. "What do I do after that?"

Daerex took a long breath. "Do as you wish. I am dying now, after such a long time. I would be upset, but I am not. Why would I be? It has been centuries. I have been waiting for someone of your bloodline, my bloodline, to free me from this life. So, I thank you, Kerstas, King of Requilit. Give this world Hell." He smiled and let out a small, weak laugh and his head turned to the side as his life faded. His body started to crack like an old pottery project and crumble into dust. Daerex, the once Mad Demon-Possessed King of Pleniris, was now but a pile of ash in front of Kerstas.

Kerstas let the ash fall out of his hands and dusted his clothes off, knocking the remains of Daerex fall to the floor of his centuries-old home. He stood up and lifted up Barnabin's body, which was on the ground a few feet away.

He attempted to pick him up, which to his surprise was more than easy. He picked him up like he weighed no more than a small bag of potatoes. He carried him through the cave, back the way they came in, and headed outside into the chilling wind on top of the Shrieking Peaks. The sound of the wailing winds was much louder than before. The cold did not make him freeze, but he knew in his mind that it was freezing. The stone was covered in snow. The clouds were swirling just below the ledge he was standing on. He laid Barnabin down. He cleared an area of snow and moved some rocks around. He placed Barnabin's body in the spot and covered him with the rocks and snow.

"Barnabin, I am sorry. I would pray for you, but I am afraid that damned man above would send you to Hell just for associating with me, so I will wish you luck wherever you are. You were loyal to me, even if it meant betraying your home. Your kingdom. I promise you that after I get my revenge, I will ensure that whatever prophecy may be about me will come true. For you I will become king. For you, my friend, I will rebuild this land. I will find Inerium and bring her home." He bowed his head down and placed his hand on the grave that he had made. "These things I promise."

Kerstas stood up and peered down into the land below as the clouds parted. He was looking to the East, and he could see an army clad in red marching towards the West. The armies of Meridine were approaching the border of their kingdom and the kingdom of Istimus.

CHAPTER 14

Inerium and Choleira fell out of the long pipe onto the wet, smelly ground of a sewer tunnel. "Are you okay?" asked Choleira, picking up Inerium from the ground.

Inerium nodded. "Yeah, I am okay. Are you?"

Choleira nodded. "Where are we?"

Inerium looked around and made a foul face, a reaction to the horrid smell emanating from the running brown waters inches from where they fell. The sewer tunnel wall was to their left, and it led down for about fifty, maybe even a hundred, feet down before splitting off into two ways. "I believe we are in the sewers beneath the city." She gagged a little. "It really stinks down here."

Choleira tried to wave her hand to perform a spell, to shield their noses from the scent, but nothing happened. "What is happening to my magic?" asked Choleira.

"Is it not working?" Inerium held her hand and poked at her palm, like a toddler when their toy stops making noises because the batteries had died out.

"No. I do not understand why." She tried to wave her hand a couple more times. No luck.

"Come on," said Inerium. "Let's go this way and see where

it leads. Surely there is a way out. Maybe even someone down here that could help us."

As optimistic as she was, Inerium was still worried about her brother. Yes, she knew that he was alive, but for how long? *How* okay was he? Is he still safe? All these thoughts were eating away at her, and she was trying to hide the feelings away from Choleira so as not to worry her. She of course knew every thought going through Inerium's mind, but she decided not to tell her and remind her that she knew because she liked seeing the smile on Inerium's face. It brought her joy, which in return brought a little more joy to Inerium. That was all they needed; the comfort of each other to reassure one another that if they were with each other, everything would be okay.

The girls started to walk down the path through the tunnel, following the right way because the left path was crumbled and had a bunch of rats crawling on the mossy disgusting stone. The path kept splitting off into different ways. Some split off only left. Some split right and some were split at a crossroads. Each time they chose the one that seemed the least gross and the least populated with rodents gnawing on the flesh and bones of their fallen kin.

Every so often the faint sound of an inhuman scream would echo throughout the tunnels. The scream was twisted and distorted, far from any normal persons. It was like a rat squealing and the raw cry of a man shouting out for help blending in a horrendous shout.

When they heard the cries echo through the tunnel, Inerium jumped and hugged onto Choleira for many minutes at a time until her nerves had calmed down. After about a half hour of traveling down the winding paths, the smell had started to mix with a small scent of cooked food. Not delicious and mouth-watering, but enough to make a hungry person beg for it. As the smell grew stronger, they started to hear whispering echoing from the next corner they were approaching. There was a light around the corner that danced around in a bright yellow-orange shade, like someone (or something) had a fire burning. They tiptoed to the corner and peered around it.

There was a person sitting in front of a small fire. No, not a person. Was it a creature? Neither of the girls were sure. Whatever it was, it was sitting in front of the fire cooking some sort of meat on a stick that was being dangled over the dancing flames.

The words being spoken by the creature were nearly indistinguishable. All that could be understood were the words "eat" and "cursed mayor."

"What is that thing?" asked Inerium.

"I do not know," said Choleira, trying to get a closer look. Her hand slipped on the brick wall that she was holding herself against and she stumbled, creating just enough noise to alert the creature.

With a quick breath, followed by a loud SKREE, the creature asked, "Who's there?"

Inerium walked around the corner, slowly making her way to the fire. The creature was very skinny. Its hands were claw-like with longer and pointier nails than a normal human's. It was crouching next to the fire in a more defensive pose compared to its relaxed, nonchalant pose it was in before Choleira alerted it. There was a cloth bag over its face with two holes cut into it. One was to see out of its left eye, which was a dark brown, and the other hole was over the creature's mouth, which had pointed teeth. (The two front top teeth were larger than the rest.)

"Who are you two?" asked the weird creature.

"My name is Inerium," said she. "We are from the city above. My friend here is accompanying me."

Of course, the term "friend" hurt Choleira more than she expected. But that was what they were, friends. "My name is Choleira. What is yours?"

The creature scratched one of its legs that was unnaturally lanky and hairy. Small hairs fell off its leg as the nails ran across it.

"My name is Rodryt. I am from the town down the road there." They pointed down the tunnel where the faintest echo of voices apart from theirs could be heard. Rodryt's voice was young. Young, like a boy barely older than Inerium.

"There is a town?" asked Inerium. The usage of the word road did not mean too much down here. Maybe the creatures down here thought of these tunnels as roads, like the humans above think of dirt paths as roads. The primary focus she had was finding help to get back up above.

Rodryt nodded. "It was a nice town known as Raitild, but one day our mayor started doing these awful things to the townsfolk. You see, he was disfigured as a child and was always made fun of it. He was born with a disease, more like a plague, which made his body partially appear like a rodent. His facial features, his body, everything about him was horrible to the eyes, and he decided when he became mayor that he would get back at us who looked normal. Human, I mean."

Choleira crouched down next to him, as did Inerium. "Did he turn you, too?"

He nodded. He clutched the bag around his head. His one visible eye started to get teary. "He hooked me and a few others up to these chairs with tubes all over them. Large sacks filled with blood were hanging, connected to the other end of the tubes. He started pumping the bags out and the liquid flooded into the veins in our arms and wrists. I blacked out and when I came to, I was… hideous." He covered his face with his hands and started weeping.

"Inerium patted him on the back. "Hey, it will be okay, Rodryt. Is there any way we can help?"

"Well, there was something about a cure that I heard when they were experimenting on me. One night, when they were prepping us up for the transfusions, I heard the mayor speaking of a cure that was being made to reverse the affliction. I believe that by now it may be made. If you can find it, please get it. I know it is a selfish thing to ask, but please. If it works on me, we can find a way to fix everyone else."

"Okay," said Inerium. "We can try to look for it. Where would we go to look for it?"

"When you enter the town, you will see a large building standing well above the rest. That will be your goal. That is the town hall, also where the experiments are held. It will be there, I bet."

Inerium and Choleira nodded. "If we find it, we will bring it back to you, Rodryt." They started to make their way down the tunnel towards the town Rodryt pointed towards.

"Hey, before you two leave, if you meet my mother, please do not tell her you met me. She would be ashamed of what I look like."

The girls nodded. It was a depressing request, but what were the odds that his mother was not already turned, anyway?

After a few more twists and turns, the tunnel started becoming brighter from the light ahead. They entered a large clearing in the sewer whose ceiling reached hundreds of feet above. There were buildings made of old rotting wood strewn all over the place connected by old rope bridges and platforms that were about to fall apart. It was like a rotting sewer version of Olmenor, but instead of floating over water, the buildings were nearly sunk into the swamp-like pond that had flooded over the once brick-populated surface. Torches lit up the pathways and homes throughout the large town of Raitild. The smell was horrid that emanated from the swamp it stood on. Rodent people were walking around the pathways. Some were carrying baskets of food and others were standing around talking to one another.

There were a few spots where some of the townsfolk were in boats rowing around the swamp to try to find a fish or drowned rat in the mess to eat, for food was quite rare to just buy out, unless the buyer happened to be high in the society of Raitild or simply fortunate enough to have something to pay or trade it for. In some of the shadier areas of Raitild were a few people that were sneakily exchanging things to each other, most likely substances that were not over the counter. These that were in the shady areas were peeking around corners looking around making sure they were not being watched.

Inerium and Choleira crept along the side of the wall next to them to avoid any, and all, unwanted attention. There was a boat next to a dock they had made their way to about half a way along the wall. They climbed into it and each of the girls pulled out a paddle. They rowed their way across, keeping their heads down.

Choleira tucked her cloak in to hide her bow and arrows on her back. She wondered if the magic in the bow would still be of use since her own magic was somehow nullified.

"How are we going to stay hidden?" asked Inerium. We cannot use your concealment magic."

"Trying to work that out right now," she said. She was trying to plan it out with poor progress. "We can make our way to the mayor's place by taking the long way around."

"That could work," said Inerium. The wood on the paddles was damp and partially layered in moss and nastiness.

They had made their way across the water to the dock near the Southeastern part of Raitild, thankfully undetected. They set their paddles in the seats of the boat and tied it to a post on the dock, which was on the brink of collapsing from rot. They started to make their way up the set of five steps up from the dock onto the main structure that made up the city of Raitild. No people (hybrid or non) had noticed that they had infiltrated their city. As they passed each building, they looked behind them and around the corners to make sure no one was there to see them. They did not know if any of the townsfolk were trustworthy, and they did not wish to find out either.

After passing many buildings and nearly getting caught twice, (once when Inerium almost tripped over a barrel and again when she had to sneeze from the overbearing smell and was extremely loud) they had made it almost the entire way to the mayor's place.

When they had gone as far as they could go along the outer edge of the city, the girls started to head towards the midline of the city, where a great set of stairs trailed up to the larger buildings elevated above the rest. They waited in silence in between a few large crates for a couple minutes while a large group of rodent people made their way across the streets, barely inches from where they were hiding.

When the coast was clear they started to sprint up the stairs when a loud "STOP RIGHT THERE!" erupted from the throat of a rodent man standing at the top. Three more followed behind him, drawing out large pieces of metal they had sharpened into swords.

The girls ran into the city, weaving in and out of crowds of rodent people who pointed at them, making comments of both "who are they?" and "they are not turned yet."

As they ran farther and farther into the city, more and more rodent soldiers (as what Inerium labeled them as) started chasing after them. Choleira ran around a corner to the left and pulled Inerium with her. They fell over a pair of non-turned humans who were hiding in the corner the girls had just run into.

"Watch where you…" one started to say but cut himself off when he had noticed the two were not turned.

"Please help us," said Inerium. "They are after us."

The two men looked at each other and nodded. They grabbed a barrel leaning against the wall and told them to get inside it. They did swiftly and the man closed the lid over them. He knocked four times in a scattered rhythm on the door of the building they were next to, and he let out a long sigh. He ran out of the corner and onto the street, shouting as loud as he could to get the soldiers attention and ran off, leading them away from Choleira, Inerium, and the other man who was left behind by his friend.

The door opened and another non-turned human opened the door. "Come inside," he said.

"Sir, there are two girls here." He pointed at the barrel next to him that they were hidden in. "They were being chased by the Snatchers. Dailen led them off. I am afraid that the worst is to happen to him before the night's end.

The man at the door nodded, followed by a hand motion beckoning the three inside. The girls crawled out of the barrel and followed the two men inside the house. The door was shut and locked behind them after a quadruple left and right take outside.

After they were made comfortable, Inerium and Choleira were sitting together in a large, cushioned chair with dried stains whose origins were unknown. (The stain was from an old drink spilling from a drunkard who had went too hard on his liquor and missed his mouth entirely while trying to down his flagon.)

There were an even ten people sitting in the room, making a three to seven ratio of women to men. They were all middle aged, two of the men rather older with graying hair and unflattering wrinkles. The two oldest men were at a small table against the wall playing a card game that had them slightly heated and clutching the cards to the point they were creasing between their skeleton-like fingers.

The three women were sitting in the corner. One of the three was sitting in a rocking chair having her hands held by the two beside her, who were dabbing her face with a cloth that dried her tears away. A younger-looking man with a black beard that held a few gray hairs was leaning against the wall next to the woman with his head held down, rapidly tapping his foot on the old floor. (The floor was making a creaking noise every few taps of his foot which started to annoy the others in the room, which did not calm anyone down any more than they already were.)

Three of the men (two brown-haired and one black-haired) were gathered around a round table in the middle of the room, which was wholly lit by the candles and lanterns on the tables. There was a bright lantern hanging by a hook from the ceiling in the center of the room. On the table the three men were at was a large piece of paper that stretched from one end to the other. It was a map of Raitild that was drawn out by them that even included the hiding spots under the frames of the town that tunneled and pathed their way throughout it.

Inerium adjusted her legs, and her left thigh moved the sheath of Solef and her twin dagger. She had completely forgotten they were there. Even Choleira's bow had slipped her mind because it was covered the whole time by her cloak. Inerium caressed her ring of water magic, pondering on the idea that it might work, but the thought was cast away when she remembered that Choleira's magic water bow did not work earlier.

The man who had let them in was standing before the girls. "So, how did you all get here?" he asked.

"We were in the city above ground, and we came down here through the sewer tunnels."

"There is no city outside of these tunnels, my lady. They end after a mile or so in every direction. We have mapped them out for months and every way leads to a dead end." His face showed doubt and confusion. Of course, it sounded ludicrous, two strangers appearing from a supposed city from above when nothing outside of the tunnels around Raitild exists.

"We are telling the truth, sir," said Choleira. "We do not understand it either. When we fell through the tunnel from above, it closed off after we fell out.

The man paused to think for a bit. "I see. Maybe you are from a different layer. Perhaps."

"What do you mean by layer?" asked Inerium.

"You do not know about them?" He sighed. "Well, to be fair we did not know either as of a few weeks ago. Whenever the mayor started his damned experiments on the people of this town, we were greeted by a small group of people who called themselves 'Verraks'. They told us that there were these layers of different places or worlds that connected to each other, and that they travel them to save those of us that have not been corrupted by the taint that is the curse of the Shadowed One."

"Who is the Shadowed One?" asked Inerium. She had heard of Hellruler, which was known by everyone, but this name was not familiar to her, nor to Choleira or even Kerstas. "And what curse did he place?"

"We were not exactly told. We were just told that a curse was placed on the creator of this place, along with the other layers, and it caused them to turn evil."

He walked over to the table that the map was sitting on. Choleira studied it and analyzed the shape of the circular city, with four distinct paths cutting through them by gaps above the sewer lake below it. She noticed the familiarity of the outline and tapped on Inerium's arm, pointing it out. "It looks just like…"

Inerium then saw it. The whole city's outlined shape was in the same form as the relic she picked up in Nellenor, the evil relic that had corrupted the elves who mistakenly found it. She was tempted to take it out of her small bag she had on her. She was almost *tempted* to.

Small whispers started flowing from her bag. Low whispers that were grainy and malicious. "Come on. Take it out and reveal it to them." There was a secondary voice with it. Behind the understood speech that was being whispered was a strenuous croaking tone speaking a different language entirely, like the primary voice was the translator for it.

Choleira could hear it, too. No one else could, however. "What is that?"

"I think it is the relic."

"Well do not take it out. Whatever it wants, we cannot let it have."

Inerium nodded and ignored the voices emanating from the relic. And it was a good reason she did not take it out.

The man traced the gaps in the city. "This city is mapped

out in this odd shape. Almost resembles an eye, doesn't it? None of us know what it means, but the leader of that group of Verraks said that it was the symbol created and used by the Shadowed One. He did not give us a straight or clear answer, but to be fair what he told us was already too much to comprehend, so I do apologize to you both if it is the same for you as well.

"It is okay. We have been told a lot of things that we were told were too great to comprehend."

Inerium was mainly referring to Spenzser back at the Blooming Gorgot. He had, of course, told them a great many things, some that they still could not wrap their heads around. Spenzser was very knowledgeable, yes, but not even the Lord the people of Pleniris worshipped could comprehend how knowledgeable he was.

"Okay, well that helps a bit, so I do not sound totally crazy."

One of the old people playing cards slammed his four-card hand down on the table, shouting "HA, FUCK YOU, ASSHOLE!" He laid down his cards and flipped both the birds at his rival. He turned in his chair towards the girls and the man talking to them. "In my opinion, Marqael, I still think you are batshit, and I was there when he explained it." He laughed and started to shuffle the cards, starting another game.

The old men kept a sheet of paper next to them, tallying each of their wins on it. The old man who had won and made his very loud outburst was farther behind than his opponent by five, so it was understandable why he would react the way he did.

Marqael turned towards Inerium and Choleira. "That right there is Philip. His opponent in cards is Fredrik. The three men at the table here are Dustin, Robert, and Austin." (Austin was the black-haired man. The other two were the brown-haired ones.) He pointed towards the corner where the three women and one man were all standing. "The man standing against the wall there is Jakson. His wife Rose is the one in the chair. Her son was taken from her yesterday by the snatchers you almost got taken from. The blonde woman with the blue dress on the left of her is Mary. The redhead with the crimson dress sitting on the right is Bethany. They are sisters of hers. Not by blood, but they were raised together by Fredrik over there."

"And I assume your name is Marqael, right?"

Marqael nodded. "And what are your names?"

The rest of the room raised their heads a little waiting for their answers. Some were skeptical about them being there, as if they could be pawns or serving the mayor, but they knew that they would be rodent hybrids if they were.

"I am Inerium, princess of Requilit, the land where I came from."

"And I am Choleira…" she paused, wondering if she should be careful about her words. Would these people act ill-willed towards an Elf? Possibly. She was not for certain. "I was born from a small village in the forest near Inerium's land."

"I see. Well, welcome, Inerium and Choleira, to the safe house of the Resistance of Raitild. We are the only ones left that have not been turned into those things. We did have Dailen, but he used himself as a diversion to save you two and Robert. Dailen and Robert were best friends, some would say even more, but we could not for sure say."

"I am sorry about him," said Choleira.

"Don't be," said Robert, standing up. "He did the right thing. As much as I do miss him and am pissed off about him being taken, I do not hold it against you two. You just happened to be in the wrong place at the very wrong time."

Marqael leaned over the table, peering down at the map,

and pointed at the large building towards the back, which Inerium and Choleira assumed to be the mayor's residence, or at least where the experiments were held. (It was both.) "What is our next move?" he asked.

"We were thinking of using the lower levels here," Robert pointed at the Eastern edge of the city and traced it along the border until it reached the spot right behind the large building. "And we can travel through this path until we get behind Town Hall. We infiltrate the building and find him, then kill him."

"Where are the weapons?" he asked.

Robert pointed at a small building on the map labeled SHED. "Here. Stored safely inside. The path will take us right by the door."

Marqael nodded. "Good. Then we leave soon. It is about time that asshole paid for what he did."

The men at the table stood up and readied themselves. Jakson stopped tapping his foot and rolled back his torn sleeves. "Let's do this. They took our son from us. I must know that he is alive, rodent or not."

The old men were to stay due to their feeble bodies. They could not be a burden on their mission, and they were far too into their game of cards to leave anyway.

Rose reached her arm out to Jakson and held his hand. "Please return our son to us. My dear Rodryt." She started sobbing more and the other two women started comforting her again.

"We will go," said Inerium. "There is something there we must get. We hope it can help us get out of here."

Marqael thought on it for a moment. "Fine," he said. "But stay safe and out of the way. We do not want you two to have the same fate as the others."

"I think we will manage," said Choleira, smiling and nudging playfully at Inerium's arm. "I've got her with me."

The comment caught Inerium by surprise. She got a little flustered and fell short of words. All the men started to head towards the door, lining up and ready to leave. Choleira and Inerium stood behind them as well. Marqael opened the door and did a triple left and right take of the area outside to make sure no one was there. There was not. They all left one by one while Marqael stood guard of the alleyway. They stepped over the railing and hopped down to a boarded platform just above the murky waters below them.

⎯⎯◇⎯⎯

The men had helped Inerium down to keep them from falling in the muck. They traveled along the path made by boards placed on the supporting frames of Raitild. There were many paths trailing off from their main one, but this one was marked with red paint so that they would not be led astray from it.

"Just a few more seconds and we should be right below the weapons shed," said Jakson. The group made their way further down the red-painted trail until they stopped next to a support beam with a red string tied around it. "Here it is," he said, feeling around the wooden surface above him.

Jakson hit his fist on an area that was more worn down than the other parts of the wood. A square cut out with hinges on it swung down like an attic door. A rope fell and landed in his hands. He climbed up, disappearing into the space above.

A few moments passed and his hand appeared with a sword in his hand, sheathed in an old leather scabbard. "Take one and pass it to the next man." One by one Jakson handed swords down until the five men each held a weapon. Jakson had an axe, Robert had a large sword, Marqael had two small daggers, and the last three had average-sized straight-swords. Choleira had her bow but could not use the arrows. Thankfully, Jakson had a bow and a quiver of arrows stored away just in case. She received these. Inerium kept Solef and her smaller twin as she did not need any extra weapons.

"Town Hall is about three minutes away from this point," said Marqael. "Let's move. Quickly but silently." They made their way across the makeshift path towards the Town Hall. They made their way across the makeshift path, trying to keep their balance so they would not fall into the filthy waters below them.

The path stopped right at the edge of a drop off into the murk below. To their left, nailed to the supporting boards, was a ladder that had been taken from a painter who was repainting the town hall not even two days ago. It still had white paint on some of the lower steps. One by one the men climbed up the steps into the city above them.

When Inerium and Choleira climbed up the ladder and stepped out into the city of Raitild, they were near the back corner of the Town Hall. From where they were standing, they could see the bottom few steps that led up to the building they were now standing next to. The whole city could be seen from where they were. The rodent people walking along the bridges, the soldiers patrolling the streets most likely searching for them, and the small rodent-turned children playing in the streets tossing rocks into a five-ringed circle trying to score higher points than the other. Then, just barely visible, was the flickering dim light of Rodryt's fire bouncing around in the tunnel in the far wall.

Choleira looked to make sure that Inerium was not looking

and pulled out the vial on her neck with the tears in it. She clutched it in her hand and closed her eyes. She whispered something under her breath in her old Elven speech that sounded something like, "E Layovay Yayou," which she spoke low enough that only she could hear.

The tears started to swirl around like a whirlpool and glow a bright blue. The light faded and she put the vial back in her shirt. It was a curious thing. Even she did not know how the tears glowed. Her magic was not supposed to work here, at least as she had assessed so far. She wondered how it was possible, and frankly she did not care. What she did with the tears was no binding spell or any kind of charm. All she did was simply say I love you in her speech and that was all, so maybe the emotional power held in the tears was far more powerful than Choleira had been told.

"The true power held inside emotion-driven magic was beyond any basic form. It draws out the raw essence of a person or being's soul and pours it into the element affiliated with it. Like a rage-filled flame or a joyful wind gust, any form of magic produced by raw emotion is the most powerful form it can take. Of course, there are beings who can use more powerful forms and states of their magic, but the emotions elevate the power put into it and therefore the output poured out from it." An excerpt from "The Nature of Essence" by a scholar who remained nameless but was renown as the "Scholar of Essence."

There was, in fact, a copy of "The Nature of Essence" in the massive library back at their castle in Requilit. Inerium never read it or seen it, but it was placed with the older books that Kerstas used to read, actually directly next to the one that spoke about D'vilsik and Nelivesk. This book was one of the highest references for witches in covens and practitioners of dark magic throughout Pleniris.

"It is well past the resting hour by now," said Marqael. "They should all be asleep so it will be easier to get inside."

The other men nodded, and they started to creep up the stairs. The lights in the windows of Town Hall were flickering dim flames from the nighttime candles the people of Raitild would use when it was their resting hour, which were the eight hours of the day they deemed nighttime due to the lack of sun or moonlight to reference the actual time. There were spots on the walls that were not fully painted, showing the previous ugly tan coating (which at one point in time was the same white that was being added currently.)

"That spot was the only one left to paint before we stole their ladder," whispered Jakson, chuckling under his breath. "It held a better use for us anyway." He took a glance at the ladder they climbed up on.

The others reached down and pulled the trap door closed and covered it with a nearby tarp on the ground, which had also been stolen the same time the ladder had been. They stopped right before the great doors of the Town Hall. They had two large, knobbed handles on it that were old, rustic as well.

"Are you ready?" asked Marqael to the others.

The men nodded. Choleira and Inerium nodded.

The men all lined up in front of the door, scattered slightly so that if there happened to be guards waiting, they would be ready. Their weapons were held up, prepared for use, and the doors were opened. A low creaking sound groaned out of the doors as they swung open. No one was at the doors. They made their way inside, closing the giant doors behind them. The doors closing made a loud THUD that echoed throughout the main room they stood in. The men all flinched, waiting for a hoard of guards to come with weapons held high. But there were none. Up a small set of steps, counted seven, were two large tables lined with chairs that led up to a larger chair that was set in the center of the end of the room. The small candles on the tables, along with the ones that were hanging from the chains on the walls, were flickering and dancing along the spaces of the room their orange lights reached.

"Stay on your guard," said Marqael. "I am getting an odd feeling about this."

The other men grasped their weapons tighter and squinted their eyes to get a more focused look around them.

"Do you know where his chambers are?" asked Inerium.

"No, but I believe it may be there to the left. In that room." He pointed to a hallway that led off to the left from the large chair.

They headed down the hallway, which was decorated with twisted pictures of creatures that appeared rodent-like. Were they pictures? Inerium and Choleira examined them as they went by, carefully looking at the images. There were noticeable strokes on the canvas, which appeared like paint brush strokes. Did the mayor paint them? Did he get someone to paint them? They must have been painted one way or another, it was just the thought of *why* they were.

"That sick fuck," said Robert. "What the living hell is wrong with him?" He glared at the paintings he passed. "He acts like the things he does to these people is art. Ugh."

The other men were glaring at them. One in particular was very carefully examining the features of the paintings, almost like he was looking for something, or someone. It was Jakson, Rodryt's father.

"Horrific, are they not?" asked Dustin, patting jakson on the shoulder.

"As long as one of them is not my son, they will not be." He took another careful look at the painting in front of him. It was a large fat rodent man wearing a pair of trousers barely hung up by red suspenders that held down his white sweaty shirt.

Inerium and Choleira passed by the fat rodent man's portrait and looked in disgust at the others they passed by. There were dozens of them, all (by surprise) done with much talent nonetheless. Despite the morbidness of them, the color schemes and realism captured in them was worthy of being held in a museum. There were colors inside the paintings that the men had never even seen or thought of.

Then, as they reached the end of the hallway they reached the last paintings, which two stood on each side just before the framing of the doorway leading into whatever room awaited them beyond the hall of portraits.

The portrait that Inerium and Choleira looked at was the one that Jakson was looking for... There was Rodryt sitting in the chair he described. There were little red wires running into his arms, his face only half transformed into a rodent. The one human part left was pale. His hair was neat and a pretty brown. His eye was a dark brown as well, matching his hair. As for the other side, it was rodent-like. His mouth was elongating and growing sharp teeth and whiskers. There was a singular tear trailing down the human half's face.

"Inerium, it's him."

Inerium nodded. "I know." She picked it up and stared at it, remembering the poor boy in the sewer tunnels hiding from the rest of the town. He had thought so much that his parents were ashamed of the way he looked and that they wanted nothing to do with him. This, however was clearly not the case. Jakson was searching for him, any sign of him. His mother was grieving for him and missing him. Inerium wanted to just tell Jakson that their son was okay. That he was hiding in the tunnels safe and scared. But she could not. She promised... *Why the fuck did I promise...*

She turned the portrait of Rodryt around and put it on the ground out of sight. None of the other men saw her do it. Only Choleira.

Marqael opened the door. As it squeaked, the men looked inside the room to see a large bed with a mass under the dark blanket. The men ran over to it and threw the blankets onto the floor. Under it was a large rodent-human man wearing only a pair of loose-fitting sleeper pants, sweat-stained, with holes in the thighs.

The rodent man squealed and tried to roll out of bed and stand on the floor. As his feet touched the floor, Dustin and Austin kicked his feet out from under him. He collapsed to the floor, causing a large cloud of dust to shoot out away from his body, like in those movies where a person would dramatically slam an ancient book on a table to talk about an elder god or forbidden spell.

Every one of the men seized the mayor and held him against the wall. "Unhand me, you fucking assholes!" he shouted, accompanied by the irritating squeaking.

The mayor was fat, very fat. He was the man in the portrait mentioned before, the one with the suspenders and white shirt. However, now, he was only wearing the pants. He reeked like the sewers he lived in. His back was covered in fur that was tangled and thick.

Jakson threw a punch at him. His fist made contact with the mayor's lower jaw and two pointed teeth clattered to the ground. "You son of a bitch. You need to pay for what you did to these people. Where is my son, you dick?"

The mayor laughed. He spit out a stream of blood that landed on Dustin's foot. "Many children come and go here. To my workshop. But one in particular I remember. What is your name, sir?" He licked his lips and felt the gap where his teeth were missing from. "Does it happen to be Jak...son?" He shortened the name, annunciating each and every syllable in his name, like twisting a dagger in the wound it made. "I remember your boy. He screamed and cried for you and that whore of a woman. And I had so much joy knowing you would not come to rescue him. I wonder what his last thoughts were when I said that there was no cure! Oh, I wonder how devastated he was knowing that he would never have been able to turn human again!"

No cure? Choleira and Inerium could not believe it. Poor Rodryt... He thought there was a cure because of what he heard. But what he *actually* heard was there *was not* a cure. Inerium wanted to cry. She did not have the heart to tell Rodryt that there was no cure...

Jakon laid in a few more punches, this time only blood came out. No teeth. "Where is he. Dead, alive, I need to see him."

The mayor squirmed, trying to get out of the other men's grasp. It was no use. "I had my guys dump his body off into the water below Raitild. Good luck finding him. There's too many to count down there, so by the time you find your son's body it will already be so decomposed you won't even recognize him!" He started howling with so much laughter that he even pissed himself. A puddle formed on the floor from the urine, and it stunk up the room.

"Ugh, God, man, control yourself." Marqael said. He kicked the mayor in the groin. "You stink."

The mayor grunted and coughed up a large amount of saliva and blood. "You guys will not survive any longer once the others get here," he said. "I will watch and drink as I personally conduct your transformations!"

Inerium and Choleira just sat and watched the men pummel the mayor until his face started to swell up and turn red, until there was so much blood and swelling that it was impossible to tell which parts were covered in blood and which parts were bleeding. Austin and Marqael grabbed his arms. Dustin and Jakson grabbed his legs. They all gave a one two three and threw him into the window by his bed.

The mayor flew through the glass, which shattered upon impact, and he slammed onto the wooden street below. The screams the mayor cried out were so loud that all the doors in the nearby houses opened up. The residents inside the houses peered outside to see what was happening. When they saw who it was that was struggling to get on his feet in the road in front of the Town Hall, they started to run towards him.

"Everyone," shouted a well-dressed rodent man. "The mayor has been thrown out of his window!"

The other residents of Raitild started to come outside and run down the street towards the mayor. From the sides of Town Hall came groups of soldiers charging at the people with their weapons raised in the air.

"No. They are going to protect him," said Dustin.

Inerium walked to the window to get a better look. "No, I have a feeling something else is playing out here."

They all watched as the guards circled around the mayor. Their swords and spears were pointed outwards.

"Thank you. Took you all long enough," the mayor sneered.

A few of the guards exchanged some glances and head nods. The ones standing in the front stepped aside, making an opening in the front of the circle. They all turned around and now pointed their weapons at the mayor.

"You did too much to us. You turned us into these abominations because your parents birthed a monster. Fuck you and fuck them for creating you. You should have been drowned in these sewers the moment you breathed your first breath." The soldier looked at the crowd of people, eagerly waiting to rush at the mayor. "Come and get him!"

The crowd of people started charging at the mayor, grabbing whatever rocks or objects they could get their hands on. The people started grabbing at the mayor and pulling on him, smashing him with their rocks and whatnots. Many more people joined the crowd until it was just a mass of swinging arms and yelling. After a few seconds, body parts started flying. An arm. A leg. A few chunks. They all started flying about and landing wherever they decided to. The mayor, for sure, was declared dead when they saw his head fly into the air and be impaled on one of the soldier's pikes. The people started cheering, some were even dancing on his mutilated body parts. It was horrid.

Choleira looked at Inerium. "So, what do we do now?" she asked.

"I am going to look around, see if there is anyone in the other rooms being experimented on or preparing to be," said Dustin. Austin followed him out of the room. Robert followed, too, to go see if he could find Dailen. All that were left in the room were Inerium, Choleira, Marqael, and Jakson.

"Do you want to go and find your son?" asked Marqael.

Jakson nodded. "I cannot accept that he is dead. Not until I find his body."

Inerium looked at Choleira. She wanted to tell him. There may be no cure, but his son was still alive, anyways. He has to know. "We can help you look, Jakson. I have hope, too, that he is alive."

The four left the mayor's bedchamber and headed outside. They walked past the crowd dancing in the remains of their mayor and strolled down the streets, passing by all the houses.

As they approached the edge of the town, where Inerium and Choleira had come in, Jakson started to pick up his pace.

"What is that?" he asked, running towards the tunnel.

Inside the tunnel Inerium and Choleira saw the flickering light of Rodryt's fire. It had gone dim, but it still was bright enough to shine through the tunnel entrance. It was enough for Jakson. He ran faster and faster until his heart was pounding so much that he thought his lungs were going to explode. They reached the tunnel and made their way through it, inching closer to Rodryt's fire.

Jakson dropped to his knees started sobbing. "Rodryt, my son."

Rodryt was sleeping by the fire, curled up in a ball to stay as warm as he could. He sat up and squinted his eyes, waiting for them to adjust. He rubbed his eyes, blinked. Once. Twice. Thrice.

"Dad?" he asked. "Is that you?" His voice was shaky.

"Yes. Yes, Rodryt it is me. Your mother and I have been so worried about you." He reached for the sack on his son's head.

"No," he said, sinking back and clutching the bag on his head. "They turned me into one of those things. I am hideous."

"You are still my son, Rodryt. Human or not. Show me your face."

Rodryt hesitated and finally took off the bag. His hands were shaking violently, making the bag dance around his face as it slowly raised up. He held his head down as he clutched the bag in his left clawed hand.

"Oh, my boy. My poor boy." He went in and embraced his son. Rodryt returned the embrace to his dad, both teary-eyed. Jakson picked up Rodryt. Marqael patted the boy on the back. "I am taking you home, now. Your mother is so worried." They started to walk away out of the tunnel back into Raitild, where they girls could still hear the happy cheering of the others celebrating the mayor's death.

The girls waved Rodryt away as he was carried off. He waved back and said his goodbyes to the girls. Inerium suddenly got a sinking feeling in her stomach.

A deep whispering started to speak in the back of her mind, the same one from before. The one from the relic in her bag.

"Burn it to the ground. Purge the taint that is this city. Let them turn to ash and be nothing more than embers." The words felt heavy, like a command more than a statement.

It was a command, but not one intended for Inerium or Choleira as they believed. It was not just the two girls that had heard the command, but the whole town of Raitild. A gust of wind flew past the girls and into the town.

Suddenly, a loud eruption of screams and roars came from the city's heart where they were dancing before. Flames started rising from the buildings and engulfing the whole town. Black smoke started rising into the air and collecting in the top, filling the domed ceiling above Raitild. The screams of the people of Raitild were now accompanied by the coughing of those who were choking on the smoke and ashes in the air. The smoke was so collected that it started to spill into the tunnel they were in.

"Run," said Choleira.

The girls ran through the tunnel, not paying attention to which way they were going. Were they going the way they came in? Were they lost? Were they going to die in the tunnels?

These thoughts were swarming like locusts in Inerium's mind. Choleira stayed close to Inerium. She held her hand so that she would not fall behind. A left. A right. Another right. The smoke was still following them, as if it was sentient. The water in the middle trail of the sewers was almost boiling. It definitely did not help the smell, the mixture of repulsive sewer water and the smoke growing closer and closer.

They reached the end of the tunnel. Inerium and Choleira looked at each other. Choleira hugged Inerium "We cannot die here. There has to be away out of here."

As they leaned against the wall, Inerium felt the bricks shift a little. She turned around and pushed against the wall. They pushed in more, like there was another space behind them.

"Help me push these bricks."

Choleira and Inerium pushed against the wall, kicking it every other push. The bricks started to cave in and the whole wall collapsed. Inerium grabbed ahold of Choleira until the bricks stopped falling and the dust cleared. The smoke grew closer. They could taste the bitter ash in the air. The girls ran through the opening in the wall into a large empty room. The smoke had finally stopped growing and chasing. It was as if the broken wall was a barrier between them and the smoke, as if there was a piece of glass separating the two.

The girls fell to their knees and caught their breath. "Are you okay?" asked Choleira.

"Yeah." Inerium coughed. She had inhaled some of the smoke.

Inerium looked around the new place they were in. It looked almost like a dungeon cell. It was. In front of them were iron bars, the door wide open and broken off the top hinge. There was a small cot on the floor next to them. A bucket was in the far corner of the cell for urinating and shitting.

"It looks like we are inside of a dungeon," Inerium said. "One like my parents had under their castle back home."

Choleira looked around. She held up her hand, which was blistered and bleeding from the bricks she had pushed. "Hee-alay." The wound started to heal itself. The blood evaporated and the cuts closed. She turned to Inerium, grabbed her hands, and did the same for hers. "Hee-alay." Her hands and other wounds were healed.

They walked out of the cell into the large room where guards would normally sit to watch the prisoners. There were seven other cells besides the one they stepped out of. There were four on the opposite side and three others on theirs. The other cells were empty as well, but the doors were closed. Locked. A set of stairs led up to the floor above.

The girls walked up the stairs. On the second floor was a hallway, coated in an uneven layer of yellow paint. They passed by a door on their left, which was also locked, and continued on down. As they walked through the hall, they started to hear voices echoing from the other side. They were male, almost familiar.

Choleira gasped and grabbed Inerium's hand. "Stand behind me."

From around the corner came Vanitar and the other soldier, who still could not speak. "Well, what do we have here?" He started to laugh. "I have been searching for you two everywhere."

Suddenly, the door in the hall that was closed behind them opened and a pair of guards came out. They were Vanitar's. They grabbed Inerium and Choleira, tying their arms behind their backs.

"Let us go!" Inerium cried out, trying to break free of the man's grasp.

"I don't think I will," Vanitar smiled a wicked Grinch-like smile. "You are valuable, Princess Inerium. Far too valuable. I need your brother dead. And what better way than to hold you hostage for him to show? He already slipped my grasp once, but he will not this time. I guarantee it."

He looked up to the soldiers and nodded his head, making a motion with his hand like he was holding a hammer putting in a nail. The girls felt a sharp pain hit the backs of their heads and their vision went black.

As they started to fall unconscious, they heard Vanitar say the words, "We will take them when he the moon starts to set. We do not want any unwanted attention." The soldiers picked up the girls and took them away into the room they came out of.

CHAPTER 15

Kerstas had started to make his way down the mountain. The trail was steep and slick from the snow and ice. His body ached. His eyes burned. The new power his body was adjusting to was immense. He could not use it. Not yet anyways. In due time it will.

Kerstas could see so much even from halfway down the mountain. The nearby villages below looked so small from up high. He knew they were large villages, housing nearly a hundred people in some.

He had traveled to one of them once as a younger boy with his parents. They were away on business. Kentrin was discussing information on attacks being made on their village and the ones nearby. They suspected it was Meridine. They said the soldiers came in armor decorated in red capes and red plumes on their helmets. It was, after all, the color of Meridine's kingdom. While they were there Kerstas played with the other kids. Inerium was not old enough to run around just yet. She was swaddled in Eleana's arms. Kerstas did not know what happened that day in terms of what his father discussed, but he remembered his father was in a hurry to leave and return home. He said it was important. They returned home and the rest had fallen into Kerstas' mind distant from conscious memories.

He traveled farther down the mountain. It was getting warmer thankfully. He stopped shivering and chattering his teeth. He could see the main road below him. The soldiers that were approaching from the West were getting closer. He could see each individual one now. There were three horse-drawn caravans, all guarded by six soldiers. A soldier on a horse stood on each side of the three caravans, as well as another one riding in the front. He was for sure the leader of this party.

The traveling group reminded Kerstas of Malgrin and his group of soldiers he had gotten separated from back in the cave, right near the border. The great golden trees were dim, but still with what little glow they had were still shimmering brilliantly in the foggy air. They had not withered, nor had any of the leaves fallen yet. Kerstas missed his home, his parents, his friends. He missed Inerium and wondered if she had gotten away. If she was safe. On top of all these thoughts was still that burning desire. The desire to enact his revenge on the ones who did those awful things to him for so many years. They survived; he knows they did. He knew it in his gut, in his soul, that they had survived the attack.

—⟫◆⟪—

He reached the bottom of the mountain. The party was still marching towards the border, which was close to where Kerstas was currently at. He hid in the bushes nearby and waited for them to pass by.

As they passed, he heard various conversations throughout the party. Some were about how they could not wait to return home or what they were going to eat for lunch. There was one conversation that caught Kerstas' attention.

"Are you on board with this?" asked one of the soldiers walking beside the second wagon.

"Not at all. We received a letter from Venirit declaring war if we did not hand over the young prince of Requilit. Kerstas was his name I believe. They also said with little explanation that we were being accused and held responsible for the murder of the king and queen of Requilit."

"But we didn't do it." The second man's voice was higher than the first, almost like he was going through puberty. The cracks were distinct like a hiccup during a lecture.

"I know we didn't, but the kingdom of Venirit believes we did. And Istimus is probably allying with them to fight us as well. That damned fool of a king they have has been trying to find an excuse to take our kingdom down for ages. Even my dad told me when he was in the ranks that Istimus' king was plotting to take our land from us."

"Do you think *he* is responsible?"

"For the king and queen's death in Requilit? Absolutely. That asshole did not even attempt to come to the boy's coronation. We ran out of the building the moment the chaos started. I saw a bunch of guards standing around the sides of the building. Maybe they were his, you think?"

"Yeah," the cracking-voiced boy said. "I do not know who else's it could have been. And who better to blame than us? Our land is directly below theirs. That coronation would have been the perfect opportunity to wipe out the boy's family, as well as him."

Kerstas was carefully listening in to the conversation being held by the two men. He could tell the one with the non-crackly voice was much older, maybe mid-forties. He crawled through the bushes along the road avoiding detection from the party of soldiers. He had walked quite a way parallel to the party crouched down. His thighs were burning as he crouch-walked along the bush and tree lining next to the road. He stopped for a moment to give his legs a break.

What he did not notice was that the party had also stopped moving a few yards ahead from where he stopped. He suddenly heard footsteps approaching around the area he was hiding in. He stepped away from the bush he was behind and laid stomach-down on the tall grass that stood just barely above him.

The soldier approaching was one from the wagon that Kerstas was listening in on. It was neither of the ones he was hearing, though. The soldier opened up the flap on the front of his brown pants and started to urinate. The stream trailed through the air and started to splash on the ground barely two feet from Kerstas' head. He backed away from it when the pool started to grow closer to him. He accidentally crawled over a stick, and it snapped.

The soldier jumped and quickly put his dick away. "Who is there? He looked around and saw the spot where Kerstas was. The grass above him was just barely moved away, but just enough so that the soldier took notice. "Stand up."

Kerstas stood up. The grass line now stood up to his calves. "Don't attack. I do not mean any harm."

"Who are you?" Asked the man. "And, um, did I accidentally piss on you?" He looked around on Kerstas and the area around him, checking for any wet spots.

"My name is. My name is Kerstas. And no, you did not."

"Kerstas? As in Prince Kerstas?"

Kerstas nodded. The soldier quickly turned around and called out for the others. Within seconds, a dozen soldiers had all joined the one who found him.

"What is it?" Asked the deep-voiced man who Kerstas

heard talking earlier. He saw Kerstas standing in front of the crowd. "Who is this kid?"

"It is him, man. It's the Prince."

"Kerstas?" Asked another soldier who was on the larger side.

Kerstas nodded once again. "Yes, I am Kerstas of Requilit. Who are you all?"

"Come with us, first. The captain must meet you before anything more is said or explained."

The men led Kerstas onto the road and up to the rest of the party. The horses were feeding on the grass and drinking from a small pond about two yards from the main road. They had set up tents to lay down in and get out of the shade. The leader of the party was sitting on the ground next to a large campfire cooking a rabbit with four others, who had their helmets setting next to them.

"Who is this?" Asked the leader of the party. He was clearly in charge from the decorated patches on his uniform's chest. There was a total of eight, which Kerstas did not find it important to analyze them. His helmet was sitting beside him. It had a long red set of horsehair coming out of it with silver strands in it. The mouth cover was lined with gold over the silver, and it was pulled up on the forehead portion of the helmet.

"It's Kerstas, sir. We found him in the bushes over there."

The party leader looked up. "Prince Kerstas, well then. To be honest I thought you were dead. News spread out all over Pleniris that you were dead, that you had been killed during the attack."

"I am alive. Who do you side with? What kingdom?"

"With Meridine, of course. Does the red not show that already?" He patted on his helmet.

Kerstas suddenly understood. He remembered that Malgrin was wearing a red cape on his uniform. The other soldiers in the group were also wearing at least something that resembled red.

"Vanitar's men took me. The day of the attack. We went inside a cave a few miles to the West and got trapped inside. Only I survived. They were wearing red as well."

Some of the men by the captain looked at each other and exchanged a few words behind their cupped hands. A few eyes widened and a lot of words were spoken, but Kerstas understood none of it.

"That helps a lot. Thank you, Kerstas."

"What do you mean?" Kerstas was confused. The cogs in his brain were slowly turning one by one, increasing speed as he thought more about the situation.

"The men who took you wore red, yes? At least some sort of red?"

Kerstas nodded.

"Well, they were not our men. They were Vanitar's men from Istimus. For years the nearby villages had been afraid of us, running as soon as they saw our red banners. My assumption, now proven to be true, is that Vanitar has been sending men after his own territories posing as ours to cause conflict between the kingdoms. There have not been any battles between the kingdoms of Istimus and Meridine, but there certainly has been little brawls between our soldiers from time to time over the years." He turned his rabbit a few times to cook the other side. "What happened to you, Kerstas? The attack on your kingdom happened days, maybe weeks, ago. I've lost track."

Kerstas explained the events that happened after the events of the massacre at the castle. How he was taken by Malgrin's men and was aided by Barnabin and Geremi and the others. He tried to explain the cave that turned into crystal and how he met Spizser, but that portion was understandably difficult to explain to them. He skipped over it once the men started to look at him like he was insane, and he moved on to when he exited the cave at the top of the mountain. He lied about what happened inside of the cave, though. Instead of telling the soldiers that he had drank the blood of the Mad Demon-Possessed King, he told them that "the creature in the mountain attacked Barnabin and I was lucky to make it out alive." He then followed up the events that just passed only minutes ago.

Once the soldiers were finished listening to Kerstas recount his story, they started eating on the food that had been cooking over the large fire.

The captain took a bite out of the leg of his rabbit. It was a little burnt, but it still looked really tasty to Kerstas, who had not eaten in hours, maybe even a day at this point. "So," the captain said in between bites. Bits of the rabbit meat flew out of his mouth, along with the juices that sprayed out and sizzled in the fire. "What did the creature look like? I had heard rumors, but to be honest I did not even believe there was a creature in that mountain, at least one that was still living at least."

"It was a man. Sort of. A demon in human form. He looked like a man on the surface, but nothing can mistake the sinister look in the eyes of a demon. They are cruel and filled with darkness."

The soldiers beside the captain had a look in their eyes like they were scared. It was because they were. Whenever the soldiers of all the kingdoms in Pleniris were told about the famed creature of the Shrieking Peaks, they imagined it like a werewolf or some kind of monster that would have been featured in an 80's movie, kind of like a cave troll with multiple arms. An arachnid cave troll? That would have been terrifying to think of, even for the strongest-willed people.

However, their speculations about the creature in the Shrieking Peaks were wrong, and they did not even think to assume that a demon, in flesh, was the creature in the mountain. A near immortal being residing only miles away from their family and home. They most likely believed that the creature was still alive. Kerstas had left out the part of him drinking the blood and absorbing Daerex's power.

The soldiers were now frantically looking up at the mountain's peaks, like a driver does when a car almost hits them for recklessly driving and then they are looking carefully at every car in their vision thinking they are going to do the same thing. *What if it comes to us in our sleep* they wondered as they stared at the peaks, hands shaking as they put more food in their mouths. They chewed faster, trying to let the taste distract them from their paranoia for a creature that was not alive anymore. The fact that they should have been truly afraid of was that right in front of them, telling his story, was a boy who now had an unawakened form of the power that the creature once held.

"What is your name, if you do not mind me asking?" Kerstas had been talking to the captain of this party the whole time and had not even asked his name. He apologized for not asking beforehand while he was asked his.

"My name is Moredir, captain of Meridine's army." He held out his hand. Kerstas shook it. We were heading to the nearby village of Neuten to camp stay at, hopefully to clear our name and explain to them that it was their own kingdom's army that had attacked them many years ago."

"Let us hope they listen," said two soldiers to Moredir's left. He was a bit on the larger side. Not fat, but muscular. He had a giant battle axe resting on the log he sat on. His beard was braided down to his chest. His hair was a dark brown that matched his eyes, and it, too, was braided down so that the helmet would not tangle or pull on it when he removed it. "I mean how would you feel if someone came to you and told you your own kingdom was betraying you and slaughtering your friends and family?"

Moredir nodded. "You do have a point." He looked at Kerstas. "But we now have something we did not have before. We now have Kerstas. He can back our claims up, and he was kidnapped by them. All of these things do not make Istimus look good at all, and they will surely understand once King Kerstas tells his story. If he wants to aid us." He turned to look at Kerstas.

Kerstas nodded. "I can." He kept eyeballing the rabbit that was being cooked a few feet away from him. He wanted to just take it from the others' hands and devour it, but he did not.

Moredir took notice of Kerstas' eye movement from him to the rabbit, so he picked up one of the rabbit carcasses that had just been cooked through and handed it to him. Steam was rising from the body of the charred meat. Kerstas took a long sniff. It made his mouth water and wish he had a potato soup to pair it with. That sounded so good. Tsuin and Tsuon cooked it for him many times back home. He had not thought of the twin cooks since the attack. He wondered if they were alive. He hoped so. He hoped to come back to his kingdom one day to them having a whole feast prepared for him and his sister when he brought her home.

Kerstas tore the rabbit apart. Back legs first. Then front. Then the breasts, thighs, and then whatever of the carcass was left that was barely hanging onto the wooden stick it was impaled on. He had not eaten in a long time, so whatever food was available he feasted on. There were pot-boiled potatoes and loaves of bread as well that the soldiers brought out. Kerstas ended up eating four potatoes and almost an entire loaf of bread, washing it all down with a pouch of water. He refilled the pouch at the nearby water source the horses were drinking from. The other soldiers did the same when he did.

"Moredir, right?" Kerstas asked. "Did you know my father?"

Moredir smiled. "Very well, young king. We were close when we were young. And older, of course. When he became king, I did not see him as often outside of important meetings and land-wide celebrations. We were best friends. We met because his father and my father got along very well. Of course, not many people were very fond of your grandpa, Kerstas."

"Yeah, I heard he was not favored by really anyone, not even his own family. My father for sure was ashamed of what my grandfather made our kingdom out to be. He made a promise to redeem Requilit, and I wanted to do the same. Starting with the state of the church and those who preach in them. I swore years ago they would be the first to be executed after my coronation."

Hey, you cannot just execute priests, Kerstas," said the soldier directly to the left of Moredir. He was fit as well, but he had a belly with it from excessive drinking. A beer belly as some would call it. "It would give yourself and your kingdom a bad name."

"Not if I explain what happened to me. They violated me. Raped me. For years and years until I turned sixteen. My father... I believed back then that my father knew about it all. He would send me to them after nearly every service to see if it would help. For the first year or so I believed my father put them up to it and I was alienated from him." He drank another sack of water while suppressing the memories of it. He still felt the sting. The awkward and excruciating pain in his ass that he felt every week for so long. "But then, I heard them talking after they thought I had passed out from the pain. They were saying that they believed that they would be executed on the spot if Kentrin, my father, were to hear about it. I wanted to tell him everything, but I was too scared to. The rage was so strong in me that I promised that I would do it myself." He wiped tears away. The memories were coming down hard on him. His body ached from the memories. His heart was racing. "So, I endured the torturous acts until the day came, the day of my coronation. I was so excited to see the faces of them as I ordered their executions, bringing their horrendous, sinful acts to the light."

The men were in shock. They could not believe a word they heard. They did, of course, but it was impossible to comprehend. A son of a king being mistreated for so long by those who claim to by closest to God.

Kerstas and the soldiers had stopped eating and drinking. He helped them take down the tents and ready the horses for the trip to Neuten. Neuten was around a three-mile trip from where they were. It would not have been a long trip by a car, which would have only been maybe three minutes, but since the carriages were much slower than an automobile, and some of the soldiers were on foot, it would take hours. Once the wagons and soldiers were ready, and the fires were extinguished, they headed on to the East.

⟫◆⟪

Hours passed. They stopped once or twice for bathroom breaks. Neuten was maybe half an hour away now as Kerstas predicted, prying his memory of maps he had seen of Pleniris that were kept in the library and conference rooms at the castle in Requilit. Every kingdom's capitol, where the king and queen reside, had maps in it. They had to for strategizing things or for long travels for meetings. Maps could be found about anywhere, really. Traders had them, taverns had them, even brothels had them mounted in some of the bedrooms where the men would take the workers to fuck.

Kerstas had studied the map a lot because his grandmother told him many stories about the various things in the lands, and he liked to reference the locations on the map so he could visit them and experience the stories and tales for himself. He had heard the stories of the Woodland Elves of the forest dividing Requilit and Venirit. The tale of the dragon who had scorched the lands between Venirit and Istimus, which still, as the stories go, to this day still burns and smokes from how hot the dragon's flames were.

There was even a story that his father told him many years ago, before the priests did the awful things to him, about a fishing village in the Southeastern corner of Pleniris. The woman who became the first witch by making a deal with a demon. He had met her son, he now realized, the spawn of that witch and the demon she dealt with. Daerex, also known as the mad demon-possessed king, son of Sybralem the witch and Grigori the demon.

Kerstas turned his head and stared up at the great mountain he had scaled down. It no longer terrified him, now that the creature inside was no longer there. Now it was just a giant mountain with only rumors to scare people away. Kerstas closed his eyes and rested his head on the corner of the wagon he rode on.

He started to dream. In the dream he was standing in a large field of ash. His hands were trembling and tingling like they would after falling asleep on them. His eyes were burning and his whole body was twitching like it was trying to lash out. He was holding his body back, but the unnerving urge to swing his arms out and kick his legs, almost in a violent manner, was nearly overpowering him. The Shrieking Peaks were standing before him, taking up the horizon. The sun was rising behind it, nearly at the peak.

He started to hear a voice in his head, one Inerium and Choleira had heard twice now. It was a malicious voice, but no longer whispering. More like talking quietly. The grittiness of the voice shook Kerstas' body, even outside of the dream.

"It is nearly finished, young Kerstas. The time is almost upon us," the voice said.

His body ran cold. He started seeing visions flash before him. An ancient dagger decorated with unknown symbols dripping with a dark green liquid. An artifact in the shape of an eye with crossing oval irises that met in the middle to one open pupil. The artifact was now lying in the large field of ash under the light of a now bright red eclipsed moon. The sky almost seemed to bleed from it from how the flares danced under the bottom of the lunar celestial body. It was what was calling to him. The voice was coming from the artifact.

"Come, Kerstas," it said. Come."

The moon started glowing a brighter and brighter crimson until he had to shield his eyes from it. He woke up from his short nap, covering his eyes as the sun bore down on his face.

One of the soldiers was shaking him awake. "Are you okay, Kerstas?" he asked.

Kerstas rubbed his eyes. He was sweating. The soldier who woke him grabbed the water pouch on Kerstas' side and made him drink nearly half of it.

"You were shaking, like something was attacking you. He and I Had to hold your arms steady just to keep you from hitting us," he said, gesturing at the soldier on Kerstas' right side. He was lanky but still had a little muscle on him. Enough to hold his own in a fight if he were to be in one.

"Are you okay, young lord?" the lanky boy asked, releasing his shaking grip off of his upper arm.

"Yeah, just a nightmare, that is all. I can barely even remember it." He grabbed his head, which was pounding and pulsating with his heartbeat. Every beat made it worse, almost making his vision darken with each progressing beat.

"We are here," he heard Moredir said from the front of the party, which was now starting to come to a halt.

Kerstas looked up and saw the village of Neuten. It was a larger village, roughly around the size of Raitild, but of course not located in a sewer system. There were a bunch of little houses strewn about on the grassy landscape to the right side of the main road. There was a church near the center of the town square, centered by a fountain gushing out water that reflected the light of the sun. Across from the church stood the town hall, which had a small staircase leading up to its two wooden doors. A path led straight down the town into the square, which then trailed off another path to the left where the marketplace was.

The party unloaded, keeping their supplies on the wagons. They left two soldiers to stand guard to keep the goods and everything else safe while the rest were in the village. They were told that if any commotion were to arise in the village they were to put all the supplies they could on one wagon and head back to their last campsite, where the others who made it would meet them.

The party took an organized formation to walk into the town. It appeared scattered, but it was an organized scattering. There were about seven rows, each with about five to six soldiers in them. They were not in an even block formation. They were just spread out uneven enough to appear random, while it was just the opposite. The formation allowed each soldier to see almost directly to the front so that if something were to happen to one of the rows towards the front, they could see it and react. They could also, if they were archers, fire their arrows at any attackers they had without risking impaling one of their comrades.

In this formation Kerstas stood near the third row. Far enough back to not be targeted first, but far enough forward in the formation as to not get ambushed from behind without the other soldiers being aware. They had given him a set of spare armor they had so he would not stand out in the formation. It had a short red cape that was ripped a little on the right side. The plated legs were a little loose-fitting, but they were held up with a leather belt he already wore. His chest-piece was not a "knight in shining armor" kind of piece, but it was a light tan leather with chainmail underneath it. The cape was clasped on to the shoulders by two metal buttons colored red as well to match. He had on a pair of leather gloves with the pinky and ring fingers missing from the right glove.

The question of why all the tears and rips were on the right side of the set and none on the left swam through Kerstas' mind, but he did not think on it too much to worry himself. He also wondered, even if it were not his primary thoughts, what powers he would receive from Daerex's blood. Of course, there was the dark magic he would receive, but Kerstas had no clue what element he already possessed beforehand. He did not even know he could possess one. Magic, of course, was nearly on the level of myths and legends as people talked about it and what the old heroes of the past did with it.

They walked through the village down the main path that

led directly to the center. There were some people standing in front of their houses talking to one another or just staring to the horizon without another thought in their head.

Maybe they are trying to pray to their god to ask for a fortune or a year's supply of food thought Kerstas. *Not like he would answer them. He did not even answer my prayers when his followers defiled me and ruined any chance, I had of even thinking about following him and worshipping him.* He had thoughts like this a lot. Sometimes they even felt like they were being drawn out of him.

The people in the village took notice of them walking through the center. Some paid little attention, but those that did glared and almost seemed to be in defensive stances, as if they believed that the soldiers were about to break out and start slaughtering them all. Of course, what they saw were not just soldiers. They saw the red banners, the red capes, and the red accents on their armor. Some of them took notice of Kerstas. They did not know it was him, but because he was not fully armored and he had no helmet on, he was a person of interest to the ones eyeballing every soldier in the party.

They reached the village's center. A pair of people came out of the village's meeting hall. They were all older. Not white hair and feeble, but slight greying and light wrinkling. Early sixties maybe? Could be. The two were wearing nice clothing. Not royalty-tier, but like a middle to high class kind of wear. Their white button-up shirts were tucked into their tailored pants that fit them seamlessly. The one on the left was wearing small glasses that he had to tilt his head slightly upwards to see out of. The one on the right had a cane with an angel's wing carved at the handle, with carved feathers falling down the shaft of it. His eyes were brown, the other's green.

"What brings you here?" asked the one with the cane. His voice was weak, a heavy smoker possibly. He was. Kerstas looked and saw a pipe sticking out of his pocket, with a sack hanging from the pants loop behind it.

"We are coming from Meridine," said Moredir. "Istimus and Venirit are allying against us. They say we are responsible for the deaths of Queen Elena and King Kentrin, along with the kidnapping of Prince Kerstas."

"And you are saying you did not? Your armies come to our doorsteps every week, demanding tax money and raping our women. Two days ago, you red-caped assholes killed one of our men for not giving up his wife for your desires," said the man with glasses.

"Sir, if I may," said Kerstas, stepping to the front of the party next to Moredir.

"And who are you?" The man with on the left adjusted his glasses.

"I am Kerstas, son of Kentrin, prince of Requilit. And I know the truth of what happened."

The man with the cane started to step forward. "So, the armies of Meridine are responsible after all."

Kerstas shook his head. "No, they are not. The armies of Istimus are to blame. I heard it from the mouth of their captain, Malgrin. He told me that king Vanitar was paranoid, believing in some prophecy he thought was about me. He told his men to come and kill my parents and take me back to him. I escaped and ran into these men here, who have come to clear their name."

Moredir stepped forward, putting his hand on Kerstas' shoulder. "We have been told that our armies have been coming here and terrorizing you and the other villages. And by what I am now hearing, it is a lot worse than we believed."

"Are you saying that your kingdom is not responsible for this? We saw the red on your armor. Everyone knows the colors of the kingdoms! You are red and Istimus is yellow! Venirit is green and Requilit is blue! A group in red has always come here demanding us of things. That is *your* kingdom, sir."

"I have proof that it was not us. Ever since the attack on Requilit, my men have stayed guard of our kingdom. We have gone out and hunted for food for our barracks, but we have not gone within a mile of our borders. This is the farthest East we have been in months, even years."

"We know it was you. When you came from there, we saw you from miles away. You and your red outfits. You even took some of the plating off to avoid excess noise." The man with the cane pointed behind him.

Moredir and Kerstas looked at each other. It had clicked for both of them what had happened. "You said from that direction, correct?" Moredir pointed to the East.

"Yes, you came from the back to surprise us. You all were not there too long, but one of your men killed one of our elder women, part of our medical workers." He tapped his cane on the ground as he said the last two words.

"Sir, listen to your words. Think about the facts. You saw us come from the West. It is a straight road for miles and miles. There is no way we could have circled around to the back of your village without being seen."

Kerstas raised his hand in the air like a student about to ask a question. "And, if I may add, Malgrin was wearing a red cape when I was in his party's custody."

"He was wearing red?" The glasses-wearing elder asked.

Kerstas nodded. *It's not like I did not just say that already.*

The elders looked at one another, whispered a few things to each other, and then returned to their positions. "A meeting will be held tonight, when the sun sets. Then, we will continue." They turned around and headed back into the Town Hall.

"So what now?" Asked Kerstas.

"We wait. We will camp outside of the village. When the sky starts to darken, me and you will return here and talk to them about everything. I hope it will work out for us and they will see the truth."

Kerstas nodded. "I hope that as well."

CHAPTER 16

"Are you okay?" asked Inerium.

Inerium was sitting next to Choleira on a wagon being drawn by two horses. A large tarp covered the top of the wagon, like one that would be seen transporting cargo or supplies in old Western movies or Oregon Trail.

"Yes," said Choleira. Their hands were locked together, the heat between their palms caused them to sweat a little. Even with the tarp overtop of the wagon, the sun was still sending heavy waves of heat on them. It felt like they could not breathe.

The girls' heads were covered by vegetable sacks, much like the one Rodryt had on in the tunnels. They could not see anything besides the light of the sun that shone through the opening in the back of the wagon tarp. The air stunk. They were most likely going through the swamps circling around Venirit. The stench of the swamp was unforgettable, and this was that stench. It was almost suffocating.

They could not see if there were any others in the wagon. They only knew that they were there. In their minds that was all they ever needed, but a threat being amongst them was also concerning.

Inerium tried to move her legs. They were tied together

with some king of rope. When she moved her legs, Choleira's moved as well.

"I think they tied us together," said Inerium.

"They did. Only our legs. Our hands are free, though." She reached her other hand over and covered the back of Inerium's hand. Inerium used her right hand to do the same.

Inerium felt her sides. Her bag was gone, along with Solef and her smaller sister. When Inerium felt Choleira, her cloak was missing. Her bow and arrows were also not with her.

"I know," Choleira said. "They took all of our stuff. I am not sure where they put it."

"Your ears, did they see them?"

Choleira let out a quick breath, like one does when they are startled. "I did not even think about that." Her head turned towards Inerium. "Do you think they are going to try to sell us?"

The smell finally went away. They had passed through the swamps and were now on the grasslands between the swamp and the Scorched Lands of Vestyr. Inerium sat in silence for a moment to breathe some clean air. The idea of them being sold was haunting. She did not even want to consider it. It was a high possibility as much as Inerium did not want to admit it. Knowing there was an Elven girl in their custody, any soldier or person would consider the price for them. A creep would try to buy her to use her for his own pleasures and fantasies. Traders would love to see how much gold he or she could get for her ears or even strands of her hair for "good luck" if they could sell the idea. Any idea was on the table for what a person could do with a magical creature's body if they bought it.

"No. I would hope not. He said that we were valuable, but I believe he meant it in another way. Not financial value, but maybe to get to my brother. I know he is searching for me.

He has to be. I know if I were him, I would travel across this whole country just to know he was safe."

"What about that one soldier?" she asked.

"Which one?" Inerium asked. She was trying to prod her memory, but it was hazy where she was hit over the head.

"I think she means me," said a familiar voice from the opposite side of the wagon.

The girls froze. "Who are you?" Inerium asked. Her voice was shaky.

"Malgrin. We spoke at the Blooming Gorgot in Venirit. I believe you read my note."

Inerium remembered the note. "What do you know about Kerstas?" she asked.

"I was the captain of the party that took your brother." He paused and let out a deep sigh. "As well as the same party that is responsible for your parents' deaths."

"It was you?" Inerium asked furiously. She tried to stand up but fell over as her legs were tied. Choleira helped her steady herself.

"I want to apologize. It does not mean a lot now. I know it is too late, but can you forgive me?"

"Did you kill my parents, Malgrin?" Inerium's tone was malicious, almost like Kerstas' got when he talked about the priests who violated him.

"No." He tapped his feet on the ground a couple times. "I did not tell your brother this, but the ones that killed your parents are dead. I killed them myself after I saw them do it. I did not wish for the death of your parents. I did not want any of this. I honestly intended to set your brother free once we reached a certain point, but complications happened. We — we stopped near a cave at the base of the Shrieking Peaks, near the Southern Road. We sent in some men to make sure there was nothing inside of it. The cave collapsed and we tried to get in. When we finally cleared the rubble, there was no one there. Just an empty space, aside from a fat soldier of ours who most likely caused the cave in trying to fit through a small space in the cave that his body was squeezed in."

"Do you think he is dead?" Choleira asked. "We had a run-in with a man at the Gorgot who said he was okay."

"I believe so," he said. "That boy has got a strong pair on him, that is for sure. With a will as strong as his, I do not think anything God throws at him could kill him. Hell, I would even say he could kill God, too, if he was determined to."

"Where is our stuff?" Inerium asked. Suddenly, a thought came across her mind. The relic. What if they got ahold of it...

"I have it right here next to me. It is safe, I promise. Your weapons, a painting that was tied up in a ribbon, and there was also something else in your bag. I could not tell what it was. It was made of bone and looked very eerie. I did not take it out, but what is it?"

Inerium had completely forgotten about the painting that Choleira had shrunken down for her back in Nellenor. The beautiful swan painting.

"I do not know," she said. "I got it a while back in the Northern Woods. It done terrible things to the last owner of it. And i watched it influence an entire city to burn itself to the ground."

Malgrin glanced over at the bag sitting next to him. "I see." His hand almost seemed to reach out to the bag without him realizing. He saw his hand digging through the bag and he quickly pulled it out. "I am sorry. I do not know what happened. My arm was acting on its own."

"It is that relic in there. It has an influence over people.

It has not done anything to me or Choleira, though. I am thankful, but curious as to why not."

"Do you think it might be a relic of Hellruler's?" Malgrin asked, glancing at the bag.

"I doubt it. With the stuff the two of us have seen on our journey, this makes Hellruler seem like a child. Whatever that thing is, it is evil — pure evil."

The wagon hit a large rock in the road, and it bounced, knocking Choleira and Inerium off their seats. Inerium hit her head on the wooden floor.

Malgrin helped them back up. He pulled off the sacks. They could see again. There was a little bit of dried blood on Inerium's forehead.

"Ineri, you are bleeding." She wiped the blood off her forehead with her sleeve. "There you go." She smiled. It was a small yet cute smile. A very warming one full of care. "All better."

"I forgot to ask. You are an elf, right?" Malgrin's question was one of curiosity, not ill-intentioned. Choleira knew this.

"Yes. I am from the Northern Woods as you call it. From an Elven city named Olmenor."

"Were the woods not cursed?"

She nodded her head. "They were. Those who strayed off the main path would be lost forever. The curse is lifted now. But, if I may, I would like to keep that a secret. My people are terrified of humans. We are the only ones left here in Pleniris. The rest of my kin have left to the Promised Lands far to the NorthEast where the sun sets."

He nodded. It was a reasonable request, of course. It would make it harder for ambushes from the woods by bandits and others up to no good. "It will be our secret. What caused the curse in the first place?"

Choleira and Inerium both glanced at the bag sitting next to him. "That thing you keep reaching for. That is what did it."

He glanced at it again, this time with a little more fear in his eyes. "This little thing, not even bigger than a hand, caused so much?" His hand started inching towards the bag again. "With that kind of power, who knows what could be done..."

A whispering started to come from the bag. No words were spoken. It was more like a long icy breath that gave chills to the the three in the wagon. Malgrin's hand started trembling, like he was fighting it to keep it from grabbing ahold of the relic.

Inerium quickly stood up and grabbed the bag. She grabbed Choleira's cloak and stuffed it inside the bag as well, covering the relic. She placed the bag between her and Choleira's hips, moving closer together to hold it in place. "We will hold on to it, Sir Malgrin."

"Th—Thank you, girls." His voice was shaky. "I cannot help myself. It is like my own body is trying to take it, despite my mind telling it not to." He sat in silence for a few minutes, staring at his hands and occasionally up at the bag, sandwiched between the girls' hips.

"Where are we going?" Choleira asked. She tried to lean over and grab her bow and quiver of water, which was sitting in the bottom in its pouch that kept it from spilling out.

Malgrin grabbed it, along with Solef and her younger sister. "I cannot let you have these. Not yet, anyways. I still have to pretend that I am the enemy."

"Do you not serve them?" Inerium asked.

Malgrin nodded. "Orders. I have to."

"But they are just orders. You can ignore them, Sir Malgrin. Like you could have chosen to leave those bags on our heads or take the relic from the bag instead of fighting it."

He laughed. It was short yet felt like a relative who had just heard a funny joke. "You sound so much like him. Like your brother. He said the same thing to me when he was with me. He told me that following orders blindly was no honorable thing to do. It is not as simple as doing or not doing. Sometimes there are other things going on behind the scenes that influence the person to do bad things."

"Is something happening to you, Malgrin?" Inerium leaned forward a little.

Choleira did the same. She had a look about her that she knew something. She did. "Sir, they will be okay. He will not hurt them."

He looked over at Choleira. "Can you guarantee that?" he asked. His eyes were a little teary.

"I cannot fully guarantee it, but I do not think even he will go that far. Not with you and not with any other men under his command."

"What is it?" Inerium asked, looking at Choleira and back to Malgrin.

He nodded to her. "Go ahead."

She took a deep breath. "King Vanitar has threatened to kill his wife and kids if he betrays his kingdom. He was paranoid of some prophecy about Kerstas and said that if anyone were to aid him, their families—as well as they—will be killed."

"Oh. Surely he cannot mean that. What king would say such a thing?"

He held his head down. "He would. He is scared of your brother, Princess Inerium. There was a prophecy he was told. I think he may have misheard it a little or may have connected things too quickly and convinced himself that the prophecy was about Kerstas."

"What is the prophecy?" Inerium asked.

Choleira suddenly was a little scared. Not because of what was in Malgrin or Inerium's head, but what was in hers.

Choleira and the other elves had heard of a prophecy, one similar to the one Malgrin was referring to. Perhaps even the *exact* one he was referring to.

"It said that when a new heir would be born, the four would fall and become one under him. King Vanitar assumed that because your mother, Queen Eleana, was pregnant with a son that the prophecy was about him. And that when he would assume the throne, the four kingdoms of Pleniris would be all under his rule."

Choleira was rocking back and forth at this point, her hands and legs trembling. "Ineri, your ancestor—Sybralem—-do you remember her?"

Inerium nodded. "Yeah, why?"

Malgrin glanced at Inerium. "You are a descendant of the witch Sybralem?"

Inerium nodded. "Yes, but why does that matter?"

Choleira took a deep breath with a shaky exhale. "My people know of a prophecy, most likely the one he was mentioning." She looked up from Inerium and then to Malgrin. "When the heir of the demon's blood comes of age, the Sanguavis will awaken. The six will fall and under his rule they will be one."

"Six?" Malgrin asked. "I thought it said four."

Choleira nodded. "It got misinterpreted by the prophets who came to our lands. Before the wars. Back when the mad demon-possessed king Daerex terrorized the land. They heard the prophecy and assumed that ours was wrong, interpreting it as the four kingdoms rather than whoever the six was a reference to."

"I still do not understand. How does it reference Kerstas?" Inerium asked curiously yet cautiously. "What is the Sanguavis?"

"I do not know. But that is the name that they used. They were almost terrified to use it, like the name was cursed."

"But how does that relate to Kerstas? Does he have some demon blood in him or something?" Malgrin asked.

"Sybralem was a witch. The story of how she became one is rarely truly known. She was met with a demon during the last eclipse this land has seen. They slept together and conceived a child. Generations passed and it all trailed down to your parents Kentrin and Eleana. Her ancestor was Sybralem, and Kentrin's ancestor was the demon king Darren, the son of Sybralem."

"How do you know all of this?" asked Inerium.

"I am also curious about this. How do you possess so much knowledge on this matter?" Malgrin asked.

Choleira stayed silent for a moment. The wagon rolled over a few ruts in the road. "He let me in. He let me know things." Her eyes started watering. They quickly dried up. She remembered she was not allowed to cry. Elves do not cry unless they are in front of someone extremely important to them. And only them.

"Who?" Inerium asked.

"The man at the Blooming Gorgot in Venirit. Spenzser. Spizser. Whatever his name was. Our waiter. When he talked to us one on one, he opened his mind to me. I could not read it, but he spoke to me. He let me in on some extra information about your ancestry and why Kerstas was so important to Vanitar. I was just curious. There are things in that man's mind that no one—absolutely no one— should think about. I do not know what he is, but there are no words that can describe him besides utterly terrifying."

Inerium wrapped her arms around Choleira and held her.

Choleira buried her face in Inerium's chest, slightly embarrassed about it.

"It is okay," said Inerium. "Let the thoughts stay in the back of your mind. They cannot hurt you."

Suddenly, as the words came out of Inerium's mouth, the thoughts in Choleira's mind about the terrors she saw in Spizser's head trailed away, hiding in the farthest places of Choleira's memories, even behind the ones she could not remember.

Choleira sat up. "What did you do?"

"What do you mean?" Inerium asked, confused.

"What you just said. You told the thoughts to go away—and they did. Like magic. Even my magic is not capable of doing that. Sure, I can cast illusions, summon water and fire, but nothing close to what you just did."

Inerium was still confused. She did not understand what happened. It was an odd concept to wrap her mind around, telling someone's thoughts to go away and have them obey. It was powerful magic. Very powerful magic that was of the mind and not of the elements. In the old books and tales that Kerstas had read her, she could not remember a single moment of hearing about a hero or person who had the ability to alter or command the mind of another. She was still unconvinced that what she just did was real. Any sane person would think the same.

"I do not understand, Choli. I'm confused."

"Ineri," she said, putting her arms around her. "You possess magic. By the way it looks it is powerful. Maybe even more so than my own. Try it again."

Malgrin joined in on the conversation. "It may come In handy, princess." He thought for a moment. "Try and tell me to do something. Put your mind to it."

She thought for a few seconds. An idea came to her. "Give us our weapons."

He froze. His arms immediately shot over to Solef, her little sister, and Choleira's magical bow and quiver. "Here you go."

She took them, handing Choleira her quiver and bow and strapping Solef and her little sister to her waist. "Thank you, Malgrin."

"Holy shit. I could not even fight it. I could not even think against it, either. That is some powerful fucking stuff you have there. Excuse my language, princess. I am just astounded that you possess such a gift."

Choleira held Inerium's hands. "You have to be careful. One wrong phrase could cause a lot of problems."

Inerium understood. She still could not comprehend what she was capable of, but she knew it was great. The ideas of what she could do started swimming around in her mind. She thought of making the wagon driver turn around and take her back home. She thought of telling the guards at the castle in Istimus to kill King Vanitar when they arrived. She thought, as embarrassing as it was, to tell Choleira to hold her hand again. She did none of these things. She would feel terrible if she made Choleira do anything against her will. She would feel like a terrible friend to her and would never expect any form of forgiveness for it.

Just then, Choleira held Inerium's hands in hers. Not out of command by Inerium's thoughts, but because she wanted to. Her hands were warm. They were soft. She liked holding them. "You do not have to worry, Ineri. I do not believe the thoughts will affect me if you truly do not mean them. I know your heart. You do not have to worry about me."

Inerium smiled. "Thank you, Choli. I would not want to do anything to hurt you."

"I know." They embraced each other in a tight hug.

Malgrin smiled, king of like a proud father. He assumed what was happening between them, but he did not say anything. He just sat there smiling waiting for them to finish their moment.

<hr />

The wagon stopped. Malgrin quickly grabbed the bags and put them back over the girls' heads. "I am sorry. When we start going again I will remove them."

The girls nodded. They handed the weapons back to him. He reached for the bag. Inerium quickly grabbed it, shaking her head.

"No. It stays with me."

Malgrin straightened up, almost like a robot that was given a command. "As you command, princess."

"Damn. I am sorry, Malgrin. I did not mean to."

"It is okay, Inerium," he said. "Take it out of there if you do not trust me. I understand fully. But I have to at least have the bag. They will think something is up."

Inerium nodded. She grabbed the sack of Errych berries from the bag and emptied them into her hand. The two girls scarfed them down, as they were starving and had not eaten in Lord knows how long.

Malgrin had himself a few. "These are pretty good. I will have to get some of these some time." He shook his head and went serious again.

Inerium put the bone relic in the now empty bag that held the berries in it. She put it in her pants, tying the strings to the waist of her pants. The ropes on the bottom of the bags were tightened, just enough so that it did not choke the girls, and they pretended that they did not know where they were and who they were with.

A guard stepped up on the wagon where the tarp opened up. "Alright, it is time to get off. We are taking a short break so the horses can drink and you can relieve yourselves if you need to."

They all stepped off, assisted by Malgrin and the other soldier who they assumed was the driver of the wagon. A thought crossed Inerium's mind. Did the driver hear anything they talked about? Did he suspect that Malgrin was helping them? She was not sure. Choleira and Malgrin wondered the same thing.

The sun was bright, even through the sacks on their heads. Malgrin walked them through a grassy field until they stumbled upon a line of bushes. It was quite difficult with their feet tied, but they managed with small steps (which were more like scoots or shuffles.)

"You can relieve yourselves here, girls. When you are done holler at me and I will come get you. Take your time."

"Thank you," said Inerium and Choleira.

The girls struggled to squat to the ground and take their bottoms off, but they managed with a lot of struggling. They finished their business and called out for Malgrin. He walked over and picked them up, averting his eyes so he did not see either of their nether regions. They were children, after all. With how much they had been through even they forgot that they were not even in their teen years yet. Inerium had to grow up very fast in the time between her peaceful life in the castle to being on the other end of the country, having been on the run from those trying to capture and maybe even kill her. She was thankful, however, for all of it. If it were not for meeting

Choleira, she believed that she would not have even made it past the Northern Woods alone.

She suddenly remembered her horse. Snowfire, who was left behind at the stables in Venirit. Was he okay?

"Do you know what happened to Snowfire, Malgrin?" Inerium whispered, as to only let him hear her.

"He is safe, Inerium. I took him when we left Venirit after that guard hit you over the head. I also took care of him when they were not looking. He accidentally took too far of a look in the swamp outside of the city walls and drowned. You did not see him, but Snowfire is one of the two horses drawing the wagon. I could not leave him. He is too magnificent of a horse."

"Thank you so much. He is my favorite horse. I do not know what I would do if something bad would have happened to him."

"They do not know he is yours. They think I just stole him from the stables."

They continued walking towards the wagon. They did not know how far away it was. Inerium or Choleira did not bother counting the steps or judging the yardage of the bush from the wagon. One of the guards stopped them.

"What are you doing, soldier?" Malgrin asked.

"Sir, I— I heard the talking in the back of the wagon. I cannot let you betray our kingdom. King Vanitar ordered me to spy on you. He said something about seeing you pass a note to the princess at the dinner table."

Malgrin stepped in between the girls and the soldier. They could not see what was happening. They only saw his figure in front of them, blocking out most of the sunlight bearing down on their bagged faces.

"Is that so?"

The solider nodded. "Yes it is." Inerium heard him draw his sword from his side. A reflection of the sun danced on his blade as he rose it. "I cannot let you live anymore, captain. Traitor."

He started charging at Malgrin. Malgrin pushed the girls out of the way. Their legs tensed up as they tried to run (forgetting they were tied) and they fell to the ground.

Inerium and Choleira started to inchworm crawl away, using their hands to feel in front of them for anything in the way.

"Help me untie this bag," Choleira said. She sat up next to Inerium.

The sounds of swords clashing rang in the air, followed with exclamations of "TRAITOR" and a few "BASTARDS" to try to throw Malgrin off. They did not. He remained calm, deflecting the blows from the soldier and sending some back at the openings he made. He did not intend to kill the soldier, that much was clear. He was a skilled soldier. He could have easily disarmed the soldier and gutted him, but he did not. He kept the fight going, perhaps missing a good duel from his training years at the camps in Istimus.

Inerium felt around Choleira's body, tracing up her back and to her neck. She found the rope tying the sack over her head. She found the knot. It was loose, and easily undone. She pulled on one of the open-ended parts of the knot and tugged on it. The string came undone and she took the bag off. She quickly turned around and undone the bag on Inerium's head. She and Choleira untied their legs, freeing them. It was like taking off an ankle bracelet that was so tight it cut off the foot's circulation.

They both could see now. The sun was blinding. Once their eyes adjusted, they could see, not just hear, the soldier and Malgrin fighting. Their swords clashed. Sparks flew in the air like flecks of the sun bouncing off the reflection in the blades. Dirt was flying through the air as their boots kicked up holes in the ground.

"You are getting rusty, captain," said the soldier.

"I will let you think that. My skills are just as sharp as ever. You still have much to learn."

Malgrin blocked an attack, parrying the soldier's sword to the left. Malgrin used this opening to thrust his sword forward, aiming it down and catching the tip of the blade under the cross guard of the soldier's sword. He twisted the blade and pulled his sword back. The soldier's sword flew out of his hand and clanged to the ground. Malgrin pointed his sword at the soldier, touching the tip to his throat.

"Do not underestimate me, soldier. I have my reasons for what I am doing. Vanitar is a paranoid asshole and he has already caused enough chaos in these lands."

"You are still a traitor, Malgrin."

Malgrin laughed. "I am only a traitor to a king who is trying to claim this whole country as his own by starting a war he knows he can win. That is who I am betraying. I am as loyal as ever to my kingdom. Not my king." He picked up the soldier's sword and handed it back to him. He took it from Malgrin.

"You will rot in Hell, Malgrin," said the soldier. He cried out a battle cry, which was not that impressive due to the cracking his voice did during it, and ran at Malgrin with his sword raised in the sky. "Die, traitor!"

Malgrin quickly spun around, raising his sword up and deflecting the attack as simply as he did the last ones. He kicked the soldier in the stomach and hit him over the head with the butt of his sword. The soldier dropped his to the ground once again. "I will not kill you. As much as I should, I will not. You are fighting a losing battle. You lost the moment you sided with Vanitar over your captain."

"I sided with my king," he said, grunting and clutching his stomach. I am a soldier."

Malgrin shook his head. "Your king is a fool. As is mine. As they may be the same, I only see Kerstas as a king. That boy has spirit and more willpower than any king before him has. His attention may be diverted for now, but his heart is to his kingdom and its people. Not to himself and his power."

"He is just a kid," said the soldier. "And King Vanitar will see his death by his own hands. And he fully intends to use *her* to get that wish." He glanced at Inerium.

As his eyes flashed to Inerium, he lunged at her. She tried to run, but in the small moment that passed he kicked Choleira to the ground and grabbed Inerium. He held a small knife to her throat.

"I will kill her myself and hang her body from my wagon if that is what will make my king happy! Do not test me!" His voice had suddenly changed. It was more sinister now, like a crazed madman spouting about his gods and about how they gave him visions and powers. "Stand down, Malgrin! Surrender!"

Malgrin nodded. He was too far to knock the blade out of his hand. Inerium would be cut, or worse, if he tried to help. Choleira was on the ground staring up at Inerium. "Don't try anything, Elf! I will cut your ears off and sell them for pocket-loads of gold!" The soldier was insane. He had snapped.

Choleira froze. She could not do anything. Inerium was in danger. She wanted to let loose and burn the soldier alive. She wanted to freeze him in place, but by the time she would utter the words, he would have cut her throat. She did not know what to do.

"Now, I am taking her to Vanitar. Neither of you will stop me or she will die."

He walked Inerium slowly to the wagon, keeping his eyes on Choleira and Malgrin. Inerium thought hard in her head. Very hard about what she wanted to happen.

Inerium then spoke. "Take that hand off." The tone she had was dark. Not evil, but hate-filled.

The soldier let go of Inerium. He held up his knife-wielding hand and started slicing away at his free hand's wrist. Blood poured on the ground and the soldier started crying out in pain. As much as he tried to pull away, the hand kept cutting and cutting. Inerium ran back to Choleira and held her. The soldier let out a loud cry of pain as he tried to saw through the bone with the blade. It would not go through.

"Must—take—it—off," he grunted, cutting completely around his wrist down to the bone. He fell to the ground in agony and leaned against the wagon. He started hitting the wheel with his wrist, crying out in pain at every strike. After about half a minute of constant hitting and agonized screams, the bone snapped and his hand fell to the ground. The soldier curled up on the ground with tears streaming down his face. He was holding his nub of an arm with the hand that took it of. "Why did I do that? Why did I do that?" he asked repeatedly. The shock had kicked into him and he was trying to process what had happened.

"I am sorry," said Inerium. It just slipped out. I do not know what came over me."

Choleira hugged her. "It is okay, Ineri. You are safe. That is all that matters to me." She squeezed her tighter and rested her cheek against Inerium's.

They walked over to Malgrin, who was in shock of what he just saw. "Inerium, what did you do?"

"I did not mean to. I was panicking and it just slipped out. I told him to take his hand off and he did. I am sorry." She tried to walk over to the soldier to apologize to him, as much as part of her did not want to because he just tried to take her away or even kill her.

"Stay away from me, demon! Witch! You and your dark magic can burn in Hell with me when I go!" He continued to cry and rock with his hand like it was a baby.

"I am sorry. It just slipped out.' She turned around to Choleira. "Can you heal him?"

A confused and concerned look came across her face. "Why? He tried to kill you, Ineri. Let him suffer for it. He tried to hurt you..."

"And I hurt him. He is just a boy. He will suffer enough when Vanitar finds out he does not have me."

Choleira refused the idea for a moment, but she gave in. Only because it was Inerium's request. She did not want to fight with her over it.

She walked over to the soldier and held out her hand. "Hee-alay," she said, pulling out her water pouch and opening the cap.

The water enveloped her hand and she clasped her hand over his wound. He gritted his teeth in pain. The water glowed a little and the bleeding stopped. The soldier used the cloth on his now-torn sleeve so cover up the nub.

"I am still not forgiving you, witch!" he called out.

"I do not expect you to. I am only not allowing you to die." Inerium took a deep breath and closed her eyes, concentrating on her words. "Walk to your king. Tell him you failed to bring us to him and forget about my magical abilities. Your hand has always been gone. You were born without one."

The soldier nodded. He stood up and turned towards the

East. He started walking. No head turning, no other thoughts in his mind besides arriving at Vanitar's doorstep with his news. He would not make it. His body would soon give out from the pain and he would be eaten by wolves at the border of the Scorched Lands of Vestyr, just a few miles away from Istimus' castle. Inerium nor Choleira nor Malgrin knew of his future demise, but they soon forgot about him.

Inerium and Choleira walked back over to Malgrin. "What do we do now?" Inerium asked.

Malgrin looked around. "You are a terrifying young lady, princess. You scare me a bit."

Inerium looked over at him. "I do not mean to be. I am sorry."

"It is okay," Choleira said, hugging Inerium tightly. "I love you, scary or not."

Inerium froze up. Choleira realized what she said. "I—um—I." She could not speak. Her face was red. Errych berry red.

"Are you okay?" Inerium asked.

"You are red as those berries we ate, Choleira," said Malgrin. "Damn."

She hid her face in her sleeves. Inerium pulled her hands away. "It is okay, I promise, Choli. I do too."

They returned to the wagon. Inerium saw Snowfire, hooked up to the left of a black horse connected to the wagon.

"Hey, boy, you ready to go?" Inerium asked, petting Snowfire." He excitedly stamped his hooves on the ground. The other horse stood there mindlessly.

"I will take that as a yes," said Choleira.

They all hopped on the wagon. They took the tarp off the top of the wagon so they could see where they were going. They put the tarp in the aisle between the benches of the wagon, making a large flat surface they could lay on during the travel. Malgrin took the reins. They placed their belongings under a flap in the tarp to keep hidden. The eye was pushing into Inerium's side.

"Oh yeah, I forgot about this." She pulled it out of her pants, untied the sack, and placed it into her side bag, hiding it again under the flap in the tarp.

The sun was starting to go down, falling behind their horizon on their left.

"Girls, get some sleep," Malgrin said. "We will be taking a long trip. We will head to one of the villages more to the West. I believe it is called Danur. It is a small village that lies near the border of Venirit and Istimus, right near the Scorched Lands."

"Okay. We will be back here," Choleira said.

Malgrin let out a chuckle. "I would hope so. Goodnight and sweet dreams to the both of you."

The girls closed their eyes, hugged up to one another like best friends at a sleepover and fell asleep.

CHAPTER 17

Kerstas was woken up by Moredir. He had fallen asleep in one of the cots placed outside in the camping grounds for the soldiers. The sun was just going over the edge of the horizon, leaving the sky a sea full of stars.

A fire was crackling some ways away from him where a few of the men were cooking some small animals they caught when night fell. One of them managed to even kill a deer by sneaking up on it and shooting it in the heart with an arrow. That soldier had gutted the deer and sectioned its meat, holding the various pieces on sticks over the flame to cook it through.

Kerstas smelled the cooking meat and his stomach had started to growl.

"Here have one," said Moredir. It's damn good. Ordys over there was the one who killed the thing."

Kerstas looked over at Ordys, who was a tall and slender soldier who had black hair that curled down to his ears. A large bow and a quiver of nearly a dozen black-feathered arrows sat by him. He waved at Kerstas. "Enjoy!" he called out, chomping on another hunk of meat on a stick. He burned his mouth and started fan-waving his hand into his mouth to cool it down. The other men around him laughed when he did this.

Kerstas took the meat from Moredir. It was about the size

of his hand with some good char bordering its shape. The cut was thick. The steam flew up Kerstas' nose and he inhaled it deeply. He took a bite out of it and it tore without any pulling force. His teeth sank straight through like he bit into a cake.

"This is really good," he said.

"Glad you like it!" Ordys hollered, waving a piece of raw meat in the air, which looked very phallic. He shoved a stick through it and laid it overtop the flame with a the others.

"When you are finished with that, meet me at the entrance to the village," said Moredir. He walked away towards the village.

Kerstas was handed a cup of some type of liquid. "Here," said the soldier, strings of meat dangling off his long black beard. His eyes were nearly covered by the hair on his head laying over them.

"What is it?"

"It is man's drink. Drink up. You are a young king, after all. You will have to get used to it eventually."

Kerstas took a sip from the cup. It was bitter and made his face scrunch up like a child eating a sour piece of hard candy. When he swallowed it the liquid burned his throat and stomach. He coughed. He tried another sip. A little flavor came through. A flavor of berries and sweetness, accompanied by the burning and bitterness. He started to put the cup up to his lips, ready to down it all, but another soldier grabbed the cup from him.

"Not yet, Kerstas. You have a meeting to attend. You cannot show up drunk off your ass. They definitely would not believe a word you say if you did. When you come back, and you convince them that it was Istimus' kingdom and clear our name, you can have this."

Kerstas smiled. "You have got a deal. Save that cup for

me." He finished his food and stood up. He headed towards the village, following the same path Moredir took.

———◆———

"There you are," Moredir said. "I was beginning to worry the men might have tried to get you to drink with them beforehand."

"One tried, but the rest convinced him to let me wait until we returned with good news."

Moredir nodded. "Well, if we manage to convince them, I will drink with you, Kerstas." He smirked. They walked through the village down the center path.

Once they reached the center of the circle, they turned right and headed up the set of stairs leading up to Town Hall, which was now the only building whose windows were illuminated by the light of candles and lamps inside.

Moredir opened the doors and the two walked in. There was a circle of podiums around the center of the room. A singular podium stood in the center. The two elders stood at the front two podiums. As for the other five, there were middle-aged members of the village standing behind them, glaring at Moredir and Kerstas. They reached the center podium and looked around the room, sitting in awkward silence waiting for the first one to speak.

Finally, the elder with the cane spoke after tapping his cane three times on the wooden floor. "Let us begin. State your names."

"Moredir, captain of Meridine's army."

Kerstas cleared his throat. "Kerstas of house Requilit. Prince and heir to the throne of Requilit."

"You are technically a king now, are you not?" Asked a

woman two podiums to the left of the elder wearing glasses. She was a larger woman with matted greying hair, which was more brown than grey but did not give her any benefits to her looks. She was wrinkling and her hands were fat as they rested on the sides of the podium, most likely trying to keep herself balanced. In terms of relativity, she would be at would have been at Kerstas and Moredir's ten o'clock.

Kerstas looked at her. "Technically no. I was almost coronated, but Istimus' armies interrupted it. As my father was placing the crown on my head the soldiers attacked, killing my parents in front of me."

A man at Kerstas' three o'clock spoke up. He appeared younger than the previous woman. His beard was neat and kept well. His hair was combed over to the right and he wore a nice-looking outfit, one not obtained from the village. "How can you be so sure that it was Istimus' armies?" he asked. "Were they not wearing red?" A few of the members of the other podiums whispered a few things to one another.

"Order!" hollered out the elder with the cane, tapping it multiple times on the floor. The room went silent.

Kerstas turned to him. The man's face was glowing with confidence that he had already won by saying that. He was wrong. "How do you know what they were wearing?" The other members of the podium turned to him, curious as well to hear his answer.

"I—I heard the rumors. Vanitar told me the ones that killed your parents were wearing red."

Kerstas shook his head. Moredir knew why as well. After all, he was present at the ceremony and knew what he saw. "Actually, Vanitar is a liar."

The ones behind the podiums all let out a synchronized

gasp. "How dare you speak that way about our king!" the snobby blonde-haired man shouted.

Moredir spoke up. "He is right. I was at his coronation, and by my soul I am telling this as the truth. Vanitar was not present. Everyone noticed. He even told thee other kings that he had matters to attend to elsewhere, saying he was too preoccupied to attend the crowning of another kingdom's king."

"Where did the rumor of the attacking soldiers wearing red come from, then? Tell us that," said the large woman, slinging spit all over the podium in front of her, choking on a little of it.

"I recall the events in my head," said Kerstas. "They were wearing their yellow-plated armors, which so happened to have splotches of red paint on parts of it. Some of their helmets and armor pieces were accented red, unlike Meredine's who were mostly red with little opposing accents on them."

"You saw my men. They were wearing red. All red, not little red. We wear our country's given color proud all over us, so that everyone knows how much we care for our country."

A few of the members on the right side started whispering to each other, nodding between statements.

The elders looked at each other, and then to the rest of the ones standing behind the podiums. "Bring her. Let her see if they are telling the truth." The members of the council got wide-eyed, whispering even faster between one another.

"She is mad. You cannot entrust her with this," the well-dressed man said.

"She can see," said the glasses-wearing elder. "And she will know what truly happened." He looked at the farthest member of the council to his left. "Get her."

Nearly twenty minutes to half an hour passed, Kerstas had no idea how long it truly was. Moredir had no idea either. He started to doze off, sitting on the floor and holding his head between his knees to prop it up so his neck would not cramp. Kerstas had actually dozed off, now sitting in a chair turned backwards with his head resting on its back frame.

The doors swung open, letting a chilling air in. It woke up Kerstas and Moredir. The council members who were not already standing in their places walked over and took them.

An old woman walked through the doorway; her hand being held in balance support by the council member that was sent to fetch her. She was wearing a large cloak with a hood over her face, which was covered by her ghost-white hair falling out of the hood. All that was visible through the shadow of the hood was a singular black-irised eye above a long nose with little white hairs growing out of the nostrils. She was barefoot, exposing her wrinkly feet with extra long, talon-like toenails that had not been cut in who knows how long. By Kerstas and Moredir's surprise, she did not stink. She smelled like various herbs and some spices.

"Who is this?" Kerstas asked.

"This is Majosei. She is not from here, but she happened to be visiting our village to pick up some spices for her practices back at her cabin near Fairy's Woods between Requilit and Meredine."

Majosei approached the center of the room. She held onto Kerstas and Moredir's podium to keep herself upright. "So," she said in a feeble voice, "King Kerstas and Meredine's captain Moredir trying to prove Istimus is responsible for the death of Queen Eleana and King Kentrin." Her one visible eye reflected Kerstas and Moredir's reflections. It was almost like looking into a black pool of still water.

"You know us?" Kerstas asked.

She smiled and cackled a little. "I do. And you, boy most of all. Your life is one worth knowing for someone like me. A seer. A witch, if that term would be more befitting. Your mother came to me many years ago asking for answers. I told her about her ancestry and the importance it held. But that is not the matter in question, now is it?" She turned her head to the elders of the council. "What do you need of me?"

"These two claim that the ones responsible for the deaths of the king and queen of Requilit, along with the kidnapping of Kerstas, was done by the armies of Istimus. We say it is Meridine because they had red on. They have also been attacking the nearby villages as well as ours for a while, more so after the murder of the king and queen." The elder with the glasses coughed after speaking. Maybe because of age. Maybe he inhaled some dust.

"Were you there?" Majosei said, licking her dry lips. Her one showing eye reflected the elder with the glasses.

"No."

"Can you prove that it was Meridine's army?"

"They wore red."

"That is not what I asked," snapped Majosei.

"He answered your question," said the blonde-haired man, butting in.

Majosei twisted her neck to look at the blonde man. The few teeth she had reflected the flames dancing from the candles in small flashes, like a child sees their parents when playing peek-a-boo.

"Did he?" She looked at one of the women next to the elder

with the cane. "If I looked at your blue dress and said you were from Istimus, would I be correct?"

The woman shook her head. She was younger than the other members. Not too much younger, but enough to stand out among the others. Majosei looked around at the other members of the council. They still did not seem convinced.

Majosei sighed, her breath whistling as it came out. "Always have to do it the difficult way."

She reached into her cloak and laid a few objects on the podium in front of her. Kerstas and Moredir stepped out of the way. She laid down a small stone pot the size of her hand. Beside it she placed a dried circular object that was a tan-white color that had a small, shrivveled cord-like thing trailing from it. A darker circular spot laid on the opposite side of it, faded into the rest of the object's color. Kerstas thought it looked a little like an eyeball, which it was. Who or what it belonged to did not concern Kerstas; he was just disturbed that it was there. A few wilted purple flowers were placed next to the eyeball.

Majosei placed the eyeball and flowers in the pot. She pulled out a pestle made of the same stone as the pot and ground up the materials. The eyeball squished and juiced as she circled the pot. The flowers mixed in with the paste that used to be an eyeball, creating a disgusting mess in the pot.

"What are you doing?" Kerstas asked.

"They wish to know the truth. They refuse to listen so they will see instead."

She continued mixing the eye and flowers. She reached into her cloak and pulled out a small jar of a grey powder, along with another jar of a dark liquid. She poured a small splash of the liquid in and a few dashes of the powder, putting the jars back in her cloak.

"Layet tayhemay sayee fayour thaira sayelvysc," she said,

waving her hands over the pot. The contents inside started to boil and steam. "Move the podium," she said to Kerstas and Moredir. She picked up the pot, which to everyone's surprise was not hot despite the boiling contents and threw it on the ground. "Look. See for yourselves."

The contents of the pot had turned into a large pool of thick black liquid that took up the entire center of the room. The council members looked down into the pool, waiting for something to happen.

"Rayveallay," she said.

The liquid bubbled and rippled. The liquid started to assume other colors and forms until an entire scene was happening inside of it, like watching a movie on the floor. There were soldiers wearing yellow-plated armor with red paint on them standing next to a large wall.

"Do you think anyone will find out?" asked one of the soldiers. He had a lot redder paint on his helmet compared to the rest of his armor pieces.

"They shouldn't," said the one beside him. His chest plate and boots had a lot of red paint on them. "We have been raiding our own villages for weeks at this point. It should be a piece of cake to blame all this on Meredine. King Vanitar wants them all dead."

"Even the boy?" the one with the red helmet asked.

"No. The king has other plans for him. Something about a prophecy he heard about. He was really shaken up by it."

"Do you know what it was about?"

The soldier with the red chest plate shook his head. "No idea. But if it was bad enough to make him to go to *this* level, I do not believe I want to know."

"Agreed," said a third soldier who was just listening in. He had a face guard on, which was painted red, along with a red pair of trousers matching a red shirt under his armor (which was still its yellow color.) "I thought I heard King Vanitar mention something about the kingdoms falling and being ruled by the kid, but he is just a boy. Sixteen right? How could he take over this whole country at his age?"

The one with the red chest plate and boots shook his head. "I do not know. But it is the king's orders. As much as I do not agree with this, we have to."

They looked inside the window above their heads. Kentrin was about to place the crown on Kerstas' head.

"Now," said the soldier with the face guard.

The three soldiers ran around the building to the front to meet up with the others waiting outside with their weapons drawn. There were other soldiers slaughtering each other down the large steps of the castle. Blue-armored corpses were scattered all over the streets. The soldiers burst the doors open and started killing all the people inside.

The pool on the floor of the town hall started to fade away. Right before it fully faded, Kerstas saw his parents murdered once again before his eyes, watching himself watch them collapse to the floor.

The images faded away and the liquid on the floor started turning into mist, dissipating into nothing. The council members whispered to one another. They other council members turned to the elders and waited for the response.

The elder on the right tapped his cane on the ground. "Thank you, Majosei. This—clears up some." The elder's face looked almost like a kid's when they were told they did not get the toy they wanted for Christmas. "You may go."

Majosei turned around and placed her hand on Kerstas' shoulder. "I know you are in there, Daerex," she said. "You may not be consciously present, but your power is in there no doubt." She smiled and walked away. The doors shut behind her. Kerstas walked her out the door, his mind now flooding with questions that will never be answered.

"We of the council would like to apologize for any ill manners towards you or your men." He sighed. "In our place you would have understood."

Kerstas stepped forward, centering himself. "I believe that you knowing the truth is all that matters. I think Moredir would agree."

Moredir nodded. "Thank you. Hopefully the word can spread of Istimus' plotting against the kingdom of Requilit, as well as all of Pleniris."

"We will send word out when the sun rises. Every village from here to Civit will know of King Vanitar's schemes."

"Thank you." Moredir and Kerstas did a head-bow motion and turned to leave the town hall to return to the camp.

"Oh, and Kerstas," said the glasses-wearing elder.

Kerstas turned back towards him. The elder walked from behind his podium and stood in front of Kerstas. "It is good to see you. I was praying that you were alive."

Kerstas forced a smile, nodded again, and left. A small queasy feeling turned his stomach. That word. *Praying.* It reminded him of how he had prayed every day for help from what the priests did to him but never received salvation. He knew it was not the prayers that saved him that day. It was the prophecy that Vanitar heard that saved him. It was Malgrin, Barnabin, and Geremi that saved him. They protected him even against orders, and *that* is what saved him. Without them he would have most likely died during the attack, or even during one of the nights when he was with Malgrin's party.

They returned to the camp. The men were all asleep, besides one that stood watch by the dying fire. He kept feeding the flame small twigs and leaves nearby.

"Welcome back," he said, poking the embers with a branch. "How did it go?"

"Very well." Moredir sat down on the ground next to him, warming his hands up. Kerstas sat next to him. "They know the truth that Istimus is responsible for this mess."

"How? Did they just believe you?"

Kerstas shook his head. "Not at first, but they brought in this old witch name Majosei who showed them everything that happened that day. Including the murder of—mom and dad."

Moredir patted him on the back. Not hard, but in a comforting way. "Do not think about it, kid. It will only bring you down further. I am sorry." He looked at the solider. It was the one with the large axe who sat next to him earlier in the day. "They believe us now. When the first light starts to show, they will send out couriers to all the villages from here to Civit, as we were told."

"Good. The whole land will know soon that Istimus is the true enemy."

Suddenly, the sound of galloping approached from the East. "Sir, sir!" It was a soldier in a red shirt and a pair of black pants on. A lantern was lit on the left side of the horse, dangling from the brown saddlebag. The horse was grey with a few black spots on him. He was a large horse, well taken care of that was for sure. He hopped off the horse.

"What is it, Deivan?" Moredir asked.

"I rode out with Samuil as you asked, to scout out for any camps. We were ambushed on the road leading to Danur. Both Istimus' and Venirit's armies were camping around there.

Hundreds, if not thousands, of soldiers are all armed and ready. They mean war, sir. I barely made it back with my own life."

"Good work, Deivan." He paused, like he wanted to ask something else. "Go get some food," said Moredir. Deivan ran off to a smaller group of soldiers who had woken up and were cooking some small catches they made during their travel.

The man with the axe looked over at Moredir and Kerstas. "It does not add up," he said.

"What does not add up?" Kerstas asked.

"Only two of them left. One came back. If there were two kingdoms camping together, and they ambushed those two men, they should both be captured. If not dead."

"I see what you mean," said Moredir. He looked over at Deivan. He seemed a uneasy. He was holding a piece of cooked meat in his hand, but he was not eating a bite of it. His cup sat beside his foot untouched.

"You do not think that he would betray us, do you?" Kerstas asked.

"I do not wish to believe it, but I suspect it," said Moredir. "Why would he be back without even a scratch from an ambush orchestrated by two kingdoms?"

The axe-wielding soldier cut in. "He said ambush. How would they have been ambushed if they had no idea he was coming?"

"It does not make sense. Hey, Deivan, get over here!" Moredir motioned Deivan to come over.

Deivan walked over slowly. "What is it?" He stood next to Kerstas, rocking back and forth on his feet.

"What happened to him? To Samuil."

"We were riding up around the villages near Venirit. We found the camps of Venirit and Istimus' armies and when we tried to get closer, we were spotted. I ran off but they got him. I rode straight here after that."

"You said you got ambushed. That they caught you by surprise," said Kerstas. "If I remember correctly."

Deivan started to sweat a little. He started rocking a bit more, fidgeting with his hands and picking at his nails. "Yeah. Yeah, that is correct."

"Then how could they have ambushed you if you were sneaking up on them? Surely you all were quiet enough. That a bunch of soldiers in an *open field* could have gotten the jump on you."

Deivan started fidgeting faster. He was dripping in sweat and his breath started to accelerate. His voice became shakier. "They—I—."

The axe-wielding soldier jumped in. "They what? They what, huh?"

Deivan started to back away from them. Moredir stretched his foot out and tripped him. He fell to the ground. He crawled on the ground barely illuminated by the lights of the campfire and the moon above. He reached into his pants, pulling out a small horn. He took a great breath in and released it full force into the mouthpiece of the horn. A loud shrieking noise bellowed from the tiny horn, sounding similar to the wind blowing through the Shrieking Peaks. The sounds echoed across the land, bouncing off of the great mountain, almost harmonizing with the symphony of shrieks that came from its peaks.

Moredir ran over and tackled the soldier, pinning him to the ground. He threw the horn from his hand and crushed it with his foot. The horn made a crunch noise under his boot, and it broke into pieces. The echoes stopped.

"What the fuck are you doing, soldier?" Moredir shouted.

He grabbed Deivan by the collar of his shirt and shook him, like a parent waking their child.

Deivan smiled. "It is too late." He started laughing.

Kerstas looked around. It was too dark to see anything. The light from the fire caused the darkness to be obscured, making it impossible to see anything in the shadows.

The sound of whistling started coming from the distance, from the northeast. Kerstas remembered that sound. The same one from when he was with Malgrin's group. "Get down," he said, pushing the soldier with the axe over onto the ground.

"What did you do that for?" he asked.

Suddenly, just as he asked the question, arrows sailed through the air, impaling many of the soldiers huddled around the smaller fires in the camp. Moredir ran back to Kerstas and the soldier with the axe.

"The bastard betrayed us! He brought them here!"

"I just knew something was off," said the axe-wielding soldier.

"What do we do?" Kerstas asked.

Moredir shook his head. He looked at the soldier with the axe. "Are there any places to hide nearby, Selmic?"

So that is his name

"Yeah," Selmic said. The village. You know, the one you all came from not too long ago."

"Okay, smart ass, thanks," Moredir said.

"No, there should be a place we can hide there. Every village has at least one paranoid old timer who has a basement full of supplies they stashed away, ready for the end of times to come jumping around the corner."

"Do you know which house?" Kerstas asked.

Selmic shook his head. "Not exactly, but it is usually one that is older than the rest."

"I think I saw one earlier. It was near the center of town. I saw it on the way through," Moredir said, pointing roughly towards the inner circle of the village.

"Let's go, then. Quickly."

They ran towards the village, the sounds of metal clashing and people screaming filled the air behind them.

As they passed a bunch of bushes huddled together, a bunch of soldiers jumped out, knocking Selmic to the ground. He fell and they drove their swords into his neck and chest.

Moredir spun around. "Selmic!"

He drew his sword and impaled one of the four soldiers that jumped out of the bushes with it. Another soldier bashed his shield against Moredir's head, making him dizzy. Kerstas tried to run in and help, but the other two soldiers grabbed him and tied his hands behind his back with a rope. They kicked him to the ground and did the same to his feet, this rope with a long end for them to hold on to.

They pulled on the string and dragged him across the grass. He watched Moredir try to fight off the two soldiers, but failed. The shield-wielding soldier hit Moredir against the head once more, and while he was trying to reorientate himself again, the other soldier drove his sword into his stomach. Moredir coughed up a small but of blood, clutching the sword.

The soldier drove it deeper and twisted it around. Moredir groaned in pain and coughed up more blood. The soldier pulled his sword out and cleaned the blood off of it using his oversized shirt. He and the soldier with the shield walked away towards the other soldiers who were dragging Kerstas away, making sure no one could cut him free.

Kerstas reached around to try to grab at any roots or jarring objects lodged in the ground, but anything his hands clung to either slipped away or came loose with the dirt around it.

He was dragged by a few small trees, no taller than ten feet or so. He grabbed onto the trunk of it, which his hand wrapped fully around. He pulled himself towards the tree, turning his grip around the trunk to both of his arms wrapped completely around it, holding his chest to the wood.

"Quit that," one of the soldiers said, tugging on his legs. It did not work. Kerstas' hold on the tree grew tighter.

Another soldier came and tried to pull his arms apart. "Stop struggling, boy, it will be a whole lot easier for all of us."

The soldier freed one arm. The other soldier tugged on his legs again and Kerstas collapsed to the ground. His head hit a small rock on the ground. It started bleeding a little from the impact on the sharp edge. Kerstas' vision was a little blurry. He tried to grab for the tree again, but it was too far now. He was being dragged once again by the soldier holding the rope that tied his ankles together. The other soldiers watching him were standing closer now, almost stepping on his hands while they walked.

One of them stepped on his hair and ripped out a few strands. "That hurt, damnit," Kerstas said, hitting the leg of the soldier who stepped on his hair.

The same soldier kicked Kerstas in the side of the head. His vision started to blur and then blacken.

"That should shut him up for a while."

CHAPTER 18

Inerium woke up from her nap she had. Part of the gold branches and vines on her clothes had gotten snagged and ripped off. She had forgotten that she was wearing the nice clothes that were laid out for her so many days ago back in Olmenor, when she had first met Choleira. She was still wearing her same outfit as the day she met her. Her beautiful fiery dress that had stayed so clean despite of their adventures they had been on. She assumed it was most likely her magic keeping her clothes clean and in tact. She stared at the linings of the dress for a little bit, admiring how it looked like she was wearing a flame on her flawless skin.

Choleira was curled up beside her, quiet and asleep. Her arm was stretched out under Inerium's neck, wrapping around her shoulder. She looked so peaceful while asleep. Her hair looked beautiful in the light of the moon, which was starting to disappear. Daylight was coming along shortly. The village that they were headed to was also coming closer as well. Perhaps another half hour or so would finish the trip. She was not sure, and she did not care. At the moment the only thing on her mind was looking at Choleira peacefully slumbering cuddled up to her. She did not want to move any of her body in fear of disturbing her sleep.

The carriage ran over a bump in the road, and it shook a little. Choleira groaned and opened her eyes. She turned her head and looked at Inerium. She smiled.

"Hey," Inerium said.

"Hey, where are we?"

Inerium shrugged her shoulders. "I am not sure. I have not been paying much attention to anything else."

"What had your attention?" Her eyes reflected the stars. The red and blue hues in them beautifully reflected the starts in a multi-colored void in her eyes.

Inerium could hardly get any words out because she was too drawn in to Choleira's eyes. "I—You—."

She smiled and let out a little giggle. She bunched her hair together with her free hand and laid it on her shoulder. "Well, I can't hold onto it forever, can i?"

"Well—." What she wanted to say was *I would not mind if you did. Please do.* But she did not. She was far too embarrassed to say it. Choleira knew what Inerium wanted to say, but she played along like she did not. She enjoyed seeing Inerium flustered and stammering.

"Yes?" She let out a little giggle again, this time smirking. Her teeth reflected the moonlight. The open-mouthed smile completely took Inerium by surprise. She knew it would.

"Y—You." She hid her face.

Choleira moved herself closer to Inerium, hugging tighter around her with the arm wrapped around her shoulder. "You know I already knew that." She scrunched her nose. She raised her hand and started to fiddle with the vial necklace hiding under her dress. She did it a lot, Inerium had not noticed. Whether Inerium would notice or not, Choleira would sit and stare at the vial holding Inerium's tears in it, with the slightest smile on her face that could be hidden easily if Inerium were to glance at her. Inerium's necklace hung around her neck as well. Thoughts came across her mind a few times of the possibility of holding Choleira's tears inside it, creating the bond she had mentioned. A soul bond created by the purest, most raw, form of emotional magic.

Inerium's face grew red. It could not be seen too well in the dark of the night, but she could feel it burning. "I keep forgetting that you do." She hid her face.

Choleira pulled her hands away from her face with her free hand, putting one of them in her hand under Inerium's neck. She held that hand while holding the other with her other hand.

"Don't hide your face, Ineri. I am awake now, so I cannot dream about it."

Inerium smiled. "Well, here it is, then, Choli."

"Thank you," Choleira said.

"We are almost there," said Malgrin from the driver's seat of the carriage. "Are you two awake?"

"Yeah, we are," Inerium said. She reached in her bag, feeling for the relic.

There it was. She pulled it out. The bone was cold in her hand. The relic laid in her hand, almost staring up at her. It was just a simple thing but held such a weight to it. Not a weight in terms of mass, but in terms of the power, the burden, it held. A pit filled Inerium's stomach as she stared at the eye of Inanis longer. She put it back in her band.

Choleira grabbed her hand once more and squeezed it. "Do not think about it. That thing is evil, you know that. Do not let it corrupt you, Ineri."

"It will not, Choli. I promise. I have other things keeping my mind straight. My brother and you."

"Thank you."

The two girls laid together and stared into each other's eyes for a few minutes. No words were exchanged, but there did not need to be. They laid together in silence staring into one another's souls and lost themselves in their thoughts and imaginations.

———◦◦———

The carriage suddenly stopped. "What is that?" Malgrin asked.

The girls sat up and looked where Malgrin was looking. There was an army, a large one in fact, traveling down the main road through the ashen lands, which was roughly a half mile or so from their position. They had recently turned off the main road to the side road that headed West to Danur, which was their destination. They were about a quarter to maybe halfway down the side road to Danur.

The sun was starting to rise over the horizon. The grass was starting to turn from its dark green to its light, beautiful green it gives off when the sun shines on it. The small drops on the grass blades reflected the morning light as the sun rose.

"It looks like an army," said Inerium. "But why?"

"They are actually going through with it."

"What do you mean?" Choleira asked. "Who?"

"Venirit and Istimus appears to have teamed up. Their armies are traveling to go to war with Meredine's army. Do you see the green and yellow banners?" He pointed to the army, whose banners of green and yellow could be seen in the slowly increasing sunlight.

"Yes." Choleira said. "She turned her gaze to the right a little. "And who are they?" She pointed to the distance, almost right around the bottom of the great mountain.

Another army was marching down the main southern road, holding banners colored red. There were a great many of them, too.

"Oh no," Malgrin said. "That would me Meredine's armies."

"Why do you say oh no?" Inerium asked.

"Meredine's army is strong. Their soldiers are built like oxen. One of their soldiers is equal physically to two if not three of ours. They train their soldiers from very young ages, almost breeding them for war."

"Oh," Choleira said. "But they are not against us, are they?"

"Against me, Inerium. My soldiers. I am from Istimus. This war is Meredine against both Istimus and Venirit. Requilit's army of course is out of the picture, so I would imagine another war would be soon to follow to see who gains control."

"But Kerstas is still alive. *He* is the king of Requilit. *He* controls Requilit's territory," said Inerium.

"I believe they intend to change that fact," Malgrin said. "If they know he is alive, I have no doubts that they are going to try to execute him as a statement to not fuck with them. If Istimus were to gain control of Requilit's territory, they could easily have the advantage by taking out Venirit, controlling three quarters of the whole country. All that would be left is Meredine. By allying with Venirit for this war, they have made the odds two to one against Meredine. If they could take them out now, they could simply take Meredine and Requilit's territories just like that. Then nothing could stop them."

"I will not let that happen," Inerium said. She shook her head. "My brother will not die. He will live. Whatever prophecy is about him will come true, and he will rule over this country. It will all happen. The other lands will fall and be under his banner. The one true king of Pleniris, Kerstas the Sanguavis."

Choleira smiled. Her eyes had a slight look of fear behind them, though. She appeared happy for the words Inerium said, but they almost terrified her at the same time.

"We have to save him."

"We do not even know where he is, Inerium," said Malgrin. "Even if we did, how could we?"

"Take the reigns." Inerium said. Her voice felt heavy, like each word was a weight. "Take us to your camp." Inerium could not explain why she was telling him to do this, but that sinking feeling was sitting in her stomach. That feeling she got, like when one has a hunch about something they just *know* to be true.

Malgrin did as he was commanded without a word. He nodded his head and readied the reigns. Choleira and Inerium got comfortable again and they rode off towards the marching camps of Istimus and Venirit.

CHAPTER 19

Kerstas' head was throbbing. His hands and legs were tied together as he laid over the saddle of a horse. He stared at the ground passing under him as the horse clopped and trotted.

The soldier in front of him held onto the reigns of the dark brown horse with leather gloves. His yellow cape blew in the wind and hit Kerstas in the face a few times. Kerstas tried to shake the cape off his face.

"Hey, quit that squirming," said the soldier riding the horse.

"Your cape keeps getting in my face," Kerstas said, shaking it away once again.

"Stay still. Or you are walking behind me. Ill make sure you step in every pile of horse shit on your way, too, if I feel like it."

Kerstas stayed still. He let the soldier's cape slap against his face without a word said, as much as he so wished to rip the cape off his back and suffocate him with it.

"Where are we going?" Kerstas asked.

The soldier turned his head slightly. He grunted and did not say a word. The wind blew the soldier's cape out of Kerstas face for a moment, long enough to see them approaching a large camp settled in the great valley of ash and dirt, which was known as the Scorched Lands of Vestyr.

The horse stopped near the edge of the camp, where other horses were feeding and drinking. Kerstas was being led to the large tent in the center of the camp, decorated with both yellow and green banners, belonging to the two kingdoms residing on the eastern half of Pleniris. They really had allied together against Meredine. He walked through the flaps of the tent's entrance to see a large table with the map of Pleniris on it.

There were red-painted wooden figures placed on the southern road of the map, just past the town of Neuten. The yellow and green figures were bunched up together in the center of the scorched lands, which is where Kerstas currently stood. Small wagons were placed in the crowds of painted figures, painted accordingly to whose army they belonged to. Some of the yellow and green wagons had to be stacked atop one another so they did not crowd too far away from their true locations.

"What are our orders?" The two men standing at the table staring at the map had not even noticed Kerstas come into the tent. The soldier on the right was the once who spoke. He donned a green cape on his back, just how Malgrin and Moredir wore theirs.

"The armies of Meredine are marching here as we speak," said the soldier on the left, who was wearing a yellow cape draped over his shoulder. He was most likely a rank underneath Malgrin. "Our soldiers are ready for them whenever they show up. Our letter was clear enough. We have the entire eastern half of the country believing that they are responsible for what happened in Requilit."

"And what about him?" The soldier wearing the green cape pointed at Kerstas, who up until now thought he had been brought in unnoticed.

"Vanitar wants him alive for now. Before the fighting starts, he says we will have something of value delivered to us."

"What is being delivered?"

The soldier in yellow smiled. "Our captain has two in his custody. One an elf, one a certain runaway princess. They were picked up a day or so ago, as said by a letter we received by one of the guards in his party."

"Inerium?" Kerstas asked. He lurched forward. The soldiers who escorted him in had to hold him back. "You bastards have her?" His voice was strained, almost like he was growling the words out like a feral beast.

"We do, and if you do not want anything to happen to her, I suggest that you do everything we ask with no resistance."

Kerstas stared at the soldier. His eyes were filled with a hatred that sent a chill down a demon's spine. A fire was burning in his soul that could not be put out. Rage was building up inside him. "Do not harm her," he growled.

A small twinge of fear filled the eyes of the soldiers in the tent. The grips of the soldiers holding him loosened for a second, then tightened once more.

The two caped soldiers nodded. J—just do as we say and she will not be," said the green-caped soldier.

Kerstas nodded, the fire still burning inside him. He almost placed them on the same level as the priests back in Requilit. They were damned close to that, but not as much.

"Good," the soldier with the yellow composed himself. The soldier in green's hands were still shaking a bit. He placed them flat on the map table to try to calm down.

Suddenly another soldier, who was wearing a set of leather armor with a green tunic underneath it, came running through the entrance of the tent. "Sir!"

"Yes, soldier?" The green-caped soldier stood up straight and walked to the one who had just came in, keeping distance from Kerstas.

"They are here."

CHAPTER 20

The wagon was approaching the camp. It was maybe five minutes away, close enough to see soldiers in yellow and green walking and preparing for battle. Some were sitting by fires cooking up food, most likely cooking up what might be their last meals. For some, it would be true.

Choleira was sitting by Inerium watching the clouds pass above them. The sun was setting, at least she thought so. It had just been a few days, maybe a week, since she had met Inerium. Every second she had spent with her she cherished. To an elf's life, a week was like a minute compared to a human life, but with Inerium, it was different. It was almost like time froze when she was next to her, as if the universe and everything in it stopped for them.

"That one kind of looks like a bird," said Inerium.

Choleira looked over at the cloud Inerium pointed to. It was shaped like a dove flying through the air. The wind picked up and almost seemed to move its wings as it soared across the blue sky. "Hey, that one looks like a circle."

Inerium looked around in the sky to see what she was pointing to, but could not see it. "Where?"

"There, silly." She inched closer to Inerium, shoulder to

shoulder, and pressed her cheek against hers. Inerium's face was hot, assumingely from how close Choleira was to her.

Choleira pointed up to the sky at something circular inching towards the sun. It was not moving in the same direction or speed as the wind. It was slow, but it was closing the distance with the sun.

"Is that the moon?" Asked Inerium.

Malgrin, who was sitting silently steering the horses chimed in. "It appears to be. But why is it so high at this hour?"

"I do not know," said Choleira, "but I am getting an odd feeling about it."

Inerium nodded in agreement. Looking at the moon inching towards the sun made her stomach turn. Something in the back of her mind was telling her something bad was about to happen.

"Tahee-tayeemay-issay-cayomayingay," said a sinister voice echoing in the air, shaking the wagon as it spoke. It was the relic's voice. Inerium knew it in her gut as she thought it.

"What was that," asked Malgrin.

Inerium pulled the relic out of her bag. "What did you say?"

The voice groaned out the words as it spoke. "The time is coming." He laughed. The echo of the horrid laugh blew the dust away as they drove over it, like the voice created a shockwave around them.

The voice put a pit in Inerium's stomach. It shook her bones as it spoke and laughed. She wondered how something could be so evil, so dark, that it made so many terrible things happen around it. Just the sound of its voice made the ground quiver in fear.

The camp was nearing. The soldiers were running about, scrambling to get their weapons and unequipped armor. Inerium, Choleira, and Malgrin looked over to see a large army of heavily armored and weaponed men marching towards the camp. Their numbers were large. Hundreds of them. If Inerium gave it more thought, she honestly would have considered there even being over a thousand men approaching. Their banners were held, bearing the eight-sided red crest of Meridine.

"Stop the wagon," said Inerium.

Malgrin did so instantly. The horses bent their heads to try to find some water, but there was none to be found anywhere nearby due to the ground being so dried up. The soldiers of Istimus and Venirit gathered and lined up near the edge of their camp. They parted down the middle, making a path to the large tent in the center.

"That's," Inerium started to say, looking at the ones who came out of the tent. The two caped soldiers walked in the front. Right behind them came Kerstas, still being held by the other two soldiers. "Kerstas."

CHAPTER 21

Kerstas stood at the front of the combined armies of Istimus and Venirit. His arms were held by the two soldiers still, which now had started to make his hands tingle and go numb. Before him stood the giant army of Meredine. Their red armor gleamed in the sunlight as it shone down. The moon in the sky, as Kerstas saw as he was being led to the front, was moving closer and closer to the sun. The wind was picking up a little. The great mountain stood up high, staring down at them. The sun was just starting to touch its tip. The moon about two fingers away from it, if measured by hand.

The one at the head of Meredine's army was a scary-looking man well-suited in red armor. His sword was massive, sheathed in a golden scabbard that matched its hilt. His helmet had a red plume of horsehair trailing down from the front to the back. The helmet hugged around the man's cheeks and stopped at his chin. The center of his face was visible. He looked familiar, but Kerstas could not remember why.

"Kerstas, so you are still alive. Thank God." The soldier's voice was deep, rough. He seemed like he had led many battles and had used his voice enough to have it be so gritty. "I thought you were dead." As menacing as his voice seemed, it had a kindness to it when he spoke to Kerstas.

"It is so nice that the king of Meridine himself could show up," said the stuck-up annoying voice of Vanitar, who was now walking up the open path behind Kerstas.

That was where he knew the man from. He was at his coronation. He was the scary king who he thought was death-glaring him that day. The one he originally thought responsible for the death of his parents. Now he knew that for sure not to be true. It was all because of the asshole that had just stepped in front of him.

"I did not expect to see you here," he said.

"I could say the same, Vanitar. I assume you are the mind behind this whole thing?"

Vanitar smirked. "What ever do you mean?" He chuckled. "After all you were the one who murdered the boy's parents. You started this." The soldiers behind him started to whisper to each other.

The king of Meridine took a deep breath. "I did not want this. There does not have to be any bloodshed here."

Vanitar shook his head and clicked his tongue a few times. "It is too late now. Blood will be shed. But it will not be mine."

"Wait!" Called out a female voice approaching from Kerstas' right. He turned to see Inerium, running down the open field towards him and the two kings. Behind her was Choleira, who Kerstas of course did not know yet. Behind her was Malgrin, his hand clutching his sword, ready to draw it at any moment.

"Inerium!" Kerstas tried to run towards her. The soldiers gripped his arms tighter and kicked the backs of his legs, knocking him on his knees. They pinned him. There.

Vanitar turned to look at Kerstas. "Stay put. You move, she and you both die."

Kerstas gritted his teeth. His gums started to bleed a little from the tension. A low growl started to form in his throat.

The burning flames inside him grew stronger. A voice started echoing in his head, laughing and telling him to kill every last one of them. The voice was sinister, evil, not the same one as the voice of Daerex in the mountain. This voice was evil... malicious. His eyes started to burn from the fire burning hotter and hotter from his soul. Even his breathing started to feel hot.

Vanitar snapped his fingers and pointed at Inerium. Four of the soldiers ran at her and Choleira and held them down to the ground just a few feet away from Kerstas. Inerium started to shout, to give the soldiers the order to let go of her, but they tied a rope around her mouth that kept her from saying any words.

"You said you would not touch her!" Kerstas shouted.

Vanitar shrugged his shoulders. "They may have said it, but I did not. And if I did," he paused to let out a small laugh, "oh well."

"Bastard!" Kerstas shook from side to side to break free from the soldiers' grips, but it did no good.

Choleira held out her hands, her eyes filled with rage. "Let her go!" She held up her hands and flames flew from her palms, engulfing the soldiers pinning down Inerium.

The soldiers cried out in pain as their bodies were covered in fire. Flames coated every open space on their bodies, leaving only fire and smoke taking human shapes. Rage, the emotion that made fire its rawest, most powerful form. Flames that could not be put out until the target was nothing but ash.

Choleira picked Inerium off the ground and dusted off her clothes, which had some tears at the legs, exposing her pale skin underneath.

"Thank you, Choli." She looked over at the two soldiers, who were still running around screaming in pain as their bodies burned. "Will those flames go out?"

Choleira smiled. "Once they are dead, the flames will cease. I got a little angry. Anger and rage are to fire like sadness and joy are to water. It fuels it. Those flames are flames of hate. Nothing could put them out, not even an ocean of water."

The soldiers finally stopped screaming in agony and collapsed to the ground. The flames started to die out as the charred bodies of the soldiers crumbled into the dust.

"So, you have magic, elven girl?" Vanitar smirked and turned to his army behind him. "It seems, my soldiers, that we have an elf among us! She took the lives of two of our men! Will we let her get away with that?"

The men all shouted out, "NO!"

Meridine's king stepped forward. He motioned Inerium and Choleira to come to his side. They did.

"Unhand my brother, asshole," Inerium said to Vanitar.

Vanitar shook his head. His punchable face grinning. "No. Your brother killed my men. He cannot live without punishment for that."

"I did not kill them," Kerstas said. "The cave collapsed on them."

"Sure, sure," Vanitar said. "I know the truth. Malgrin, there you are!" Malgrin had finally caught up and was standing by Vanitar. He stared down at Kerstas and then up to Inerium.

Inerium looked at Malgrin. "Please. Save him."

Vanitar looked at Malgrin and laughed. "He is my captain, foolish girl. He only takes orders from me."

Malgrin slowly walked over to Inerium. He stood by Meridine's king. "Orders are only orders. They mean nothing when the person making them is not fit to give them." He gave a slight look to Kerstas and smiled.

"Traitor!" Vanitar snapped his fingers and pointed at Malgrin.

One of the archers in yellow near the front of the army knocked an arrow in his bow and fired it. The arrow sailed through the air and pierced Malgrin's chest. He fell to the ground.

"Malgrin!" Inerium kneeled to the ground next to him. Choleira did the same.

"I am sorry, girls. Please forgive me. I wish I could have been a better man. I have failed you."

"No. You did more than anyone else would have. You betrayed your kingdom for me, Choli, and my brother. Even with a king's orders not to. You have not failed, Malgrin."

He smiled. "Thank you, Inerium. I will tell your father that you are safe when I see him again." He stared in the sky. "I will be with you all soon." A tear fell down his face as he let out his final breath.

"Move his body," said Meridine's king, speaking to a soldier wearing a long red cape that was torn at the end. He was not the captain. No, Moredir died by the hands of Vanitar's men.

He picked up Malgrin, closing his eyes, and packed him to the wagon sitting nearby. He returned next to Meridine's king. "I am sorry, your highness. Father."

The king of Meridine closed his eyes and whispered a prayer. He opened his eyes and stared at the soldier who had fired the arrow. "You will be the first to die." The sound of a bowstring being pulled filled the silent, tense air. An arrow was let loose from it, sailed past his head and landed in the throat of the soldier who had killed Malgrin.

The soldiers started screaming and shouting out at each other. Vanitar's lip quivered in rage, his eyes twitching. He motioned at the soldiers holding down Kerstas and they brought him over. They knelt him to the ground in front of him. "Bow down to me, and give me your kingdom, boy."

Kerstas laughed. "Burn in Hell."

He smirked. "Not yet. Not until my work is done." He looked at another one of his archers and nodded his head. "Take her out."

The sound of a bowstring drawing could be heard. Kerstas watched the archer's eyes stare to someone behind him. He watched the arrow release from the bow and sail past his head. He heard a yelp of pain and a shriek from another girl. The soldiers of Venirit all froze in place and turned their heads to look at Istimus' army.

Kerstas turned his head just enough to see Inerium laying down on the ashen ground, an arrow protruding from her chest. Choleira was laying over top of her. Her hands were trembling. Her eyes were filled with malice.

But even Choleira's rage could not match the rage that Kerstas was feeling. The flames inside him were burning out of control. His heart was racing. He started growling and shaking like a wild beast.

"You bastard! Why the fuck did you do that?" Kerstas' was roaring. His voice was straining from the burning hatred growing inside him.

"Now you will join her." Vanitar held out his hand. A soldier handed him his sword and he thrust it into Kerstas' stomach. Kerstas coughed up a pile of blood and collapsed to the ground, staring at Inerium just a few feet away from him.

CHAPTER 22

The soldiers of all three armies stared in shock as Vanitar started cackling. "Finally! Now there is nothing to stop me!"

"You forgot about something," said the king of Meridine. "Meridine stands against you." He drew his sword, and his men raised their weapons in the air and started shouting and roaring battle cries.

"Not for long." Vanitar held up his hand. "Soldiers, it is time to fight!"

The soldiers of Istimus readied their weapons. The soldiers of Venirit were hesitant. Some went for their weapons, but a great many did not. They stood still.

"Soldiers of Venirit, why are your weapons not drawn?"

The soldiers stared at him. The captain of Venirit spoke up. "You lied to us, Vanitar. You told us that Meridine is responsible for the deaths of King Kentrin and Queen Eleana.

Vanitar paused. He started to sweat. "I—yes—they did."

"If that is the case, then why the fuck did you just kill their daughter and stab their son?" The captain of Venirit stood waiting for an answer whether it was the truth, or some bullshit lie. Vanitar had no words. No excuses. Just unintelligible stuttering.

The captain of Venirit waved his hand, motioning the

soldiers still loyal to him to come with him. The soldiers who had raised their weapons for Vanitar walked over to join Istimus' army. The rest of them, which were quite a few, but many less than Vanitar's army now possessed. Venirit's captain stood by the king of Meridine. His men joined the ranks of Meridine.

"Thank you, sir," said Meridine's king.

"Please, your majesty, you can call me Oryth."

"Well, Oryth, you can call me Merryk. King Merryk if you are not comfortable with just the name."

"Thank you, King Merryk. I am sorry that my men and I believed you were responsible for this mess."

Merryk studied the army standing against him. They were great in numbers, there was no doubt about that. And nearly half of Venirit's army had stayed on their side. Meridine's army now had the remaining half of Venirit's army.

Merryk turned to look at Oryth. "Take them away," he said pointing at Inerium and Choleira, who was kneeling over Inerium's body trying to stop the bleeding. She was using the flames on her fingertips to cauterize the wound. She had pulled out the arrow.

Oryth nodded. He walked over to Choleira. "Come on. Bring her, too. We have to get out of here before the chaos starts." He carefully picked up Inerium's body. She was not breathing, at least by what he could tell. Choleira was carefully watching every move he made with her. There was no emotion in her eyes, at least none that were visible. Inside she was shocked. She was panicking and was almost on the verge of tears, but she could not show them, not around anyone but her. Only around Inerium.

"You do not get to just walk away with them!" Vanitar tried to signal his archers to take aim at them, but Merryk made his move. With a swift movement he swung his sword and sliced off the fingers on Vanitar's raised hand.

Vanitar cried out in pain as he clutched his bleeding hand. "If you harm her again, I will make sure that I will cut off more than just your damned fingers, Vanitar!"

Vanitar grunted in pain. More blood poured out of the stumps on his hand. "Damn you, Merryk! Damn you to Hell!"

"Get them out of here," said Merryk to Oryth.

The moon was getting closer and closer to the sun by the second. The edges of the giant spherical bodies were touching, the sun slowly starting to be shadowed by the moon. Oryth walked away with Inerium in his arms, Choleira walking right behind him, holding Inerium's hand. She was holding the vial that held Inerium's tears in her other hand. Her hair had fallen down. She did not bother trying to braid it again or lay it back. Her focus was only on Inerium.

As Inerium was being taken away, a small, hand-sized object fell out of her bag on the ground near Kerstas, who was trying to keep still from the pain. He looked up as he watched Inerium be taken away in Oryth's arms. Then, his vision focused on the object laying in the ashen dirt.

CHAPTER 23

Kerstas stared at the object laying in front of him. It was a few feet away, just out of reach. The rage burning inside of him was almost overwhelming him, causing him to sweat.

"Kill them," said a voice. The voice was dark, evil, the same one that had told Kerstas to murder all of the ones who stood as his enemy. "Destroy your enemies. Lay waste to them."

The moon had started to creep over the surface of the sun. The soldiers had started to notice when the land started being shadowed by the great lunar body. The more superstitious ones started to panic, because they had ears the stories and tales of how demons would walk the lands while the sun was covered by the moon.

Kerstas grunted in pain as he pulled his body across the ground. His arms and legs were weak from the wound in his stomach that was still bleeding all over the ashen ground. He reached his hand out, but as his palm rested on the relic, he felt another sharp pain impale him through his shoulder. One of Istimus' soldiers had stabbed Kerstas in the shoulder with his spear. He winced in pain, which the muscles tensing in his shoulder caused the blade to cut deeper.

"Kerstas, no!" Merryk raised his sword in the air and pointed it at Vanitar. "You will die." Merryk's soldiers cried out and charged at Vanitar's. Vanitar's soldiers charged in as well, weapons raised.

Weapons clashed and blood spilled all over the battlefield. Soldiers cried out in pain as their limbs were severed and bodies impaled. Vanitar stood at the back grinning as he watched the soldiers fight and shed each other's blood. He knew his secret was out, but if there was no longer an army to oppose him, he knew that the land would be his.

"Get off of him!" Merryk kicked the soldier away from Kerstas. He pulled the spear out of Kerstas' shoulder and used it to decapitate the soldier who had stabbed him with it. He knelt down next to Kerstas and tore off a piece of the soldier's shirt. He used it to cover Kerstas' shoulder wound. He pressed hard on it to keep Kerstas from losing any more blood. "How are you?"

Kerstas coughed and winced at the excruciating pain. "In a fuck load of pain, what do you think? I am alive, thankfully."

"Yes, thank God for that."

Kerstas rolled his eyes. "I would not. I refuse to thank him for a single thing."

If it were not for the giant battle being fought around them, Merryk would have asked Kerstas his reasoning for saying such a thing. "Keep pressure on that, Kerstas, and stay alive for me. For all of us." He drew his sword again and charged into the fight, cutting down any soldiers in yellow he saw, along with any soldiers in green that tried to kill him.

Kerstas clutched the relic in his hand. The muscle in his shoulder was throbbing in pain. His heartbeat could be felt in his hand as it held onto the relic. The moon was now halfway covering the sun. A large shadow had covered most of the battlefield.

"Kill them," said the voice from the relic. "Release all of your hatred on them."

The flames of hatred were burning wildly inside him. It was like each word fueled his rage more and more. His hands were trembling from the rage and the now unbearable pain he was feeling. His fingertips started to darken, turning black. He stared at them as they turned black up to the knuckle of both of his hands. A low laugh started echoing in his head. The ground started to shake below him, making some of the soldiers lose their balance. The battlefield was covered in blood and the corpses of soldiers in red, yellow, and green.

Kerstas' wounds started healing themselves. The pain had numbed, and all that was left for him to feel was rage. He did not know what to do, but he felt another part of him awakening. A power that laid dormant ever since he had left the cave in the shrieking peaks. The power given to him by Daerex. The moon had now covered the sun completely. As the land was completely covered by the great shadow, the soldiers looked up in fear as all their hopes were drained from them.

Kerstas held out his right hand and let out a long breath. His fingers were tingling. One of the soldiers of Istimus saw him and charged at him, holding his sword out to drive it through him. Kerstas twisted his hand and curled his fingers. The soldier levitated up into the air. Kerstas closed his eyes. He could feel something inside the soldier as the soldier was suspended in the air.

"What is that, that odd presence that I feel in you?" Kerstas asked.

"You can feel it?" The voice echoed in his mind, making his vision blurry. "That, Lord Kerstas, is his blood."

"Interesting," Kerstas said, his mouth twisting into a wicked grin.

Kerstas pulled his hand towards him. The soldier started to cry out in pain as his pores started to bleed. A cloud of blood trailed out of the soldier as his skin started to dehydrate. His limbs shriveled up and his skin turned a dark grey. The soldier's corpse fell to the ground as the cloud of his blood circled in the air. All the soldiers stared at the sky to see the blood circling above their heads. They looked at Kerstas in fear as he stood grinning in the center of the battlefield.

"Demon! The boy is a demon," cried out a soldier from Venirit's army that had sided with Istimus. Vanitar was standing in the back, his eyes widened. He looked up in terror at the cloud of blood swirling above.

Kerstas looked over and saw Vanitar. He started to make his way towards him. A small handful of Vanitar's barbarian soldiers stepped in Kerstas' way, holding their giant axes in their bear-like hands.

"Do not stand in my way." Kerstas' voice was like a monster's growl, one that would haunt someone's dreams. "Or your fates will be the same."

The soldiers laughed. "You are just a boy," said the first one, "just a boy with some magic."

"I may be just a boy." Kerstas swirled his index finger around in the air, and the blood cloud followed it. He pointed at the soldier who spoke to him. The cloud flew through the air and enveloped the soldier. Blood poured out of his pores and increased the thickness of the crimson cloud. His body shriveled up just like the last one and collapsed to the ground. Kerstas' fingertips were burning hot. The power in them was immense.

"Yes. Yes. Kill them. Show them what you are capable of," the voice of the relic said. The words became heavier and heavier as they were spoken, like a weight was added to each syllable that was iterated.

The next barbarian soldier came charging at Kerstas halfway through a swing of his great axe with a yellow ribbon tied around the gripping point of the handle. "Die!"

Kerstas shook his head. "If you say so," he said, forming his hand into a claw.

The cloud of blood wrapped around the soldier's arm and tore it off in one pull. The blood that sprayed from the severed limb joined the cloud. The soldier's arm hovered in the air and started arching into a swing. The axe swung through the air and severed the head of its owner. the arm rotted away as the blood was seeped from it and the axe collapsed to the ground.

Kerstas was almost having fun with this newfound power of his. Yes, the acts he was doing were barbaric and demonic, but a part of him in the back of his mind seemed to find relief as he did them. The voice kept echoing in his head, getting louder and louder. His hatred and anger grew stronger as the voice spoke to him, pouring oil on the fire inside him.

Kerstas walked towards Vanitar, who was on his knees staring at Kerstas. His eyes were filled with terror, so much so that he was nearly paralyzed from it.

The remaining barbarian soldiers lowered their weapons. "Spare us," they said.

Kerstas looked at them as he passed by them. "Hold him for me," his voice growled. They nodded and ran to Vanitar. They grabbed his arms and dangled him in the air. Kerstas walked to Vanitar and looked him up and down. The blood cloud evaporated.

"I—I am sorry." Vanitar's voice trembled as he said it. Tears started to form in his eyes. "M—Monster."

Kerstas twisted his grin into a wicked smile. "Maybe so, but who is the one that murdered my family? Who robbed me of my home, my kingdom, my life, my title? You murdered my parents and my sister in front of me!" He snapped his fingers. The soldiers holding him suddenly lost control of their bodies and started pulling on Vanitar's arms. A loud popping noise sounded from each of his shoulders as his arms were snapped. They were not ripped off, but they were useless now. "And you are the one sitting here crying?"

"What are you going to do?" Vanitar asked.

"Your tears have no meaning to me, but they will be of use to me." He held up his hand and curled his fingers into a pinching position.

The tears forming in started covering Vanitar's eyes until they were completely covered. He smushed his index and thumb together, and Vanitar's eyes popped out of their sockets, mushing into a paste. Vanitar cried out in pain, a crackling wail that made the men holding him cringe and cover their ears. Vanitar's arms fell limp, causing him to let out another awful shriek.

Vanitar fell back down to his knees and attempted to look up at Kerstas with his empty sockets. "Kill me—kill me please. End this suffering of mine."

Kerstas laughed. "After all that you have caused, do you really expect me to just let you die? No, your suffering will last for a long, long time, Vanitar. I promise that."

"Soldiers of Istimus, hear me now!" Kerstas' growling voice echoed across the battlefield. All the soldiers stopped fighting to hear Kerstas. Some were terrified of him, but the ones under Meridine's banner were not. They were just shaken up a bit. "Vanitar's life is now in my hands! If you do not wish him to be slaughtered along with the rest of you, lay down your weapons and swear allegiance to me! Those who refuse to do so will suffer the fate of those who will be buried after this battle!"

The soldiers of Istimus and those of Venirit that joined Vanitar all froze in place. They dropped their weapons on the ground and knelt, bowing their heads to Kerstas.

Kerstas' rage had started to lessen. His bloodlust was fading away. The voice of the relic had stopped echoing in his ears and all malicious thoughts inside had ceased. The battle was over. They had won.

CHAPTER 24

Choleira hovered over Inerium as she laid in the back of the wagon, which was being driven by Oryth.

"Please, Inerium, you cannot die. You cannot." Choleira was holding both of Inerium's hands. "Please. You are my best friend. I have only known you for a short time, but I would take it over everything in my life that has come before that. I..." Choleira paused. The feelings she was feeling were getting too overwhelming for her. But she did not care. Oryth was not looking. He kept his eyes forward, watching for any soldiers who might try to come and ambush them.

"I—I love you." Choleira's eyes started to water. The tears started falling on Inerium's face, trickling down her cheeks. "You cannot leave me. I will not let you."

She pulled out the vial around her neck and opened it, Inerium's tears from Nellenor sitting inside it. She collected her tears that were falling off Inerium's face and from Choleira's eyes. She mixed the tears together and shook the vial, mixing them together. The water started to glow a bright, transparent silver. She pulled Inerium's vial out and poured half of the mixed tears into it.

The mixture in both bottles were glowing brightly, as if the tears inside were shed by gods. Inerium's chest started rising and falling. She was breathing. Choleira noticed and gasped. "Ineri?" Inerium's eyes fluttered open. "Choli, hey, what happened?"

"I thought I lost you. A soldier shot you with an arrow and you—you died." She smiled, her tears still falling a little. She wiped them away. "But now you are back."

Inerium looked at the vial around her neck. The liquid in the vial was still glowing. "You—did it?"

Choleira smiled and nodded. Her tears had finally stopped falling. "Yes. I love you, Inerium."

Inerium gasped. "I—I love you, too."

The sun was still covered by the moon. In the distance she could see the blood cloud swirling in the air created by Kerstas. "Wh—what is that?"

Choleira looked at the cloud. "It looks like blood. But a cloud."

Inerium saw the blood cloud fade away into the darkened sky. For a few minutes no words were spoken. Inerium and Choleira just stared into each other's eyes, smiling and getting lost in them. They did not even realize that they were holding hands until the silence was broken by a shriek of pain that echoed from the battlefield, soon followed by a second one.

"What was that?" Oryth asked. He turned around and smiled. "Welcome back, princess. I see you are in good hands."

"The best," Inerium said tightening her hold on Choleira's hands. Choleira returned the tightening grip.

The silence was broken again a minute later by a booming voice that made the horses stop trotting altogether. The wagon stopped.

"Soldiers of Istimus, hear me now!" Kerstas' voice rumbled the ground. Inerium was shocked when she heard it. It had such hatred in it. "Vanitar's life is now in my hands! If you do not wish him to be slaughtered along with the rest of you, lay down your weapons and swear allegiance to me! Those who refuse to do so will suffer the fate of those who will be buried after this battle!" She knew his words were true. She felt them in her soul, the malicious intentions behind every word.

"Kerstas," Inerium said. "What happened to you?"

"Ineri," Choleira said. Her voice had a fearful tone to it.

"What is it?" Inerium saw Choleira looking through her bag. She had taken it off, along with Solef and her little sister, when they got into the wagon so she could peacefully lay down.

"It is gone." Choleira looked scared. Her hands were shaking. "The eye of Inanis is missing."

Inerium looked around in the floor of the wagon, pilfering around the bags and straw laid across it. She checked her bag as well to see if it was just hidden in the bottom. It was nowhere to be found.

Then, when she had the thought, her stomach started turning. She knew it was true the moment she thought it. "Kerstas has it." She quickly looked up to Oryth. "Take us back. Hurry." Her voice was layered once more as she gave her command to Oryth. He immediately turned the reigns to the left and the horses turned around, steering the wagon back to the battlefield, where they could see the soldiers clad in yellow kneeling down, bowing to Kerstas.

CHAPTER 25

Kerstas stood at the front of Meridine's army. King Merryk stood by his side. Istimus' army was kneeling in front of them, with Vanitar kneeled on the ground. His limp arms were dead by his sides. His sockets had dried blood under them.

The fiery rage in Kerstas was starting to lessen. It had not completely died out yet. There was still something—someone—fueling it, and he was right in front of him.

"Vanitar, in front of all your men. In front of all your soldiers who so blindly obeyed your orders, I, Kerstas, king of Requilit, order you to take your life in front of them." He tossed a small dagger on the ground in front of him that Merryk had handed him.

Vanitar felt the ground for the dagger. He touched the blade with his fingers and felt around for the handle. He picked it up and stared at it, even though he could not see it.

"How could I do such a thing?" His whiny voice was still as irritating as it was before. Him being in agonizing pain did not help it at all. If anything, it made it worse. "I cannot do it. God would never forgive me."

Kerstas' voice started to turn into a growl. "Do not worry yourself of God's forgiveness—because I will send you to Hell myself." His voice shook the ground. There was another voice layering with his. It was *that* voice, the one from the relic. He was speaking through Kerstas. His hand still clutched the relic.

Vanitar's eye sockets started filling with tears and they started pouring out of them. It was a very uncomfortable thing to see. "Please."

"You did not offer them mercy. You killed them. And for what? A plot to take over Pleniris? A prophecy you heard about me?"

"That prophecy—It is how it said it would be."

"Fuck your prophecy. We would not be in this situation if you had not heard it. You would still have your eyes and arms. You would still be a king."

"I am still king!" Vanitar quickly stood up. His arms swung around like a puppet's. "I even poisoned that lazy fuckup of a king in Venirit. He should be dead by now. Venirit was going to be mine!"

"Tell that to them," Kerstas said smiling. He started to point at Istimus' army behind Vanitar, but he did not after he realized he could not see him pointing.

The soldiers of Istimus remained knelt down. Their heads tilted up to see Kerstas intimidatingly standing over top of their king, who they no longer considered to be one.

"I can never forgive you, Vanitar. Let these be the final words you hear." He knelt down in front of Vanitar and whispered in his ear, "I damn you to Hell. Burn."

He grabbed the hand that was holding the dagger and drove the blade into Vanitar's heart. He coughed up some blood and let out a final gurgled breath as his life faded away.

Kerstas heard the sound of a wagon approaching. He turned around to see Choleira and Inerium standing in the back of the wagon. They were holding hands trying to keep their balance and not fall out.

Every bit of darkness inside of him suddenly vanished from his body. Inerium jumped out of the wagon and ran to him. She hugged him so tight that it took the breath from him.

"How are you alive?" Kerstas asked. "You were shot by the arrow." He put the relic in his pocket.

"She brought me back." Inerium turned and smiled at Choleira.

Kerstas looked at Choleira. "Thank you. Thank you so much for saving her."

Choleira smiled. "I would do anything for her." She reached out and held Inerium's hand again. Both of their faces were red.

"You are an elf, right?" Choleira nodded. Kerstas' eyes lit up and he suddenly had a big smile on his face. "No way. No way." The excitement in his voice was very apparent. "So, you can do magic?"

Choleira nodded. "I can actually use many forms of magic. There is Elven speech magic, water magic, and fire magic."

"That is so cool. Can I, um, see some of it? If that is okay to ask."

Merryk was bewildered. Kerstas, the boy who had just single handedly ended a great battle, was now acting like a nerd who had just met one of his favorite characters.

Choleira giggled. "Sure." She held out her hands. In the left hand, a small ball of water formed from the sweat in her palm. In the other hand, a small flame ignited from her palm. "These are the water and fire magic. There is a lot more I can do with them, but I would rather not harm these humans, especially mine." She glanced over at Inerium with a cute smirk on her face, which caused Inerium's face to redden more. "And this is an example of the Elven speech magic." She closed her eyes and concentrated on her breathing. She fixed her eyes on Kerstas' tattered outfit. "May-Enday-Andae-Imprayoovah."

Kerstas could not understand a single word she said. But as she finished speaking the words, his clothes were enveloped a cloud of grey and black smoke. When the smoke was cleared, Kerstas was wearing a blue set of armor with golden accents on the places where the plates met. His head was still uncovered, though. His bright blue eyes went very well with the dark blue armor he now wore. There were a pair of black pants underneath the blue plated leg braces. He had on a short-sleeved black shirt on underneath his torso armor piece. His arms were no lingered covered in blood and ashes. They were clean, and to his new discovery, he had gotten a tan. He thought the whole time his arms were just dirty.

Kerstas looked over at the great mountain, which was starting to become visible again as the moon finally moved away from the sun. The lands were bright again, and the soldiers became less anxious. He felt his pocket and the relic was still sitting inside. He wondered what it was that was speaking to him. There was a word that lingered in his mind that was almost carved into his thoughts.

Sanguavis.

He did not know the meaning of it. He thought maybe it was one of the foreign words like Choleira had used, but he was not for certain. What he did know was that the word kept creeping into his thoughts.

King Merryk placed a hand on Kerstas' shoulder. "You did good, kid. Your father would be proud of you. I am sure he is."

Kerstas smiled, choking back a few tears at the thoughts of his father. "Thank you, King Merryk."

He nodded his head. "King Kerstas." He knelt to the ground and bowed his head to Kerstas. His men did the same. Then, with proud smiles on their faces, Inerium and Choleira did the same.

Kerstas looked around to see every soldier around him kneeling and bowing their heads to him. He was speechless. "Why are you bowing, sir?" Kerstas asked Merryk.

"My sons were killed. Malgrin and Moredir were my only children. I have no heirs. When I lost my wife many years ago, I had nothing besides my two sons, and that asshole Vanitar took them from me." He glared at Vanitar's corpse. "I figured, since you are now the only heir in the land to a throne, you deserve the title."

"I cannot take the title of king from you."

There were only two kings left in Pleniris now. Technically there was only one. Kerstas had not officially become one because his coronation was interrupted abruptly. Venirit's king was currently being prepared for his funeral service. The poison that Vanitar slipped into his drink caused his heart to stop after it had been fully ingested. And Vanitar was now laying dead in front of Kerstas. The four kingdoms each needed a king to rule them. There had never been any more or any less than the four, even when the chaos unleashed by Daerex was happening.

"You do not have to, my king." Merryk took off his helmet and placed it on the ground. "As king of Meridine, I hereby renounce my title as king, and choose my successor as Kerstas of Requilit. If he would have me as his captain."

Kerstas nodded. "Are—Are you sure?"

"One hundred percent. My king." He smiled.

The other soldiers all shouted out in unison, "Hail King Kerstas!"

Kerstas stood proud. He tried to put on a brave face despite the fact that he was terribly nervous. He was being cheered on by the armies of three kingdoms.

"Your coronation, King Kerstas, will be held back where it

should have been. Back in Requilit. Where you will live and rule over all Pleniris."

Home. Kerstas was finally going home. After all this time he had almost forgotten what it looked like. Suddenly, all the memories of home started flooding back. He remembered the great hall where he would enjoy meals with his family, as well as where his original coronation was held. Tsuin and Tsuon. He forgot about the twins. Did they survive? He really hoped so. Then he remembered Rengeon. His friend and servant. Did he survive as well? Kerstas hoped that all of them survived. His parents did not even get a proper funeral. What happened to their bodies? Were they still laying in the great hall, or were they moved with all the other corpses that littered the castle.

Inerium stood up and hugged her brother. "I am so proud of you. I am so glad you are alive."

"I am too, little Ineri." She had missed her brother's voice, like how one misses the voice of their mother singing them to sleep or telling them a bedtime story. "Come on, let's go home."

"Your coronation will be set the day after you arrive in Pleniris, Kerstas", said Merryk. He stood up and all the other soldiers did the same.

"Soldiers of Pleniris!" Kerstas' voice was not as booming and fierce as it was when his voice layered with Inanis', but it reached every soldier standing around him. "Collect the dead of your brethren! Return home, and let their families know what happened here today! They did not die a coward's death! No, they died as soldiers, who fought bravely until their last breaths!"

The soldiers in unison shouted, "Yes, King Kerstas!" They started picking up the bodies and collecting them, arranging them in sections for Venirit, Meridine, and Istimus. After about an hour the bodies had been accounted for and identified. The wagons stationed around the battlefield were loaded up with them and set off in the directions of their kingdoms. The soldiers marched back to their kingdoms to prepare for the new age of Pleniris, ruled by a singular king.

There was only one wagon left, which was for Kerstas, Inerium, and Choleira. The horse that would be pulling the wagon was none other than Snowfire, Inerium's horse. He was still alive. Inerium ran over and pet his fiery mane. His white coat was a little dirty from the ashes that coated the ground of the Ashen Lands the battle took place in.

The three climbed into the wagon and Snowfire started trotting down to get onto the Southern Road.

CHAPTER 26

An hour or so had passed. Kerstas and the girls were catching up and talking about the adventures they had. Choleira talked some about her home in the forest and some of the ways of her people. Inerium talked about their time in Nellenor and what the relic did to them, which made Kerstas a little wary of it sitting in his pocket. He anxiously patted his pocket, like someone patting a dog's head to get it to calm down.

"And then we met this really strange guy at a restaurant called the Blooming Gorgot in Venirit. He froze time and helped us escape before we ended up in this giant city in the sewers below the city."

Kerstas thought for a moment. Spizser came to mind when she mentioned a mysterious guy, especially with power to manipulate time. "Spizser?" Kerstas asked.

"You know him?" Inerium asked. She straightened up, curious to know more. "I mean he called himself Spenzser when we met him."

"Yes. Me and Barnabin ran into him in the crystal cave I mentioned. He had resurrected this guy who impaled himself on his weapon for mentioning him. The guy got so scared that he took his own life."

"Oh wow," said Choleira. "So do you think he is the same guy?"

"No doubt about it," said Kerstas. "There is no way that two people that happen to have that much power, not to mention with very similar names, were not the same person."

Inerium nodded. "It is very interesting, if not a bit suspicious, that he happened to be in the right place and right time for all of us."

"I do see what you mean," said Choleira. "How was it suspicious?"

"Well," Kerstas started, "he happened to be at the Blooming Gorgot and in the Krysyn Depths at moments we would have either been killed in or taken away in. We happened to be saved right at the moments everything could have changed. I could have been killed by the Krysalians, and you two might've been taken by Vanitar and held as ransom to get to me."

They all agreed on it and got off the topic of Spizser and their encounters with him. They were now nearing the place where the Southern Road meets the Western Road that connected Requilit and Meridine. The trees surrounding the great mountain were all glowing tremendously. Kerstas had noticed that they were doing so even when Vanitar and Venirit's king had died. Did they somehow know that Kerstas was going to rule over all Pleniris? It was most likely. It was true after all.

The rest of the ride to Requilit's border was silent. Choleira and Inerium sat staring into each other's eyes, and Kerstas stared off at the great mountain, the one that not even a week ago had terrified him. He knew now that the rumors of the creature lurking in the great mountain were at least true enough. It may have been a human-demon hybrid that was once the king of Meridine, but a creature, nonetheless. Kerstas now had the power of Daerex, as well as whatever powers came with possessing the relic still sitting in his pocket. Throughout the ride he would occasionally caress the relic in his pocket like it was his pet, whether he realized he was doing it or not.

They had made the turn onto the Western Road, and they could see the lining of trees in front of them. Majosei the witch resided in these woods, and they were by some nicknamed the Fairy Woods. Kerstas' grandmother would sometimes tell him and Inerium stories when they were really young about the woods. She mentioned that there were creatures in the woods that could change their shapes to be birds or beasts whenever they pleased. They did not know if she had meant *fairy* or *faerie*, but they honestly did not know the difference to know which was more fascinating to them.

"There are the woods grandmother mentioned, Kerstas." Inerium pointed to the woods as they neared the lining of the trees.

They forest's edge stopped right next to the Western Road. The edge had some nice camping grounds that a lot of hikers or explorers would stay at during the nights. They were too scared the venture any further into the woods than a mile or so because of the rumors that they had heard circulating them. There were the rumors and stories that were told about the Elven Woods, so it was most likely that the stories and rumors of the Fairy Woods were true as well.

"Those woods are best avoided," said Choleira.

Inerium and Kerstas turned to look at her. "What is there to avoid in them?" Inerium asked.

"They are called the Fairy Woods because of those who live inside them. They are a few of a large race called fairies, or *faeries* as the old tongues called them, residing in that forest.

"What are they?" Kerstas asked. He had read stories about fairies the size of a bird with butterfly wings that could grant wishes or use magic, but never any that would seem bad. "Are they bad?"

"They are a sworn enemy of my people. The Elves and Faeries had been at each other's throats for centuries. When my people left to the Far Lands, they left to another place even further past the edges of the Southern Lands. Some of them stayed behind, and they were woodland, just like my people are."

Do they have any magic?" Inerium asked, inching closer to Choleira. She moved her hand onto Choleira's lap to try to ease her stress, which she suspected she was experiencing.

"Yes they do." Choleira took a deep breath. She placed her hand over Inerium's and wrapped her fingers around her palm. "There are some who can change shape and appear as an animal. I am not sure if one can change into multiple, or that they can only change into one, but I do know that they can do it. Evindal once told us that he encountered a pair who had taken shape as a large bear and a large wolf. This was many many centuries ago, before the chaos that mad king brought to these lands."

"I see," said Kerstas. He scratched his chin, which he had noticed started growing small hairs on it. His cheeks and lips had started doing the same. It was nothing to brag about, but he was proud that he had started growing some. "Will they attack us?"

Choleira shook her head. "No, they do not attack unless they are provoked, or if they are on the hunt and someone happens to be in the wrong place and wrong time."

Inerium nodded her head in sync with Kerstas. They did not speak any more on the subject. They all stared at the forest as they drove by it, watching the trees shrink as they passed further away from them.

The day was finally coming to an end. The sun had fully set beneath the horizon nearly an hour ago, and the moon was returning to its place in the sky, without the sun to intrude on its time. Kerstas stopped the wagon on the side of the road near a small stream so they could rest and Snowfire could drink up and get rest as well.

Inerium and Choleira had snuggled up together under a warm blanket on the wagon, and Kerstas fell asleep near the foot of it, letting the girls have their time. He did not have any urge or desire to find someone to spend his life with. His only goals in life up until now were to get his revenge on the priests who violated him, and to reclaim his kingdom. He had done the second, and after he was officially the king, he would ensure the first goal would be met.

<hr />

The sun had started to rise above the horizon. Inerium and Choleira were still asleep. Kerstas smiled at them and let them stay asleep. He enjoyed how peaceful they looked curled up next to one another.

Kerstas hooked Snowfire up to the wagon and they started moving again towards Requilit. Inerium turned a bit when the wagon jolted forward, but she remained asleep and scooted closer to Choleira, wrapping her free arm around her.

After a bit passed, the sun was fully above the horizon, shining across the land of Pleniris. They had passed the village of Maciv and were nearing the wall of Requilit's capitol.

Inerium and Choleira sat up and stretched their arms. Inerium yawned and Choleira moved her neck to loosen it.

"Where are we?" Inerium asked, looking around. She could see the woods a fair distance behind them.

Kerstas turned around and smiled at the girls. "Good morning," he said amused. He turned forward and took a deep breath in. The walls of Requilit were just a minute away.

"We are home."

CHAPTER 27

They were finally home. They had parked the wagon at the large wooden gates of Requilit. Snowfire was eating at the stables. The three walked up the street, passing by many buildings that were all empty. They used to be filled with people conversing, buying things, and trading amongst one another. The streets were littered with trash, and they were overgrown with moss. How long had they been gone? Surely it has not been that long...

Kerstas looked around to try to see if there was someone, anyone, to be found.

"Hello, is there anyone here?" Kerstas' voice echoed. Surely someone could hear it.

Suddenly, a rustling came from behind one of the doors to the house on their right. They stopped and walked up to it. Kerstas knocked on the door.

"Go away," said the voice of a woman behind the door. "We do not want you Istimus fiends here anymore."

"What are you talking about?" Kerstas asked.

"Do not play with me." Her voice made it apparent that she hated whoever she believed she was talking to. "You and your other soldier buddies have taken advantage of us long enough! So how are you going to play dumb with me, soldier of Istimus?"

Kerstas stood in shock. The shock then turned to anger. "Miss, I am no soldier of Istimus. I am Kerstas."

"Kerstas is dead," the woman said. "They made sure of that. They went parading around the streets about how they had murdered him and were going after his sister next." Kerstas tried to open the door. It was locked.

Inerium stepped forward. "Hey, I am still alive, ma'am. My brother is as well. You do not have to worry about anything else."

The lady cracked the door open and looked out. She was an older woman. Not elderly, but she was starting to wrinkle at the eyes. She had brown hair with some gray ones intertwined in the mess. Her clothes were dirty and ragged. "Inerium?"

Inerium smiled. "Yes, it is me." She pointed at Kerstas. "And he is alive, too."

"Hello," Kerstas said. He greeted her with a warm smile. "As I said. I am Kerstas. I am alive still."

Tears formed in the woman's eyes. She opened the door fully and hugged the two. "We have been waiting for so long. We thought that the day would never come that we would be freed from them."

"How long has it been?" Kerstas asked. The question puzzled him greatly. It felt like the attack had happened roughly a week ago, but the way they were talking about it made him think otherwise. But how would that be possible? It surely was not. Was it?

The woman shook her head. "It has been a month. Maybe more? I do not know. Time has gotten away from me. Most of us have forgotten what day of the month it was."

Kerstas' questions remained unanswered. Even they could

not tell him how long it had been. "Where is everyone else? You mentioned others."

"Inside their houses. They are afraid of the soldiers. They come breaking down our doors in the middle of the night to satiate themselves at times. They rape us and steal from us. They are horrible." She started crying even harder.

Inerium hugged her. "I am so sorry this happened to you all. My brother is home now. And he has been granted the title of King of Pleniris."

The woman looked up at Kerstas. Her eyes were widened. "Of *all* Pleniris?"

Kerstas nodded with a smile. "Go round up the others. We will head up to the castle. I need my throne if I am to rule over this land. And by the sound of it, there are some in there occupying my home."

They set off down the street towards the castle, which was high on the hill with a long set of stairs leading down to the street they were walking on.

Kerstas opened the double doors of the castle and stepped inside. He stared at the large throne at the end of the room. The tables had been thrown to the sides of the room, opening the center. In the throne was a soldier with a thin cape draping over his shoulder. He was sitting sideways letting his legs dangle over the arm of the throne.

He turned his head towards Kerstas, Inerium, and Choleira. "Who the fuck are you three?" His voice was obnoxious. It was high-pitched and cracking. It almost sounded like…Vanitar's.

"You first. You are in my spot," Kerstas said.

He straightened up. His feet stamped the ground. It seemed like he had stomped his feet on the ground to make him seem more threatening. It definitely did not work. "*I* am Vanitar the

Second! *I* am the son of King Vanitar of Istimus, and I have been given Requilit as my own kingdom!"

Kerstas laughed. "You voice annoys me like your father's voice did. I can tell you are related."

"Don't you dare disrespect my father! Guards, we have unwanted guests!" From the side rooms came a handful of soldiers with yellow accents on their armor.

"Who are you three?" The soldier who spoke was larger than the others. He held a large spear in his hand with a yellow ribbon just below the blade.

"Names should not be important, soldier. You no longer have a leader to give out your orders. You would really take them from this pathetic excuse of a man? He is barely even a prince." Kerstas let out a little laugh. He turned his head to Inerium. "Step back, sis, I do not want you or Choleira to get hurt by me or them if this gets ugly."

Inerium nodded and stepped back with Choleira. Inerium was hugging on to Choleira from behind. She held Inerium's hand in hers over her shoulder.

"What are you talking about?" The soldier raised his spear, pointing it at Kerstas. His voice was rough.

"That is my throne you are sitting on, Vanitar. Ugh, your name sickens me. It reminds me of your father. You both are whiny as all Hell."

"Keep your mouth shut, peasant. Just because you have that blue armor on does not mean you have any authority here. Just a soldier of Requilit, that is all you are. We locked the rest of you that we did not decide to murder in the dungeons below. I guess the last free one came to beg for their freedom."

Kerstas was relived to know that his soldiers were still alive. Imprisoned, but still alive.

Inerium stepped forward. Choleira grabbed her hand.

Inerium turned around. "It is okay. Trust me." Her face grew serious, and she walked next to Kerstas. She looked at one of the soldiers in the back of the group "You there, go free them." Her voice was firm.

The soldier nodded and immediately ran off to do as he was told. The other soldiers stared in shock as he did so.

"What did you do?" Kerstas asked. There was a bit of disbelief behind his surprised look.

"I told him to free your soldiers, big brother. Your highness." She mockingly curtsied and giggled. Choleira giggled behind her hand at Inerium's movement. "I can give commands to people, and they listen without a single thought in their heads."

"That is interesting," Kerstas said, smirking. "Thank you." Kerstas raised his arms up towards the soldier. "I do not wish to harm any of you. You all can be on your way home to your families." He looked at Vanitar II. "Except you, of course. Your family is gone."

"What the fuck are you talking about? What do you know of *my* family? I am royalty, you are a mere soldier! You know *nothing* of royal families and living the life of a royal!"

Kerstas clicked his tongue a few times. The sound of many footsteps echoed through the hallway to the side. From the opening came dozens of soldiers dressed in blue accented armor. They all took one look at Kerstas and knelt down on one knee and bowed their heads.

"I know *everything* there is to know about it. I have not properly introduced myself yet." He smiled and stepped forward. "I am Kerstas of Requilit's royal family. I am the heir to the throne of Requilit, and as of now, *all* of Pleniris."

"Bullshit!" Vanitar II's voice cracked as he shouted. "My father is the king of Istimus! He is going to rule over all of this land! It is his plan!"

Kerstas let out a loud laugh that hurt his throat as he let it out.

"What is so damned funny?" Vanitar II asked. He huffed and stomped his foot on the floor.

"Your father's plan is no longer in motion," Kerstas said. "I saw to that myself. Your father is dead."

"No. That cannot be." Vanitar II's voice broke even more. Inerium laughed at it. Choleira slightly smiled at her giggling. "You lie!"

Kerstas shook his head. "No, I speak the truth. He died crying. As will you."

Vanitar II started throwing his arms around like a bratty child throwing a tantrum. He pointed at Kerstas and ordered his soldiers to kill him. They started walking towards him with their weapons raised. The soldiers of Requilit immediately stood up and guarded Kerstas, Inerium, and Choleira.

"You will not harm her," said a soldier in the front who was wearing a thin blue cape over his right shoulder. He drew a rapier from the scabbard on his hip. They had most likely recovered their weapons as they came up.

"Thank you, sir," Kerstas said.

"Of course, my lord. It is good to see you again. And you, too, Princess Inerium."

"I will give you this one chance, and this one chance only, to surrender yourselves and pledge your loyalty to me. If not, well, you will join your father," Kerstas said.

"I will never surrender to the likes of you! Murderer!"

Kerstas shook his head. "Then you doom your men as well as yourself, Vanitar II." He held up his hand and closed his eyes. He concentrated on the water on the soldiers' bodies. The smelly, putrid sweat leaking from their bodies. He twirled his hand around and the sweat all gathered in a large ball in front of him.

"Witchcraft!" Vanitar II fell to the ground in a panic. He was backing away while crawling on the floor.

Kerstas felt the rage return to him again. The bloodlust. "Yes," said the voice of the relic in his pocket. "Kill them. Suffocate them." The voice echoed in his head.

The bloodlust increased drastically, and he curled his fingers into a choking position. The water streamed out into little strands of water that tangled themselves around the throats of the soldiers of Istimus. They were picked up off the ground and were suspended by the strands. Vanitar II watched in horror as his men were being slowly killed. The sounds of necks snapping echoed in the hall, making the soldiers of Requilit cringe and wince. The bodies of the Istimus soldiers collapsed to the stone floor.

Vanitar II's eyes were filled with terror. "Please, have mercy."

Kerstas shook his head. "Just like your father. Begging for mercy and begging for your life when all else is lost." He charged up to Vanitar II and grabbed him by the throat. His scrawny body was not hard to lift from the ground. He pried Vanitar II's mouth open with his free hand and let out an evil chuckle, layered with the voice from the relic, which echoed in the main hall. "Say hello to your father in Hell for me."

Kerstas closed his eyes and all the water still hovering in the air floes into Vanitar II's mouth and continued to stream through his body. The water started pouring out of his eyes and nose. He started flailing out in pain and horror as his body began to fill with water. His stomach started to swell up like a balloon. And just as a balloon does, Vanitar II's body burst open, leaving a large mess of guts, water, and bones all over the stone floor.

"Sorry about that, guys. I went a little overboard," Kerstas said, breathing and calming himself down.

In the back of his mind Kerstas could faintly hear the echoing of the relic's voice laughing. The bloodlust and dark feelings inside him crept away just as the voice did. It honestly frightened him a little, but he was more concerned on what his men and the girls thought of him.

"A little?" The soldier wearing the cape let out a short-breathed laugh. "Since when could you use magic, Lord Kerstas?"

"I just found out myself during the battle in the Ashen Lands." He wanted to keep the part about the relic and Daerex's power a secret. He did not want his reputation as king to be tarnished by him possessing demon and dark magic. He did not want to be like his grandfather, feared and hated by the people. "It turned out that I have water magic."

"We are glad to have you back, my lord. It has been so long."

"How long exactly?" Kerstas asked.

The soldier shook his head. "Hard to say. Time got away from us in those cells."

This puzzled Kerstas even more. Even the soldiers of Requilit did not know how much time had passed since the attack. It concerned him even more now that they all collectively could not tell him a straight answer.

"What will you have us do, your majesty?"

Kerstas looked around. "It would be nice to have this place cleaned up. After all, there will be people from all over Pleniris coming to watch my coronation."

"Your coronation, my lord?"

Kerstas nodded. It was finally going to be official. He had not forgotten his promise. He was going to seek revenge on those priests who wronged him for so long. No matter what. "After the battle, King Merryk of Meridine stripped himself of his title and claimed me his heir. It was after that when he said that I was to be crowned the king of *all* Pleniris. To rule over all four kingdoms."

"Oh wow. Congratulations, Lord Kerstas. That is a very heavy title to hold."

"Indeed, it is. But it is one I will wear, for the fallen kings of Pleniris who had fallen by the hands of Vanitar and his schemes."

The soldiers all knelt down in front of Kerstas and bowed their heads. "Hail, Lord Kerstas, King of Pleniris!"

Kerstas could not help but smile when they all said this. How could he not? He turned around to see Inerium and Choleira kneeling as well. "Stand up, you two. You do not need to bow to me. Not my sister and her partner."

When he called her that, Inerium's face turned a bright red. "P—Partner?"

Choleira giggled and hugged Inerium tightly. "Hey, there, my partner. I guess we can call each other that, huh?" She let out another giggle, which made Inerium's face redden even more.

Kerstas looked at his throne and walked up to it. He sat down in it and looked at everyone before him in the great hall. He was finally in his seat. Finally back in his home. Yes, it all needed some touching up to return it to its full glory, but nonetheless it was his home. And he was happy to be back in it.

CHAPTER 28

A few days had passed since the three returned to Requilit. The castle had been cleaned top to bottom by the townspeople, who were ecstatic to have Kerstas and Inerium returned to them. They were overjoyed just to be in the castle, let alone the honor of being entrusted to clean it. Kerstas did not see their appeal in cleaning it, but he did not complain about it.

Inerium and Choleira both slept in her bedroom. Kerstas slept in his, not fully ready to sleep in his parents' room yet. He got out of bed and remembered when Rengeon would come in and help him dress and get up. He did not have that luxury, that friend, anymore. He had found out that Rengeon died trying to protect the castle during the attack. And the twins Tsuin and Tsuon had also died in the attack. They were buried alongside Rengeon in the grass fields around the capitol. Kerstas and Inerium were devastated to find out they had passed protecting their home, but they died with honor no doubt.

Kerstas left the bedroom and walked towards Inerium's room. He knocked on the door a few times before entering. Inerium and Choleira were already awake looking at the straw dolls and figures scattered about the room. To his surprise they were all still there.

"Good morning, Ineri and Choleira. You sleep well?'

They nodded. "She is showing off her dolls," Choleira said with a little laugh.

"Hey, they are not dolls," Inerium said with a bit of a playful tone in her voice. "They are figures of people and creatures in my dreams I used to have."

"What is that, then?" Choleira pointed to the large mass under the sheet that Kerstas also asked of before.

"Yeah, what is it?" Kerstas asked, curious as well. He had completely forgotten it with everything that has happened.

Inerium walked over to the sheet. "Oh yeah. I forgot about this thing. It was never finished, but I can explain what it was supposed to be."

Inerium ripped the sheet off to reveal a large mass of straw, sticks, and other small crafting materials she had found. The mass that they looked at almost looked like the unfinished body of a dragon, with six distinct parts coming out of its back for wings. The straw and other materials it was comprised of were painted black. The wings were not fully finished. Three of the six were done. The wings had tears in the parts that caught air as it flew. There was a lower jaw formed for the head, but the rest was unfinished.

"This is Dorgy, the dragon from the stories Kerstas told me as a child. My favorite story by him."

Kerstas smiled. "Yes, I remember. The story of the golden city and the dragon.

She nodded. "Yes, and I remember after the first night you told me the story, I had a dream about him. He was sleeping in a field of ashes. He had six wings and big green eyes. He had many horns on his head as well."

"It looks really good, Ineri. I wish I could have seen the final product."

Inerium did a cute smile one gives off when they are told

they did a good job, and she started showing off more dolls to Choleira.

"I will leave you two alone, then." Kerstas left the room and walked around the castle, looking at all the paintings and rooms it held. He remembered all of it. He visited his grandmother's garden, which was still well-taken care of to his surprise. The trees lining the border of the garden were shimmering a bright red and orange. He walked around a few times reminiscing the times he would explain all the flowers and plants to Inerium, who had taken Choleira the day before and gave her the tour that Kerstas gave to her.

Kerstas returned to the main hall and sat in his throne. His soldiers were patrolling the castle, making sure no one got in. The city of the capitol was booming again. Trading had returned to normal, and the people of Requilit were all talking about how Kerstas was going to rule over the whole land.

A knock came from the large doors of the castle. The two guards standing at them opened the doors and let in a man who was out of breath.

"Good morning, Lord Kerstas. I have received news that Merryk of Meridine, as well as the highest-ranked people of the kingdoms are on their way. Your coronation is to be held here in the main hall of Castle Requilit tomorrow evening when the sun is at its highest point. The people here in the capitol will help decorate the castle for the coronation. Have a good day, my lord." He left the room and the doors shut behind him with a loud, echoing thud.

"Tomorrow," Kerstas said, grinning. "I will be king."

CHAPTER 29

The day had come. Kerstas woke in his bed, the sun shining through his window. The great mountain was staring at him, but not as threatening as it used to be. Now, it was just a simple giant mountain that he could view outside of his window. His blue armor made by Choleira's magic was hanging on a mannequin in the corner. Then, a knock came at the door.

"Good morning, Lord Kerstas," said Merryk. He had a giant warming smile on his face. "Today is the big day. You finally can become king."

Kerstas was nervous. Very nervous. He had stayed up a good amount of the night because of his nerves. He was so nervous about the thoughts of him being a bad king or if he would not be cut out for it. Or that the people would hate him. He shook the ideas from his head. He did not want to have that mentality, especially not on the day of his coronation.

"Do you think I will make a good king?" Kerstas asked.

Merryk nodded. "Without a doubt. Your father was a close friend of mine. He was a great king, better than any other I had met. I have no doubts that you will be the same."

"Thank you, Merryk. It means a lot."

Merryk smiled and held out his arm. "Come. They are waiting for you."

"They are already here?" Kerstas' voice was shaky from anxiety. "I just woke up. I am not properly dressed for this or prepared at all."

Merryk clapped his hands. A pair of women walked through the doorway behind him holding a handful of clothes. They were young. Not too young, but at least twenty years old. The one on the left had brown hair braided down to her shoulders, and the one on the right had blonde hair that was held up in a high bun. They were both wearing blue dresses.

"They will take care of that." Merryk bowed and walked out of the room. "When you are done, Lord Kerstas, I will be waiting right out here."

Kerstas nodded. The girls immediately started preparing Kerstas for his coronation. They had used makeup to hide any of Kerstas' scars or wounds he received in the battle. They combed his hair over but left it a little messy to make it look natural, but professional. They slipped the clothing onto him. It was a black dress shirt and dark pants, followed with a blue coat with gold accents and buttons on it. The buttons had the diamond crest of Requilit on them that shimmered in the sunlight. After a few minutes of dressing and touching up, Kerstas was about as ready appearance-wise as he could be. As for his nerves, he could not be any more nervous and scared for the coming moment.

The girls walked out of the room. When he knew that they were gone, he walked over to his bed and reached under his pillow closest to the window. He pulled the relic out from under it and put it in his coat's breast pocket. He walked out of the room and Merryk was standing on the wall by the door.

"You ready, My Lord?"

Kerstas nodded. They walked down the hall and down the

stairs, and continued until they stood right at the doorway into the main hall.

"I will go and take my seat. You come out when you are ready." Merryk walked through the doorway and closed the door behind him.

From the small glimpse Kerstas got, the room was filled with people, both royal and common. The room was decorated exactly as it was for his first coronation. The walls were lined with branches and vines covered in golden leaves glistening in the sunlight. It was magnificent, considering how little time had passed since he had come back home.

Kerstas took a deep breath in and a shuttered breath out. He closed his eyes and cast away his nervousness. When he had calmed down enough, he reached for the door handle and opened the wooden door.

Kerstas walked into the main hall and stood in front of the throne. Inside the hall were people crowded in both the seats and the free flooring. There was not a single spot to see the floor besides the elevated part he was standing on at the front of the room. In the front row were Inerium, Choleira, and Merryk, along with a great many others he did not recognize. The soldiers of Requilit all stood guard at the pillars in the room and doors. The people inside poured out the doors, climbing over top of one another to get a view inside. The people were whispering to one another about how Kerstas was truly alive and he was going to be great. Not one negative comment was made about him. High-ranked soldiers of Istimus, Meridine, and Venirit all stood around the room as well near the first three rows. They could be pointed out by the colors of the shoulder capes and color of the armor pieces they were wearing.

"Hello, everyone. As you know, my name is Kerstas." His nerves were coming back. His hands started to shake. He looked down at Inerium. She gave him a warm smile and a gesture to get him to keep going. "I did not expect to be back in these halls again. I could have sworn I was going to end up with the same fate as my parents. I can say that I am grateful that I am still alive. And I am thankful to two men in particular for my life. They both died trying to keep me safe. But I would not even be standing here now if it were not for Barnabin and Malgrin, both soldiers of Istimus."

Merryk's eyes started to tear up. He wiped them away before any of his men could see.

"But isn't Istimus responsible for this mess?" A man in the crowd had raised his hand up to get Kerstas' attention as he asked this. He was one of the commoners.

Kerstas nodded. "Yes, they were, but they disobeyed their orders and chose to protect me instead. Malgrin had also saved my sister and her dear partner Choleira."

"You mean that Elven girl?' The man had tried to push his way through the crowd. The people stopped him. "I bet those ears of hers could sell for a pretty penny. Or maybe in the sex trade."

Kerstas stepped down. He held his hand out to Choleira. Inerium stood up with her and Kerstas led them to the throne. They stood by it. Merryk joined them, his hand resting on his sword.

Kerstas looked at the man. "There will be no such thing in my kingdom. No sex trades. And you are not to lay a finger on her or any of her people, or else I will have you executed for attacking a member of my household." The man nodded and calmed down. He left the building.

Kerstas did not know what to do next. He did not know how a coronation went. He did not know if he was going to just get his crown and title, or if there had to be a ceremony beforehand.

Merryk, seeing Kerstas' confusion, stepped forward. "Men and women of Pleniris, I am pleased to see you all here today. I am Merryk, the former king of Meridine. I am proud to say that Kerstas of Requilit will be receiving the title of king for all four lands here. He will rule over all four kingdoms under his name. What has been happing all across our country this past while is inexcusable, all done by the hands of Vanitar of Istimus. We will not have any more wars within our lands. Our kingdoms will unite as one under Lord Kerstas' rule, and he will bring peace to our lands. For Pleniris!"

The people all started cheering at Merryk's speech. Even Kerstas almost started to clap, but he did not. He gave Merryk a smile and a deep head nod, which he understood as a thanks.

"Thank you all," Kerstas said with a smile and a few tears in his eyes. "This means so much to me. I wish my father and mother were here to see this. I miss them so much."

Merryk walked over to Kerstas and placed a hand on his shoulder. "I miss them too. I wish they could be here today. They would be so proud to see how much their son has grown." Merryk looked over at the wall on the opposite side of the room that Kerstas came in on.

The two girls who had helped him. Get ready were walking in through the other wooden door holding a pillow carrying a golden crown on it. The crown held six towers on it with a gem in them, which were colored blue, red, green, yellow, white, and black. The white and black stones stood in the front, over a large pattern in the image of a dragon molded into the metal of the crown. The dragon's body curled up and down the flat surface of the crown.

The girls knelt down as they stood next to him, reining

the pillow higher in the air. Merryk picked up the crown. He turned to face Kerstas. Kerstas knelt down on one knee and bowed his head.

"Lord Kerstas. I am known your father since he was a boy. He was the best friend I could have ever had. And it is my greatest honor to grant you the title of king of all Pleniris." Merryk placed the crown on Kerstas' head, and he stood up, raising his head high. Everyone in the room cheered for him, clapping and roaring with praises for him.

Then, Kerstas saw them walk in. Dressed in their black robes with the white collars. The priests, the exact ones from his youth, were walking through the center of the hall up to him. They bowed to him and started to say a prayer.

"Do not waste your breath." Kerstas' voice was dark. Not evil or malicious, just dark and heavy.

The priests looked up at him. "Excuse me?"

"You know what you did all those years ago to me. How could I forget it? You. Every one of you."

"I—I do not know what you mean, Kerstas." The priest speaking was the head one. The one who was in charge of doing it all.

"Oh, but you do." Kerstas looked to the crowd. "People of Pleniris, I as the now king of this land, will give out my first order! These men these priests these *monsters* will pay for their crimes once they confess!"

The people in the crowd were whispering to one another. They were wondering what he was going to do with the priests. Some were afraid that he had snapped and was going to kill them all. Others were thinking that he was going to announce new churches or something holy, which was far from accurate.

"Confess your sins, fathers." Kerstas' voice was darker now, almost seemingly amused now, like he was enjoying it.

"We—we have no sins, my son."

Kerstas shook his head. "To them you do. Holy bastards." He pointed to the crowd and could see that the children had hid behind their parents when the priests were near them. "Confess or be forever damned as a monster."

"Fine I confess." Tears had started to form. "I—I am sorry to all of you young ones in the crowd that can see me and hear me. I have done awful things to your children, men and women of Requilit. I said it was cleansing or even studying, but I was playing with them. Defiling them. Including our new king standing before you now."

The crowd gasped. Words flew around from one wall to the next in seconds. The other priests sank their heads, showing that they were also responsible for so much trauma to the children of Requilit.

"I will have new priests here after tonight. I am not apologizing for what I am about to do." He turned towards the crowd, who were horrified of the news they had just received. Many parents were holding their children and apologizing multiple times to them to calm them down. "I hold these men, these *holy* men, accountable for the molestation and rape of every child in Requilit. The trauma you all caused those kids could never be undone. And for that, the price shall be death. You will hang for your sins. But until that day comes, you will be in the dungeons downstairs so that you can try to make your peace with God. I doubt he will be listening."

Kerstas looked at the guards on the left wall and nodded his head at them. They walked over and picked up the priest who had confessed. "Actually, you confessed your sins first before any of the others. In front of me, in front of God, and in front of them. I will at least honor you with a quick death." He knelt down next to the priests ear so that only he could hear. "Even if

I think you should suffer for what you did to me, you confessed and apologized. I thank you for that. I will make it quick."

Suddenly a rush surged through Kerstas' body. Was it evil? He was not sure. It was like adrenaline, but it burned. It did not hurt, but it did not feel good either. It was just there. He knew what feeling it was. The relic.

"You know the word, Kerstas. Say it. Place your hand upon his head and speak the word of death."

Kerstas closed his eyes and placed his hand on the priest's head. His eyes started to tear up. "Thank you for your mercy, King Kerstas. I am so sorry. Could you ever forgive me?"

Kerstas opened his eyes. "Only you, confessor. Only you. I should not, but I will for your confession."

The priest smiled. "Thank you. Thank you. God will be proud."

Kerstas shook his head. "No, he would not. The things I have done. The things I will do. There is nothing to be proud of." He closed his eyes again. "Dayethay."

The priest gasped as the life started to drain from his eyes. His body started to collapse to the floor. Kerstas caught him and eased his now lifeless body to the floor. "Take the rest of them to the dungeons below. They will answer for their sins soon." They were taken out of the room.

The people in the hall were all cautiously looking at Kerstas. They looked from the priest's body to Kerstas.

"What did you do?" Merryk asked.

Kerstas stood back up and faced the people. "I gave him a quick death for confessing. I am so sorry that you all had to witness it. And I am also deeply sorry for what they have done to your children. They will pay. I promise."

"You said that there were going to be more priests

tomorrow," a person in the crowd said. "What if they do what they did?"

Kerstas straightened himself up. The golden accents in his outfit started shimmering. "I will not allow that to happen. If any priest commits this unholy act to any child, they will suffer for it. If they confess to me as he did, they will be honored with a painless, quick death. Let this be known throughout all Pleniris! I am merciful, but I will not tolerate this any further! Not in my kingdom!"

The people in the crowd all stood up from their seats and started cheering and applauding. Kerstas expected them to be terrified of him—of what he just did, but no. They may have been scared, but the hope they had of Kerstas redeeming their land far outweighed their fear of his powers. Why would he use it on them? They knew he would not. That was what made their fears settle down.

"Thank you all. I promise to make this country a better place! As your king—king of Pleniris, I vow to make you all proud of what I will do. I will not let you down!"

They all cheered once again. Inerium had walked up to Kerstas and gave him a giant hug. "I am already proud of you, Kerstas. You will be a great king."

Kerstas smiled. "Thank you, Ineri." He looked up at Choleira. "I will talk to your people, Miss Choleira. They will not have to worry about us invading their territory or going to war with them. If the high lord would speak with me, I would appreciate it."

Choleira nodded. Ineri and I could head there today if she would want to. I am sure she would want to see Olmenor again."

Inerium nodded. "I would. That would be great."

Kerstas sat down in his throne. It was not entirely

comfortable, but the power that came with it made up for it. He stared at the golden leaves sprawled along the walls, pillars, and ceiling. It was like being inside an elven palace with how decorated it was. Choleira would not *entirely* agree with that thought, but she could see where he came from at the thought.

Merryk stepped forward on the floor and held up his hands. "Thank you all for coming today to see King Kerstas' coronation. Now, return to your homes and continue your daily activities. Tell those that were not there today of what Kerstas said. Let Pleniris know who their new king is."

The people all started walking out of the building, talking amongst one another and planning to go and drink to Kerstas' good health and to a new age for the land.

Once the room had cleared Kerstas let out a long sigh of relief. "I can finally relax. I have been so tense. So nervous."

"You looked as stiff as a board, Kerstas. Were you really that nervous?" Merryk had a joyous look on his face.

Kerstas nodded. His hands had been shaking the whole time. They had just started to steady. "Also, I would like to appoint you as the head of the guard, Merryk. The leader or my armies, my soldiers."

"Sir?"

"You heard me. I appoint you to be captain of the guard of Pleniris, Sir Merryk. You will be in charge of the soldiers of the four lands of Pleniris. You can assign titles to those you believe deserve it."

"Thank you, my lord. I am honored." Kerstas did not realize how different Merryk's voice was now versus when he was on the battlefield. He sounded civilized, almost gentleman-like. "I feel like I do not deserve it."

"You do. As a former king, you definitely do. And you can still lead your men, who trust you more than anyone in this land. They do not have to look to another to guide them."

Merryk's hard face twisted into a warm smile. "Thank you so much, My King. It means a lot."

Kerstas patted Merryk on the back, which was a weird thing to do as a sixteen-year-old boy to a well-grown man. Merryk appreciated the gesture, though, and took it as a sign of the highest respect.

"I will start searching for worthy captains for the lands immediately, King Kerstas. I will train them to be soldiers under your name."

"Thank you, Captain Merryk. You may go now." Merryk bowed and left the room.

Inerium and Choleira walked up to Kerstas holding hands. "Hey, we are going to go and set up that meeting with High Lord Evindal in Olmenor, if he will have one. I am sure he will."

"Thank you, Ineri. And you, too, Choleira."

Choleira smiled and bowed her head. They turned and walked, occasionally skipped, as they left for Olmenor.

Kerstas leaned back in his throne. He took in all of the sights of the room. The doors of the castle were closed so no one could see inside. He took out the relic sitting in his pocket. He stared at it for a while, almost entranced by it—like the way the great mountain used to. He stared out the window towards the great mountain. The feeling of being called to it no longer existed. The darkness inside it, after all, was inside him now. And now another darkness was resting in his hand, cold as a Winter's wind, staring at him. A pit formed in his stomach when we would look at it for too long. Dark thoughts would start to cloud his mind until there was nothing else but them swimming in his head. He put the relic away and the thoughts dissipated. He felt calm again, no longer having to fight an urge to kill someone or harm someone.

It was a new day for Pleniris. Kerstas was king. He had gotten his revenge against the priests who had wronged him and so many others. He was going to set his kingdom right. He was going to make sure that he would earn the right to be called King of Pleniris.

FIVE YEARS LATER

CHAPTER 30

Five years had passed. The year was now 869 and the Cold Seasons were rolling in. Everyone was hurrying to pick all their crops and stock up firewood for the chilling months to come.

Pleniris was thriving as a country. The tensions between the four kingdoms after almost a year had resolved. The people had never been happier. Kerstas had made sure that every village and citizen of Pleniris would be treated fairly and none would feel like they were lesser than another. There were still rich, average, and poor classes, but Kerstas did not see them any differently from one another. The new priests in the churches of Pleniris preached the word of their Lord to the people. Kerstas kept quiet about the secrets that he still held that his father had told him.

He had a meeting with Evindal and the other high council members of Olmenor. Evindal had agreed to Kerstas' terms on the treaty they had agreed on. He wrote the treaty in front of Evindal so that there were no secret messages or loopholes hidden in the words. The agreement was that no man should step foot into Evindal's territory unless they were to be summoned personally by him or another member of the council. In return, Evindal would ensure that there will be no hostility held against the humans, unless one were to provoke an Elf and try to harm them. Evindal's lands would remain untouched by man. Kerstas had even offered to let them expand their lands further and spread to other forests, but Evindal refused due to the danger of the faeries in the Western Woods and the old witches in the woods near Sylahm.

Choleira ended up staying and living with Inerium in the castle in Requilit. They of course were not married, at least not yet. Choleira dropped the question on Inerium one night on their trip to visit her brother in Olmenor. He had already pre-approved of it, and Evindal had blessed it when Choleira asked him if it was allowed. Kerstas had also given his royal blessing to her, as both king and brother. She was so happy when she received the blessings that she could hardly contain herself.

When the morning came for them to leave Olmenor and head back to Requilit, Lady Aylisen had done her morning water show. She had pooled a large wall of water around the circle Inerium and Choleira always sat on, just like they did the first time they met, and she knelt down and proposed with a beautiful silver ring with three round gleaming moonstones set in it. Inerium's eyes had filled with tears and she of course said yes. They thanked everyone who had blessed them and supported them. When the wedding would be, they were not sure, but it would be attended by humans and Elves. They returned home to Requilit so that Inerium could tell her brother the big news.

CHAPTER 31

Kerstas woke up in his bedroom to the sound of a knock at his door. Kerstas rolled over in his bed. His crown was laying on the bedside table, the relic under his pillow as it always was when he slept.

"Who is it?" He buried his face deeper into his pillow, making his voice muffled and almost entirely incomprehensible.

"There is someone here to see you, my lord." The voice was from one of his soldiers, one of the ones that stood guard of his hall at night to keep any potential assassins from strolling in and taking him out.

"Can they come by later?" Kerstas tucked himself deeper into bed, wrapping himself up like a burrito in the blankets.

"I am afraid not, my lord. He made it very apparent that he would see you now."

"Did he give a name?" Kerstas rolled over and sat up in bed, groggy from being kept up by the images that the relic put into his dreams. His head was throbbing. He wanted to just shoo the soldier away and go back to sleep, but then the next words the soldier said made him get out of bed.

"No, but I can describe him. Short, round, and has red sideburns."

Kerstas immediately leaped out of bed. He grabbed the relic

and put it into his pocket. He put his crown on his head, pulled the hair out of his eyes, and ran to the door. "Take me to him."

The soldier led Kerstas into the main hall, where all the tables were lined in the center, creating a long table where Spizser sat. A chair was placed at the head of the table, adjacent to where he was sitting. He was wearing a very simple outfit— white shirt with black pants and an orange vest over his shoulders. He was smiling, his hands placed on the table with his fingers interlocked. There was a large silver platter with a dome lid sitting in front of him. The smell coming from the platter was similar to an animal pen.

"Hello, old friend. Congratulations on the new title. The land seems to be doing great with you in charge." Spizser's voice was casual—too casual—but there was something off-putting about the situation that made Kerstas' body shake. He was not sure if it was Spizser's voice or if it was the mysterious, foul-smelling platter in front of him.

He cautiously sat down. "Hello, and thank you, Spizser. It has been quite a few years since we last spoke."

"Yes—it has. I apologize for my absence. I meant to visit sooner, but it took me a while to catch him—it." A small grin formed in his lips as fast as it faded away, another thing that made Kerstas more nervous.

Any encounter he had with him always ended up uncovering some new information about the world he lived in, or the god he once believed in that would be way to vast to comprehend.

"What would that be?" The caution in Kerstas' voice was easy to notice.

Spizser reached over and lifted up the dome lid. Underneath, sitting tied down on the silver platter, was a lamb. A young lamb, not yet an adult, but past its adolescent days. "This is a lamb, Kerstas. A very *rare* lamb. He—it—is very hard to catch.

It might as well be the only one of its kind with how difficult it is to even lay eyes upon. You are the first to see one in thousands of years."

A lump was forming in Kerstas' throat, his stomach was forming a pit as well. Every cell in his body was screaming for him to bolt out of the room and get away from the creature, but he stayed seated, staring at it. The white coat on it was flawless, not a single black or non-white spot to be seen anywhere on it. The eyes were blue, very unusual for a lamb, but maybe that was the part that made it so rare.

"What do you plan to do with it?" Kerstas' voice was shaking. He held his hands in his lap so that he could not show that his hands were shaking. Spizser was well aware that they were.

He looked down at the lamb, which almost seemed to frighten the creature. It kicked its legs to try to get away, but it seemed stuck in place on the platter. No amount of kicking or squirming could help it. "We are going to eat it. He is, after all, the rarest delicacy this world has to offer. Hell, *any* place has to offer."

Kerstas nodded. He had not eaten that morning, so he could use some food. And what he had heard from Inerium and Choleira about Spizser's cooking, he was eager to try it. "When will it be started?"

"Well, young Kerstas, there is a tradition when it comes to this specific meal. The one being offered the meal has to do the killing and carving of him—it."

Kerstas stayed silent for a moment. It did not set easy with him how Spizser would pause and rephrase *him* to *it* when talking about the lamb. He did not want to question it. The potential answers in his head were too much to handle. "What do I use to carve?"

Spizser smiled. He reached under the table and pulled out a large object wrapped up in a dark red cloth. "This. I brought it from The Ashen Dragon, a bar of mine far from here." He unfolded the cloth to unveil a large dagger with a curved black blade. The handle of the dagger was wrapped in a leather strip that had foreign golden letters etched into it. The sharp edge of the blade was silver, which gleamed in the sunlight that poured into the hall.

"What kind of blade is that?" Kerstas leaned closer to try to make out the letters on the handle. He could not.

"It is a special carving blade, used a long time ago for offerings." He caressed the flat edge of the blade. The lamb kicked more and more at the sight of the blade, belting out a hideous cry through the red cloth tied around its mouth. The cloth also had the golden markings on it that the blade's handle did.

Kerstas picked up the blade. It was heavy, very heavy. He looked down at the lamb, who was staring fearfully at him and the blade. "Do I kill it, too?"

Spizser nodded. "Yes."

Kerstas gulped. His hand holding the blade was trembling. He could not explain why, just that he knew he was terrified of something. The situation? The lamb? Spizser? He was not sure. It was something, though. He had never felt so nervous and scared about anything in his life, not even being crowned king of the whole country.

"What is the best way to go about this?"

"Heart, throat, head, whichever you prefer. As long as it is dead."

Kerstas was sweating, his hands shaking. He did not even think about hiding it now. It was too bad—too apparent. He aimed the tip of the blade at the lamb's exposed chest, where the heart was located. "Hold him for me?"

Spizser smiled and nodded. His eyes flickered down to the lamb. The look he gave it almost seemed hateful, like he wanted it to die. He grabbed the lamb's body and turned it to make it easier for Kerstas. Kerstas drove the blade into the lamb's chest. It made a loud screaming noise that almost sounded human in a way. It made Kerstas' body run cold and sent chills down his spine. He drove the blade deeper.

The dark feeling of the relic started creeping over him again. "More. More. Make him hurt," it said. Kerstas thought for just a second that the entity inside the relic knew this creature, calling it *he*, like Spizser did.

Kerstas started twisting the blade inside the lamb's chest. The lamb let out more human-like shrieks of pain as its life started to fade. When it did, the body went limp, and the shrieks of agony ended. Kerstas let go of the blade, leaving it inside the lamb. The malicious feeling the relic gave him faded away.

"Good. Now I can have it prepared," Spizser said, lifting the platter off the table. The blood splashed off the rim onto the table. He looked down at the spillage. "Oh, my apologies." He waved his hand and the spillage disappeared. He walked into the side hall that led to the kitchen and was gone for a few minutes.

When he returned, he was cleaning his hands off with a white rag. Blood stained the rag as he cleaned his hands. He tossed the rag in the air, and it disappeared like the spillage did. He sat down in his chair.

"Now we wait. Not long, though, I will most likely get impatient and speed up the process."

Kerstas was confused by what he meant but did not question

it. When it comes to a man that knows everything and more, and can do so many unexplainable things, he learned not to question it. "How are you cooking it?" It was the only thing that could come to his mind. He was too anxious, too scared, to think of anything else. The fear he was feeling started to make his joints ache.

"Roasting it. I promise it will be delicious. The dish, if I recall, was called Geeyod-Rayostay in the old tongues. Now, I cannot recall. We will just call it a 'roast lamb', okay?"

Kerstas nodded. "Sounds good. I cannot wait to try it."

Spizser smiled. "I cannot wait for you to try him, either. He *is,* after all, a very *precious* lamb. The old way of preparing this dish is to take the lamb right when it gets out of its youngest years, at the point of boyhood. The parents are usually very territorial of their babies, so that is why it took so long to capture him. With some effort, I managed to snag him in the night." He almost seemed to emphasize certain things, like he was referencing something much greater than what he was letting on. Something much more important than simply a rare lamb.

"Thank you, by the way. I do not think I ever thanked you, Spizser. For helping Inerium and Choleira."

"You are welcome, Kerstas. Forgive me for not calling you *my lord* or *king.* When you get to a status such as mine, you forget these kinds of titles. Hell, I do not even call Deusir *Lord* Deusir or *God.* I just cannot bring myself to it."

"What are you, if you do not mind me asking?" Kerstas, as nervous as he was, had managed to compose himself enough to start asking questions that had been running through his head since he had first met him.

"There is a very old word that used to describe it. *Remutarean,* I believe it was."

The relic started shaking in Kerstas' pocket. He felt fear emanating from the relic. Not malice or hatred. Just fear. He placed it on the table, where it continued to shake.

"What does that word mean?" He glanced at the relic, wondering what was going on.

Spizser smirked as he looked at the relic on the table. "A very powerful form of what you all call magic. Let me put it this way. Some of the most powerful gods, like yours, have the power of creation magic, to create something from nothing." His silver eyes seemed to almost be burning like a fire as he spoke to Kerstas. It scared him more. "*I* have the power to create gods, Kerstas. At least, that is a small part of it.

Small? *That* was a small part? Kerstas' head started spinning. He felt dizzy. He grabbed the table to steady himself. "You call that small? I do not believe it. There is no way something can have that much power."

Spizser shrugged his shoulders. "You are right. Nothing *should*, but yet here I am. Believe me or not, the timeline will remain true. That is all that matters."

More questions flooded Kerstas' head. There were too many to ask at this point. He wanted to blurt them out one by one and get them all answered, but they would be there for an eternity.

Spizser tapped on the table twice, the same thing he did back in the crystal cave with those men. A rush surged through Kerstas' body, like he was falling at a high speed.

"It is done," said Spizser, standing up from the table.

"What is?"

He turned around. He was already halfway to the hall that led to the kitchen. "Geeyod Rayostay"

Spizser returned from the kitchen holding a large silver platter, the same one from before but clean now. On the platter were two plates and two wine glasses filled with red liquid, most likely wine. On the plates were a scoop of mashed potatoes, some roasted greens, and four lamb lollipops. The food looked delicious, and the smell was unlike any other meal Kerstas had smelled before. The aroma coming off the plates was beautiful. He could taste the savory flavors on those plates before they even reached his mouth. His mouth started to water. He licked his lips, preparing to bless them with the meal being brought to him. He had not eaten anything close to this in such a long time, if ever at all.

Spizser placed a plate in front of Kerstas. "Enjoy," he said.

Spizser placed the other plate down in front of where he sat and placed the wine glasses on the left-hand side of the plates. He sat down in his seat and waved his hand over the blank space on the right of his plate. A folded napkin appeared holding a set of golden eating utensils. The fork, spoon, and knife were all glistening in the sun. They were all equal lengths, which did not seem like much, but to a diner it made a much cozier experience. Something about the simple things like that improves every aspect of a dinner. If a customer was already satisfied with where they would be eating before they even touched their food or drink, they were almost guaranteed to enjoy their meals. Spizser knew this, that is why he presented everything the way he did.

Kerstas dug into the meal. Everything was delicious. The potatoes melted in his mouth; the greens were seasoned beautifully. And the lamb was like no other. The juices sent chills down Kerstas' spine and made his tastebuds cry out in thanks and begged for more.

Spizser watched gleefully as Kerstas ate the food and drank

his wine. He started to dig into his own plate. Not as fast as Kerstas, but he did eat rather swiftly.

"I must confess, Kerstas, I have not been entirely open with you about what is going on here today."

"What do you mean?" The last lamb lollipop was sitting in his hand. The juices were dripping onto the plate. He wanted to fill his mouth and savor every flavor coming out of it.

"This meal was not simply just a meal. The lamb was not simply just a lamb."

"What are you saying?" Kerstas started to put the meat down back onto the plate.

"It is a sin, Kerstas—an unforgivable sin—to consume the flesh of a being with superior power. Such as an angel or a demon... or a god."

"Yes, I am aware of that." He came off a little sassier than he meant to. He apologized for it. "I did it to Daerex. He told me the same thing. As well as the story of Sybralem, where she had eaten that fish demon thing."

"Well, this lamb was no ordinary lamb, Kerstas."

"What was it? Was it a divine being or an evil one?"

"In a way, he was both. You saw him as evil, while he was divine. *Very* divine. You see, when Deusir gets bored every few thousand years or so, he places a part of himself inside a vessel to roam around for a while to check in on the world. After he did, I took it. I took the vessel and brought it here today. For you."

"Why me? What does any of this have to do with me?"

"Everything." Spizser breathed the word, like it held a giant weight under it. "Kerstas the Sanguavis." He held his hand up in the air and danced it around, like a composer does when performing his symphony. "The six will fall and the Sanguavis will rule." He sang the words as he danced his hand in the air.

"You hold a very crucial role in this timeline, Kerstas. The Sanguavis is no simple title."

That word. It kept echoing in his mind when the eclipse happened. It was carved into his mind. "What does that word mean?"

"The six will fall and the Sanguavis will rule." He sang the words again. "That is the prophecy. It means that you are to be a vessel, Kerstas." His eyes darted to the relic laying on the table. He quickly wiped the smirk off his face. "I cannot give many details, but I can tell you that it is an important role, if not *the* most important role, in this timeline."

Kerstas grabbed onto the table. His head was pounding, making his vision blurry. His stomach was flipping so much that he felt he could vomit at any second.

Spizser waved his hand and Kerstas' glass filled with water. "Drink."

Kerstas nodded and drank the glass. It was just water, but it helped with the nausea. He stood up and walked around to try to clear his head of all the questions swimming around.

"There is still another piece on your plate, Kerstas." Spizser pointed at Kerstas' plate. The piece of lamb was still laying there, laying in all the juices and blood on the plate. "Are you going to let it simply go to waste, or will you consume it?"

Kerstas stared at the lamb piece sitting on his plate. He walked over to the table and leaned over. The piece of lamb left was enticing, almost like it was begging to be eaten. Or perhaps begging not to be.

"You have a choice, Kerstas. This final piece is everything. Consume it and renounce him as your lord. Or waste it and never know what *true* power is." Spizser's voice had gotten deeper as he spoke more. It scared Kerstas a little.

Kerstas thought about his choice. A part of him wanted

to just leave the lamb piece on the plate and forget it ever existed. That part of him wanted to tell Spizser to get out and let him live in peace without any disturbances from gods or anything else that was unnatural. But another part of him thought differently. That other part of him wanted to consume the meat. It wanted to savor every chew and swallow that he made eating it, knowing that it was the flesh of God. Such a being that could be called so loving was nowhere close to it. Even his followers were irredeemable. They assault and rape children while still calling themselves holy men of the lord. They made Kerstas sick with how much they preached good words about their lord. Ever since he had made the order that any priests would be put to death if they did such a thing, they stopped, but they still had the desire—the urges—to.

He looked down at the piece of meat and smiled. The malicious feelings were coming back, the ones that the relic gave him. He picked up the lamb piece and held it into the air. "I will consume." He tore into the last piece like an animal. He cleaned the bone and licked off the juices on it. He threw the bone down onto the plate with the others.

Spizser smiled. "Good. Now the toll."

"Toll? What toll?" A chill surged throughout Kerstas' body. His eyes started to burn, and his arms and legs started to tingle. "What is happening to me?"

"My apologies. You have just consumed the flesh of a god, my dear Kerstas. Your body is now adjusting to the sudden change in power."

Kerstas took another drink of water. Spizser waved his hand and the plates disappeared, leaving only Kerstas' glass of water and the relic. Kerstas slowly walked over to his throne and sat down in it. His body was aching.

Spizser smiled and stood up from his seat. He started

walking towards the doors. "I oughta get going now. It is not time yet, but when the time comes, the Sanguavis will need to fulfill the prophecy."

"What am I to do until then? Will I be ready?"

Spizser let out a little chuckle. "Rule your kingdom, Kerstas. The time will come."

"And when will that be?" Kerstas watched Spizser turn around with a smile on his face, one that was filled with mystery and so many secrets.

"Soon." He took one last glance at the relic and one more at Kerstas, and then he walked out the doors.

Kerstas looked at the relic on the table. A low humming sound was coming out of it, making it vibrate on the table. Then, out of the silence of the room came a deep, quiet voice that let out a single whispered word.

"Soon."

Printed in the United States
by Baker & Taylor Publisher Services

.